STARFIST
FIRESTORM

FIRESTORM

BOOK TWELVE

DAVID SHERMAN
AND
DAN CRAGG

BALLANTINE BOOKS • NEW YORK

Copyright © 2007 by David Sherman and Dan Cragg

Published in the United States by Del Rey Books, an imprint of The Random House Publishing Group, a division of Random House, Inc., New York.

DEL REY is a registered trademark and the Del Rey colophon is a trademark of Random House, Inc.

Library of Congress Cataloging-in-Publication Data
Sherman, David.
Firestorm / David Sherman and Dan Cragg.
p. cm.—(Starfist ; bk. 12)
ISBN 978-0-345-46056-1
1. Marines—Fiction.   2. Life on other planets—Fiction.   I. Cragg, Dan.   II. Title.
PS3569.H4175F56 2007
813'.54—dc22   2006036422

Printed in the United States of America on acid-free paper

www.delreybooks.com

2   4   6   8   9   7   5   3   1

First Edition

Text design by Julie Schroeder

For Tom Carhart
Soldier, scholar, friend

PROLOGUE

Commandant of the Marine Corps Anders Aguinaldo listened intently as Lieutenant General Burbage Weinstock, his chief of staff, delivered the morning briefing on the status of Marine FISTs on deployment.

"Are any army units also headed to Ravenette?" Aguinaldo asked when Weinstock said 29th FIST was en route to Ravenette and 17th FIST was about to embark for deployment on the same campaign.

"They'll be joining the Army's 54th Infantry and 87th Heavy Infantry Divisions to form the 10th Corps."

"Who's commanding 10th Corps?"

Weinstock thumbed his notepad, then shook his head. "Admiral Porter hasn't decided yet."

Aguinaldo's eyes lit up for a moment, then he asked, "Any unofficial word from Sturgeon at 34th FIST?"

Weinstock bit down a grimace. "Only more of the same. General Billie refuses to listen to any advice from a Marine." He shook his head. "It seems Billie is even ignoring his own deputy commander, Lieutenant General Cazombi. Cazombi would have made a good Marine."

Aguinaldo nodded, he too had a high opinion of Cazombi. "What is Godalgonz doing these days?"

"Mostly hanging around, trying to keep out of the way while keeping up with what everybody else is doing." Weinstock shrugged. "What else can a lieutenant general without a job do?"

"Try to keep out of the way while he's trying to keep up." Aguinaldo stood. "Do you have anything else for me?"

"No, sir, that does it for current deployments."

"Very good. I'm going to see the chairman, I might have a job for Godalgonz. Have someone inform the chairman that I'm on my way."

A landcar was waiting for the commandant when he exited HQMC.

At the Heptigon, Commandant Aguinaldo was ushered directly into the office of Admiral Joseph K. C. B. Porter, Chairman of the Combined Chiefs of Staff. Admiral Porter was standing at the side of his desk, looking as if he were waiting patiently for Aguinaldo's arrival. His evident patience, though, was merely a mask for the nervousness he felt. It wasn't every day that the Commandant of the Marine Corps paid a visit to the Chairman of the Combined Chiefs. When he did, the visit usually meant a headache for the chairman.

"Andy, welcome!" Porter said, stepping forward and extending his hands to grip Aguinaldo's right hand in a hearty shake. He needed to use both hands to disguise their tremble.

"Thank you, Admiral. Good to see you." Aguinaldo didn't grip Porter's right hand firmly enough to steady it, allowing him to feel the tremble. He hid a smile; he was going to get what he wanted.

"Have a seat, Andy," Porter said, steering the Marine to an intimate seating group—two comfortable chairs at a round-topped table in front of a large window. "Cognac? Colombian coffee? Cigar? I have some Davidoffs."

"The coffee sounds good. Black. And thank you; I'll indulge myself as long as you have Davidoffs."

By the time the two men were seated, a steward was rolling a service trolley into the office. The steward deftly unloaded the cart onto the table: a fine silver coffee set and a pair of fine china coffee mugs—one with the emblem of the Confederation Navy emblazoned on its side, the other with the Eagle, Globe, and Starstream of the Confederation Marine Corps. He placed a humidor near Porter's right hand and a silver ashtray midway between the two men.

"Thank you, I'll pour," Porter told the steward as soon as everything was laid out. He waited for the porter to withdraw before pouring the coffee and opening the humidor.

The two men took a moment to savor a sip of the coffee and go through the ritual of clipping and lighting their cigars. Then Porter decided to bite the bullet and get it over with.

"What problem are you bringing me today, Andy?"

Aguinaldo shook his head. "No problem, Admiral," he said. "I'm bringing you a *solution* to a problem."

Porter leaned back and gave Aguinaldo a look of mild disbelief. "A *solution* to a problem?"

"You're sending two army divisions and two of my FISTs to Ravenette," Aguinaldo said. "They've been provisionally designated the 10th Corps. I don't believe the army has a spare lieutenant general to send as the corps' commander. Am I right?"

"Well, I do have someone in mind for the job."

Aguinaldo nodded. "I'm sure you do, Admiral. And I'm equally sure that the three-star you have in mind is already filling a vital function on the staff of the Combined Chiefs."

Porter blinked. "Who's been talking?"

Aguinaldo shook his head. "Nobody's said anything—at least not to me or any of my top people. All I've heard is that you're about to make an announcement. There are no names attached to what I heard. But when I look at who's locally available, every one of them is serving in a vital function."

Porter looked at him quizzically for a moment, then leaned forward and tapped the ash off his cigar into the sterling ashtray. "I know what you're going to say, Andy," he said in a conspiratorial tone. "But it won't wash, the army won't stand for it."

"Sure the army will. The 10th Corps is provisional, so give it an acting commander." A smile fleetingly cracked Aguinaldo's face.

"And you have just the man for the job."

"Indeed I do." This time Aguinaldo's smile was less fleeting. "You have a need for a lieutenant general, I've got one without a billet to slot him into. Make him Acting CG, 10th Provisional Corps. The army will complain, but they won't go after your head as long as they believe the appointment is temporary, just to oversee the transit."

Porter leaned back and eyed Aguinaldo. The Marine had a valid argument; while the army would strenuously object to a Marine commanding a corps that was mostly army, they wouldn't fight a transitional appointment too strongly. Besides, he felt he owed Aguinaldo. "You know, Andy, I do believe you're right. I'll have the orders drawn up immediately, appointing Kyr Godalgonz as Acting Commanding General, 10th Provisional Corps. Jason can stand the corps down when it reaches Ravenette and reassign its elements." He cocked his head. "Hmm. He'll have three FISTs and a Marine lieutenant general. He can designate them as a Marine amphibious expeditionary force." He smiled at the commandant. "Well, Andy, it seems that you *did* come to see me with a solution to a problem." His smile widened to a grin. "And solved a problem of your own as well, I suspect."

"As the admiral says."

"Take that with you," Porter said when Aguinaldo reached to put his cigar in the ashtray. "Take a couple more." He picked up the humidor and opened it before extending it to the Marine.

"Thank you very much, sir," the commandant said, taking three Davidoffs.

The two men rose and shook hands.

Aguinaldo held his own grin until he was back inside his landcar for the return to HQMC. He certainly had solved a problem of his own.

Newly promoted Lieutenant General Kyr Godalgonz had followed two highly successful tours as a FIST commander with a promotion to major general and tours on the staffs of 1st and 5th Fleet Marines, then one at Headquarters, Marine Corps. For which exemplary service he was rewarded with promotion to the three-silver-nova rank. However, HQMC didn't have a three-nova billet immediately available. Now the problem of what to do with an excess lieutenant general was solved.

As was another problem.

General Jason Billie—commander of the Confederation forces on and around Ravenette—had a chestful of medals, but the majority of them were "attaboys," medals given not for heroism under fire, but for job performance in support positions. To Marines, any outstanding job performance that didn't involve serious risk to life or limb was simply doing one's job—the Marines didn't award attaboys. Furthermore, Billie hadn't earned any of his campaign medals by getting anywhere near the pointy end of a campaign. Ravenette was his first combat command. As sometimes happens when career staff officers attain high rank and receive their first combat command, Billie refused to listen to advice from his more experienced subordinate unit commanders. Even though Billie felt comfortable ignoring his own division commanders and a Marine brigadier, Aguinaldo didn't think he'd have the guts to shrug off a Marine lieutenant general. Particularly not one who had nearly as many medals as Billie did—every one of which was a decoration for heroism under fire, or a campaign medal earned at the tip of the spear.

He got out his comm and called Lieutenant General Burbage Weinstock. "Please inform Lieutenant General Godalgonz that the commandant requests the pleasure of his company at his earliest convenience. You be there too."

Even to a lieutenant general, "the commandant requests the pleasure of your company at your earliest convenience" means "drop whatever you're doing and see me *now*." So Lieutenant General Kyr Godalgonz was waiting with Lieutenant General Burbage Weinstock when Commandant Aguinaldo returned to his office.

Lieutenant General Kyr Godalgonz was tall and lean and graying at the temples; he looked exactly like what a trid director would want for the role of a heroic Marine lieutenant general in a war epic.

Commandant Aguinaldo got to the point before he reached his desk. "Kyr, how soon can you be ready to ship out?"

"Sir?" Godalgonz asked, taken by surprise. The question was too broad for a simple answer, so he gave the extremes. "If I'm shipping out for a permanent change of station, a week will be more than enough. My wife's been through almost as many as I have; she can handle most of it. If it's for a deployment, two hours."

"It's for a deployment. Admiral Porter is having orders cut now assigning you as Acting Commanding General, 10th Provisional Corps, which is en route to Ravenette."

For an instant, it was as though Godalgonz had been struck by a bolt of lightning—assignment to a corps command wasn't something he'd ever considered, not even remotely. But he recovered fast. "I can have my wife grab my mount-out bags and meet me."

Aguinaldo chuckled. "No need to do that," he said. "The orders haven't arrived here yet. Take your wife out to dinner tonight, then have some private time with her. You'll probably leave tomorrow. Now sit, please, both of you." He led them to a small cluster of chairs away from the windows.

"All right, Kyr. You'll have the Army's 54th Infantry and 87th Heavy Infantry Divisions, along with 17th and 29th FISTs. They're all en route now, except for 17th FIST, which you will rendezvouz with at its first jump. General Jason Billie is in command of the Confederation forces on Ravenette. I know you weren't here very long before he shipped out, but did you ever meet him?"

"No, sir, I never had the pleasure."

Aguinaldo and Weinstock exchanged a look.

"Jason Billie is a kwangduk's ass," Weinstock said when Aguinaldo nodded for him to speak. "I know, that's a strong term to use to describe a brother officer, but Billie isn't exactly a brother to us. I mean aside from being Army, and not Marine. To begin with, he's a career staff officer." Weinstock smiled at the expression that washed over Godalgonz's face at that bit of news; the Marines had career staff officers, but it was impossible for a Marine to reach flag rank without extensive combat-command experience.

"Ravenette's his first combat command?"

"Exactly. All of his subordinate commanders, including his deputy commander, have experience. But the only one Billie seems willing to listen to is his chief of staff—another career staffer."

Aguinaldo picked it up. "That's why I went to the chairman and got you assigned to this corps command. Billie won't be able to shrug you off as easily as he does army two-stars and Marine brigadiers."

"But it's acting CG of a provisional corps," Godalgonz said. "What's to stop him from standing the corps down and eliminating the corps commander billet?"

Aguinaldo gave Godalgonz a wolfish smile. "A Marine lieutenant general."

For his part, Lieutenant General Godalgonz was delighted with the assignment. Seven years earlier, when he had been promoted to major general, he assumed he'd never again be in command of Marines in the field, the reason many Marine brigadiers declined promotion to two-nova rank; major generals got field command only on the rare occasions when two or more FISTs were on deployment together. Despite

Aguinaldo's briefing about General Billie, Godalgonz looked forward to meeting the army commander—and to being a corps commander under him. And if he could get 34th FIST moved to his corps, he'd have Brigadier Theodosius Sturgeon as one of his subordinate commanders. Sturgeon was the only active Marine to have commanded a corps in combat.

Delighted? Lieutenant General Godalgonz was thrilled.

Newly promoted Lieutenant General Kyr Godalgonz, Confederation Marine Corps, arrived on Ravenette with the 10th Provisional Corps much earlier than General Jason Billie, Supreme Commander, Confederation Armed Forces, Ravenette, had anticipated. General Billie was not pleased. As much as he appreciated getting two additional divisions, two more Marine FISTs would only get in the way. And he suspected that a Marine lieutenant general would be a far greater pain in his nether end than that damn Cazombi, his deputy commander.

STARFIST
FIRESTORM

CHAPTER ONE

Marines strive to have everything shipshape, the Marines of 34th FIST no less than other Marines. Shipshape can mean spit-and-polish, everything as clean and neat and shiny as humanly possible—and then some. These are Marines we're talking about, after all. In a deeper sense, shipshape means having one's body and mind in peak condition, and all of one's gear, equipment, and—most important—weapons in the best possible condition. Getting himself and all his equipment—most important, his weapons—shipshape in all regards is one of the most important things a Marine can do to increase his odds of winning and surviving his next firefight.

Thirty-fourth Fleet Initial Strike Team had been on Ravenette for close to half a year, standard, running hither and yon to plug holes in the porous Confederation Army defensive line, living in vermin-infested bunkers that had been thoroughly trashed by the soldiers who'd inhabited them before the army had moved to less severely in-fested bunkers. They'd just fought off a division-size assault, a battle they'd won only because the Confederation Army's 27th Division—in contravention of orders from General Jason Billie—had turned its artillery onto the flank of the secessionist soldiers just as they were about to overrun the Marines' positions.

No, 34th FIST wasn't shipshape, it was . . .

"*Shit*-shape!" Sergeant Tim Kerr shouted as he barged into the bunker occupied by second squad's second fire team. "This whole damn squad is in *shit-shape!*"

Corporal Rachman "Rock" Claypoole, second fire team leader, spun about to yell back at Kerr, but froze with his face twisted in anger and his mouth open. He froze because he remembered that Kerr was no longer *Corporal* Kerr—another fire team leader just like him, although a good deal more senior and experienced—but *Sergeant* Kerr, his squad leader. Even though the squad leader was a good deal lower in rank than Ensign Charlie Bass, the platoon commander, when a squad leader was in the kind of mood Kerr looked to be in, he wasn't much junior to God.

Claypoole shut his mouth with an audible *clack* of teeth and un-twisted his face, stifling his anger. He stood a little more erect and looked about the bunker. The room had been crudely gouged out of the coral-like wall of the escarpment that rose above the beach on the north side of the Bataan Peninsula, and its walls roughly smoothed; at least the worst of the protrusions had been knocked off. That was all the fin-ishing the engineers had had time to do when they were preparing the defensive positions for the war now being fought here on Ravenette. Any protrusions they'd left had been replaced by gouges and pits, the result of fire from the attacking Coalition division that had nearly over-run the Marines.

One good thing about the gouges and pits was that they'd replaced much of the crud the Marines hadn't been able to scour off the walls when they took over the bunkers from the army. A bad thing was the re-sulting stony debris scattered about. Not to mention the expended mu-nitions that littered the floor.

When Kerr barged in and roared his displeasure, Lance Corporal Jack "Wolfman" MacIlargie jumped as though he'd been caught doing something he shouldn't, then just gawped at his squad leader, uncertain of what was coming next—he'd never seen Corporal Kerr so angry. He guessed that an extra ration of anger was issued to new sergeants.

Lance Corporal Dave "Hammer" Schultz had been leaning on the embrasure, looking out over Pohick Bay—just because the Marines, with help from the 27th Division, had defeated a reinforced division didn't mean the Coalition wouldn't order another assault. When he heard Kerr, he casually glanced over his shoulder at the squad leader, then just as casually turned back to his vigil and spat a thick stream of saliva onto the glasis that led from the beach to the escarpment. After the battle, the glasis had been carpeted with bodies, parts of bodies, and unidentifiable bits and chunks of gore, all of which had since been removed for mass burial. The detritus knocked from the face of the escarpment still lay on the glasis. Schultz rolled his shoulders. His back hurt from the wound he'd received weeks earlier when a metal facing-sheet from a trench fell on him while the Marines were beating off a major assault.

Kerr's fury really wasn't at the condition of his squad's bunkers, rather it was a mechanism to distract him from his anguish over casualties. He'd become squad leader only because the previous squad leader, Sergeant Linsman, had been killed a few weeks earlier. He was in anguish about that, and about having had one man in each of his three fire teams wounded on the operation—so far. For that matter, he'd been wounded himself. Right, five of the ten Marines in his squad were already casualties, and as far as he could tell there was no end to the campaign in sight. That kind of thinking could lead to despair. Kerr didn't want to despair, so he turned his emotions to fury, and took it out on his men.

Besides, if his men were uncertain about him, and they kept busy making their bunkers shipshape, they'd be less likely to dwell on the things that had *him* so upset.

"Look at this sty!" Kerr shrieked, kicking at the rubble strewn on the floor. "I want this bunker shipshape when I come back." He glared at the three Marines of second fire team in order—he even glared at Schultz's turned back. "And I want you and your weapons and gear clean and ready to stand inspection on my return." One more glare and he spun and left the bunker as suddenly as he'd stormed in.

After a lengthy moment of silence, MacIlargie murmured, "What crawled up his ass and died?"

"Wants us too busy to think," Schultz rumbled.

Claypoole stopped staring at the bunker entrance where Kerr had vanished and slowly turned toward Schultz. "Uh, too busy to think about what?" he asked.

"Half casualties."

Claypoole mulled that for a moment, wondering what might constitute a "half casualty." Then it clicked; half of the squad had been casualties so far in the defense of the Bataan Peninsula. "Right," he said. Damn good idea. Let's get busy cleaning up this shithole." He grabbed a push broom from a corner and tossed it to MacIlargie. "Start sweeping up, Wolfman."

MacIlargie deftly caught the broom, but instead of sweeping the floor, he cocked his head in thought. "Rock," he said slowly, "we barely have enough water to drink. How are we supposed to get ourselves and our gear clean enough to stand inspection?"

Claypoole gave MacIlargie a that's-a-dumb-question-but-I-don't-expect-anything-better-from-you look and said, "We're Marines. When we don't have what we need to accomplish a mission, we improvise. When we don't have what we need to improvise, we simulate."

MacIlargie blinked a few times. He understood improvising, but "How do we simulate cleaning ourselves and our gear?"

"Fake it," Schultz grumbled.

MacIlargie quickly glanced toward the big, taciturn Marine, then started pushing the broom. After a couple of minutes he looked at Claypoole and said, "I could use some help here, you know. Why don't you do something?"

"I am doing something," Claypoole retorted. "I'm the fire team leader. I'm supervising. You missed some shit over there." He pointed at a patch of floor that MacIlargie had just swept.

"Supervising, yeah sure, supervising," MacIlargie grumbled. He didn't look at Schultz, still looking out over Pohick Bay. A few minutes later, though, all three Marines were working together to clean out their bunker.

First squad hadn't suffered quite as badly as second squad; four wounded and none killed. And, unlike second squad, two of its fire team leaders were both senior and experienced enough to be in line to be slotted into squad leader billets—should one become vacant. As a matter of fact, Sergeant Lupo "Rabbit" Ratliff, the first squad leader, believed that if 34th FIST had not been quarantined, and if its Marines had been rotated out to other units like everybody else in the Confederation Marine Corps, Corporal "Dorny" Dornhofer, his first fire team leader, would long since have been promoted to sergeant and made a squad leader. But it wasn't Ratliff's place to question the decisions of higher-higher, not even when he believed higher-higher was clearly in the wrong.

No, Sergeant Ratliff had more immediate concerns than howcome-forwhy nobody was moving on to other duty stations. Word had filtered down that a Marine lieutenant general was on his way to Bataan to take over combat operations from General Billie. Of course, that word was scuttlebutt, and probably as accurate as the idea that Ensign Charlie Bass was the secret love child of Confederation President Cynthia Chang-Sturdevant. Not that Ratliff thought a Marine lieutenant general wasn't on his way, but the idea that an army general commanding a major operation would give up combat operations command to a Marine was just too absurd to consider. Sure, sure, a Marine had relieved the army combat commander on Diamunde. But in that case, the overall commander was a navy admiral, and *he* had removed the doggie and replaced him with the Marine. Here, the doggie was the overall commander and the admiral was subordinate to him. So there was no way—short of all the army generals getting killed—that a Marine would get command.

The straight scoop—and Ratliff knew it was straight because he'd gotten it directly from Charlie Bass, who had been in the squad leaders' meeting that had just broken up—was that a Marine lieutenant general *was* on his way. Bass didn't know what the three-nova's function would be once he delivered the two divisions and two FISTs he was bringing. If it came to the worst, he'd be an inspector general.

Nobody ever wanted to stand an IG inspection, especially not in the middle of a shooting war. But, dammit, Charlie Bass thought third platoon should be as ready for one as it could be. So Ratliff called his fire team leaders together and told them to get their bunkers ready to stand a round of inspections. "I don't *care* that you don't have the shit you need to get your bunkers properly cleaned," he said when they objected. "Do what you can with what you've got!"

When he dismissed his fire team leaders, he went in search of the other squad leaders.

"How'd your people react when you told them to get ready for an IG?" Ratliff asked Sergeant Kerr when he found him.

Kerr gave him a blank look. "What IG?"

Ratliff returned the look. "The IG Ensign Bass told us about."

"He did?"

"I had a feeling you weren't listening during the squad leaders' meeting," Ratliff said, shaking his head. "What's the problem?"

Kerr looked into nowhere in particular. "No problem. I was, I was thinking about casualties, that's all." He hung his head.

"Look at me, Tim." Ratliff put a hand on Kerr's shoulder and drew him close. "Come on, lift your head and look at me." When Kerr's head stayed down, Ratliff squeezed his shoulder and gave it a shake. Kerr slowly raised his head and looked into Ratliff's eyes from a distance of just centimeters. Ratliff shifted his grip to the back of Kerr's neck and pulled until their foreheads touched.

"Listen to me, Tim," Ratliff said softly. "I know you feel like shit because of how you got your job. So what? Most of our fire team leaders got their jobs the same way—someone above them got killed or too badly injured to come back. We're Marines and that's life for us."

"B-but I, I . . ."

"Yeah, yeah, I know. You were almost killed on Wanderjahr and it took a long time for you to make it back to where you could be returned to duty. And then you had to deal with your own mortality. You've done a pretty good job of it, you didn't let it get in the way of doing your job when you were a fire team leader. Now you've got more lives to be concerned about. That comes with the big bucks. You're a good Marine, you were an outstanding fire team leader. Now be the outstanding squad leader you can be."

Before Kerr could respond, Sergeant Kelly, the gun squad leader, boomed out "What's this, kissy-face between squad leaders?"

"Up your ass with a railroad tie, Kelly!" Ratliff boomed back.

"Nah, Rabbit's trying to teach me squad leader's contact telepathy," Kerr said.

"Squad leader contact telepathy? Never heard of it."

"That's because you're a gun squad leader," Ratliff snorted. "Gun squad leaders don't have enough brains for anybody to read their minds."

"So what do you think of that IG happy horseshit?" Kelly asked in a more normal voice when he reached the other squad leaders.

"Happy horseshit about says it," Kerr replied.

Ratliff nodded at him sharply, glad to see Kerr was coming out of the funk he'd been in. "Whatever's going to happen, it won't be like the IG we missed by coming here in the first place." The Inspector General of the Marine Corps was at Camp Major Pete Ellis, home of 34th FIST, when the orders for the deployment arrived and the inspection was canceled.

"Better not be," Kelly muttered. "Ain't a man jack in the FIST could pass a fire team leader's inspection right now, much less a proper IG."

"Damn straight!"

"So what are we going to do about it?"

"Improvise."

"And what we can't improvise, simulate."

CHAPTER TWO

Heb Cawman, former Chairman of the Coalition Committee on the Conduct of the War, sat inside his comfortable cell in the brig of the CNSS *Kiowa,* twiddling his thumbs and humming an old folk song popular among the farmers of Ruspina, his home world, where he sincerely wished he were. But he would be willing to settle, instead, for a bottle of Old Snort bourbon.

"Sittin' by the roadside, on a summer's day. Chattin' wif muh messmates, passin' time away," he sang quietly. The cell had no bars and was more like an efficiency apartment than a detention facility. It measured about four meters by ten. The door to the companionway that ran down the row of cells was always open, but the prisoners couldn't go through it because a strong detention field blocked the way. Guards carried electronic devices that neutralized the field so they could come and go, but unless a prisoner had access to one of the things and knew the codes, he was stuck in his cell. Besides, even if he could've gotten out, what could a man like Cawman do aboard a navy starship except get himself put right back in the brig?

A hatch hissed open down the companionway, out of Cawman's sight, and he sat up. As far as he knew, he was the only prisoner in the brig and visitors, even a guard bringing him something, broke the monotony. Since he was under constant video and sensor surveillance, he often amused himself by making ugly faces and passing gas—weak substitutes for even casual human contact.

"Mr. Cawman?" A woman dressed in a navy officer's uniform, but without badges of rank, came into view on the other side of the field. She filled her uniform in a most delightful manner. She was petite, with a very pale complexion, and she looked to be no more than twenty. Actually, she was in her forties, a highly trained intelligence officer who'd been at the business of prisoner interrogation for more than fifteen years.

"The one 'n' only, Missy." Cawman stood up and grinned. He bowed deeply to bid her enter.

"My name is Fatimah, Mr. Cawman, and I have some questions to ask you." She passed through the field and Cawman graciously offered her the only chair in the cell; he sat on the bed. Smiling, she sat down and popped open a case that she placed on her lap. Her knees were kept primly together.

"You gonna hook me up to that thing 'n' turn on the juice?" Cawman nodded at the case. He could not see what was inside.

"Oh, Mr. Cawman," Fatimah said, and laughed, "you know the Confederation, as well as your own government, is a signatory to the Richmond Convention on Treatment of Prisoners of War and Other Detainees! Torture, threats, intimidation—they're illegal! Even you, Mr. Cawman, a noncombatant taken on the field of battle, are to be afforded every courtesy and treated humanely. While we're together, Mr. Cawman, I want you to consider me in the same light you would, say, your niece, not a nasty old interrogator." She smiled broadly, revealing perfect teeth.

Cawman grinned, revealing the dirty stumps of the few teeth that remained in his mouth. "Niece is fine but third cousin'd be better." He leered. "Missy, I was snatched by your Marine pirates 'n' drug up here against my will! I want to file a protest!" He continued to grin. "Hey, you got any other names besides Fatimah?"

Fatimah only smiled and said, "Of course, Mr. Cawman, I will help you file your protest as well as help you file any other complaints you may have about the way you are being treated here. Do you feel like answering a few questions now, Mr. Cawman?"

"I'll letcha know," and he gestured at the case on Fatimah's knees, indicating she should proceed.

"I'm going to record your remarks, Mr. Cawman. I'll stop recording anytime you like. Is that all right with you, Mr. Cawman?"

"Sure."

"First, do you have any complaints?" She smiled again.

Cawman noted that her eyes were brown. Her auburn hair was cut short, conforming to the contours of her head. Her tiny nose tilted upwards slightly. *She's looking mighty good,* he thought. "Naw," Cawman answered. "Them Marines, they was pretty rough at first, but what the hell, I been roughed up even worse in some o' the best bars back home." He laughed and slapped his knee.

"Mr. Cawman, you were the Chairman of the Coalition's Committee on the Conduct of the War. Is that true?" Cawman nodded and Fatimah smiled. "Can you tell me what your duties were on that committee?"

Cawman shrugged. "Hell, Missy, my only duty was to be a big pain in Gen'ral Davis Lyons's behind! The folks back home wanted to believe we was keepin' the ol' boy's nose in the manure, so to speak, so we harassed 'im without really interferin' too much with the way he ran his army. He ran it pretty durn good too, I'd say! He even put some of the boys in the hoosegow!"

Fatimah smiled. "I heard about that. It doesn't seem to me, sir, that your government was, er, well, very well organized."

"It weren't. Mostly we sat around throwin' spitballs at each other 'n' drinking Old Snort to kill the boredom. Ol' Preston Summers, the president, 'n' Gen'ral Lyons, they actually run the war. The rest of us, the senate, jist rubber-stamped their decisions."

Fatimah was silent for a moment. "Mr. Cawman, I have the impression there's a lot you're not telling me. Now, we have to be honest with each other here." She leaned forward, eyes locking with Cawman's. "What happens to you depends on how cooperative you are with us."

"Are you intimidatin' me, Missy?" Cawman grinned.

Fatimah smiled. "I have the authority to restrict some of your privileges, sir, if you give me a hard time." She shrugged. "Cut down on your smokes, for instance, turn off your closed-circuit vid system for another."

"Well, yer smokes is much inferior to what I'm used to, and those vids are for kids, so go ahead, cut 'em off." Cawman leaned back and put his arms behind his head. This girl, he could see, was a pushover.

Fatimah smiled. "I have some Davidoffs here and a bottle of Old Snort and they're yours if you promise you'll try to get along with me."

"Holy Martin Luther in hell!" Cawman yelled, sitting upright. "Where do I sign?"

"Let's talk first, all right? You were a senator and the chairman of an important committee, sir, so we think you are a high government official of the Coalition. That makes you a very important prisoner. Moreover, you are a high-ranking member of a government that is in rebellion against the Confederation of Human Worlds, and your forces have mounted an unprovoked attack against one of our garrisons. That makes you subject to charges of high treason and you know what that could mean."

"Miss Fatimah, let me straighten you out here. First, I am well aware of the legal niceties involved in any definition of war. Who attacked whom first, who provoked that attack—that is open to question. Eventually you'll have to try me on charges of treason; no way you can shove me under a rock somewhere, so I'll make lots of noise. Second, in my person you have a mere functionary of the Coalition government. Yes, I voted for the war, along with several hundred other people, but we thought at the time that we had been provoked by your forces, that our citizens had been fired on and killed by them. Third"—

So, Fatimah thought, *the old windbag can speak Standard English when he wants to. Is his country hick persona just an act?*

—"I am not really as important as you think. Other people are more important in what transpired on Ravenette and in the Coalition government than I ever was. I had nothing to do with the attack on Fort Seymour, when all those demonstrators were cut down. No. What you have in me is a nobody." There was a noticeable tinge of bitterness in the way he said that.

Attack on Fort Seymour, Fatimah thought. *What a curious phrasing.* She also inferred from his remarks that Cawman was not happy with his role in the Coalition's government. Was there something here she could exploit? Cawman's vanity? "Mr. Cawman, where is President Preston Summers now?"

"Ah, Missy," Cawman drawled, shifting his position on the bed, glancing downward at the deck before he spoke, "I cain't rightly say."

Fatimah knew he was lying. His body language expressed surprise and nervousness at the question and glancing downward like that indicated to her he was gathering his thoughts before he responded.

"But you must've had a contingency plan, in case Gilbert's Corners came under attack, or the battlefront shifted and required the government's evacuation."

"Um, no, no, actually, we didn't," he said, looking away sharply as he spoke.

Fatimah smiled to herself but kept her pose of youthful innocence. Oh, yes, he was lying. "Well, there's no one there now, Mr. Cawman. Certainly Mr. Summers is no longer there. Where do you suppose he went?"

Cawman thought that question over for a few moments. He despised Preston Summers, his airs, his highfalutin music, his reputation, everything about the man. Why should he care what became of him? The war was lost anyway, and it was far better that Summers go on trial than Heb Cawman. On the other hand, dammit, Heb Cawman was no sniveling coward who'd betray a man just for a bottle of whiskey and a good smoke. Nosiree! "Well, I'll tell ya this, Missy, ol' Preston, he's gonna soon be far away and deep in the ground, where you cain't get at him, but that's all I kin say."

Fatimah decided it was time to conclude the interview. "Mr. Cawman, you have been a great help to me and I appreciate your cooperative spirit. I'll see that my superiors know about that, and it will certainly count in your favor. Meanwhile"—she withdrew a bottle of Old Snort and a Davidoff from her case and handed them to Cawman— "I think your help deserves a reward." She smiled broadly.

"Holy hasenpfeffer hallelujah!" Cawman exclaimed, twisting the cap off the bottle. "When I get outta here I'm gonna marry you, lil' girl!" He toasted her and took a long swig from the bottle. Fatimah smiled.

"Do you have anything for General Cazombi, Ruth?" Admiral Hoi asked.

Ensign Ruth O'Reilly, also known as Fatimah, smiled. "Yes, sir, I do. I'm pretty sure about two bits of intelligence I got from this Cawman creature. One, what's left of the Coalition government is planning to be evacuated to a mountain retreat, someplace where there are caves. I think it is most likely in the Cumbers, sir, precisely where I'd expect General Lyons would choose his fallback position if our breakout from Bataan is successful and we divide his army."

"So that'd mean he'd be fighting his war on two fronts, Billie in front and his own politicians in the rear."

"Yessir." She glanced up at the vid screen. Heb Cawman lay on his bunk, a half-finished bottle of bourbon in one hand, a Davidoff between his teeth, keeping time with his free hand to some ludicrous tune he was humming. "I'll confirm that in the next interview, sir, which I shall commence in about fifteen minutes."

Admiral Hoi arched his eyebrows in surprise. "Hell, Ruth, he'll be so drunk by then he won't even be able to talk!"

Ruth smiled. "Actually, no, sir. That 'whiskey' wouldn't get a kwangduk drunk. He's just experiencing euphoria at the thought he's drinking the real stuff. He's been sober for so long now just the whiff of alcohol is all he needs to get high."

The admiral laughed. "Well, I hope that cigar is a fake too. Seems a shame to waste a perfectly good Davidoff on a man like that."

"Sorry, sir, the cigar is genuine. Sir, the second thing. You know we've suspected all along that the massacre at Fort Seymour was a setup, that secessionist elements in the Coalition wanted an incident to justify an attack on the fort and an ordinance of secession. Well, I sense that Cawman knows something about that. It's just something in the way he mentioned the attack on Fort Seymour while emphasizing that he had no responsibility for it. I know that's a lot to conclude from what was just a nuance, but I have pretty good instincts and I believe I'm onto something here."

"If that's true, Ruth, we want to get our hands on the responsible parties. Can you get Cawman to talk?"

"Yes, sir. Within the next hour I'll have the truth out of him."

"How're you gonna do that?" Admiral Hoi was genuinely perplexed at Ensign O'Reilly's confidence.

"Sir, I'm going to use the oldest trick in the book. I'm going to tell Cawman that another prisoner has put the finger on him. Even now guards are 'dragging' one of our men into the brig. Cawman can't see him, but he'll hear a lot of shouting and cursing. I'll simply walk down to his cell and tell him the jig's up, that he was identified as the mastermind, 'So if you don't want to hang, give up the others.' Believe me, this guy's a pushover. I'll have names within the hour. Or I'll have whatever it is he knows—and he knows something."

Admiral Hoi shook his head in wonder. "Well, go get him, then." He chuckled.

CHAPTER THREE

"Company L, now hear this," Captain Lewis Conorado said into his helmet's all-hands circuit. "By platoons, assemble in your platoon assembly areas. Bring all weapons and field gear. I say again, assemble in your platoon assembly areas. Bring all weapons and field gear."

"Oh shit!" Lance Corporal Isadore "Izzy" Godenov, on radio watch, exclaimed. "We're moving out."

"Moving out to where?" asked his fire team leader, Corporal Joe Dean.

"How do I know?" Godenov retorted. "All I know is the Skipper just came on the horn with orders to assemble at the platoon areas, and bring weapons and field gear."

Dean grimaced and strode the few steps to the entrance of the bunker, grabbing his blaster as he went. He leaned out and looked up and down the corridor that ran behind the defensive positions. "Looks like you got it right, Izzy," he said as he pushed back in and went to his field gear. "I saw some other members of the platoon heading for the assembly area. Now *move* it—I don't want to have to explain to Ensign Bass why first squad's third fire team was the last to show up." Working by feel, he grabbed and donned his gear. Loaded up, he checked his men, Godenov and PFC John Three McGinty. It felt like they had everything; he had to check by feel because their gear was as chameleoned as their uniforms and he couldn't see any of it in the dim light inside the bunker. "Let's go." He led the way, carrying his helmet in his hand so people could see him. Along the way he rolled up his sleeves to increase his visibility. Godenov and McGinty followed suit.

Third fire team, first squad, wasn't the last to reach the platoon assembly area; basically, the Marines reached it in order relative to the distance they had to travel. All of them had their helmets and gloves off, most also had their sleeves rolled up.

Ensign Charlie Bass and Staff Sergeant Wang Hyakowa were waiting for the platoon. Ration cartons and water containers were at Hyakowa's side. The platoon formed up, facing the platoon commander and platoon sergeant. The Marines didn't stand at attention, but their postures were tense in anticipation of learning the reason for the assembly. They didn't have to wait long.

"The Supreme Commander," Bass said with a peculiar emphasis on the title, "has decided to mount a breakout. He wants to break through the Coalition lines facing us, and he wants the break to be in the center of the enemy line—the strongest part of the line. Three guesses who gets to be the point of the spear, and the first two don't count." He paused to let groans and curses ripple through the platoon, then continued, "That's right. Thirty-fourth FIST's air, and all the artillery will pound the enemy lines before we advance." He checked the time. "If you listen carefully, you should be able to hear the barrage starting right about now." The Marines didn't have to listen carefully; the barrage was heavy and not all that far away—some of the artillery pieces firing were on the ridge top directly above them.

"The battalion will advance in a column of companies on line. The 'honor' of being the lead company falls on Company L. Third platoon will have the left flank." Bass looked at Lance Corporal Schultz. "Don't worry, Hammer, second squad gets the left of the platoon."

Schultz always wanted to be in the most dangerous position when the Marines moved, whether that position was the point or an exposed flank. He wasn't suicidal, he just believed he was the most alert Marine in whatever unit he was in, the most able to spot danger before the enemy had time to react, the most able to hurt the enemy first. He believed that improved his chances of survival in a firefight and saved the lives of other Marines.

"Staff Sergeant Hyakowa has a day's rations and water for everybody. Squad leaders, move your people to him in good order, and make sure every one of your Marines has a full ration of food and water. Do it, first squad, second, guns." Bass stepped out of the way as Sergeant Ratliff led his men to Hyakowa and oversaw their supplying. The Marines had their food and water and were back in formation in less than fifteen minutes.

"The Brigadier," Bass said when they were ready, "has arranged for transportation to take us to our jumping-off point." He stopped talking and looked over the disembodied heads and arms standing in three ranks in front of him, then roared out, " 'TOON, 'ten-*hut*!" The Marines snapped to attention, and there was a brief clatter of blaster butts clanking to the deck next to the Marines' right feet.

Bass marched toward Ratliff, with Hyakowa a step to his left and rear. Briskly, with the certainty that came from years of standing and conducting inspections, he went from one Marine to the next and checked each of them. Every one had everything he was supposed to, and the weapons he examined were in proper working order. When he finished with PFC Emilio Delagarza, the assistant gunner in second gun team, the last man in the formation, he returned to his front and center position. He looked pointedly at the three squad leaders and said, "It's nice to see that the squad leaders conducted their own inspections before their squads got here." The squad leaders, still at attention, neither looked at him nor changed expression.

"At ease," Bass ordered. "We don't have anything else to do before our transportation arrives. So you may as well fall out, but don't leave the area." He looked toward the overhead as the thunder of the artillery barrage stopped. "That's odd," he murmured. "The barrage was supposed to last two hours. It's only been"—he looked at Hyakowa.

"About half an hour," the platoon sergeant said.

"It wasn't supposed to stop until after we jumped off."

Hyakowa looked at him blandly, but didn't say anything. If Charlie Bass didn't know what was going on, Wang Hyakowa certainly didn't.

A new sound pierced the air, the scream of Essays nearing the end of the powered dive from orbit. A combat assault landing! Bass looked at the overhead again, as though he could see through the ridge above to the sky. Had the Coalition somehow come up with Essays to make its own assault into the defenses of the Bataan Peninsula? Or had the reinforcements—and the rumored Marine lieutenant general—arrived earlier than expected? He looked at Hyakowa and shrugged. For now, he'd wait patiently. But there was a limit to Charlie Bass's patience.

Charlie Bass engaged in small talk with Hyakowa for a few minutes, then called the squad leaders up and reviewed known enemy emplacements and tactics with them for a time. Then he got up from where he'd been sitting on the floor of the tunnel and began pacing. After almost an hour of decreasing patience, he put on his helmet to call Captain Conorado. But a call from the company commander was already coming in on the command circuit.

"Three Actual," Bass said into the circuit, informing Conorado he was there. First platoon's Ensign Antoni had already reported, and Lieutenant Rokmonov of the assault platoon sounded off right after Bass. Ensign Molina of second platoon was the last platoon commander on the circuit.

"Don't ask for details," Conorado said when all four platoon commanders were on, "because I don't have any. The only word I have, and I stress *only* word, is 'Stand down.' That came direct from Commander van Winkle. He said that was all he knew. I'll let you know what's up the minute I have any information to impart. Six Actual out."

Bass was left with the nearly inaudible hum of a radio on standby in his ears. Slowly, he lifted his helmet and looked around the platoon area.

"Third herd," he called out, "gather 'round and listen up." In a moment the Marines were standing in front of him, but in a group rather than a formation. "Don't ask, I can't tell you what I don't know," he said to the the faces looking at him for information or instructions. "All I know is, the battalion has been ordered to stand down. So go back to your bunkers. I'll let you know when I know more."

Questions began pelting him.

"Ensign Bass, is the war over?"

"Has the breakout been postponed?"

"Did the army decide to use its own troops for the spearpoint?"

"Did that lieutenant general show up, was that what the Essays were?"

"Is the Marine general in command now?"

"*I said don't ask!*" Bass roared. "*I don't know!* Now get back to your damn bunkers." He turned to Hyakowa with an expression of feigned disbelief.

For his part, Hyakowa held back the grin that was trying to split his face. "You knew they were going to ask, no matter what you said about not knowing anything else." He looked at the backs of the heads of the Marines returning to their bunkers, then back at Bass. "Now that they're gone, you can give me the rest of the word."

"Not you too, Wang!" Bass said in a tone of shocked disbelief.

Hyakowa could no longer restrain himself and burst out with a belly laugh.

"Corporal Dean, what do you think is happening?" PFC John Three McGinty asked his fire team leader on the way back to their bunker.

Dean shook his head. "All I know for sure is, the ritual sacrifice of a Marine FIST has been called off—at least for now."

McGinty swallowed. "What do you mean, ritual sacrifice?"

Lance Corporal Godenov snorted and asked, "Can I hit him?"

"No, you can't hit him. That's *my* job." Dean reached out and smacked Godenov on the back of his head.

"Hey, what'd you hit *me* for?" Godenov squawked, rubbing the back of his head.

"For not knowing that only the fire team leader gets to smack the new guy upside the head for asking dumb questions." Dean smacked the back of McGinty's head. "All right," he said before McGinty could object, "now that the head smacking is done with, I'll answer your dumb question.

"General Billie wants a frontal assault to break through the middle of the Coalition lines. He knows that whoever goes first will get chewed up, maybe totally wiped out. He also knows his soldiers can't do it, so he wants us to go and get killed to weaken the enemy line enough for his soldiers to finish the job. *That's* what I meant by ritual sacrifice. Understand?"

"He couldn't want that!" McGinty gasped.

Dean smacked him upside his head again. "Billie's a doggie. Doggies don't like Marines. Billie *particularly* doesn't like Marines. You better believe he'd want to get us wiped out."

* * *

Corporal Doyle was visibly shaking when he and his men reached their bunker. PFC Lasha Summers had seen his fire team leader like that before, and he understood that it didn't necessarily mean anything. Nonetheless, he found it unnerving, so he went directly to the bunker's aperture and stared out over Pohick Bay rather than glance at the corporal, who looked like he was about to throw up, or loose his sphincter, or do something else unpleasant and probably malodorous.

PFC Lary Smedley, on the other hand, was entirely too new to third platoon and Corporal Doyle to know anything other than that his fire team leader looked frightened enough to shit himself, which put him in an similar frame of mind and digestive distress.

Fortunately for the state of Smedley's intestinal urges, Sergeant Kerr had noticed Doyle's trembling while on his way back to the squad's section, and followed third fire team to its bunker entrance where he caught Doyle's eye. Kerr crooked a finger at Doyle, and backed into the corridor.

"Y-Yes, Sergeant K-Kerr," Doyle stammered when he joined the squad leader.

"Let's keep this quiet, just between you and me," Kerr said quietly, almost a whisper.

Doyle nodded rapidly and sucked on his lower lip.

"You've got two new men," Kerr said. "This is Summers's first deployment, and Smedley joined us in the middle of it. You've got the new men because I know how good you are with them, how good a teacher you are. Do you understand that?"

Doyle nodded again, and found his voice. "Y-Yes, I know you th-think I'm good with the n-new men."

Kerr shook his head. "I don't think, I *know.* I've seen you with them. But right now you're scaring them."

Doyle blinked. "Sc-Scaring them?"

"Look at your arms."

Doyle lifted an arm and looked at it. It was trembling. He raised the other and looked at it as well. "I l-look like I c-can't hold my blaster," he mumbled.

Kerr nodded. "Your men see that and it scares them. Especially Smedley. He hasn't been with us long enough to know you. And Doyle," he put a hand on Doyle's shoulder, "when Ensign Bass told us what we were going to do, I knew the general was sending us out to get killed. I just about shat myself."

Doyle started shaking more. "I-I know. That sc-scared me half to d-death." Then the last thing Kerr said clicked and he looked at him. "Y-You were scared? It didn't sh-show."

"That's right, it didn't show. Every man in the platoon was probably just as scared as I was, as you were." He looked toward Doyle's bunker, where two not very experienced Marines were waiting, and probably wondering why their squad leader had taken their fire team leader away. "Except maybe for the men who're new enough they don't know.

"The men who are experienced enough to not show their fear are the Marines who will do their best. But when a leader shows his fear, it's contagious. Get hold of yourself, don't let it show. When a good leader doesn't show fear, his men think they have to live up to his standard. You're a good leader. Now get hold of yourself. All right?"

Doyle stood more erect and took a few slow, deep breaths. "You're right, boss. I'll do it."

Kerr looked down. "Look at your arms now."

Doyle lifted them. The tremor was almost gone.

"Now go and let your men see they've got a strong fire team leader."

Doyle took another deep breath. "I'll do that."

Kerr didn't say anything, just pointed at the bunker door. Doyle left him and was almost marching by the time he disappeared through it.

Kerr looked up and down the corridor and saw he was alone. He shuddered and leaned against the wall, took a moment to let his own fear show. Then gathered himself together and moved on to check his other fire teams.

CHAPTER FOUR

Lieutenant General Kyr "Killer" Godalgonz, Acting Commander, 10th Provisional Corps, strode purposefully up the ramp from the landing bay followed closely by his "retinue"—a grim, heavily scarred ensign. Several passing enlisted men, noticing the silver novas on Godalgonz's battle dress, came to attention as he passed. "Stand easy, people." He growled, "This is a goddamned combat zone. Besides, I'll be in the area all day." The men grinned at that. This was a very unusual lieutenant general!

Godalgonz stopped at the top of the ramp. "Cooper, where the hell do we go from here?" he asked Ensign Cooper Rynchus.

"Well, we're several days early, sir, maybe the brass band is still practicing." Rynchus wrinkled his nose and smiled. "These guys have been cooped up in here quite a while, sir. Reminds me of the Siege of Mandelbaum, 265 days of shitting in our mess kits."

General Godalgonz laughed. "Well, Cooper, that's the smell of fighting men." He breathed deeply. "We're right where we always wanted to be, eh, Cooper?"

From a passageway to their left they could hear someone running toward them. Godalgonz looked at Ensign Rynchus and raised his eyebrows. "Guy's got flat feet," he said.

The flap-flap-flap of someone's destroyed arches drew nearer. Major General Balca Sorca appeared, panting heavily, snapped to attention, saluted, and gasped, "Welcome to Bataan, General, Godlylganz, sir!"

"Godalgonz, General, *Godalgonz.*" Godalgonz returned the salute and held out his hand. "You must be General Sorca, General Billie's chief of staff."

"Sorry, sir. Yessir, I am. Er, where's your staff?" Sorca glanced around nervously as they shook. Sorca's hand felt limp and damp in Godalgonz's grip, which was so firm it made Sorca wince. That told the Marine all he wanted to know about Balca Sorca.

"Back in orbit. I want you to meet my ADC, Ensign Rynchus. Cooper, this here is Major General Sorca, chief of staff to General Jason Billie.

Sorca only nodded at Rynchus. He was too low-ranking to merit a handshake. Sorca did not know what to make of this pair. The lieutenant general, tall, whipcord thin, emanating energy and determination. When Godalgonz talked he fixed his listener directly with piercing blue eyes, his prominent jaw protruding like a boxer daring his opponent to strike the first blow; the iron gray hair at his temples lent character to his distinguished appearance. Overall, he impressed people as a figure who had just stepped out of a history vid of Marine Corps heroes.

Ensign Rynchus was another matter. Shorter than the general, broad in the shoulders. Sorca judged his age as nearly fifty, rather old to be an ensign. Then he remembered that in the Marines all officers had been enlisted men. Evidently this ensign had been an experienced noncommissioned officer before he got his commission. Also evident was, that he'd been around—the scars on his face testified to that. To Sorca he appeared a dangerous and disagreeable person. Sorca, like most army officers, never could understand why the Marines insisted on some enlisted service before officers were commissioned. Marine officers never seemed to lose the rough edges they acquired in the barracks.

"Well, sir, if you will follow me, I'll take you directly to General Billie."

"General, you're early," General Jason Billie said, rising from his desk. The statement was more an accusation than a welcome. Lieutenant

General Godalgonz came to attention and saluted smartly. "Lieutenant General Godalgonz, acting commander, 10th Provisional Corps, reporting as ordered, sir!" Ensign Rynchus had been unceremoniously asked to wait outside.

Billie returned the salute. "Be seated, General. Have a Clinton?" He offered the cigar. Godalgonz shook his head. "Balca, please get General Cazombi. When he gets here we'll have a closed-door conference. Well, General Godalgonz, we didn't expect you for a few days yet."

"The troops were ready for embarkation, so we left early. My philosophy is get to the battle early, fight early, go home early."

Billie arched his eyebrows at that. "Ah, well, yes, yes, General, I take your point. Good to have you on board."

"I brought two army divisions, sir, the 54th Light and the 87th Heavy plus two Marine FISTs, the 17th and 29th. Equipment, personnel, all combat ready, itching to go. Sixty thousand men, sir. At your disposal. May I ask what your battle plan is?"

"Now that you're here, we're ready to break out of this hole. I want to wait until Lieutenant General Alistair Cazombi gets here, General. You know him? Army officer, my deputy commander. Had we known you were coming today, we'd all have been waiting for you at the ramp." Billie smiled tightly.

"No problem, sir."

"Your staff? When will they land?"

"They're in orbit with the fleet, sir. I'll land them when you say you're ready to bring down the troops."

"Excellent. That ensign? Your aide?"

"Yessir. Ensign Cooper Rynchus. Good man, sir. Been around. He got the Marine Medal of Heroism at the Siege of Mandelbaum. Were you there, by any chance?"

"Uh, no, General, I wasn't."

"Good man, that Rynchus."

"I see. Ah!"—Billie stood—"Here's General Cazombi at last! Alistair, come in, come in! Meet Lieutenant General Godlygonz, newly arrived 10th Provisional Corps commander."

"*Godalgonz*, sir." He shook hands with Cazombi.

"Bring any Davidoffs with you?" Cazombi grinned.

"Don't smoke, General."

"Pity." Cazombi took a seat. "Well, General," Cazombi said to Billie, "let's go to war."

"Close the door, Sorca. Cigar?" Cazombi shook his head.

General Godalgonz did not miss the exchange between Billie and Cazombi. No love and less respect there, he reflected. He remembered what Commandant Aguinaldo had told him about Billie. "Not worth a kwangduk's ass."

"Alistair, General Godalgonz is here a bit early," he said, emphasizing *early*, "so we've had no time to prepare a full briefing on the situation. But I just wanted us to get acquainted here first, then we can discuss my plans for the breakout. Later. Tell us about yourself, General." He turned to Godalgonz.

Godalgonz shrugged. "I never expected to command a corps, even provisionally, much less get in on this fight, sir. But now I'm here, I want to fight. That's what I do."

"Um, yes. Well, General, tell us something about yourself personally. Married? Children? Education, the usual."

"Yessir, all that crap." Godalgonz stuck his jaw out aggressively and fixed General Billie with those blue eyes. Billie rapidly shifted his glance to avoid the piercing orbs.

Billie realized he was getting nowhere with this man. "Alistair, would you show General *Godalgonz* to his quarters, work with him to get his staff and commanders landed? Let's keep your combat units in orbit until we're ready to use them, but land your logistical and support people. Alistair, find someplace to stick them. Very good, gentlemen. We'll have a full staff briefing when your people have arrived and been situated."

Cazombi and Godalgonz stood, saluted, about-faced and marched out of the office. "Close the door, Balca," Billie ordered. Then: "Jesus on a haystack, Balca, just what I *don't* need, another goddamned jarhead-kick-'em-in-the-ass Marine!" He slammed a fist on his desk.

"We can use the reinforcements, sir," Sorca ventured.

"Yeah." Billie was silent for a moment. "Sorca, I have an idea."

"Nice place you have here." Godalgonz grinned at Cazombi as they negotiated the narrow passageway. They paused at an intersection. Tunnels ran off in different directions, each marked with arrows and symbols that pointed the way to various parts of the underground fortress. "A guy could get lost down here."

"You get used to it. Mind if I call you Kyr?"

"Not at all. Alistair okay with you? My aide's Cooper, old NCO." He nodded at Ensign Rynchus.

"Cooper." They shook hands. "Well, we're at the heart of Bataan. These tunnels"—Cazombi gestured at the passageways branching off— "lead to every part of the fortress. This place was a storage depot when I arrived here. It was huge and almost empty. Our engineers did a wonderful job of deepening the chambers and fortifying the place. Three problems: too many men in here; we're surrounded by water that seeps in everywhere; and we've been stuck down here far too long."

"How do you handle all that water?"

"Filtration systems recycle the stuff and we consume the product. The seepage from Pohick Bay is our major source of drinking water, actually. Sewage is also filtered and the, uh, 'results' are used to supplement the nuclear generator that provides electrical power to run the air-filtration and climate-control systems, such as they are." He wrinkled his nose. "The detritus the engineers produce from their excavations is broken down into its constituent elements in special furnaces installed for that purpose. The heat that produces is used to thaw this place out. Believe me, it can get mighty cold and damp down here and you'll come to appreciate the warmth that system generates."

"Vermin? I've heard of creatures called slimies."

Cazombi permitted himself a twitch of his lips that on him passed for a smile. "We've got them under control. Nasty buggers. What the engineers couldn't exterminate, well, we were short of rations for a while and the troops . . ." He shrugged.

Godalgonz gave Ensign Rynchus a knowing look. They both had been there, done that at Mandelbaum. "Hell," Godalgonz said, "you've got a whole field army down here and in orbit. Why haven't you broken out yet?"

"Well, that's up to our"—he hesitated—"commanding general." That pause told Godalgonz volumes about the relationship between the two general officers.

"How is Billie to serve under?"

Cazombi hesitated again, looking evenly at Godalgonz before he spoke. "You'll find that out, General," was all he said. Godalgonz smiled to himself. He remembered what Aguinaldo had told him. Obviously Cazombi was a loyal subordinate who wouldn't say a bad word about Jason Billie to a stranger, even though he despised Billie.

From down a shaft running deep into the rock came the noise of many men working in a closed space. "What is all that, sir?" Rynchus asked.

Cazombi glanced at the markings stenciled onto the rock. "I have to remind myself every now and then who's where," he apologized. "Down there are several regiments from the army's 21st Corps. It's one of several huge caverns we've managed to cram several thousand men into, with all their gear. We're about a hundred meters below the surface here, so this area is impervious to enemy fire. The men can relax and work in relative comfort. We've been rotating the brigades and regiments between these rest areas and the surface fortifications. Just before the Big Push, whenever in the hell that'll be, we'll move the designated assault units into the fighting positions topside. Care to go down and take a look?"

"Thanks, Alistair, but let's wait till I get my bearings. I want to visit my Marines first chance. Um, Alistair, do you think you could drop me off at Ted Sturgeon's HQ?"

"They're on the other side of Bataan from here. Don't worry, we ain't gonna have to walk. Just ahead is the shuttle system we use to get around fast down here. I use it to visit the corps and divisional commanders every day. All the engineers had to do was expand and improve the system that was installed when this place was a storage depot. Once you get to know how it works, it's very efficient. When his nibs calls one of his staff conferences we've all got to be there ASAP, so you'll get to know the shuttle routes very well before we get out of here."

"Kyr! Cooper!" Brigadier Ted Sturgeon leaped to his feet and stuck out his hand. The three Marines shook hands enthusiastically.

"I found these two jarheads wandering around looking for a way out of this place," Cazombi said. "Couldn't think of a better place to dump them than on you, Ted. Gentlemen, excuse me now."

"Hell, Alistair, we're *all* lookin' for a way out of this friggin' hole!" Sturgeon laughed.

"Well, let me know if you find it." Cazombi grimaced, as close as he ever came to allowing a full smile, and left them.

The three Marines had all served together at one time or another and enjoyed that easy camaraderie of men who knew each other well and had shared the same hardships and triumphs. For a while they traded memories, talked of men they'd known and places they'd been. Then General Godalgonz got to the point. "Tell me about this Billie."

Sturgeon shook his head. "He's a disaster, Kyr, a pure disaster. And he hates Marines."

Godalgonz nodded. "Anders warned me of that when I talked to him before coming out here. Is he *that* bad, Ted?"

"Worse. He's snatching defeat from the jaws of victory," Sturgeon answered bitterly. "He has fucked up this war and gotten a lot of good men killed, and he's fixing to get some more killed, mark my words."

Godalgonz did not show the surprise he felt. This was Ted Sturgeon, for heaven's sakes, morale on the floor. Things had to be bad if Sturgeon felt like this. "Well, Ted, we've been through shit like this before and survived. We'll pull through again. Hell," he said, changing the subject, "remember that navy captain who was in charge of that troop transport—what the hell was his name? The most unmitigated disaster ever to wear a uniform?"

"They should have put Cazombi in charge of this mess," Sturgeon muttered. "The way General Billie hides out down here, there's no chance the enemy will oblige us with a change of commanders."

"I'm beginning to get the picture," Godalgonz replied. The morale had to be extremely low, he realized, if a man like Ted Sturgeon was giving in to talk like that. "Buck up, Ted! Now that I'm here, we're going to kick some ass. I'll handle this Billie guy, you bet!"

"Balca"—Billie leaned back comfortably—"I'm gonna rid myself of these damned Marines."

"Sir, that might be easier said than done," Major General Sorca replied.

"Mebbe not. Look." Billie called up a 1:100,000 vidmap of the battle theater. "See here, Lyons's got a full division here, at Phelps, and another one here, at this little town just outside Gilbert's Corners. Those troops are locked and loaded; Lyons's reserve as well as the protective screen for the Coalition's government. I'm gonna take this hard-charging three-star and the 17th, 29th, and 34th FISTs and send them on a raid against Gilbert's. They'll be outgunned and outnumbered. Keep them busy out there saving their asses from annihilation and out of our hair while we prepare the main thrust. What do you think?"

Major General Balca Sorca hesitated before he replied. "Well, um, sir, that would mean we'd have to sacrifice some of our own men, just to get them out of the way?" That was as close as Sorca would ever come to questioning an order from his mentor, but privately he was beginning to wonder if he'd hitched himself to the right set of stars in this army.

"It'll also pin down those reserves and disrupt the Coalition government. Come on, Balca! You play chess. You know that to win you have to sacrifice pieces, even some valuable ones!" Billie regarded his chief of staff through a cloud of cigar smoke. Was Balca losing his nerve? Was *every* officer in this hole except Jason Billie himself unable to see the Big Picture? "You chop wood, Balca, you get chips. Issue the order."

CHAPTER FIVE

At a hundred-plus kilos and standing only about 180 centimeters, Major General Golda Clipper was almost as broad as he was tall. But once given a mission, he pursued it like a boulder rolling down a mountainside.

"Mr. President"—General Clipper ran a hamlike palm over his closely cropped head as he spoke; it came away wet with perspiration mixed with the dust of the road he had taken to get to Gilbert's Corners—"I believe an attack is imminent and I suggest you communicate this intelligence to your gov'mint 'n' evacuate to a safer location."

Preston Summers, President of the Coalition of Independent Worlds, gazed silently at the rotund figure. Slowly he removed the cigar from the side of his mouth, fished out tobacco shreds with a finger, and said, "Gawdam cheap seegars, fall apart on ya before they's even halfway smoked." He wiped his finger on his trousers. "So ya think this place is gonna turn into a battlefield, Gen'ral?"

"I know it is, sir."

"Then we're fucked, aren't we?" Summers squinted through the cigar smoke.

"Wouldn't put it quite that way, sir."

"Don't shit me, Gen'ral. They've awreddy attacked us here once, 'n' they's plannin' on doin' it agin, ain't they? Only this time they're comin' with a force big enough to hold this place. Well, we survived that first attack so what makes you think we won't weather this one you think is comin' now?"

"That was just a probe, Mr. President, to prove they could attack you at will; to scare you to keep you off balance—"

"Sure scared the stuffings outta me!"

"They even kidnapped some of your officials that time, didn't they?"

Summers laughed. "Hauled ol' Heb Cawman off like a sack o' sticks, they did! I wonder what he's tole 'em by now? Y'know, we did talk about evacuatin' Gilbert's Corners some time ago, Cawman, some others 'n' me. He was against it at the time, as I recall. Best thing ever happened to this war for us was them capturin' that ol' galoot."

"General Lyons also arrested some of the other members of that Committee on the Conduct of the War, didn't he?"

"Sartinly did, sartinly did, 'n' he had reason to do it too. After this war is over you'll know why, Gen'ral Clipper. Now answer me this: They's gonna land on the coast 'n' take Phelps too, ain't they?"

"They already have. A coast-watcher spotted them and notified General Lyons. He believes they're headed straight here and my job is to stop them. I can't protect you folks and do that at the same time."

Summers's heart skipped a beat at that news but he only nodded. "What's the size of the force they landed?"

"Big enough to do the job, Mr. President."

Summers was silent briefly, thinking, *Why the fuck didn't Lyons beef up the coastal defenses instead of putting that goddamned useless MP battalion out there?* But when he spoke, he said, "Well, I ain't no strategist but seems to me Phelps is our back door." He sighed. "Have a seegar, Gen'ral? 'Scuse me for not offerin' you one sooner. They's not top-quality smokes but they's all I got right now. Gawdam blockade's cut off my supply of the really good stuff. Now bourbon, different matter." He produced a bottle and two glasses. "Join me."

"We don't have much time, sir," Clipper responded, lighting his cigar and accepting a glass of whiskey from Summers. In his hands the glass looked like a thimble. He toasted the president. "Damned good stuff, sir!"

"It oughta be. Comes out of my own distillery. So why they comin' here 'steada straight up the road to Ashburtonville?"

Clipper shrugged. "This here is the head of the beast 'n' they is gonna try to cut it off."

Summers guffawed loudly. "Gen'ral, lemme tell you a couple things. First off, this ain't the head of nothing, it's the ass end! Gen'ral Lyons is this war—he's what's holding it all together. All we do back here at Gilbert's Corners is palaver, drink whiskey, 'n' act big all day long. Why, the Confederation'd be crazy to attack this place 'n' end all the confusion! And second, if they really is comin' down here to attack this place, we have lost this war."

General Clipper finished his whiskey and stood up. "Mr. President, my orders, and they come directly from Gen'ral Lyons, are to reinforce the garrison here and prepare for a major assault on this place. I am informing you now that I am removing you and your government to a safer location where you may continue carrying on the Coalition's business."

"Okay! Okay!" Summers stood and held out both hands in a placating gesture. "I'm not the enemy here, Gen'ral Clipper!"

"I am going to carry out my orders, sir. Most expeditiously. I request you inform your government immediately—"

"Gawdam, Gen'ral, you military guys don't have no sense of humor, do you?" Summers shook his head. "I'll make the announcement but I want you there with me when I do."

"Very good, sir."

"Now, how much time do we have?"

"None, sir. We have to move right now."

"Damn! Well, where are you gonna move us to, then?"

"To some caves in the Cumber Mountains. I have aircraft and surface transportation standing by. I'll send the most important people and their staffs first, then get the rest in subsequent transports until you're all there. Then I'm turning this place into a fortress. I think I can screen your movements from the enemy. They still don't have their satellite observation platforms fully up and running."

Summers swore volubly, then said, "Y'know, that's just what we discussed some time ago. It was left up in the air as a possibility because so many of the Coalition's representatives didn't like the idea of living in caves. Like we're too civilized for that." He snorted, "So we're gonna wind up this war a bunch of troglodytes . . ." He shook his head.

"A bunch of what, sir?"

"Never mind, Gen'ral. Come on, let's git the boys together."

It took some time but eventually the delegates and their key staff personnel sat in chairs around the walls in the old tavern where General Lyons had last faced the Committee on the Conduct of the War. The congress hall that had been erected to accommodate full meetings of the Coalition government had burned during the Marines' recent raid. But the tavern was "homey" and still smelled of stale beer.

"Folks," Summers began, "we are under the threat of an imminent, large-scale attack"—several of the assembled delegates gasped in surprise and horror but Summers hurried on—"Return to your offices at once, gather up ten of your most important people, whatever equipment you'll need to do business, and assemble on Main Street. General Clipper's troops will evacuate you to our new seat of government in the caverns located in the Cumber Mountains—"

"Aaaahhhhh!" Bela Raipur Gwalior, a delegate from Chilianwala screeched. "It is all over! We are dead! All is lost! Aaaaahhhhh!"

Summers grimaced, "Damn it, Bela, pipe down! It ain't over till I says it's over." He turned to General Clipper and muttered, sotto voce, "Damn woman was all for this war till it turned sour." He turned back to the delegates who were in a state of agitation. "Now y'all get back to yer offices 'n' gather up yer rods 'n' staffs and git yer damned asses out into the street—"

"See here, Preston!" Zozor Yella, the delegate from Kambula shouted, stepping forward, "what gives you the authority to address us in such a disrespectful and very ungentlemanly—"

"*Awwriiight!*" General Clipper's voice echoed off the timbers as he rolled forward. "You heard the man! Git yer behinds and yer shit into the goddamned company street and do it right goddamned now or I will have my men drag your asses out there 'n' load you up. Move! Move! Move!"

Miraculously, nobody was hurt in the rush for the door. After silence had settled over the old tavern, Summers wiped his forehead theatrically, turned to Clipper and laughed. "Geez, Gen'ral, you sure do have a way with politicians!"

"Well," he explained, "I used to be a company first sergeant."

CHAPTER SIX

The next time word of what they were going to do came down, the Marines of third platoon knew it was the straight scoop because Captain Conorado assembled the company in the open area behind the coral ridge their bunkers were in, and gave them the word himself. If the open area looked like a battleground, well, it had recently been one. Coalition forces, during their ill-fated amphibious assault on the Marine section of the Bataan defenses, had airlifted troops and equipment on the reverse side of the ridge; the ground was littered with the shattered remains of Coalition vehicles and artillery pieces. When Conorado told his Marines to gather close, many of them found perches on Coalition equipment.

"I know that you've all heard the scuttlebutt that a Marine lieutenant general has come to Ravenette," Conorado said when his Marines were settled in front of him. He himself sat high on the side of a self-propelled artillery piece. The company's officers and most of the senior NCOs had arrayed themselves around his back and sides. "It's true. Lieutenant General Kyr Godalgonz has come from HQMC. He traveled as Acting CG, 10th Provisional Corps. Two of the elements of 10th Corps were 17th and 29th FISTs. There were also two army divisions." If it sounded to a non-Marine observer that Conorado casually dismissed the two army divisions as less important than the two FISTs, well, Conorado was a Marine, and Marines are *always* dismissive of army units. Many of the Marines Conorado addressed, on the other hand, were just this side of thinking he spoke too well of the two army divisions.

"There's been scuttlebutt," Conorado continued, "that Lieutenant General Godalgonz was taking over combat operations for ConForRav." Military-speak for Confederation Forces, Ravenette. "That hasn't happened. At this moment, the lieutenant general is ComMarForRav." Commander, Marine Forces, Ravenette. "MarForRav is about to conduct its first multi-FIST operation, with Lieutenant General Godalgonz in command.

"Force Recon discovered that the Coalition government has established itself in a farming village 150 kilometers southwest of Fort Seymour. The village, a place by the name of Gilbert's Corners, is defended by as much as a reinforced regiment. In addition to the government's own defenses, the Coalition's 9th Division is close enough to give assistance in event of an attack on Gilbert's Corners." Conorado paused to emphasize what he was about to say. "Thirty-fourth and Seventeenth FISTs are going to give the 9th Division an excuse to react to Gilbert's Corners.

"That got your attention, didn't it?

"The operation will be a raid in force, and will utilize all the Dragons and hoppers of the three FISTs. We will board Dragons, go out beyond the horizon, and swing around to make a landing southeast of Gilbert's Corners. There we will be met by hoppers for the final leg of our movement-to-objective. We will strike fast and hard, and do everything we can to disrupt the Coalition government's operations, up to and including destroying the government.

"Twenty-ninth FIST, if you're interested, will be picked up by the hoppers as soon as they drop us at Gilbert's Corners and they will transit it to the landing beach, where it will be on standby in the event that it is needed.

"Lieutenant General Godalgonz and the staffs of all three FISTs are finished with the basic plan for this operation, and are now working on contingency plans. I haven't seen all of the primary plan, but I can tell you that it calls for us to get out of Gilbert's Corners before the 9th Division can get there.

"When you are dismissed, head back to your assigned areas and get ready to mount out. You will be briefed in more detail as I have the details to give you. In the meanwhile, get your weapons and gear in order, and get some sleep. There will be a chow call at zero-dark-thirty. We can expect to move out before dawn."

Conorado suddenly stood erect, and platoon sergeants and squad leaders called their men to attention.

"Platoon sergeants, dismiss your men!" Followed by the other officers, Conorado turned and headed into the ridge, back to his command post. As soon as he was out of sight, the platoon sergeants sent their men back to their areas.

The "chow call at zero-dark-thirty" was a hot meal delivered to the bunkers by the enlisted personnel of the mess sections of both the FIST and the battalion. The promised briefing didn't come until the Marines had boarded the Dragons and were headed out to sea under the cover of darkness. The briefing was fragmentary; each platoon in the company was given only the plans for its own part of the operation. Given the time constraints, Captain Conorado had only briefed the platoon commanders and platoon sergeants, and most of the briefing was the transmission to their comps of each platoon's portion. It was then up to the platoon commanders and platoon sergeants to brief their Marines.

This wasn't a fully effective method of briefing the troops. Even though each platoon commander and platoon sergeant was top man in a Dragon with half of his platoon, each of the Dragons also had a few extra Marines from either the FIST or battalion companies. Which meant *those* Marines didn't necessarily get a briefing germane to their parts of the operation. It wasn't to be helped, though. Between General Billie's desire to get the Marines out of his way immediately, and Lieutenant General Godalgonz's desire to show Billie that he was an effective combat commander, the raid in force had to go *now,* with no time for thorough briefings or rehearsal.

Staff Sergeant Hyakowa made sure the Marines in his Dragon were hooked into his Bravo unit circuit, then briefed them on what they'd be doing when they reached the beach, and then on their part of the upcoming raid. He added what little he knew about the rest of the raid, and finished up by uploading the necessary map overlays to Sergeant Kerr and the team leaders. All he could tell the two squads from the company's assault platoon was, "Keep close to me until you get further orders." Hyakowa's unhappiness with the situation didn't show in his voice.

Once the briefing was over, Kerr told his men to study the plan, then try to get some sleep. It didn't take him long to absorb the small amount of briefing material, then he closed his eyes and tried to follow his own advice. But unwelcome thoughts of casualties kept him awake during the long ride to the landing beach.

Private Lem Bob Stanley was bored. Out of his skull. Like with an auger. Yep, that was it. Bored like someone took an auger and bored a hole right through his skull. That's how Lem Bob Stanley told himself his head felt. It *hurt.* Dangnabbit. Aside from not having nothing to do besides watch that there beach, Lem Bob couldn't do anything else, either. Couldn't even go over to the creek and do some fishing. Not even sit here and catch some sleep, because Private Stanley had to pick up that radio there and call in to report ". . . ain't got nothin' to report . . ." every half hour. No sir! Colonel Sedge Mossby'd been right definite about doing nothing but sit in the shade of this here tree looked something like a cottonwood and watch the beach. Hell, nothing to see on the goddamn beach. It'd be right interesting to watch the beach if there were some naked womenfolk splashing in the water down there. Of course, Lem Bob knew if there were some naked womenfolk splashing in the water, he'd be a-hauling his ass down there to do some splashing with them. Huh-huh, and more than just splashing, you can bet. But damn Colonel Mossby'd get a wild hair up his ass about that too. Dang him! Lem Bob didn't know why Colonel Mossby thought this bit of beach was worth watching, weren't nothing around here to make the Confederation military to come this way.

Private Lem Bob Stanley's unit was the Mylex Militia, not the regular army. Lem Bob thought the militia should go back to the *old* way and elect its officers. They'd elect that Colonel Sedge Mossby right back down to private! Put someone else in as colonel, someone who'd have enough sense to give men duties what didn't bore them out of their skulls. There wasn't no *dang* thing to look at on that beach, nothing to keep a man's mind occupied except for that . . .

What *was* suddenly riling up the water like that? The waves hitting the beach about half a klick off were acting plumb loco, throwing spray like there was monster trucks running through them, but there wasn't anything there to rile them. And now on the beach, there was sand flyin' everywhere! And what's that thrumming in the sky now?

Lem Bob looked and had to use his hand to push his jaw back up before it fell off. There were many strange-looking aircraft heading straight toward the beach from over the ocean—Lem Bob didn't know it, but they were three squadrons of Marine hoppers. The hoppers landed just inland from the beach and opened their hatches. The Marines, already racing off their chameleon-painted Dragons, sped into the hoppers, which took off again, headed northwest. The things he couldn't quite see quit spraying sand and headed back over the water.

It wasn't time for Lem Bob's half-hourly report, but he surely had something to report. Lem Bob was so excited about finally having something to report—and something he couldn't explain—that the Mylex Militia's radiowatch noncom couldn't understand what he was trying to report. When the radiowatch noncom told him to try again when he sobered up, and that he was on report for drinking on duty, Lem Bob blew up and demanded to speak directly to Colonel Mossby. Lem Bob was shouting loudly enough that the duty officer, on the far side of the headquarters tent, heard his demand. The duty officer quickstepped to the radio station and demanded the noncom tell him what was going on. When the answer was, "Damn 'f I know, he's drunk an' I cain't figgur out what he's sayin'," the duty officer—who knew that whatever Private Lem Bob Stanleys other shortcomings were, drinking on duty wasn't one of them—took the microphone from the noncom and began talking.

That calmed Lem Bob down enough for him to give a garbled but intelligible account of what he'd just witnessed. The duty officer thanked him, told him to maintain position and immediately report anything else unusual, and then raised Colonel Mossby, to pass the report to him.

Unlike many members of the Mylex Militia, Colonel Mossby knew about the Marine chameleons and their vehicles. He wasted no time contacting General Lyons and reporting to him that it appeared the Confederation forces were launching an attack in the direction of Gilbert's Corners.

General Lyons immediately contacted Major General Verkas

Nonbrite, commander of the 9th Cabala Division, at Grenoble's Shop, a mere twelve kilometers southeast of Gilbert's Corners, and ordered him to move his division to intercept an airborne assault on the government center there or, failing that, to launch a counterattack. Lyons ordered a dozen of his remaining satellite killers into action to blow a hole in the Confederation's string-of-pearls, to disable the satellite surveillance system enough to allow the 9th Division's movement to go undetected until its elements were in position to counter the Marine assault that he was certain was about to hit Gilbert's Corners.

Major General Nonbrite was ahead of the curve; following the Force Recon raid on Gilbert's Corners, a raid in which Chairman of the Committee on the Conduct of the War Heb Cawman was captured, he had initiated a program of rotating his regiments to reinforce the garrison at Gilbert's Corners. Currently, the 819th Regiment was situated two kilometers northeast of the government center, and the 259th Regiment was ready to mount out to replace the 819th. The 589th Regiment was midway through its refitting rotation and could move out with twenty-four hours' notice. His artillery was zeroed in on all approaches to Gilbert's Corners. And the 125th Brigade was on standby at the base camp, ready to move wherever it was needed on less than thirty minutes' notice.

Twenty-four hours wasn't enough time for the regiments at Grenoble's Shop to prepare in detail, but the 9th Division didn't have to move; two of its three regiments were directly in the path of any attacker coming from the southeast.

General Nonbrite alerted Task Force Osper, the reinforced security battalion at Gilbert's Corners, of a possible Confederation assault.

The Marines knew the 9th Division was on the direct route from their landing beach to Gilbert's Corners, so the hoppers swung farther south to avoid overflying the division before they cut inland. The hoppers flew low, following roads, not quite as far above the ground as the tallest treetops to reduce the chance of being spotted. Three kilometers from Gilbert's Corners, they rose thirty meters above the trees and moved line abreast for the final approach. At the same time, the eighteen Raptors of the three FISTs' squadrons, orbiting at forty thousand feet above Gilbert's Corners, heeled over to plunge toward the surface. At ten thousand feet, two of the squadrons began firing plasma cannons at predesignated targets in the Coalition defenses, while the third squadron sought targets of opportunity along the roads on the route from the 9th Division's base at Grenoble's Shop to Gilbert's Corners. None of the squadrons looked to the northeast, so they didn't see the 819th Regiment begin its move to intercept.

The aerial attack caught Task Force Osper by surprise; it was the first use of Confederation attack aircraft, other than against the Coalition forces attacking the defensive perimeter at the Bataan Peninsula, since the war began. Still, the plunging fire from the Raptors' plasma cannons didn't have as much effect as it might have. After the Force Recon raid that destroyed many of the battalion's barracks and resulted in the capture of Heb Cawman, Task Force Osper's combat losses were quickly replaced and the battalion was reinforced so it was nearly two thousand strong. Construction of new barracks had been canceled, and all construction efforts were directed to building new strongpoints for the defenders—many of those strongpoints held defensive weapons systems designed to be operated remotely; some even automatically, after a command to sweep an area. General Lyons didn't want to risk a repeat of the slaughter of the force that had been tasked with protecting the Coalition government. Close-in security, previously neglected, was built up to make it nearly impossible for anyone who managed to evade the patrols and sensors in the forests beyond the farm belt to approach undetected—even Marines in chameleon uniforms. The only significant loss to the defense from the air assault was a five-room subground complex that included two bunkers; its ferrocrete roof hadn't cured properly and half melted, half collapsed when it was hit by a burst of aerial cannon fire, causing the loss of two squads.

The Marines landed less than a minute after the Raptors broke off their attack.

CHAPTER SEVEN

When Lieutenant General Kyr Godalgonz landed north of Gilbert's Corners with 17th FIST, it was the first time in the memory of anyone in Marine Forces Ravenette that a three-nova general had participated in an assault landing.

"If we're going to capture the leaders of the rebel government," Godalgonz had explained to his FIST commanders, "I believe it's important that those leaders have someone of high rank to surrender to. They might construe being forced to surrender to someone of lesser rank to be an insult, and they won't cooperate as well as they might—or they might even resist, causing unnecessary casualties among them and to us."

Neither Brigadier Sturgeon of 34th FIST nor 17th FIST's Brigadier Nuemain could argue that point, though both thought Godalgonz was taking an unnecessary risk. They also both felt that their own commander's belief that they might be too low-ranking to accept the surrender of rebel leaders was a bit insulting. But they were Marines; when given orders they fulfill them.

Brigadier Sturgeon did not envy Brigadier Nuemain's having Lieutenant General Godalgonz with him on his sweep to the north to capture the Coalition leaders. Neither was he very fond of the call signs Godalgonz assigned them. Nuemain was Boomer, 29th FIST's Brigadier Devh was Pitbull, and Sturgeon was Viper. Godalgonz himself was Killer.

Lieutenant General Godalgonz, of course, had another, unspoken, reason for wanting to make the landing with 17th FIST: This was a fully unexpected—and almost positively his last—chance to make an assault landing with a FIST. He was disappointed when 17th FIST's landing was opposed by just three easily neutralized watch posts.

The farmers, shopkeepers, and construction workers at Gilbert's Corners had learned the hard way what happens to untrained people when they take on Confederation Marines, and they weren't about to make the same mistake twice. As soon as they realized the Marines were landing, they began scrambling for shelter behind locked doors.

The hoppers carrying 34th FIST's infantry battalion landed a kilometer west of the southwest extremity of Gilbert's Corners, from where it could block a reaction force heading to the northern edge of the town or itself enter the town from the south.

Sergeant Kerr jumped from the hopper when it was still more than a meter above the ground and sprinted away from the bird. The Marines of second squad followed him, using their infra screens to identify their squad leader. Kerr hit the dirt fifty meters away, and the squad went prone on line with him.

"Fire team leaders, report!" Kerr barked into his squad circuit.

The fire team leaders were already in contact with their men.

"First fire team, ready," Corporal Chan answered immediately.

"Second fire team, we're here," Corporal Claypoole said as soon as Chan finished.

"Th-Third fire team, present and accounted f-for!" Corporal Doyle reported.

Sergeant Kerr listened to the platoon circuit while his fire team leaders were reporting. As soon as he heard first squad's Sergeant Ratliff report, he spoke into the circuit with, "Second squad, all present and ready." Then Sergeant Kelly called that the gun squad was in position.

"Guns," Ensign Bass said as soon as all three squads reported in. "One gun lay down fire on the objective. Two, you know what to do. Everybody else, wait for targets." One gun began streaming plasma bolts at a bunker in front of second squad's position; knocking out that watch post was third platoon's first objective.

Kerr peered through his magnifier screen at the uncamouflaged bunker five hundred meters away. No fire had come from it yet, and only someone suicidal would try to fire from it; it was being washed by a stream of plasma. No incoming fire, no casualties; it was time to go.

"Second squad, on your feet, forward at the double," Kerr ordered. He pushed himself erect and began trotting toward the bunker. "Watch your flank, Doyle. We don't want any friendly casualties here."

"R-Roger," Corporal Doyle answered. He sounded as if he was already panting from the exertion of running.

Kerr slid his infra into place and looked to his right. The stream of fire from the gun bathing the bunker scorched a brilliant line across his vision, almost blanking out the red blotches of the men running along with him. Still, he was able to make out the three Marines of his third fire team—they weren't in the gun's line of fire, and if they didn't drift to their right, wouldn't be in it until the squad was fifty meters from the bunker.

"Keep tight with the rest of the squad, Doyle," he ordered.

"Y-Yes, Sergeant Kerr." Doyle was definitely panting, but Kerr now thought his shortness of breath might have been hyperventilation due to fear, rather than from running.

Corporal Kindrachuk's voice came over the radio. "Gun one, changing barrels."

"Second squad, hit the deck!" Kerr ordered. "Hit that bunker!"

Plasma bolts from the blasters of the ten Marines of second squad began hitting the bunker just as the bursts from the gun team stopped washing it. Most of the bolts hit in or near the bunker's firing aperture.

Before the Marines could get into a rhythm, Kindrachuk's voice came back: "Gun one resuming," and the gun again bathed the bunker with bursts of plasma bolts.

"Second squad, up and at 'em!" Kerr lurched to his feet and looked left and right through his infra to make sure his men were back on their feet and trotting forward. Assured that they were, he faced front again and maintained pace with them. They'd cut the distance to the bunker in half. With less than a hundred meters to go, Kerr ordered, "Second squad, halt in place and go to your knee." The squad stopped and each man raised his blaster to his shoulder from a kneeling position. "Wait for my command, then open fire," Kerr told his men. Then, "Gun one, cease fire!" As soon as the gun stopped shooting, he ordered, "Second squad, fire! Stand, advance firing!" The ten Marines rose as one and moved forward at a brisk walk, firing their blasters at the bunker. Their fire wasn't as accurate as it had been when they stopped to let gun one change its barrel, but it was accurate enough that it would have been suicide for anyone still alive in the bunker to approach the aperture to fire out of it.

But there was nobody alive in the bunker when they reached it.

"Whooh! Crispy critters!" Lance Corporal MacIlargie exclaimed when he reached the bunker and looked inside.

Crispy critters, indeed. Four charred husks were all that remained of the Coalition soldiers who'd been on duty in the watch post bunker. They were unidentifiable to the naked eye beyond "probably human."

"Never mind that," Kerr snapped. "Let's get some security here while the rest of the platoon comes up."

"You heard the man," Corporal Claypoole said. "We've got the middle. Second fire team, with me." He slipped off a glove to show MacIlargie and Lance Corporal Schultz where he was, and began walking away from the bunker, toward Gilbert's Corners. A hundred meters away he stopped, and the three Marines took positions watching the approach from the village.

"That's weird," MacIlargie murmured into the fire team circuit.

"What's weird?" Claypoole asked.

"Nobody's there."

That was true. Not only were no soldiers rushing toward the recent sounds of battle, no people of any sort were visible in the village.

"Hiding," Schultz rumbled.

"Makes sense to me," Claypoole agreed. The civilians heard firing close to their north, and now sounds of a raging firefight to their southeast. Anybody who didn't absolutely have to be out would be in hiding, to avoid getting accidentally shot. He continued to watch. The wait wasn't long.

"Second squad, on your feet!" Ensign Bass barked when first and gun squads reached the bunker a couple of minutes after second squad declared it secure. "On line. Gun two with first squad, gun one with second. Check your dress, keep it staggered."

"Stand up!" Claypoole ordered as he rose to his feet. He looked through his infra to see the rest of the squad angling toward his position, then looked to see where the rest of the platoon was. There, to his left when facing the village. He swore silently when he realized what that probably meant, and which fire team was to his right. Sergeant Kerr confirmed his suspicion a moment later.

"Doyle," the squad leader said on the squad circuit, "Kilo Company's coming up on our right flank. Tie in with them."

"Me?" Corporal Doyle squeaked. "M-Me tie in with Kilo?"

"I didn't stutter, Doyle, you heard me. You can do it. Take a look, here they come."

Doyle looked to his right rear. His infra showed red blotches that weren't Marines of Company L approaching. "R-Right. Tie in." He thought for a couple of seconds, then said, "S-Summers, identify y-yourself to the Kilo flanker and m-maintain contact w-with him."

"Roger," PFC Summers said crisply.

In moments, 34th FIST's entire infantry battalion was on line, advancing on Gilbert's Corners and past its sides. South of the village, the Raptors of all three of the FISTs on Ravenette plunged down in their firing runs, to bounce back up for another go. The sounds of the fight on the ground grew.

Lieutenant General Kyr Godalgonz was in a most uncomfortable and unaccustomed position—pinned down by enemy fire. It had been a long time since he was last pinned down; he'd been a squad leader at the time. Even though he'd survived it without injury, that did nothing to alleviate the discomfort he felt this time. Which could be due in part to the fact that he'd been a captain the last time he'd been exposed to sustained fire, and a brigadier the last time he'd faced fire of any sort.

"Lieutenant generals should get on the front lines more often," he grumbled. "Either that or stay away from the fighting altogether."

Nobody heard his grumbling, though. He was alone, pinned behind a heap of rubble that had been piled up when the debris from the Force Recon raid was being cleared out. He had full communication through his helmet with his battle staff and with his subordinate commanders, and he could monitor their communications with *their* subordinate commanders. But he was frustrated; he couldn't do anything to affect the course of the battle. His communications man, carrying his UPUD Mark III—Universal Positionator Up-Down Link—lay ten meters away, across bare ground swept by continuous fire from an automatic defensive weapon system. The sergeant hadn't moved since he'd gone down, and hadn't responded when Godalgonz called to him. Godalgonz thought the Marine must be dead. With the UPUD out of reach, he didn't have a picture of the battlespace.

Where the hell was Cooper? He twisted around, looking for Ensign Cooper Rynchus. Where was the man? He was too old and tough a Marine to be a casualty, either dead or unconscious. Godalgonz knew the man could take injuries that would kill a lesser man, and keep fighting and leading Marines. That was how he'd won the Marine Medal of Heroism at the Siege of Mandelbaum.

"Tough Guy, this is Killer," Godalgonz said into his battle staff circuit. "Where are you?"

No reply.

He tried again, then to his battle staff, "Has anybody seen Tough Guy?" All replied in the negative.

Godalgonz looked at the UPUD, only ten meters away, but it might as well have been in orbit. Only ten meters, but those ten meters were regularly showing puffs of dirt rising from the ground being pelted by fléchettes shot by the automatic defensive system that covered the area where Godalgonz was pinned down. As near as he could tell, the weapon covered an arc seventy-five meters wide. And it traversed fast, too fast for him to wait for its fire to pass and bolt to the UPUD between sweeps. The fire would reach him again before he could regain cover.

The loud *thud* of a heavy body hitting the ground next to him. He half rolled away, moving his hand blaster into position, and looked just in time to see Rynchus raising the screens on his helmet to show his face. A chewed-up area of his helmet near his left cheek was visible, showing where a fléchette burst had struck it. Godalgonz moved his hand blaster so it was no longer pointing at his aide, and raised his own screens.

"Are you hit anywhere else?" the general asked.

"Nope. And that would have missed if I wasn't wearing a helmet," Rynchus said with unintentional irony. "It messed up my comm. I can still hear, but I can't transmit. Where's Shumwray?"

Godalgonz tilted his head toward where the communications man lay. "I think he's dead."

"And he's got your UPUD." Rynchus looked at his boss. "Not much you can do without it, is there?" It was phrased as a question, but it was a statement. He kept his eyes on Godalgonz, but watched the progress of the traversing fléchettes in his peripheral vision. Without warning, as soon as the next group of dirt puffs passed, he launched himself across the ten meters of open ground and dove for the cover of a debris pile beyond the UPUD, scooping it up as he went past. He reached the cover just as the automatic weapon's traverse brought its fire back. As soon as it passed again, he darted back to Godalgonz's side.

"I always was faster than you," he said with a chuckle as he handed the UPUD to the general.

Godalgonz just gaped at Rynchus. Then he remembered that he was a lieutenant general in the Confederation Marines; he wasn't supposed to gape like a schoolboy who just watched a magician pull a rabbit out of a hat. He got control of his face, and gasped, "How did you manage not to get hit?"

Rynchus laughed. "Like I said, I can run faster than you. Now get to work and do some generaling."

Godalgonz stared into Rynchus's eyes for a couple of seconds, then said, "Don't ever do something so dumb that you get killed for me." He turned to his UPUD and quickly saw the situation.

What looked like an entire regiment was moving toward 17th FIST's right flank, and Alpha Company, on that flank, was shifting position to meet the new threat. Bravo Company, on the left flank, was maneuvering to hit the enemy forces in the defensive positions from their flank, hoping to free Charlie Company, which was pinned down in the middle, so that it could aid Alpha in fighting off the rapidly approaching Coalition regiment. To the north, 34th FIST was moving through Gilbert's Corners and along its sides. Icons indicated secured enemy positions around the village. So far, the Marines hadn't found any members of the government, though they had found some hastily vacated offices and managed to retrieve some data crystals that hadn't been destroyed.

But Godalgonz already knew all of that from listening in on his subordinate commanders' conversations with their subordinate commanders. What neither he nor anybody else in his assault force had known was that another regiment was rapidly approaching from the northeast.

"Oh, hell," he swore softly, and showed the display to Rynchus. Rynchus whistled.

"Boomer," Godalgonz radioed 17th FIST's Brigadier Nuemain, "this is Killer. Acknowledge."

"Killer, Boomer, go," Nuemain answered. He sounded rushed; he was fighting a battle bigger than anticipated.

"Patch me through to 29 Actual, my comm is down."

"Roger, Killer. Wait one."

Godalgonz waited impatiently through several seconds of soft static, then Brigadier Devh's voice came over the radio. "Killer, this is Pitbull."

"Pitbull, what is your status? I need you now."

"We're aboard and the birds are cranking. Wait one." Godalgonz heard a muffled exchange, then Devh came back. "Killer, we're lifting off. Where do you want us to go, and what do you want us to do when we get there?"

Godalgonz didn't take the time for a sigh of relief; instead he began giving orders to the commander of 29th FIST.

CHAPTER EIGHT

Third platoon went down Center Street. Not in the middle of the street, the way the armed citizens of Gilbert's Corners had in their ill-fated attempt to fight the Force Recon raiders, but along the fronts of the buildings and houses on both sides of the street, taking advantage of every bit of cover afforded by architecture or nature. They didn't bother with concealment—their chameleons kept them out of sight—except when they entered buildings or houses in search of members of the Coalition government.

Corporal Joe Dean went to a knee at the corner of a yellow brick house with a miniature portico. A shallow roof with two pillars supported it. Second squad's third fire team had already searched four houses, finding only frightened civilians who huddled away from the faces floating horribly in midair. But that experience didn't make Dean feel any more confident about searching the fifth house than he had searching the first. There had been weapons in each of the first four houses, shotguns and hunting rifles rather than military. Still, a bullet from a deer rifle will kill a man just as dead as a burst from a fléchette rifle. In three of those houses the people had been too frightened and shaken to try to fight—or even protest when the Marines confiscated their weapons. In the other, Lance Corporal Izzy Godenov had snatched a rifle from the hands of a man taking aim at Dean's back, just in time.

Then they reached another house that needed to be secured.

"Three, you know the routine," Sergeant Lupo Ratliff murmured over the squad circuit. "Do it."

"Aye aye," Dean murmured back. Then, "Izzy, Triple John, with me." He stood hunched, then dashed along the front of the house to the far side of the portico. Godenov and PFC John Three McGinty followed to the portico's near side. Dean reached in and tried the door; it wasn't locked. "Screens up," he said. The three Marines raised the chameleon screens on their helmets, exposing their faces. Dean kept his light-gatherer screen in place, Godenov kept his infra up. Only McGinty would go in with just his eyes to see through. Dean looked into his men's faces. "Ready?" When they both nodded, he shoved the door open, darted through, and slammed the swinging door against the wall. Godenov and McGinty went through the door just as fast, against the wall on the other side of the doorway.

They were in a living room with two doorways leading off it. Nobody was visible in the room. Bulky furniture stood about, none of the overstuffed chairs or the sofa against the walls.

"Izzy, right. Me, left," Dean said. He and Godenov quickly checked behind the furniture. Nobody was hiding in the room. Dean could see a dining room through the doorway to the right; there didn't seem to be anyone in it. He slipped off a glove and signaled Godenov to slide his chameleon screen back into place and take a quick look.

Godenov did, and reported no one there.

"In the house!" Dean called out loudly. "We are Confederation Marines. Come into the living room. Throw any weapons you have into the living room before you enter, and have your hands in plain sight. We aren't going to hurt you, we're looking for someone. As soon as we are sure whoever we're looking for isn't here, we'll leave you in peace."

A voice yelled from deeper in the house, "We ain't comin' to no Confed'rations. Git out'n here or ye'll be sorry."

"I'm sorry now," Dean called back. "I wish you hadn't said that. I'm sorry we might have to hurt you. Now do what I said and nobody'll get hurt."

"Fuck you!" the voice shouted defiantly.

Dean sighed, and lowered his chameleon screen. Godenov and McGinty did the same.

"Izzy," Dean said on the fire team circuit, "what's beyond the dining room?"

"Looks like a kitchen."

"Check it out. McGinty, go with him." Dean turned his ears up and listened to the faint sounds his men made as they went through the dining room into the kitchen. He heard cabinets being quietly opened and closed again.

"Nobody's here," Godenov reported.

"What about other doors?" Dean asked.

"There's a doorway into the hall we could see from the living room. Another door is right across the hall."

"Wait for me." Dean made sure his light gatherer was in place and slipped through the doorway on the living room's back wall, into a hall that led to the rear of the house. When he neared the door into the kitchen, he reached out with a hand. Godenov took it.

"Go to the rear of the door," Dean told Godenov; to McGinty, he said, "Cover us to the rear of the house. Then he stepped to the side of the door opposite the kitchen door and flipped his infra down just long enough to see that Godenov was in position on the doorway's other side. He reached out and swung the door open. He entered low and fast. It was a bedroom, but nobody was in it, not under the bed, in the closet, or in the adjoining watercloset. The bedroom had no other exits.

There were three more doorways off the hall, plus an exit at its far end. The first two opened into bedrooms that were as empty as the front of the house. They stopped shy of the last door, and Dean suddenly wished they were wearing body armor. He leaned forward, turned on his external speaker, and said, "Throw out your weapons and come out with your hands up. Nobody will get hur—"

"Fuck you!" the voice shouted again, not as defiantly this time, followed immediately by a loud *Ka-boom!* and the less loud *ka-chunk* of a fresh shell being racked into a shotgun.

Dean turned his speaker up and tried again. "Last chance before we come in."

The man didn't reply with words; his shotgun answered for him. The pellets blew a fist-sized hole in the wall next to the door, matching the hole the first blast had made.

"Shit," Dean swore. "I *hate* it when civilians want to fight us." He switched his external speaker off and turned his head toward the splotch his infra told him was McGinty. "Triple John, you're about to participate in something no Marine should ever have to do—kill a stupid civilian."

"He's too stupid to live," Godenov muttered angrily. "Let's get it over with."

Dean sighed before saying "Izzy, on my signal, burn the catch. Triple John, put three bolts through the hinge side of the door—mix them up. *Fire!*"

The relative quiet of the house's hallway was suddenly filled with multiple *CRACK-sizzles* as the three Marines opened fire. Godenov blasted away the door's catch with his first shot and fired two more through the door itself. McGinty hit the hinges with his first two shots and the now unconnected door toppled into the hallway. He put his third shot through the now empty doorway. Dean shot three spaced bolts through the wall between himself and the door.

"Cease fire!" Dean ordered over the tinkling of breaking glass and ceramics that came from the room. The three Marines listened for movement, but once the tinkling ended, the room was silent.

"In the room," Dean shouted through his speaker, "if you can, throw your weapons out. If you're too badly injured, let me know, we'll provide medical attention."

No weapons came through the doorway, no one spoke from within the room.

"Hold your fire, I'm coming in to check on you." Then on the fire team circuit, "Cover me." Carefully, silently, he eased over to where he could see through the door, bringing a bedroom into view. It wasn't a large room, and it looked like it belonged to a teenage girl who had recently redecorated it from being a young girl's room. A plasma bolt had gone through a bed with a frilly cover, now smoldering. Next to the bed was a filigree nightstand that had held a cut-glass lamp and several now unidentifiable ceramic objects, all of which were partly melted and broken. Next to the nightstand, a man sat slumped against the wall; his hands loosely held a shotgun across his thighs. A hole was burned through the left side of his chest—he was dead. From the angle of the shot that killed him, Dean thought it was from his blaster. Glass beads lay on the floor next to the man, melted from the shattered window above. A bundle of bedclothes tossed in the far corner of the room moved.

Dean almost flew through the room; he landed on the bundle hard enough to knock the wind out of whoever was hiding under it. He rolled off and roughly yanked the linens away.

A girl lay there. She looked to be about fourteen years old and was dressed in what Dean thought was local peasant garb, though of too fine a cut and quality to be authentic. A stuffed doll lay tossed aside near her. She was struggling to draw a breath.

Dean took a quick look around; no one was under the bed, the hope chest at the bed's foot was too small to hold anyone other than a child, there was nothing else a person could hide in or under.

"Izzy, the closet," Dean ordered. "Triple John, cover him." He rose to his feet and pulled the girl to hers. He slung his blaster, and holding the girl upright by her arm, slapped her back to make her cough. She did, and sucked in a deep, gasping breath, then almost wrenched herself from his grasp reaching for the doll. Dean gave her enough slack to reach it.

Then she saw the dead man and shrieked, "You killed my daddy!" The girl wildly swung the doll with her free arm, but couldn't see her target and spun so violently from the force of her swing that she would have fallen had Dean not kept his grip on her arm.

"He shot at me, girl. I wouldn't have killed him if he'd come out quietly. But he tried to kill me first! I had to."

"You came to kill us anyway. And you were going to, to—you were going to rape me!" She clutched the doll to her face.

"Shit."

"Closet's clear," Godenov broke in. "So's the hope chest."

"Let's get out of here." Dean headed for the door, pulling the girl with him. "Who told you that, girl?" he asked her. "Whoever it was lied to you. The liar, *that's* who killed your father."

She didn't listen, but screamed and tried to pull away, waving the doll as though she would fling it away. He was too strong, though, and she was dragged along with him. When they reached the living room he shook her and snarled, "Stop struggling or I'll throw you over my shoulder and carry you."

"Y-You wouldn't!"

In answer, Dean slung her over his shoulder like a sack of dirty laundry. He unslung his blaster and carried it in the hand that wasn't holding her legs.

The girl screamed again, and kicked and beat at him with the doll and one fist, but not violently enough to break away and fall to the floor. She beat her fists futilely against Dean's back. She was the only one of them who saw the glow of the flames beginning to devour her bedroom.

Staff Sergeant Hyakowa and Sergeant Kerr were waiting outside the house. Kerr's face showed. Hyakowa had his helmet tucked under his arm. The girl screamed again and began blubbering when she saw them. Being manhandled by an invisible man was one thing, seeing a face and a head hovering in midair was something entirely different.

Dean raised his screens, showing his face. "This girl and a man with a shotgun were the only people inside," he reported. He grimaced. "Someone told them we were going to kill them and rape her."

Hyakowa made a face. "Damn, I wish people wouldn't say things like that. It gets too many civilians needlessly killed. All right, bind her wrists and ankles, then leave her in the street for someone to pick up and take to the collection point." He glanced at the house, then looked at it again. Flames were starting to shoot out of the left side of the house in the back. "Belay that. Take her to the collection point yourself. It's two blocks back."

Dean shifted his blaster to the hand holding the girl's legs and gave her bottom a sharp smack. "Can you walk, or are you going to make me carry you?" he asked.

"I-I'll walk," she stammered. He let her down and tried not to look disgusted as she used a sleeve to wipe snot from her nose and mouth.

He took his helmet off and said, "Look at me. See? I'm a man, not a monster. Let's go. We'll probably find people you know, and they'll take care of you."

"W-Where are we g-going?" She hid her face with the doll.

"To a collection point, where people are being gathered to keep them out of trouble." He looked at her harshly. "And to keep them from getting hurt."

The girl looked up at Dean's hovering face. She wanted to believe what he said, she wanted to believe him *so* badly. But these Confederation Marines were the devil incarnate. She knew it was so, her daddy told her so. And they *killed* her daddy and they had her and there was nothing she could do about it. She bravely clutched her rag doll to her chest and went with the Marines to whatever hell they had waiting for her.

CHAPTER NINE

Second squad had an easier time going down West Street than first squad had advancing along Center Street; most of the residents of Gilbert's Corners who lived on the west side had fled to the imagined safety of the 819th Regiment's encampment as soon as they realized an attack was under way.

A massive firefight was raging to the southwest of Gilbert's Corners when second squad reached the south end of the village. Sergeant Kerr didn't like it, but orders were orders, so he held the squad in place when they reached the village's southern edge.

"What's happening, honcho?" Corporal Chan asked on the squad's command circuit. As the squad's senior fire team leader, it was his place to ask the question.

"We're waiting for orders," Kerr replied.

"We've got Marines in a fight over there," Corporal Claypoole said. "We should go and help them out."

"No shit, Sherlock," Kerr answered drily. "But *my* honcho said we're to hold in place until further orders. When *my* honcho gives me orders, I obey them."

"Ah, right. Okay, we wait."

"You got that right." Kerr waited, and so did his Marines.

Lieutenant General Kyr Godalgonz didn't much like what he saw. Alpha Company, on the right flank, had slowed the advance of the regiment coming from its southeast, and Bravo Company was beginning to roll up the flank of the force pinning down Charlie Company. But Bravo wasn't rolling the flank up fast enough to free up Charlie to go to the aid of Alpha. It was going to be touch and go whether 29th FIST would reach the battle area soon enough to help Alpha. Thirty-fourth FIST was just finishing its sweep and search of Gilbert's Corners, but none of its companies was close enough to help Alpha, either. Thirty-fourth had to go by foot. Godalgonz wasn't about to waste any time or energy wishing he had some Dragons. He didn't have the armored amphibians, so he simply had to make do without.

To make matters worse, he didn't know where the regiment to the northeast was now; he'd barely found it on his UPUD when the enemy started knocking out the string-of-pearls satellites and he lost his overview of the battlefield. So he took what action he could.

"Viper, this is Killer."

"Killer, Viper. Go," Brigadier Sturgeon answered immediately. He'd been listening in on Godalgonz's command circuit and was waiting for the call.

"Do you see where Alpha 17 is?"

"That's affirmative, Killer."

"Send Kilo to help them roll that flank. I need to free Bravo 17." Kilo Company was on 34th FIST's right flank, the closest to 17th FIST's action.

"Roger, Killer. They're on their way."

Commander Usner, 34th FIST's operations officer, stood close enough to Sturgeon that he was able to overhear the conversation. Sturgeon, helmet and gloves off, looked at him and gave a hand signal. Usner, also without helmet or gloves, returned a thumbs-up, and went to his own comm to call Captain Terris, Kilo Company's commanding officer, to pass the order.

"More news, Viper," Godalgonz continued. A force of probable regiment size is approaching from the northeast. Here's where they were." He transmitted a screenshot of his UPUD display made just before the string-of-pearls went down. "I don't know where they are now."

"Received, Killer," Sturgeon said as he looked at the image Godalgonz downloaded to his UPUD. "I understand your lack of current intelligence." The satellite communications of his UPUD had gone dead when the Coalition's satellite-killer guns had gone into action, the same as it had for the general. "We'll stop them."

"Killer out." Godalgonz, still pinned down, took a quick look around the edge of the debris pile and returned his attention to his personal problem.

"Any ideas on how we can get out of here?" he asked Ensign Rynchus.

Rynchus grinned at him. "What do you mean, 'we,' paleface?" he asked. Then, timing his movement, he sprang up and dashed at the strongpoint that held the automatic weapon system that held Godalgonz in place.

Sergeant Kerr listened carefully to Captain Conorado's squad leaders' briefing, and just as carefully examined the map the company commander had transmitted to the squad leaders via their platoon commanders. The briefing wasn't as good as it would have been had Conorado gathered the squad leaders, but time was of the essence.

"We move out in zero two." Conorado ended his briefing.

Kerr, like all the other squad leaders in Company L, took advantage of those two minutes to brief his men. He had so little to tell them, two minutes was more than he needed. Seconds after the two minutes had passed, word came over the company net to move out.

"Up and at 'em, people," Kerr said. "Second fire team, first, third. Remember, we're the company's right flank."

Lance Corporal Schultz grunted and headed to the head of the squad column. Everybody knew that third platoon's second squad had the company's right flank because of him. Schultz always took the most vulnerable position in movement or defense; he didn't trust anybody else to spot the enemy as quickly as he did. Nobody would ever dare argue the point with him.

"Let me know what's happening, Hammer," Kerr said as soon as the squad was formed and in motion.

Schultz's answering grunt conveyed "No shit."

In moments, the company was outside the narrow confines of Gilbert's Corners, on a line of squad columns, and headed across fields of low-growing legumes. Soon the rumble and *whir* of military vehicles became audible ahead of them.

Minutes later, Schultz spoke for the first time. "Bad guys, foot, five hundred, crossing." Enemy infantry, five hundred meters distant, moving across the squad's front. Schultz didn't bother mentioning that the enemy soldiers hadn't noticed the Marines approaching from their flank; he wasn't one to use unnecessary words. Kerr immediately passed the word to Ensign Bass on the off chance Bass hadn't heard Schultz's report; Bass had and was already relaying it to Captain Conorado.

"Company L, all elements hold in place," Conorado ordered the company as soon as he got Bass's report. Then, on the third platoon command circuit, "Give me some numbers and disposition."

Bass was examining the enemy force through his light-gatherer and magnifier screens. "Looks like two companies, moving in columns abreast. Their lead elements are already out of the forest. I hear vehicles, but don't see any yet. They sound like they're much deeper in the woods."

Conorado glanced at his UPUD, wishing that the string-of-pearls was still functioning, but he didn't waste time on it. "Are you in a position to pin them?" he asked.

Bass snorted. "We're in position to do anything we want to them."

"Wait one." Conorado transferred to the battalion command circuit.

Commander van Winkle had been listening in and didn't need to be filled in on the situation. "Have that platoon take them out," he said. "Reinforce them with half of your assault platoon to make it go down faster. I don't need to tell you how to deploy the rest of your company to block reinforcements or a counterattack. Now do it."

"Aye aye," Conorado said, then switched back to the company command circuit and began giving orders to his platoon commanders. Then he ordered his UAV team to put their birds in the air, to recon the vehicles he could hear in the trees. He needed to know how far away they were, and how many of what types in case he had to defend against them.

The company was in a line of squads in column, with third platoon on the right, a section of the assault platoon between it and second platoon, to third platoon's left. So it only took a moment for the assault section to position itself with third platoon.

Charlie Bass, using his infra screen, looked side to side at the Marines lying in the field, awaiting his command to open fire on the enemy soldiers crossing the Marine front five hundred meters distant, oblivious to the immediate and deadly danger they were in. He raised his infra and looked at the distant men and felt a fleeting sorrow that so many of them would so soon be dead. But when men go to war, men die. *His* job wasn't to feel sorry for the soldiers in the sights of his Marines, but rather to make sure that more of the enemy soldiers died than of his own men; try to see to it that enough of the soldiers on the other side died quickly enough that none of his own men paid with their lives.

Bass quickly checked with Staff Sergeant Hyakowa to make sure the squads and guns had their targets and fields of fire, then said on the platoon circuit, "You know what to do. On my mark, kill them. One. Two. *Fire!*"

As one, the blasters, guns, and assault guns of third platoon and the attached assault section opened fire on the moving column of Coalition soldiers. The targets—at five hundred meters they appeared less like walking, breathing human beings than animated targets—began falling, many with holes burned through limbs, torsos, or heads, some dropping to find cover from the horrible balls and streams of plasma that sizzled past at waist height. Gut-wrenching, soul-rending screams came from men in agony from the instantly cauterized wounds bored through limbs and guts by the crackling, sizzling plasma bolts that burned through bone, flesh, and gristle; but the *CRACK-sizzle* was all the Marines could hear from the world outside their helmets.

Less than ten seconds from when Charlie Bass gave the command to open fire, more than a quarter of the two-hundred-plus Coalition soldiers that third platoon shot at were dead or wounded. The rest were squeezing themselves against the ground, scraping hollows in the dirt to get even farther below the plasma bolts that streamed above them. Many of them fired wildly, paying no attention to the direction the bolts pinning them down came from. Only a few raised their heads above the vegetation to locate targets. Those few were hit if they didn't duck back down fast enough; even when they did, fire quickly blasted through the concealing vegetation in quest for them.

Charlie Bass saw that the enemy soldiers had gone to ground, that there were only briefly visible targets for his Marines to shoot at, and ordered a change in their firing pattern. "Third platoon," he ordered on the platoon circuit, "on my command, volley fire, four-seven-five." Everyone fire at a line on the ground, four hundred and seventy-five meters distant. "Three, two, one, *fire!*"

The blasters and guns of third platoon stopped their individual, questing fire and sent their bolts downrange to strike the ground on a line short of where the enemy soldiers lay. The bolts hit the ground and glanced off it. Some of the bolts ricocheted high into the air, but most of them skimmed the ground, as close to the dirt as a prone man.

"Left five, *fire!*" Bass ordered, and all the weapons fired again, each Marine aiming along the same line but five meters to the left of his previous shot. "Left five, *fire!*" Again, the aiming point shifted to the left. "Right ten, *fire!*" The Marines fired again, close to their original aiming points. "Right five, *fire!*" Once more, the plasma bolts shifted their strikes to the right.

The two companies of Coalition soldiers had to be suffering such heavy casualties that it was only a matter of time before the survivors would have to surrender. But where were the vehicles the Marines had heard deeper in the forest?

Sergeant Flett and Corporal MacLeash wasted no time getting their unmanned aerial vehicles aloft, even though Flett grimaced at not camouflaging them before launch. All living planets had fliers; giant insectoids, avians, reptilians, mammalian, *something.* The Marine UAVs could be disguised as almost any flier of the right size—and almost always were. The camouflage mimicked not only the outer appearance of the selected fliers, but aped their movements as well, and even their infrared signatures. Flett didn't know why Company L's UAV team hadn't been issued camouflage kits for the raid, possibly because higher-higher didn't think the FISTs on the raid would be on location long enough to need them. Whatever the reason, the kits hadn't been issued. So he and MacLeash launched their UAVs without camouflage.

The UAVs were battle cruiser gray, about half a meter nose to tail, with slightly mobile wings a few centimeters longer than their fuse-lages. The two UAVs lifted on command and headed toward the forest along divergent paths until they were a hundred meters apart. When they reached the trees, UAV 2, guided by MacLeash, flew a hundred meters above the canopy, high enough to look down into the trees in both visual and infrared, to see through all breaks in the overhead. Flett flew UAV 1 low over the canopy. The UAV team leader watched not only his own monitors, but those for UAV 2 as well, looking for places where UAV 1 could duck beneath the canopy to investigate more closely and then come back up. Less than a minute after launch, the two UAVs were over the forest, moving in the direction of the vehicle noise. Seen from above, the canopy was dense, but spottily broken. Flett ordered MacLeash into a search pattern to the right of the midline of the sounds and raised his own altitude by fifty meters to run a search pattern left of the center line.

Half a kilometer in, they began to see fleeting images of camou-flaged vehicles moving toward the fields. Flett sent MacLeash to orbit his dive area, then dipped below the canopy. UAV 1 had to go lower than Flett anticipated; seen from the top, the canopy looked like it spread horizontally with plenty of air between the leaves and the ground. But that wasn't the case below; the foliage was thick and bushy halfway to the ground, so Flett had to drop his UAV down to less than ten-meters' altitude to see more than directly below the airborne vehicle.

And had to dart right back up bare seconds later when fire from multiple crew-served weapons began to converge on the UAV. Flett had to maneuver the UAV violently to avoid crashing into branches, and to keep from being hit by the streams of fléchettes that pursued it.

UAV 1 might have been below the canopy only seconds, but it was long enough for the bird to scan an arc of almost 120 degrees of the land under the trees in visible light and transmit its findings. Flett made sure the data stream was saved as he climbed to five hundred meters and ordered MacLeash to do the same. As soon as the two UAVs were at that altitude and circling with their infrared detectors trained on the forest below, Flett transmitted his brief view of what was on the forest floor to Captain Conorado. He took a few seconds to scan the images himself, then went through it again in slo-mo, comparing it with what he saw in his and MacLeash's infrared views. What he found made him swear softly: more than a hundred vehicles were heading toward Company L's position. Half of them were troop-carrying lorries. The other half were armored combat vehicles. The infrared views from the orbiting UAVs showed even more vehicles behind them.

CHAPTER TEN

Captain Conorado glanced at the brief visual UAV 1 had acquired under the canopy, and at the infrared feeds from the orbiting UAVs, juddering as the UAVs maneuvered to avoid the streams of fléchettes that speared out of the canopy. The armored vehicles he saw were smaller than the Teufelpanzers 34th FIST had faced on Diamunde, and had no main gun turrets. Instead, their fronts sloped sharply backward to a flat top; their sides also sloped, though less sharply. Three weapons poked out of the front glasis: a small-bore cannon and two fléchette guns, all on flexible mounts that allowed them a great range of fire. Another fléchette gun was gimbal-mounted on the top; most of the vehicles had a soldier standing in a hatch on top, manning the gimbal-mounted fléchette guns. Conorado almost instantaneously saw the implications of the display.

"Lima One, Lima Two, this is Lima Six Actual," he said into the company command circuit. "Look alive. Bad guys, six hundred meters into the trees. Lima Three, the bad guys are headed toward your flank, shift squads as necessary to repel. All Lima Actuals, patch into UAV feed." Then he reported the vehicular movement to battalion head-quarters.

"It looks like you've done everything you can to prepare with what you've got," Commander van Winkle said when he got Cono-rado's report. "If I decide you need it, I'll try to divert a platoon from either Kilo or Mike to reinforce you. In the meanwhile, I'll contact FIST and request air support." He didn't mention that he wished the three FISTs had brought along their artillery batteries and Dragons. But then, nobody had expected the amount of force the Coalition was bringing against the Marine raid-in-force. What he did say was, "The prisoners are being boarded on hoppers for transit to the landing beach. As soon as the hoppers return, we'll be able to begin withdrawal." He signed off.

Commander van Winkle hadn't had to mention the lack of artillery or Dragons to Captain Conorado; the Company L commander was fully aware of the lack, and the sound reason for leaving the heavy equipment behind. The raid was supposed to be a quick in-and-out, and artillery—even towed by the Dragons—would have slowed things down. Conorado also knew that Kilo Company was helping 17th FIST, and thought Mike Company was fully involved with evacuating the captured members of the Coalition government and other prisoners. So, unless some of the Raptors of the FISTs' air squadrons could be diverted from their current operations, Company L was on its own against the rapidly approaching vehicles and the infantry half of them carried. He wished he knew what kind of armor the fighting vehicles had; his company didn't have any armor-killer weapons. If the armor wasn't too heavy, the guns of the company's assault platoon, even the guns of the blaster platoons, should be able to kill them. If the armor was light enough, the blasters could do the job—not quickly and cleanly, but they'd kill the beasts nonetheless.

Lance Corporal Schultz listened intently on the platoon circuit when Ensign Charlie Bass gave orders for the platoon to redeploy to meet the new threat. Schultz didn't bother to nod or give any other sign that he agreed with Bass's repositioning of the squads and the attached assault gun section; he knew Bass would shift second squad to meet the threat—just as he knew that Sergeant Kerr would arrange second squad so that he, Schultz, would be on the end of the squad's line. As far as Schultz was concerned, that was the natural order of things—only a fool would think otherwise, and Charlie Bass wasn't a fool.

First squad and one gun team remained in place to make sure the Coalition soldiers that third platoon had pinned down stayed pinned during the coming action. The other gun team and the entire assault-gun section shifted to face the threat from the forest along with second squad. The threat wasn't long in coming.

The forest facing third platoon suddenly erupted with massed cannon, fléchette streams, and small-arms fire all aimed in the platoon's direction. Charlie Bass hunkered as low as he could to stay below the incoming fire, and examined the download from the circling UAVs displayed on his UPUD. The infrared images weren't smooth, as the UAVs were still jinking to evade the sporadic fire aimed at them, but they were clear enough to show the Coalition vehicles forming two lines inside the forest, infantry interspersed among them. The pattern of movement along the second line told him those were the troop-carrier lorries, unloading troops for deployment into assault formations. That left the front row as the armored vehicles.

The pattern of fire coming at the Marines told Bass that the enemy knew approximately where third platoon was, but not exactly, which was why none of the Marines had been hit yet. Still, with the amount of fire coming their way, casualties *were* going to happen—and sooner rather than later.

"Kerr, Kelly, DaCruz," Bass said on the platoon circuit, "stand by for a HUD transmission." He pressed the appropriate code into his UPUD and transmitted the current UPUD image to the comps of the squad leader, the gun squad leader, and the assault section leader; three adjacent vehicles in the front row were marked. "Can you see where they are?"

The three leaders looked at the image on their Heads-Up Displays and correlated them with what they saw of the fire coming from the forest.

"I've got mark three," Kerr reported. He couldn't actually see the vehicle, it was too far back under the trees, but his infra screen showed its location.

"I see mark two," Sergeant Kelly said. He also used his infra to locate his target.

Staff Sergeant DaCruz, the assault section leader, was the last to reply. "I've got all three spotted," he said. Again, the infra screen showed the precise location of the targets.

"Second squad," Bass ordered, "kill target three. Guns, kill target two. Assault, kill target one, then shift fire as needed to assist guns and second squad. Questions?"

All three leaders understood their orders.

Kerr said into his squad circuit, "Second squad, on my mark, concentrated fire on my spot. Use your infras." He sighted his blaster on the infra glow of target three and pressed its firing lever. Before his bolt had time to reach the enemy vehicle, nine more bolts were on their way. "Fire," Kerr whispered to himself as he squeezed the firing lever again. "Fire, fire, fire." To his flanks, the nine Marines under his command were doing the same, sending hundreds of plasma bolts downrange at their designated target.

The target vehicle didn't cease its firing, but within seconds after the deluge commenced it began to move in an attempt to get out of the concentrated fire. But the Marines were looking at it through their infras and saw it move; they moved their aiming points to keep hitting the vehicle.

At the same time Kerr gave second squad his orders, Kelly told Corporal Kindrachuck, "Watch my spot, then kill that bastard." He aimed his blaster at the vehicle he saw through his infra and fired. First gun team, with Lance Corporal Tischler on the trigger, sent a lengthy stream of plasma bolts at the armored vehicle Kelly had marked. The target's cannon stopped firing almost immediately, but it wasn't dead; it went into reverse and tried to run from the gun's fire.

DaCruz gave his orders and sent his spotting round at target one. A second later, all three assault guns under his command struck the armored vehicle with plasma streams, each much heavier than the stream from the gun of third platoon's gun team. The target bucked and split at its seams from internal explosions. Satisfied that his initial target was killed, DaCruz shifted his attention to the other two targets. "First squad," he ordered, "add your fire to the gun team's fire. Second and third squads, add your fire to the blaster squads'."

The three assault squad leaders didn't reply with words; they saw where the gun and the blasters were firing and shifted their aim to assist. In seconds, all three targets Charlie Bass had designated were killed, and there was a gap in the line of enemy armor.

But the Coalition officers and sergeants had seen the Marine fire and began adjusting the fire of their own men, bringing them to bear on the Marines' locations. Bass wasted no time ordering his men to change position, and the weapons of the Marines of third platoon and the attached assault section fell silent while they moved out of what was rapidly turning into a killing ground.

Captain Conorado listened in on third platoon's orders, and saw the results of the fire on his UPUD. *Good,* he thought, *the assault guns can kill the armor.* As soon as Charlie Bass's men stopped firing and began to move away from the incoming fire, he got on the company circuit.

"All Lima elements except third platoon, fire on bandits in the forest. Assault guns kill the armor quickly. Blaster squads, use volley fire on the infantry. Fire and move before they can get your range. Third platoon, resume fire when you are clear. Do it now."

Almost as one, the Marines of first and second platoon opened fire into the forest. The blaster squads used volley fire; the squad leaders selected aiming lines short of where the Coalition infantrymen were, so the plasma bolts would deflect off the ground and skitter deeper into the trees, increasing their chances of striking targets. Not all of the bolts were deflected by the ground; some ignited vegetation and started small fires. The four guns of the two platoons added their fire to that of the blaster squads, and the combined fire looked almost like a tightly woven fiery fence slicing through the trees. The three squads of second assault section began firing at the armored vehicles, and each gun killed its target within seconds of first striking it. Third platoon's second squad, gun team, and the attached assault section reached their new positions and joined in the fire.

But before Company L's massed fire had time to do serious damage to the reinforced regiment in the trees, the remaining Coalition armored vehicles all began moving and plunged out of the trees—straight at third platoon.

Captain Conorado didn't need the UPUD display from the UAVs to see the armored assault on his right flank. "Lima three," he snapped into the company circuit, "use everything you've got to stop that attack.

Assault platoon, use all assets on the advancing armor. First and second platoons, shift your guns to help repel the armor—maintain blaster-squad fire into the trees."

In seconds, all the weapons of third platoon and the assault platoon, along with the guns of the other two platoons, were firing into the charging armored vehicles. Some of the armor stopped abruptly, dead in its tracks. Some died, but continued rolling forward from inertia. Many had to maneuver to avoid dead vehicles, yet on they came, too many for the Marines to kill them all before they closed the gap.

"By fire teams," Sergeant Kerr ordered as soon as he realized the guns and assault guns weren't going to be able to stop the armored column, "concentrate your fire on the treads. Stop those fuckers before they reach us!"

"You heard the man," Corporal Claypoole shouted over the fire team circuit.

"This one," Lance Corporal Schultz growled, and fired at the treads of an approaching vehicle.

Claypoole and Lance Corporal MacIlargie saw where he was firing and joined their fire to his. All three of the Marines fired as rapidly as they could, but the vehicle was moving too fast and the three of them couldn't concentrate enough heat steadily on one spot to damage the treads.

"Up!" Schultz barked, and shifted his aim to the gun mount on the front of the vehicle.

Claypoole and MacIlargie followed Schultz's example, and in an instant the three of them were pouring fire on the thin armor where the vehicle's gun barrel protruded through the thicker front armor.

"Got it!" Schultz yelled into the fire team circuit, and began firing at the gun mount on another vehicle bearing down on them.

Claypoole and MacIlargie were a beat slow on following him, they hadn't immediately seen what Schultz had—the metal holding the gun barrel in place weakened and gave way under the weight and jerking of the firing weapon.

The heat of the plasma bolts that struck the faceplate also weakened the barrel so that it bent a couple of degrees off true, enough to jam fléchettes and shatter the barrel. Fragments of hot faceplate, barrel, and bits of plasma flew into the crew compartment, wounding the gunner and driver, and the vehicle slewed violently into the path of a charging mass of armor and weapons. The second vehicle slammed into the first, tipping it over. The second vehicle's driver wasn't able to reverse direction quickly enough, and his vehicle rolled up the side of the first at an angle. The two vehicles' tracks hooked into each other, so when the driver of the second finally reversed the tracks, they bent and snapped; the second armored vehicle slid off and fell to its side with a bone-rattling *crash!*

When the armored vehicles broke out of the trees, Corporal Dean realized that the greatest immediate danger they presented to the Marines was their cannon fire. He ordered his men to zero in on his aiming point and keep firing at it until he told them to stop. He picked a vehicle and aimed at its barrel, about halfway down from the muzzle. Dean, Lance Corporal Godenov, and PFC McGinty poured fire onto the middle of the barrel, and in seconds the barrel overheated and bent. When the gunner didn't see the growing red spot in time and fired another burst, his fléchettes tore through the softening, bending metal and the forward half of the slagging barrel gave way. Streams of dripping metal solidified in the mouth of the remaining half of the barrel. The armored vehicle spun about and retreated back into the forest.

Dean and his fire team turned their attention to another charging vehicle.

Corporal Doyle had begun trembling when he first heard the orders for third platoon to attack the two companies crossing the fields. One platoon against two companies? That was severe odds, even if the platoon was Confederation Marines and the two companies were from no better than a second-rank army. There were just too many soldiers in two companies for a single platoon to take on.

Well, third platoon had taken on the two companies and defeated them while suffering no casualties. *I guess that's the difference between Marines and a second-rank army,* Doyle thought. He also conceded that the assault gun section made a major difference in favor of the Marines. But this was different: this was *more than* two companies of armored vehicles, and third platoon didn't have *any* antiarmor weapons. Still, he was a Marine, and so were his men, and Marines are supposed to do more with less than anybody else—and do it on shorter notice. Marines were also supposed to win all their battles. Doyle had no notion of how third platoon was supposed to win this battle, not even with the assistance of the entire assault platoon and some of the guns from first and second platoons. Well, even if he didn't know how to win this fight, Corporal Doyle was a Marine, and Marines do or d . . . belay that—Marines *do,* so even if he had no idea how, Corporal Doyle and his men were going to make their contribution to winning this battle.

Doyle looked toward the forest as an armored vehicle emerged from the trees, the vehicle commander standing in a hatch. Doyle didn't know whether that soldier was a brave man or simply stupid, but he did know that either way he was a dead man. He made sure of it by firing three rapid bolts. At least two hit, and the vehicle commander collapsed on top of the hatch.

But Corporal Doyle wasn't supposed to be searching out individual targets, he was supposed to be directing his fire team in ways that would kill the approaching armor. Now how the *hell* are three blastermen without antiarmor weapons supposed to kill armored vehicles? He saw someone firing at the tracks of one of them, and realized that wasn't going to work. Not unless . . .

"Summers, Smedley," Doyle said into his fire team circuit. "Over there." He snapped off a shot that struck the idling wheel of a vehicle running to the side of the others. "Shoot that and keep shooting it until that thing stops." All the while Doyle was telling his men what to do, he kept firing at the idling wheel. Smedley figured out what Doyle had in mind before his fire team leader even finished giving his orders and added his fire to Doyle's a beat before Summers did.

The idling wheel at the top front end of the tracks was thicker and harder than Doyle had realized, and heated more slowly. But eventually the hub gave way to the continuing assault, and smoking lubricants flowed out where the hubcap had been. After a few more turns, the idling wheel froze. The vehicle jerked when the track started to buckle, and the track broke.

It had taken so long to fracture the idling wheel that Doyle and his men didn't have enough time to disable another before the armored vehicles were among the Marines of third platoon. The big guns of the assault platoon and the lesser guns of first and second platoons had to cease fire for fear of hitting their own men.

CHAPTER ELEVEN

Ensign Rynchus timed his dash precisely and dove to the ground in front of the strongpoint a heartbeat ahead of the returning stream of fléchettes that would have shredded him an instant later. He raised his helmet screens to show his face, looked back over his shoulder toward Lieutenant General Godalgonz, grinned broadly, and mouthed, "I always was faster than you." He would have thrown his boss a thumbs-up, but would have had to remove a glove for the general to see it. He slipped his chameleon screen back into place and began crawling to the rear of the strongpoint. He was fairly certain the strongpoint was unoccupied, but that didn't mean it wasn't under observation by someone who could direct fire at him if he showed himself. Of course, if that hypothetical observer had infrared vision, nothing Rynchus did to conceal himself from view in the visual would do him a blessed bit of good.

Occupied or not, the strongpoint had to have means of access for maintenance, and the access was most likely in the strongpoint's rear, so that's where Rynchus had to go if he was to disable the weapon and free Godalgonz to move out of his pinned-down position.

He found the hatch exactly where he expected it to be; it was a plasteel panel large enough to admit a man, centered in the rear of the strongpoint. A cursory examination revealed the latch-plate protected behind a sliding panel on the right side of the hatch. Rynchus slid the panel aside and took a look inside. He didn't like what he found: a keypad. He knew that soldiers could be lazy and the hatch might not be locked, so he tried the latch-plate. It was locked. He turned to the keypad and saw that four of the keys showed signs of wear. He pressed them in random order, then tried the latch-plate again. Still locked. Rapidly, he tried four more combinations, but the hatch remained locked. Before trying more combinations, he decided to check the hinges.

The hatch didn't have hinges; it had one hinge that ran the height of the hatch. The hinge was recessed, protected by an armored strip designed to slide out of the way when the hatch opened. The design of the slide was such that he couldn't easily hold it out of the way if he attempted to break through the hinge strip. Using both his magnifier and light-gatherer screens, he went back to the keypad for a closer look. He thought that if someone used two or more fingers rather than one to open it, the keys might show different usage. They did, though the differences were subtle, and may have been a trick of the light. He watched carefully as he flexed his own fingers in a pattern that matched the keys that showed use. Each time he used his index or middle finger first, it seemed to strike the hardest. Between those two fingers, the last of the four to strike was the lightest—although his ring finger always made the lightest strike.

Four keys made for almost ten thousand possible combinations, but knowing which keys came first and last reduced the possibilities to little more than one hundred. A hundred combinations was still too many to go through quickly, but far fewer than ten thousand. He started tapping keys.

The twelfth combination resulted in a click from beneath the plate. Rynchus stopped tapping the keys and pressed the plate. The hatch swung aside.

While it was very likely that none of the defenders had noticed the cover panel open, or the brief movement of the strip protecting the recessed hinge strip, nobody even glancing in the direction of the strongpoint from its rear could fail to miss seeing that the access hatch was open. Ensign Rynchus knew that time was of the essence. He had to disable the gun and *move* before somebody saw the open hatch and realized it had been breached.

But Rynchus barked out a brief laugh when he looked inside the strongpoint. There wasn't enough clear space for him to crawl all the way in and close it from inside, but everything he needed to disable it from the hatch was right at hand. The first thing he did was smack the ammunition hopper to knock it out of alignment—the gun stopped firing almost immediately. Then he used a few carefully placed bolts from his handblaster to melt strategic bits of electronics. He knew which elements to damage, because the interior of the strongpoint was almost an exact duplicate of an automatic defensive system the Confederation army had used twenty years earlier, a system on which he had trained when the Marine Corps was evaluating it for their own use.

"Time to get out of Dodge, buckaroo," Rynchus murmured when he finished. He drew himself out of the hatch and scooted to the side of the strongpoint before checking for covering fire from other defensive positions. When he didn't see any, he began sprinting back to Lieutenant General Godalgonz. He didn't make it all the way.

The concussion wave from a massive explosion behind Rynchus slammed into him and sent him flying forward. He hit the ground hard on his shoulder, and rolled back to his feet to resume his sprint. He wasn't as fast as he'd been before the explosion.

"I guess some things are faster than you," Godalgonz said when Rynchus joined him. Now that the automatic defensive system no longer had him under fire, the general was on one knee next to the debris pile he'd been hiding behind. "Are you all right? Looked like you landed pretty hard."

"I've landed harder," Rynchus said with a grunt. He grimaced, and added, "I think maybe I broke something." He tried to rotate his shoulder, but it hurt too much. "Something grinds in there when I move it."

"Then you better get yourself to the aid station."

"I'm not hurt badly enough to need the BAS."

"Ensign, I can do without my aide long enough for the surgeon to take a look at you and put a bandage on your boo-boo."

Rynchus shook his head. "I never should have let you talk me into taking a commission. You never used to order me around like this when I was a first sergeant."

"First sergeants can often get away with doing whatever they damn well please, but ensigns *have* to do what lieutenant generals tell them to . . . and I'm telling you to get some medical attention for that shoulder."

"So what happened to that place that it blew up?"

"I was watching through my infra," Godalgonz replied. "Someone fired what looked like an antipersonnel rocket at it, probably trying to get you. It set off a secondary explosion that sent you flying. Now go see the surgeon; I can take care of myself until you get back. I'll be with either Boomer or Viper."

Unseen inside his helmet, Rynchus shook his head. Well, his shoulder did hurt like the blazes. "Aye aye, sir. I'll catch up with you as soon as I get some medical attention."

"The surgeon," Godalgonz said. But Rynchus was already gone, looking for a corpsman to secure his injured shoulder, or give him a painblocker.

Lieutenant General Godalgonz looked at the display on his UPUD; at the moment it showed an overview of the battle area. The view wasn't complete and steady, as it would have been had it shown a string-of-pearls download, but a fragmentary and jerky composite image made up of views transmitted from 17th FIST HQ Company's three UAVs. The three unmanned aerial vehicles weren't flying in synchronization, so there were gaps in their views, as well as jitters when they jinked and dodged to avoid antiaircraft fire. Seventeenth FIST's Bravo Company had begun shifting position to go to the aid of Charlie Company, which was fully engaged with the regiment that attacked from the south; Alpha Company and 34th FIST's Kilo Company had successfully flanked the defensive positions that had held Bravo in place and were rolling up the enemy's line. But Godalgonz saw at a glance that even with Bravo's aid, 17th FIST's right flank was in danger of being turned. He checked on 29th FIST's estimated time of arrival.

"Pitbull," Godalgonz radioed when he saw that 29th was close enough for his UPUD's comm to reach it, "this is Killer. Over."

"Killer, Pitbull. Go." Brigadier Devh answered so quickly he must have been listening for the call.

"Can you get the feed from 17th Actual's UAVs?"

"Looking at it now, Killer."

"Divert one company to assist Charlie 17. Stand by for instructions on the deployment of your remaining forces."

"Aye aye, Killer." Devh switched to his staff circuit and tersely told his chief of staff to send Echo company to the aid of Charlie 17, then reported, "Echo's on its way." Through the window of the hopper he rode in, he saw the hoppers carrying Echo company peel off and head on a tangent to the rest of his FIST.

"Roger," Godalgonz acknowledged as he switched his UPUD to pick up the composite feed from the UAVs of 34th FIST's Headquarters Company . . .

. . . And saw the situation there was worse than that faced by 17th FIST. Company L was fully engaged with an armored battalion that was overrunning it—not a battalion; a closer examination of the image showed that most of the vehicles between the Marines and the forest had been killed. Mike Company couldn't move to Lima's assistance because it was also being assaulted by a battalion or more of armored vehicles. Kilo 34 could be pulled back from assisting Alpha 17, but was too far away to reach Lima 34 in time.

Godalgonz looked at the sky in the direction of the ocean and saw the hoppers with the rest of 29th FIST approaching their designated landing zone. Those Marines *could* reach Lima 34 in time to help. He called Brigadier Devh again.

"Pitbull, Killer. Do you see 34's situation?" Godalgonz asked.

"That's affirmative, Killer."

"Take your remaining companies to his aid. I'm putting you under his operational command. Understood?"

"Aye aye, understood."

Godalgonz switched frequencies. "Viper, Killer. Pitbull is on his way, minus one company. He's zero two out. You have operational command. Questions?"

"Understood. No questions." Brigadier Sturgeon looked to the east. "I see Pitbull," he said.

"I'm on my way. Out." Godalgonz signed off and examined the landscape for a route to Sturgeon's command post, one that would provide him cover from enemy fire while he was on his way. As he took his first steps, he looked toward the approaching hoppers and saw them already separated into two groups, one moving toward Mike Company, the other toward Company L.

Ensign Rynchus didn't waste time going all the way to an aid station; the pain in his shoulder was bad enough that he knew a surgeon would order him sedated and probably have him evacuated. That was unacceptable to him. He was positive that if he got a painblocker and had the shoulder immobilized, he could stay active through the rest of the raid and be where he belonged—at the side of his commander, keeping the general alive and functioning. Finding a corpsman was a breeze for someone who'd been in the Marines for as long as Rynchus.

"What can I do for you, sir?" the corpsman, someone from 17th FIST, asked when Rynchus raised his helmet shields so the corpsman could see his face—everybody knew Lieutenant General Godalgonz and his salty aide.

"Hi, Doc. I banged my shoulder. Need a painblocker and some taping."

"Then come into my examination room and let me take a look." The corpsman led Rynchus into a nearby trench. "Shuck your shirt so I can get to your shoulder," the corpsman said as soon as both of them ducked below ground level. He reached for a cutter when he saw the difficulty Rynchus was having getting his shirt off.

"No cutting, Doc, I'm going right back out as soon as you patch me up, and I need my chameleons to work."

"Whatever you say," the corpsman said, and helped Rynchus remove his shirt. He whistled softly when he saw the broad bruising on the ensign's shoulder, back, and chest. "How'd you do that?" he asked as he began probing.

"You heard that big explosion a few minutes ago? It caught me."

"You're lucky." The corpsman finished probing and reached into his medkit. "A preliminary exam doesn't reveal any broken bones"—he gave Rynchus a sharp look—"which doesn't mean nothing's broken. Understand?"

"Yeah, Doc, I know there could be all kinds of stuff busted up in there."

"Including broken blood vessels, torn muscles, and disconnected tendons. Ensign, you've got to get yourself to a surgeon and get evacuated."

Rynchus gave him a grin that was half grimace. "Doc, that's why I came to you instead of going to an aid station. I need to get back to the general, take care of his ass."

"Top." He briefly ignored Rynchus's commission. "I know better than to pull rank on you, so I won't try. But I've got to give you more than a painblocker. Hang in there, this'll take a few minutes." The corpsman proceeded to give Rynchus a series of injections, beginning with a painblocker and continuing through blood thinners to prevent clots from forming and breaking loose and winding up with a coolant to prevent additional swelling. Then he applied a few patches on and around the bruising to provide time-release blood thinners and painblockers. When that was done, he covered the entire shoulder with a synthskin bandage. When the shoulder was bandaged, he helped Rynchus put his shirt back on, then applied another synthskin bandage that secured Rynchus's upper arm to his side.

"Got to keep this thing immobile to prevent further injury," the corpsman said. He shook his head and added, "Not that there won't be further injury with you running around out there instead of being hospitalized."

Rynchus looked at his immobilized upper arm. The synthskin bandage was clearly visible. He shook his head. "You know, Doc, if I get shot and killed because one of the bad guys sees that, I'm going to come back and haunt your scuzzy ass."

The corpsman laughed. "Sure you will. Now get out of my examination room before I come to my senses and hit you with a knockout so you can be medevaced and taken care of properly."

Rynchus laughed with him, then punched him lightly on the shoulder. "You're a good guy, Doc." Using only his good arm for leverage, he clambered out of the trench and went in search of his boss.

* * *

Lieutenant General Godalgonz saw that 17th FIST, with the aid of a company from 29th FIST, would be able to handle the Coalition force attacking from the southeast. Thirty-fourth FIST, on the other hand, had as much as it could manage and then some, even with the assistance of the rest of 29th FIST. Lima 34, being overrun by large numbers of enemy armored vehicles, was in particular trouble. He didn't hesitate, but headed directly toward the heaviest fighting, the place where his Marines would be most heartened by the presence of their commander—straight for where Company L was being overrun.

CHAPTER TWELVE

"Second Squad, kill them!" Sergeant Kerr shouted into his squad circuit. He knew that was a horribly inadequate command, but what do you tell a squad of infantrymen being overrun by armored vehicles? "Move, stay out of their line of fire!" The way the vehicles were milling about, that was easier said than done, but it was better than simply ordering his men to kill the beasts.

Corporal Claypoole broke in with, "Remember the Hammer on Diamunde!"

Kerr hadn't been on the Diamunde campaign, he'd been in the hospital recuperating from near death on Elneal; it took him a moment to remember what he'd heard. Lance Corporal Schultz had climbed on top of the Teufelpanzers the Marines had faced in a climactic battle, melted holes in weak spots in the tanks' armor, and fired his blaster through the openings to kill the crews and set off their armaments. By the time he remembered, most of his men were already scrambling onto the moving vehicles.

Second fire team was the first; Lance Corporal MacIlargie had been on Diamunde along with Claypoole and Schultz; they were already moving when Claypoole shouted the reminder. First fire team took a little longer. Even though Corporal Chan had been on Diamunde, neither Lance Corporal Little nor PFC Fisher had, and Chan had to tell them what to do. Corporal Doyle hadn't been in the close-quarters infantry-tank fight, but he'd been on-planet at the time and knew about it. He hustled PFCs Summers and Smedley onto a passing armored vehicle. The word spread like wildfire, and in moments all of the Marines of Company L were scrambling aboard Coalition vehicles. One Marine from first platoon tried to climb the front of a charging vehicle, lost his grip, and fell below the churning tracks, killed. Otherwise, nobody suffered worse than minor burns from grasping hot gun barrels or scrambling across hot engine compartments.

The Coalition's vehicles were armored, but they weren't tanks like the Marines had faced on Diamunde, and their armor was much thinner. Schultz instinctively understood that these vehicles would be vulnerable to rapid fire from Marine blasters at point-blank range. He hopped aboard a vehicle and straddled its main gun, then held the muzzle of his blaster centimeters from the barrel. Ignoring the heat that radiated back at his legs, he fired six bolts as fast as he could. The barrel glowed red, then white, and then bent. Schultz turned his attention to the secondary guns that jutted out of the front of the vehicle, to the sides of the now-useless main gun, and disabled them by putting two bolts into each gun's flexible mount. A *clang* from the vehicle's top jerked his head and blaster in that direction as the vehicle commander emerged through a hatch and reached for the gun mounted next to the hatch. Schultz fired one bolt by reflex, and the vehicle commander flopped backward like a broken doll. Schultz lunged forward, poked the muzzle of his blaster past the commander's hips, aimed down into the compartment, and began firing, twisting around to fire all around inside. There were brief screams, and then silence, from inside as the vehicle lurched and rolled aimlessly forward. Schultz looked through his infra for another vehicle to attack.

Lieutenant Colonel Roy Glukster, the commander of the 504th Sagunto Scout Battalion, quickly realized that the Confederation Marines he had expected to overrun easily, once his vehicles reached them, were mounting his vehicles and fighting them at so close a range that the scout cars couldn't defend themselves.

"Scouts, violent maneuver!" Glukster ordered. "You've got climbers, throw them off. Do not fire at climbers on other vehicles!" That last because he knew the armor on his scout cars couldn't withstand the fire of their own main guns—if they attempted to sweep the Marines off other vehicles, they'd risk killing their own.

Glukster watched anxiously as his scout cars began jinking and swerving violently in their attempts to throw off the Marines. He tried to observe the scout cars through the thermal sight on his own car, but he had trouble focusing on any one scout car for long enough to see clearly if the violent movements were throwing the Marines off. What he could see here and there—in entirely too many places—was guns being disabled by the close-up plasma fire from Marine blasters, holes being melted through the skin of the vehicles, and scout cars careening out of control as their drivers and crews were killed by the Marines. He winced when he saw two scout cars crash into each other. But that was nothing compared to the jolt he suffered when his own scout car collided with another and threw him from his seat into the bulkhead.

Dazed, Glukster grabbed his comm and reversed his earlier order. "All units, use secondary guns, sweep that vermin off your mates!"

One by one, then a few at a time, and finally every car began firing their secondary guns at one another, attempting to kill the Marines clinging to their sides and tops. But too few had their guns still active.

PFC Lary Smedley gripped the barrel of a scout car's secondary gun, holding himself between it and the main gun with one hand, while he fired his blaster at the driver's aperture with the other. Blinded by the damage to his periscope, and distracted by the molten glass dripping from it, the driver yanked his steering yoke wildly, careening about violently. Smedley held on with difficulty, and many of his bolts struck the armor around the aperture.

Suddenly, Corporal Doyle was on the other side of the gun mount Smedley was holding. "You've blinded the driver," Doyle said, "now knock out the main gun! I'll hold you." He grasped the flexible mount of the secondary gun with one hand, and blaster slung over his shoulder, snagged the back of Smedley's belt with the other.

Smedley fired two more bolts before Doyle's orders sunk in. "Main gun, right," he muttered, and turned his blaster to it.

"Both hands," Doyle said when he saw Smedley was still holding the secondary gun. "I've got you secure. Use both hands on your blaster."

"Both hands, both hands." Smedley sounded distracted, as if he was having trouble focusing his thoughts, or in a daze. Still, he released his grasp on the secondary gun and gripped his blaster with both hands. The violent and unpredictable movement of the armored vehicle made holding his aim difficult, but it took only ten plasma bolts to soften the barrel of the main gun enough for it to begin bending.

As soon as Doyle saw the main gun begin to bend, he told Smedley to disable the other secondary gun, which had just started firing. But before Smedley could knock that gun out of action, he heard a *clang* from the top of the scout car. "Grab a handhold!" Doyle shouted, as he released his grip on Smedley's belt and whipped his blaster off his shoulder. His toes scrabbled for a grip on the front of the scout car and he pointed his blaster at the vehicle's top, where he saw a soldier jumping up through the top hatch to grasp the commander's gun. As fast as he could, Doyle squeezed his blaster's firing lever three times, and saw the soldier drop back down through the hatch. Using his feet and one hand, he climbed to the top and thrust his blaster inside, firing as he did so. He heard screams and sizzling from within as the bolts found flesh and electronics, then his blaster jerked in his hands, followed by a fresh scream—someone inside had grabbed the blaster by its barrel but was burned by the hot barrel. He twisted around to fire in the direction he thought the scream had come from.

And then the armored car stopped its jinking and yawing and began rolling in an arc that would become a circle if nothing stopped it.

"Smedley, let's move," Doyle ordered, looking around for another vehicle to attack.

Smedley didn't answer him. He turned his head to where Smedley had been, but only saw blood-stained gouges in the armor of the scout car.

"Smedley!" Doyle called. "Where are you, Smedley!" There was no answer. Then, back along the path the scout car had taken, his infra showed the shape of a man lying broken, run over by the vehicle's tracks. Doyle lay atop the scout car, gaping at the broken body, certain it was Smedley, but still telling himself it wasn't. "Smedley," he murmured, almost whimpered.

"Doyle, move!" Sergeant Kerr's voice boomed in Doyle's helmet.

Doyle shook himself and suddenly became aware of the impact of armor-piercing rounds against the skin of the vehicle he rode. "I'm moving!" he shouted back, and rolled off the scout car on the side away from the rounds bursting through the vehicle's skin.

Quietly cursing himself for leaving the three FISTs' Dragons behind, Lieutenant General Kyr Godalgonz panted as he ran toward the close-quarters infantry-tank battle. He had run daily to keep himself in shape when he was at HQMC, and at every station since he'd been promoted to major general, but the daily run in jogging shorts and sweatshirt on a properly constructed running course was very different from running across a battlefield in chameleons and combat gear under sporadic fire—he wasn't really in proper shape to cover the three kilometers at this speed. But he didn't let that slow him down; he was in command there—the battle and the Marines fighting it were his responsibility.

Lance Corporal MacIlargie hadn't bothered disabling the guns on the first scout car he killed, he'd gone straight to the top, anchored himself to the gimbal mount of the top gun, and burned a hole through the commanders hatch. Then he killed the crew.

Now, having mounted a second armored vehicle, his tactic was exactly the same. He sat cross-legged on the forward edge of the scout car's flat top with his legs wrapped snugly around the mount and his side pressed tightly against it. He held his blaster as nearly vertical as he could, close to the far edge of the hatch so the heat wouldn't be too close to him and any ricochets wouldn't come his way, and began firing as fast as he could pull the firing lever. In seconds, the metal began to glow, turned red, then white, and sagged.

Suddenly, MacIlargie heard—and felt—the scout car's guns begin firing behind him, and became aware of guns being fired from other scout cars. *They're trying to sweep us off!* Ignoring the damage it might do to his blaster, he jabbed its muzzle at the sagging white spot at the rear edge of the hatch. Sparks flew as the muzzle broke through, and he heard a satisfying scream from inside as one of the crewmen was hit by molten metal. Keeping his legs wrapped around the gun mount, he leaned forward from the hips and thrust the muzzle of his blaster through the hole, aimed back underneath himself. He worked the firing lever as he swiveled the blaster side to side.

A *clang* sounded to the side, too close to be the hatch opening on another armored vehicle. Still firing into the scout car's interior, he turned his head toward the noise. A crewman, clutching the top of the vehicle with one hand, dragged himself out of a hatch on the side. With his other hand, the soldier waved a sidearm as his eyes sought a target. The soldier found a target when MacIlargie wrenched his blaster out of the hole he'd burned in the top of the scout car. The soldier quickly pointed and fired—and managed to hit the side of the blaster.

The impact of the slug hitting the blaster knocked it from MacIlargie's one-handed grip. The Marine almost lost his leghold on the gun mount as he reached out to catch his blaster before it tumbled off the side of the vehicle, but his fingers closed on it just in time. The soldier fired again, barely missing MacIlargie's arm. MacIlargie yanked the blaster into a two-handed grip, and screaming a battle cry, lunged toward the soldier, aiming the muzzle of his weapon at the man's face. On the wrong side of the gun gimbal, the side away from the soldier, his reach was short—instead of landing a bone-crushing blow that would slam his opponent away, he merely gouged the man's cheek.

Again, the scout car crewman found his target and shifted his aim. This time he got it right, and the slug tore into MacIlargie's right side, centimeters below his armpit. MacIlargie felt ribs crack, but didn't feel any pain when he repositioned his blaster slightly and pressed the firing lever. The bolt of plasma from MacIlargie's weapon shattered when it hit the soldier's face, and bits of starstuff sprayed all about— including three or more that landed on MacIlargie.

Now MacIlargie screamed in agony; the burning from the plasma on his leg, arm, and forehead was greater pain than he'd ever felt before. But as much pain as he was in, he let go of the gun mount with one leg and threw himself across the top of the car to lean over the side and make sure his antagonist was down. He saw the soldier receding to the rear of the vehicle, then stretched himself farther so he could bend his head down and look inside the scout car's cabin. Both the remaining crewmen were dead, each with multiple burns from the plasma bolts MacIlargie had fired before the survivor came outside to confront him.

Gasping with pain, MacIlargie looked about to see where he might safely drop off the still-rolling vehicle. There didn't seem to be anyplace he could dismount where he wouldn't have to dodge armored cars, and his wounds felt too severe to allow that much agility. He decided to stay where he was for the moment.

Ensign Cooper Rynchus, with his shoulder secured, paused in thought. Where would General Godalgonz go? He could call him on his comm, but he had an uncomfortable feeling that the Coalition forces at Gilbert's Corners were listening in on that circuit. He hadn't seen anything that told him they were, it just felt that way to him. So instead of contacting his commander directly to find out where he was, he sought him by intuition. Besides, if he called Godalgonz this soon after being ordered to a battalion aid station, the general would know he'd disobeyed the order to report to the surgeon.

So where would Rynchus's boss go? To the thickest fighting, that's where. Rynchus didn't need a UPUD to tell him where the thickest fighting was, he could hear it, three kilometers to the northeast. He headed that way at a trot slightly faster than Godalgonz had used. But Rynchus really had always been faster than his boss, and the run didn't wear on him as quickly as it had the general.

By the time Lieutenant General Godalgonz reached 34th FIST's area of operation, Brigadier Devh and the two companies of his infantry battalion were already there. Brigadier Devh and his infantry commander had deployed one company to back up Mike 34 and the other to assist Lima 34. Devh and his staff were at 34th FIST's Command Post with Brigadier Sturgeon and his staff. The CP was located at the southeast corner of Gilbert's Corners, which gave a good view of the battleground, and the surrounding houses provided some protection from stray fire.

Godalgonz quickly saw that while Lima 34 had knocked out most of the armored vehicles, the Marines of Company L were still in dire straits—the two battalions of Coalition infantry that were in support of the armored vehicles were almost on the Marines. Just before he reached 34th FIST's command center, Godalgonz finally paused for a few seconds to catch his breath. When he stopped panting heavily, he strode in and said one sharp word: "Sitrep!"

Brigadier Sturgeon already knew Godalgonz was approaching, having been alerted by his aide, Lieutenant Quaticatl, who had been told by the FIST HQ security section, and had a report ready.

"Sir," Sturgeon said crisply, adding a sharp salute, "Foxtrot Twenty-nine is assisting my Mike Company in beating off the Coalition attack against it. Golf Twenty-nine is beginning to engage the Coalition infantry assaulting my Company L. I anticipate being ready to withdraw by the time the hoppers return from the beach." He already had his helmet screens up and his gloves off, so Godalgonz saw the salute.

"Very good, Brigadier," Godalgonz said, returning the salute. He belatedly raised his screens and removed his gloves so Sturgeon, Devh, and their staff could see him. "I want to take a closer look at Lima Thirty-four."

"Very good, sir. I'll dispatch a squad from my security unit as a guard detail for you."

"Negative, Viper. An entire squad might attract attention, even in chameleons. I'll go alone, nobody will notice."

"Sir!" Sturgeon waited until Godalgonz closed his helmet and redonned his gloves, then signaled his security section commander to send a fire team after the general.

Godalgonz marched briskly to the outer edge of the lightly wooded area that surrounded the village and stopped next to a tree, to more closely observe the firefight raging half a kilometer away. He didn't notice the fire team that took position thirty meters to his right.

A few of the scout cars had survived the earlier fight against the Marines, and were now protected by infantrymen who climbed aboard to prevent chameleoned Marines from mounting them. Those infantrymen were suffering horrendous casualties, but were succeeding in keeping the scout cars in the fight. The scout cars were firing everywhere they saw movement in the field that surrounded them. Mostly they fired at wind, or fired where a Marine had just been, though they did cause some casualties. Some of their shots were simply wild.

One such wild shot went into the trees that fringed Gilbert's Corners and struck a main branch on one of them. The branch, ten centimeters in diameter where it was struck, broke and fell to the ground—right where Lieutenant General Kyr Godalgonz stood. Godalgonz didn't cry out when the branch struck, he simply dropped to the ground.

"Whoa shit!" cried Lance Corporal Russie, who was looking through his infra screen toward Godalgonz at that instant. "The general's been hit." He didn't wait for orders from his fire team leader, but sprinted toward Godalgonz. The other two Marines followed close behind.

Ensign Cooper Rynchus reached 34th FIST's CP moments after the evac team carried the general back. He didn't know if the lessened sounds of battle were because the firefight was dying down or because his hearing closed off—and wouldn't have cared if he was aware of the lesser battle noise.

"What happened?" he demanded. Two surgeons were working on Godalgonz, who was naked to the waist, and several corpsmen were clustered around, assisting them. He saw the blood and roared, "Why aren't you putting him in a stasis bag?" He moved to rush in and deal with it himself.

"Hold on there," Captain Copsen, 34th FIST's logistics officer, said, grabbing Rynchus by the upper arm to hold him back.

Rynchus wrenched his arm free, almost knocking Copsen to the ground in the process, and kept moving.

"Sir, you can't go in there," Corporal Nyralth said, stepping between Rynchus and the sheltered operating table, Lance Corporal Russie and PFC Obburst joining him. Like Rynchus, they had their screens up and their hands bare.

"But I'm his aide, I have to be at his side!"

"Mr. Rynchus," Captain Copsen said as he stepped between Rynchus and the fire team that had brought Godalgonz back from the trees, "the surgeons are trying to stop the bleeding. The general's wound is too severe to put him straight into a stasis bag, he'd bleed out before the bag can take full effect. Please, Mr. Rynchus, stay back and let the surgeons do their job, they know what they're doing."

"But . . ." Rynchus shuddered. Deep inside, he knew the general wouldn't have been shot if he'd been at his side instead of having his own shoulder seen to. "But it's my fault he's hurt. Can't you see that I have to be with him?"

Copsen flinched at the raw emotion in Rynchus's voice, but he stood his ground. "Mr. Rynchus, it was a freak accident, I don't think anybody could have prevented it."

"Accident?" Rynchus gasped.

"That's right." He turned his head to the three security Marines behind him. "Tell him."

Nyralth nudged Russie. "Tell him what you saw," he said.

Russie swallowed. "Sir, the general was standing under a tree over there," he said and gestured vaguely in the direction of the trees. "A cannon round hit a branch directly above him and it fell on him." He looked back to Nyralth.

"Sir, he was on his side when we got to him, the broken end of the branch had impaled his chest," the fire team leader reported. "I called for evac. Corpsmen came and got him." He shook his head. "I had to use my blaster to burn off the branch a few centimeters from his chest so he could be moved."

"That's right," Copsen added. "If the branch was pulled out, he would have bled to death almost immediately."

"So . . . ?" Rynchus waved weakly at the operating table.

"The surgeons know what they're doing, Mr. Rynchus. Let's let them do their job." Copsen took Rynchus by the arm and led him out of sight of the makeshift operating theater.

After a time the sound of approaching hoppers reached the medical team, still working on the general. The chief surgeon directed the corpsmen to layer synthskin over the massive wound in Godalgonz's upper chest and put him in a stasis bag. Then he went looking for Rynchus.

"Mr. Rynchus," the surgeon said softly when he reached him. "I'm Doctor Fenischel."

"How is he?" Rynchus asked hopefully as he jumped to his feet.

Fenischel shook his head. "We got the worst of the wood out of his wound, and got the bleeding under control. He's in a stasis bag now, but he lost so much blood, I doubt he'll survive until he gets back to the surgery on the *Kiowa*."

"But, but how could he not survive?" Rynchus asked, his voice cracking. "I mean, he's been wounded lots of times. He's always come back."

"Not everybody comes back," Fenischel said sadly. "Sometimes the best a surgeon can do."

"What didn't you do that you should have!" Rynchus shouted. He reached for the surgeon, but pulled his hands back and balled them into frustrated fists before making contact.

"I worked on him with an experienced assistant surgeon and several very experienced corpsmen. If there's anything that could have been done that we didn't do, well, it's something beyond the knowledge and ability of a combined century and a half of medical training and experience."

Rynchus bowed his head. "I know that, Doctor. I-I'm sorry I shouted at you. Where is he now?"

Fenischel looked over his shoulder toward the hopper landing zone. "About to be put aboard a hopper for transit back to Bataan."

Rynchus ran to catch up before his old friend and commander flew away without him.

CHAPTER THIRTEEN

The Marines of Company L limped as they returned to their bunkers facing Pohick Bay. Most of them limped; some didn't return to the bunkers at all, but were borne on flatbed lorries to Essays for transport to the fully equipped hospitals aboard one of the navy starships orbiting above—or set aside in makeshift morgues for later transport to orbit.

They limped into the bunkers, bunkers where they'd fought off a massive amphibious assault at some indefinite time in the past, a time none of them could remember clearly, whether it was hours, days, or weeks ago. An assault that most of them had thought would see their deaths, and for some nearly had. They shrugged off their gear and put their weapons down—but close at hand where they could be snatched up again to resume a fight that was ended. They slid, or slumped, or collapsed to the floor, or leaned precariously against walls, or leaned out of embrasures. They said little, and mostly avoided each other's eyes.

The respite didn't last long.

"Third herd!" Staff Sergeant Hyakowa's voice boomed along third platoon's section of corridor, ricocheted into the bunkers, "Fall in on the company street!"

Groaning or silently, the Marines of third platoon pushed themselves off walls, away from embrasures, levered and lifted themselves from the floor, gathered weapons and discarded helmets, and shuffled out of bunkers to stand in rough formation before the platoon sergeant in the tunnel that the bunkers backed onto.

Unperturbed by seeing only heads and hands, and the occasional V of chest under the heads, Hyakowa watched the Marines shuffle into position. If he noticed or felt anything about the men missing from the three lines that formed up in front of him, he gave no sign. When the Marines of third platoon finished looking left to right to dress their lines, and lowered the arms they'd extended to get proper interval, he barked, "Squad leaders, report!" Farther along the tunnel in both directions, Company L's other platoon sergeants were also calling for squad leaders' reports.

The squad leaders didn't call for their fire team leaders to report, they already knew who was there, who wasn't.

Sergeant Ratliff looked down the line of his squad. Corporal Pasquin and PFC Shoup were more visible than the others because of the blood on their chameleons, blood they'd shed themselves. He didn't expect to see Lance Corporal Longfellow; he'd seen to Longfellow's evacuation to orbit himself. "First squad, all present or accounted for!" he managed.

Sergeant Kerr didn't look; he'd counted up while his men were getting into position. Unlike first squad, second didn't have anyone visible because of bloodstained chameleons. Still, second squad's line was shorter than first squad's; Lance Corporal MacIlargie was on his way to an orbiting hospital bay, and PFC Smedley was waiting transport to a ship's freezer for later transit to the cemetary he'd designated as his final resting place when he enlisted. "Second squad, all present"—his voice broke—"or accounted for," he finished when he got his voice back. He broke discipline to look toward Corporal Doyle to see how his newest fire team leader was taking the loss of a man. Doyle looked green, but was standing at a better position of attention than anybody else in the squad.

Sergeant Kelly was the last to report. "Guns, all present or accounted for." His squad was missing Lance Corporal Tischler, evacuated, and PFC Delagarza, dead.

The squad leaders' reports complete, Hyakowa about-faced; as he turned he saw Ensign Charlie Bass approaching from the platoon's right. He raised his hand in salute when Bass reached and stood to face him. "Sir, third platoon, all present or accounted for!" Hyakowa said emotionlessly.

Bass returned Hyakowa's salute as soon as the platoon sergeant completed his report. "Thank you, Staff Sergeant," he said in a firm voice. "You may take your place." He stood looking at his platoon from one end to the other while Hyakowa marched to his parade ground position, a pace in front of the first squad leader.

"Third platoon," Bass said in measured tones, "you performed in the highest tradition of Marines today. Yes, you got hurt, but you dealt a severe blow to the Coalition forces on Ravenette. I am sorry to say that PFC Smedley and PFC Delagarza are gone, but Lance Corporal Longfellow, Lance Corporal MacIlargie, and Lance Corporal Tischler will rejoin when their injuries are healed. There are some of you, Corporal Pasquin and PFC Shoup, who will report to the battalion aid station when you are released from formation." He named the names without referring to the comp he carried loosely in one hand, or obviously looking to see who was not present.

"You may not have heard," Bass continued, "but Lieutenant General Godalgonz was also killed in action, while observing the end stages of our battle against the Coalition armored cars."

The Marines of third platoon hadn't heard, they'd been too busy trying to win their battle. At first, those who weren't too exhausted from the fierce battle they'd just fought were shocked by the news—none of them could remember the last time they'd heard of a flag officer above the rank of brigadier being killed in action. Few of them had even heard of so high-ranking an officer being on a battlefield during a firefight. Slowly, what Bass had said sunk into the others and discipline dissolved as the Marines looked side to side, front to back, at one another. A *lieutenant general* was killed on the field of battle, right near them, and they hadn't even noticed? What had they done wrong that such a thing could possibly happen? They'd thought they won that battle, but if their commanding general was killed during it, they must have . . .

Bass saw the expressions growing on his Marines' faces and knew what at least some of them were beginning to think.

"As you were, people!" he roared. "Lieutenant General Godalgonz was half a kilometer away from us, observing from what he thought was a safe distance and location. A stray enemy round was responsible for killing him. There was nothing you or anybody else could have done to prevent his death." He stopped and glowered at his Marines, meeting every eye that dared look at him. He had to move on, to distract his Marines from the fate of General Godalgonz.

"I have two more items for now," he said. "First, we will be receiving five Marines from Whiskey Company, two to replace Smedley and Delagarza, and three to fill in until Longfellow, MacIlargie, and Tischler can return. Second, you are as scuzzy as I've ever seen Marines get. When you are dismissed, you *will* clean your weapons, your gear, your uniforms, and yourselves. And you had best do a thorough job of it, because I *will* conduct an inspection later today."

Bass looked up and down the ranks again, then said, "Squad leaders, when I dismiss the platoon, you will take charge of your squads and see to it that they prepare themselves for an inspection!

"THIRD platoon, dis-MISSED!"

If PFC John Three McGinty seemed somewhat shell-shocked by the callousness of Ensign Bass in ordering the platoon to prepare for an inspection right after a battle in which two members of the platoon had been killed and several more wounded, this was the first time he'd been in an action that saw platoonmates killed. Sure, that other squad leader was killed earlier on Ravenette, and so was that corporal in the gun squad. But both of them were killed before McGinty joined the platoon. The raid in force on Gilbert's Corners was his first real action. And closer to home than the two Marines who were killed was the second fire team in McGinty's own squad, all three of its Marines wounded. One of them, Longfellow—wasn't there an ancient poet or novelist who had that same name?—was wounded so badly he had to be evacuated to orbit. McGinty thought he should feel real bad about PFC Smedley getting killed. After all, he and Smedley had both come from Whiskey Company at the same time, but he hadn't known Smedley when they were in the replacement pool. Besides, the Marines of first squad didn't associate as much with second squad as they did with the other Marines in their own squad. That was something McGinty had seen in each of the few units he'd served in during his short time in the Confederation Marine Corps: first you associate with the other Marines in your fire team, then with the other Marines in your squad. Marines in other squads come after that, and other platoons even later. He didn't think anybody ever associated with Marines from different companies. But Smedley's death *did* affect McGinty. Smedley had been in the Corps about the same length of time, and they'd joined the platoon at the same time. If Smedley could be killed so quickly, then so could McGinty, and that thought shook him.

McGinty flinched when an arm suddenly draped over his shoulder and Corporal Dean spoke softly. "Be cool, Marine. Shit happens. Good men die in combat. I don't think there's anybody who's been in the platoon for more than one deployment who hasn't lost a friend, either killed or badly enough wounded that he was evacuated and never returned."

McGinty turned his head to look at his fire team leader, but was surprised to see Dean looking off into nowhere rather than at him. He wondered what friends Dean had lost along the way, and how the older, more experienced Marine dealt with the sudden, violent deaths of men he knew and lived and worked with, and maybe called "friend," but he couldn't bring himself to ask. Not yet anyway.

Dean heaved a deep breath, then looked at McGinty and said, "But sometimes they do come back. Look at Sergeant Kerr. He was wounded so badly it took two years for him to make it back. Now he's a squad leader. Someone you didn't know was Sergeant Bladon. He was a squad leader, lost an arm on Kingdom. If he got treatment early enough, his arm will be regenerated and he'll return to duty, maybe even with Lima Company. Lance Corporal Quick was almost killed—you're his replacement. But he'll be back, maybe even soon enough to help us finish winning this war." Dean slid his arm off McGinty's shoulder and shrugged.

"Shit happens," he repeated, looking into the distance.

Abruptly, Dean stood erect and began speaking with a firm voice. "But you can't dwell on it, McGinty! That's why we're standing an inspection. To keep us so busy we don't have the time or energy to dwell on our losses. Now start cleaning your damn weapons!" He turned away sharply and marched the few paces to where Lance Corporal Godenov was cleaning his fieldstripped blaster.

McGinty looked after Dean for a moment, watched him checking what Godenov was doing, then sat to fieldstrip his own blaster. On some level, he understood that the time for grieving was later.

Corporal Doyle had been in enough action that he'd seen other Marines severely wounded, even killed. He'd suffered through the loss of men he'd lived with and worked with. But he hadn't lost any friends. Corporal Doyle didn't *have* any friends. At least not in Company L. If he allowed himself to think about it, he hadn't made any friends *at all* during his time in the Marines. If he let himself think about it, he'd have to admit that he'd spent most of his years in the Corps as a jerk nobody liked. Well, he *did* admit that to himself—but that didn't mean he had to *think* about it unnecessarily.

Even though Corporal Doyle hadn't lost any friends in combat, that day was the first time he'd lost a man for whom he was responsible, and it hurt. Seeing other Marines get killed always hurt, but losing a man he was responsible for hurt so much he wanted to cry. Especially when he began to wonder what mistake he made that cost Smedley his life. What did he do wrong? What could he have done differently?

He imagined that what he was feeling must be what it felt like to lose a friend. Sure it was, it had to be; Summers and Smedley, the men in his fire team, the men for whom he was responsible, were as close as he'd gotten to having actual friends in the Corps. He looked at Summers to see how he was doing, thinking that maybe he should go and talk to him—maybe they could comfort each other, help each other get through the loss of Smedley. But no, Summers was diligently cleaning his gear. The last time Doyle had looked, Summers was cleaning his blaster. He must have finished by now. He should go and check it out, make sure it was properly cleaned. But, dammit, he really didn't feel up to inspecting his remaining man. Maybe what he should do was seek out Sergeant Kerr. Sergeant Kerr had been in the Marines for a long time and seen a lot of action. He'd lost friends; he knew how to cope with the loss. Yeah, he should go and see his squad leader.

But Corporal Doyle didn't have to go in search of his squad leader. Before he even rose to his feet, Kerr was at the entrance to the bunker, looking in. As soon as Kerr saw Doyle look at him, he crooked a finger and stepped back into the access tunnel. Doyle got to his feet, gathered his weapons and gear, and followed.

When Doyle joined him, Kerr began talking without preamble, in a low but firm voice. "Doyle, I know how you feel. Smedley was my man too. I also lost Wolfman. I know he was still alive when the Essay lifted off to take him to orbit, so he was probably still alive when the surgeons opened his stasis bag to work on him. But he was very badly wounded, and I don't know if he'll ever return. We've lost a lot of men in this war—and I mean just in third platoon. Four men dead; think of how Ensign Bass must feel, four of his men killed. Plus three more in a hospital in orbit. Plus all the other wounded." He shook his head and his mouth twitched in the beginning of a grimace. "Hell, I became squad leader because Linsman got killed." He gave Doyle a hard look. "I've known—I *knew*—Linsman for a long time, we were buddies. He died, and I was promoted into his slot. How do you think that made me feel? A buddy died and I got a promotion out of it.

"Being a Marine is a hard job. You've been in the Corps long enough to know that in your bones. Being an infantryman in a FIST is one of the hardest jobs anybody can have. Being a leader is even harder. Leaders lose men in combat. Sometimes it's because the leader made a mistake; either he did something wrong, or he didn't do something he should have. Most of the time, it simply happens and there's nothing a leader could have done to prevent it.

"I've been watching you carefully ever since Bass made you a fire team leader. You've done a damn good job. You gave your men more training, better training, than almost any other junior fire team leader could have. It's not your fault that Smedley got killed."

Doyle blinked. How did Sergeant Kerr know what he was thinking?

"But Smedley wasn't your only Marine," Kerr continued, not noticing Doyle's reaction. "He's beyond your help now, but Summers still needs you. Right now, Corporal, Summers needs you more than ever, he needs you to be strong, to lead him, to show him what to do. Now get in there and take care of your fire team, Corporal Doyle. Show us why Ensign Bass made you a fire team leader, show us why he believes in you.

"And, Corporal Doyle, I believe in you, too." Kerr clapped Doyle on the shoulder and gave him a little push in the direction of his bunker.

It wasn't until Doyle was inspecting Summers's blaster and encouraging him to clean his gear with a little more energy, that it occurred to him to wonder if Kerr had been giving himself that pep talk as well.

The squad leaders and the more experienced fire team leaders suspected that Ensign Bass's inspection would be perfunctory, that the whole reason for the inspection was to distract everybody while giving them time to heal from the combat and their losses. So they weren't surprised when Bass did little more than walk through the platoon's lines, barely glancing at weapons, gear, and uniforms.

When the inspection was over and Bass had resumed his position front and center of the platoon, with Staff Sergeant Hyakowa standing a pace to his left, Bass got to the day's final agenda item.

"We have our replacements from Whiskey Company," he said.

"Whiskey Company." Normally a provisional company, pieced together from cooks, bakers, clerks, progammers, mechanics, anybody else not normally in a trigger-puller unit, for the purpose of providing additional combat power, usually in a defensive posture. In this case, an overstrong company specially assembled and assigned to 34th FIST to provide replacements for casualties sustained during combat; 34th FIST was getting more than its fair share of combat assignments, and more than its fair share of casualties.

Nobody in the ranks of third platoon bothered to look to the side where the five replacements stood, anxiously awaiting their assignments in their new platoon. The Marines of third platoon would meet them soon enough. And if Smedley and Delagarza were any indication, it was possible that they wouldn't last long enough for anybody to get to know them.

"I'm going to do the easy one first," Bass said, with a smile starting to form at the corners of his mouth. "Or maybe this first assignment won't be so easy—some of the fire team leaders might fight over him." He was grinning by the time he looked to his left. "PFC Quick, front and center!"

"Quick?"

"He's back?"

"Quick, already?"

Excited whispers sped through the ranks. PFC Quick had been evacuated to orbit after Company L had repulsed a major Coalition assault against the main line of resistance. Everybody looked as Quick marched from the side to the front of the formation to stand in front of Bass. Some of them noticed he moved a bit gingerly.

Quick saluted smartly, and just as smartly reported. "Sir, PFC Quick reporting as ordered!"

Bass quickly returned the salute, then grabbed Quick's hand to shake it briskly. "Welcome back, Quick. I'm glad to see you back with us. You had me worried for a while there."

"Gu—, ah, sir, I'm glad to be back. Sure as hell beats the alternative."

Bass's grin faded, but came right back. "You got that right." He looked at the squad leaders, then at first squad's third fire team. "Corporal Dean. PFC Quick was your man before he got injured. Do you want him back?"

Dean opened his mouth to shout out that he did, but he paused to think first. Quick was a known quantity, and had been one of Dean's men on Kingdom and Maugham's Station. But it wouldn't be fair to PFC McGinty to shuffle him into a new fire team right now.

"Sir," Dean said, "I'd really like to have PFC Quick back. But PFC McGinty's working out pretty well and . . ." He was about to be out of line and he knew it. What he was about to say was something he should take up privately with Sergeant Ratliff rather than bring up in a platoon formation. But if they didn't like it, what could they do, send him to war? "Besides, sir, I think Quick is due for promotion to lance corporal, and I've already got a lance corporal in my fire team." There, he'd said it.

And took Bass by surprise. Bass looked over to the new men. He had three lance corporal slots to fill, and that was the rank three of the new men already held. Unless . . . He looked into the second rank, behind Dean, at Corporal Doyle.

"Doyle, how would you like to have Quick to replace Smedley? He's a good Marine, and if he makes lance corporal, you could use one anyway."

"M-Me, sir?" Doyle answered, not quite squeaking. Bass simply looked at him. When the platoon commander didn't say anything,

Doyle sent Quick a questioning look—did he want to join Doyle's fire team? Quick gave a slight shrug. "Sure, Quick's a good Marine."

"Is that all right with you, Sergeant Kerr?" Bass asked the second squad leader.

"I think it'll work out, sir," Kerr replied.

"All right, then, that's the easy one. PFC Quick, you're in third fire team, second squad. Get in formation."

"Aye aye, sir," Quick said. He about-faced and marched to his position in the formation. The Marines who got a good look at his face as he moved through the first rank saw doubt on his face.

The rest of the assignments turned out to be easier: Lance Corporal Beycee Harvey went to first squad's second fire team to replace Lance Corporal Longfellow, and Lance Corporal Francisco Ymenez joined second squad's second fire team to replace Lance Corporal MacIlargie. The other two new men had gun MOSs, military occupational specialties, and went to the gun squad to replace Lance Corporal Tischler and PFC Delagarza; they were Lance Corporal Jayar Vargas and PFC Rolf Dias.

CHAPTER FOURTEEN

"So the chickens flew the coop, eh?" General Billie chortled. He twirled the lighted Clinton between his fingers happily and beamed at the officers gathered in his command center for their post-operation debriefing.

Lieutenant General Alistair Cazombi sat stiffly in his chair, face expressionless but mind whirling. He could not believe that his commander was actually *overjoyed* the attack on Gilbert's Corners had failed. He twisted his head slightly to observe Brigadier Ted Sturgeon, whose FIST had taken heavy casualties in the fighting at Gilbert's. Sturgeon sat there stunned, his hands clenched so tightly his fingers had turned white. He had come to the briefing straight from the field, his uniform, face, and hands still smeared with the sweat and dust of combat. He had not slept in many hours and his face was creased with the worry lines of a commander fresh from a military debacle. Cazombi sensed what was coming and caught Sturgeon's eye, shaking his head slightly, hoping the Marine understood the gesture as a warning to stay calm and not shove that foul Clinton right up General Jason Billie's ass.

"We lost General Godalgonz, sir," Cazombi said tonelessly.

Billie paused the cigar momentarily in its circuit through his fingers. "Oh. Yes. Damned shame, damned shame."

Billie's face remained neutral but he could not entirely suppress something that sounded suspiciously like a laugh covered up as a snort.

Does that sonofabitch think it's funny how Godalgonz died? Cazombi wondered. In the short time he'd known Godalgonz, Cazombi had come to like and respect the gruff Marine. Billie's callous indifference to the man's death incensed the army three-star. He shifted slightly in his seat—for anyone who knew "Cazombi the Zombie" well, a sure sign to get out of the way.

"Sir," Cazombi said, carefully, using a measured, neutral tone, "Godalgonz was a good officer and along with him we lost some good men. We should've known in advance that the Coalition had already moved its government to the Cumber Mountains and called off the whole operation."

Ted Sturgeon had also noticed Billie's reaction to mention of Godalgonz's death. He wanted to grab the four-star by the neck and squeeze until . . .

"Ahem." Billie turned to Brigadier General Wilson Wyllyums, his G2, intelligence chief. "What do you know about that?"

Wyllyums shifted uneasily in his seat. "Well, sir, I did pass on an interrogation report generated by the fleet N2 with a Heb Cawman, I believe, who was captured by the Marines on their raid. He didn't *say* the government had been moved nor did he tell his interrogator *where* it might move to, but she—"

"*She?*" Billie snorted.

"Yes, she, the interrogator, inferred from what this Cawman said that there was a plan to evacuate the entire government to the Cumber Mountains, to some caves up there."

"Sorca?" Billie turned to Major General Sorca, his chief of staff.

"Um, yessir, I recall such a report, one of many of that type we get regularly from the fleet N2. I believe I passed it on to you with the comment that General Wyllyums did not consider the information reliable. Did you, Wyllyums?"

"I gave it a three for reliability, sir, same as Fleet, information to be considered, but not confirmed."

"Well, I don't remember the report at all," Billie lied, "but if I had seen it I'd not have acted on it. I wouldn't have called off the attack just because of some secondhand supposition about the enemy's intentions. Ridiculous. A commander acts according to his own appraisal of all the factors involved in warfare. Intelligence, which is often unreliable—no offense, Wyllyums—is only one element of all that must be considered when making tactical decisions."

Brigadier Ted Sturgeon seethed with anger. *So these goddamned army pukes did know about the move in advance!* He made a supreme effort to control himself. He knew he should let Cazombi handle the meeting but every fiber of his being wanted to scream imprecations at these chairborne staff officers—particularly Jason Billie, who was using them to cover his own agenda.

"Well, I don't consider the raid a failure," General Sorca said.

"You should have been there, Balca, then maybe you'd have a different opinion," Cazombi said. Sorca's face turned red. Up to that point the other commanders who'd been on the attack had remained silent but several of them chuckled at Cazombi's riposte.

"Well, they must've heard you coming," Sorca replied sarcastically.

"You goddamned sonofabitch!" Sturgeon shouted, unable to control himself any longer.

"Gentlemen! Gentlemen!"—Billie held up his hands in a placating gesture—"I agree with Balca. The raid demonstrated our ability to strike at the enemy when and where we wish, and it may well have been the impetus to remove the Coalition government to the mountains, so we struck the fear of God into them. You might call it a 'dress rehearsal' for a much bigger operation I have in mind for the very near future." Billie beamed. The raid had been a failure in one sense, that not many civilians had been killed. He'd hoped it would've turned into a slaughter, a massacre that would have permanently embarrassed the Marines and Cazombi for having favored the operation. Nevertheless, it had failed to disrupt the Coalition's government—the enemy probably did have advance warning that the task force was coming. After all, the late Lieutenant General Godalgonz, Confederation Marine Corps, was one of those "hi diddle diddle, straight up the middle" kind of warriors. But best of all, Godalgonz was out of the way. Now only two thorns remained in General Jason Billie's hide: Cazombi and Sturgeon. He would soon start in motion the surgery to remove them permanently.

"What do you have in mind, sir?" Cazombi asked evenly, at the same time giving Sturgeon a hard glance.

"Lieutenant?" Billie addressed a staff officer who had been standing by. A huge trid of the coastline by Phelps appeared on the screen. "Alistair, I want you to get together with Wyllyums here and Thayer, come up with a plan to land a task force on the coast and roll up the 4th Division here at Phelps in a move to break down Lyons's back door. If you are successful, that will signal us to mount the breakout." Brigadier General Thayer, Billie's plans and operations officer, glanced apprehensively at Brigadier General Wyllyums, who shook his head ever so slightly.

The announcement was greeted with total silence as each officer in the briefing studied the vid. The cliffs in the vid were over one hundred meters high in most places; the beach beneath them at high tide would be totally awash, and at low tide there would not be more than fifty meters of sand and rocks to land troops on. Each officer was aware of the report Marine Force Reconnaissance had submitted on their recent raid on the MP battalion stationed there.

"General?"—Billie gestured toward Major General Cohan Briss, whose division had been engaged during the raid on Gilbert's Corners— "what is your assessment of the 9th Division's ability to reinforce the 4th if the 4th is attacked at Phelps?"

"Well, sir, Ted's 34th FIST was more closely engaged than my men were, but I'd say the 9th Division, while it was not knocked out, was badly hurt. They might reinforce the troops at Phelps, but if we send in a big enough task force and hit them hard, the operation should succeed. The only thing that worries me is how you're going to get all those troops and their gear over those goddamned cliffs. And I'd be concerned that the enemy might have anticipated this attack."

"Wyllyums?"

"Um, well, navy's string-of-pearls recon has been severely hampered by Lyons's antisatellite batteries, but aerial reconnaissance has not yet revealed any significant transfer of forces to either Phelps or Gilbert's Corners to reinforce the troops already there. So that leads me to believe Lyons hasn't done anything to protect his rear from a seaward landing—yet."

"Alistair?"

"Sir, if you want me to come up with an attack plan—"

"I do, Alistair, and I also want you to lead the operation in person. You've been too long cooped up down here and I think you have earned the right to command this task force."

"Hear! Hear!" several of the officers shouted. Sturgeon relaxed because he knew perfectly well that any task force Lieutenant General Cazombi commanded would include 34th FIST, and right now he'd give *anything* to get as far away from Jason Billie and his staff as he could, even if it meant throwing him and his men back into the line again.

"Very well, sir. I want Brigadier Sturgeon to assist me, as well as your staff, as required. And I want to pick whichever units I wish to comprise the task force."

"You have it."

"Then, sir, may I be excused to start work on the operation order?"

Billie nodded. "You are excused. Gentlemen, this meeting is over. Return to your commands and begin refurbishing them for our next and final attack. This will be the hammer and anvil play that you've all been waiting for. I want you all to coordinate fully with General Cazombi; his planning mission has precedence over everything else. Otherwise, congratulations on a job well done. Oh, there'll be a memorial service for General Godalgonz in the G3 shop at fifteen hundred sharp. Balca, stay behind for a while, would you?"

Alone with General Sorca in his small office, Billie unfastened his tunic. "Killed by a falling tree limb!" He began to laugh. "Rich! Rich! Oh, how fucking *rich*! What am I going to say at his memorial ceremony?" His voice cracked with laughter. "Will anyone be able to keep a straight face?" He began laughing so hard he convulsed over his desk, the laughter rising quickly to a shrill bray like a jackass with the hiccups—"Ark! Ark! Ark!" Tears streamed down his cheeks. He gasped for breath, pounded on his desktop. "Killed by a fucking tree limb! Oh, God, thank you! Rich! Rich! Oh, fucking rich!"

Sorca sat quietly, a small tendril of fear and doubt starting to take life inside his brain. The man commanded a huge field army and *this* is how he reacted to the death of one of his senior officers? Sorca himself had no love for Marines. He knew perfectly well what the combat commanders in this army thought of him, what they think of every chief of staff in every army.

Billie was breathing hard but he'd gotten control of himself. "And now, Balca, I'm going to get rid of Cazombi and that goddamned Marine buddy of his. Yes. I'm sending them off to bang their heads against those cliffs at Phelps, Balca. And *you*"—he pointed his finger at Sorca— "you, Balca"—he jabbed the finger into Sorca's face—"you will see that it is done! Do you understand? It will be done! *It will be!*"

Major General Balca Sorca realized then that his commander was coming unhinged.

Major General Balca Sorca sat uncomfortably in General Cazombi's little office tucked away in the bowels of Fortress Bataan. "Make it quick, Balca," Cazombi had told Sorca coldly after reluctantly agreeing to see him on such short notice. "I've got a lot of planning to do and I know you're not here to assist me."

"Yes, sir, I am here to 'assist' you. I've just come from a private conference with General Billie—"

"Lucky you." Cazombi's voice was heavy with sarcasm.

"Sir, I'll come straight to the point"—Sorca took a deep breath—"I have doubts about General Billie's mental stability and his fitness to continue in command of this army."

Cazombi's mouth almost fell open in surprise. Sorca was known throughout the army as Billie's lapdog, and until now Cazombi had listed him, if not as Billie's only ally, at least his most steadfast. "Come again, Balca?"

Nervously, Sorca cleared his throat. "You know, I wouldn't have this second star if it hadn't been for General Billie. I've served him faithfully ever since he came here. I know"—he nodded his head in affirmation— "we've had our differences, especially when it came to the defense of Fort Seymour, but those were professional disagreements, sir, and I admit your foresight should've taken precedence over my tactical decisions." He shifted his position uneasily and looked at the floor. "That raid on Gilbert's Corners was meant to fail. That's why Billie had you write that memorandum, and had General Wyllyums write his own memo setting out reasons why the mission should not have been launched. Rather, Billie dictated the memo and Wyllyums signed it. Wyllyums's reward was his star. Billie wanted these opinions on file so that when the raid failed he could put the blame on you and the

Marines. He wants you and General Sturgeon out of the picture—just like he wanted to get rid of General Godalgonz."

"Hold on a second! You mean Billie *planned* to get Godalgonz killed?"

"Not exactly, sir, but he was not unhappy that the Marine was killed. And now he wants you to go on this seaborne attack to get you out of Bataan, and possibly get you killed as well. I tell you this, sir: If the landing is not successful do not expect Billie to support you. You are being hung out to dry."

"How the hell do you know all this, Balca?"

"He told me. I am in on it. I just came from a private conference with him and frankly, sir, I am sick and tired of playing Eichmann to his Himmler."

Cazombi said nothing for a long moment. "You know, Balca," he said at last, tapping his fingers on his desk, "what you are doing is the most disloyal act a subordinate can perform toward his commander."

"I am aware of that, sir. What I am telling you now, General, I am telling you because I fear that the fate of this entire army is at risk because our commander is more interested in pursuing a personal vendetta than in winning this war."

"Hmmm." Cazombi continued tapping his fingers on his desk. "Well, I have my orders and I am going to carry them out, General Sorca. I think the landing will be a success, and once Billie sees that he'll have no choice but to launch the breakout and split Lyons's army in two and win this war. Nothing succeeds like success, General."

"General Billie should be relieved of his command," Sorca blurted out suddenly.

Cazombi stiffened and glared at Sorca. "That is plain mutiny, General, and I won't hear of it! You will *never* repeat those words again, and you will stop that line of thought immediately, do you hear me? It will be *you* who'll be relieved and face court-martial if you ever mention this to me again!"

Sorca stood to attention. "Very well, sir. I shall never mention this to you or anyone else. I've said my piece. But remember what I told you: He will not support you, General. He has no intention of doing that." He stepped back one pace, saluted smartly, about-faced, and marched out of Cazombi's office.

"Whew!" Cazombi muttered. *Who'd ever have thought Sorca had it in him to betray his patron?* But Sorca had not told Lieutenant General Alistair Cazombi anything he did not already know or suspect. Well, the landing would go off, and if necessary, Cazombi vowed, he would break the siege of Bataan on his own. But no more talk about relieving anybody of his command. Cazombi shook his head. Besides, if Billie was relieved, who'd replace him?

CHAPTER FIFTEEN

"Keep your seats, gentlemen," Lieutenant General Cazombi said as he entered the small conference room. "We don't have time for spit-and-polish this afternoon. Sergeant." He gestured for a technical sergeant sitting at a control console to activate the huge vid screen that occupied one wall of the room. At the sergeant's command, two words leaped onto the screen, OPERATION BACKDOOR.

"Does everyone know everybody else here?" Cazombi asked, perching on the edge of the sergeant's desk. "I think Ted Sturgeon knows Major General Koval, commanding the 27th Infantry Division?"

General Koval stood and nodded at the others. "They call me Korny Koval. You'll find out why once you get to know me better." He grinned and the others chuckled. "Ted there, and I, we had a grand time kicking some ass together a while back." He sat down.

"Then there's Brigadier Nuemain, 17th FIST, Brigadier Devh, 29th FIST, and the,"—he grimaced, which for him passed as a grin—"the 'irrepressible' Brigadier Sturgeon, 34th FIST." Everyone laughed at that. "Next there's Captain Bukok, our navy liaison officer."

Captain Bukok stood and bowed slightly. He was a short, stocky officer, skull almost clean-shaven, heavy jowls, cheeks dark with beard stubble. "They call me Bulldog," he said, "but that's only because I look like one." This was met with a rousing chorus of laughter. Brigadier Nuemain slapped Bukok on the back as he took his seat.

"Welcome to hell, Captain," someone said.

"Ever hear about the engineer who died and went to hell?" an older brigadier general asked. "When the devil found out who he was, he had him install air-conditioning, escalators, running water; really spruced hell up. But one day God called down and told the devil the engineer was there by mistake. 'Send him right back up here!' God ordered. 'Oh, no!' the devil replied, 'You made the mistake! I'm keeping him!' God said, 'Send him back up right now or I'm going to sue your ass!' 'Where are *You* gonna get a lawyer?' the devil asked."

Cazombi grimaced. "That, gentlemen, is our resident humorist, and when you find out what he does you'll realize his whole life in this army is a joke. But he is an essential member of our team, along with these other gentlemen. They will prepare the appropriate annexes to your operation order. Just to make sure you all know each other: Brigadier General Wilson Wyllyums, our staff intelligence expert." Wyllyums stood, acknowledging the introduction with a slight nod. He was unshaven and his tunic was unbuttoned at the collar. "And Brigadier General Thayer, our plans and operations officer." Thayer did not bother to stand, merely raised his hand self-consciously. "Finally, our logistics expert, Brigadier General Pankake."

Brigadier Pankake stood, a smile still on his face from his engineer joke. "Thank you, sir." He bowed slightly in Cazombi's direction. He was a thin, white-haired officer who stooped slightly at the shoulders. His face was creased with laugh lines, and indeed, the expression usually on his face made him look as if he were savoring some private joke and was ready to burst out laughing. "I got a rather unusual name, I know, but I was once in an office with a guy named Bacon. We used to joke that if we could get a guy named Coffee to join us we could call ourselves The Breakfast Trio."

Cazombi shook his head slightly. "You'll get to know General Pankake. Well, that's it. We are the team that is going to plan and execute"—he gestured toward the vid screen—"Operation Backdoor." He stood, walked to the front of the small room, and thrust both hands into his pockets. "We're going to pull an end run on old General Lyons, kick open his back door, light a fire under his ass, and the rest of the army's going to break out of this place. Gentlemen, this operation can put an end to this war."

* * *

Hours later.

General Koval was summing up. The small room was heavy with cigarette smoke; half-empty coffee cups and the remains of hastily eaten meals littered the place. On his own authority Cazombi had permitted smoking even though technically, that was against General Billie's orders. "We're in a goddamned war; we could all be dead tomorrow," he said. "So who the hell gives a damn about the carcinogenic content of the air we're forced to breathe down here? Besides, if you come down with lung cancer it'll have been contracted in the line of duty, so the treatment'll be free."

"So that's it, Task Force Cazombi," General Koval was saying. "So here, sir, one more time"—the other officers groaned good-naturedly—"in a nutshell, is how we recommend the operation be conducted."

"I'm honored," Cazombi said with a sigh. He sat with his legs stretched out before him, his tunic unbuttoned, a cold cup of coffee in one hand. "Please continue, General."

"We mount this attack in three phases: Phase One. A Force Recon team from Task Force 79"—he nodded at Captain Bukok—"will establish a landing zone inland, here." He pointed to an uninhabited area about ten kilometers north of the 7th Independent Military Police Battalion along the coast near Phelps. "This is where we'll land the 27th Infantry Division. From here it will be able to move forward to take Phelps supported by 34th and 29th FISTs, with 17th FIST in reserve."

"Admiral Hoi Yueng has already designated a Force Recon squad for this mission, sir," Captain Bukok interjected.

"Thirty-fourth FIST will simultaneously execute a vertical envelopment on the 7th MPs and take them out. Intel tells us"—he nodded at Brigadier Wyllyums—"that the men in this unit are incapable of mounting an adequate defense of this position. We've all studied the reports and we agree. They were put there to get them out of the way and to act as a tripwire. So even though they may be a pushover, once we hit these guys, we've got to move very fast.

"Simultaneously, 29th FIST will execute a vertical envelopment at Cranston—this little hamlet here—about fifty klicks north of the 7th

MP position. Recon has determined that there is at least a battalion of amphibs hiding there. They will eliminate that threat and then join the rest of the task force in its push on Phelps.

"Phase Two. Two brigades from the 27th Division will occupy the LZ established by Force Recon and secure the perimeter. They are followed immediately by our heavy equipment, and that includes our artillery support. For the purpose of this operation, we have agreed to combine all our artillery assets under Colonel Ramadan of 34th FIST. He will be the task force artillery commander and he will coordinate supporting fires for all the units in the attack. He will have the capability of bringing massed artillery fires on any target in the zone of operations.

"Phase Three. The reserve FIST and the third brigade of the 27th Division come ashore followed by our logistical train. We will rapidly consolidate our forces and move inland. The operation will commence at first light and by zero-seven hours we shall be moving inland against the enemy's 4th Composite Infantry Division at Phelps. Attempts to reinforce them from Ashburtonville or Gilbert's Corners will be handled by close air support, but once we have taken Phelps we should be in strength enough to fend off counterattack and push on to Ashburtonville.

"The 29th and 34th FIST will provide flank security, left and right respectively, for the main body of the task force. Their job will be to intercept and destroy any reinforcements the enemy sends against us.

"An essential element of this plan is a diversion to be mounted by the main army at Ashburtonville. Major General Sorca assures me that General Billie will mount major assaults all along our perimeter as soon as TF Cazombi is over the shore. That should keep General Lyons occupied until we can reach Phelps. Then what was a mere diversion will transition into the actual breakout. General Pankake?"

When General Pankake stood up to deliver his précis of the logistical annex to the operation order he was all business. "Gentlemen, we have calculated the level of logistical support required to keep Task Force Cazombi combat-capable for an army corps–size operation that will last five days. Ordnance, engineer, medical, and transportation units will support the organic assets of each maneuver element in the task force. You will kick off with your full combat load plus one thousand short tons of reserve ordnance to be allocated per the task force commander's directions. During Phase Three we will establish a depot in the landing zone from which your troops can resupply as needed. General Wyllyums?"

The intelligence chief, a Caporal nonchalantly lodged in one side of his mouth, got wearily to his feet. "Gentlemen, if we carry this off swiftly and without any unforeseen problems, the task force should be in the outskirts of Phelps and closely engaged with the enemy there by not later than noon on D-day. As you all know, the coast-watch MP battalion is no obstacle. The 4th Composite Division at Phelps is another matter. Its commander, Major General Barksdale Sneed, is an experienced and capable field commander. We estimate the division itself has been reinforced to about one hundred and twenty percent of its TO&E strength in personnel and equipment. It is a potent obstacle on the road to Ashburtonville. We can overcome that obstacle, but surprise is essential. Once we are on the ground, we must move quickly out of the landing zone and engage Sneed as soon as possible." He sat down.

"Gentlemen, there you have it, Operation Backdoor. You shall have the operation order within the hour. Return to your commands now and prepare your troops. Kickoff time is zero-three hours tomorrow."

The men stood, stretched, picked up their briefing materials, gathered their staff personnel, and prepared to leave. But one officer approached General Cazombi.

"Sir?" It was Brigadier General Wyllyums.

"Yes, Wilson?"

"May I speak to you in private, sir?" He spoke quietly, so none of the others could hear what he was saying. They moved over into a corner of the room. Wyllyums told Cazombi about the memo General Billie had him write before the Gilbert's Corners raid. "He thought the raid would result in civilian casualties. To avoid any personal embarrassment and to pass the blame on to you and Sturgeon, he had me sign a memo *he* wrote expressing reservations. He let that raid go off because he wanted it to fail. I signed the damned thing because he promised me my star if I'd do it, sir. I was a goddamned self-serving coward and I admit that to you now."

Cazombi was silent for a moment, thinking of the conversation he'd had with General Sorca, who thought that General Billie might be out of his mind. "Well, Wilson, in the event, the Gilbert's Corners fiasco was a flash in the pan, didn't particularly harm anyone's reputation—"

"Sir, General Billie hates you and the Marines and he'd do anything, *anything* to destroy you, even if it meant sacrificing the men in this army! I believe the man is"—he hesitated—"the man has lost his bearings."

"Wilson, we *are* going to open that back door. We *are* going to push straight up the road into Lyons's army and if we have to, *we* will break through to General Billie."

"That is precisely what you will have to do, General," Wyllyums said with conviction. "Now if you will excuse me?"

Cazombi looked at Wyllyums's retreating back. He realized it had taken courage for the man to admit what he'd done, and he respected Wyllyums for that. Sure, General Billie was a fool. Cazombi knew very well that Billie despised both him and the Marines. But so what? Jealousy was not unknown among commanders at high levels. Rivalry and personal disagreements were common among officers at all levels in any army. But not even General Billie would deliberately sacrifice his own men to destroy . . . He stroked his chin, remembering how Billie had suppressed his *laughter* when someone had mentioned General Godalgonz's death. *Who is the fool here, Billie or Alistair Cazombi?*

"Lost in thought, sir?"

Cazombi started. "Oh, Ted. Yes, yes, I guess so, the 'burden of command,' you might say." He grinned slightly. "Ted"—he put his arm around Sturgeon's shoulders—"we're going into the shit tomorrow and I can't think of a better man to have at my side than you—and your Marines. This operation is going to succeed. I'm going to make sure of that. I'm going to do whatever has to be done to ensure success tomorrow. I need you to stand by me, Ted."

"Hell or high water, sir, we'll be there."

Cazombi looked steadily at Sturgeon for a long moment, nodded, and walked off, leaving the Marine standing there, a quizzical expression on his face. He wondered what was bothering Cazombi that he had to reassure himself of Sturgeon's "support." Sturgeon shook his head. There was no time for second thoughts or worries, no time to think of momma and the kids. No, now it was "hi-diddle-diddle, straight up the middle," just where Brigadier Ted Sturgeon liked to be.

CHAPTER SIXTEEN

Jane Beresford Posterus, "J. B." to her intimate associates, did not smoke or drink or carry on with loose company, and was always in bed by ten o'clock each night of the week. She had obeyed those rules all her long life, until she went into politics, and even then the only rule she violated was the last.

Posterus discovered very soon after being elected to the presidency of the Mylex Union that the most important events in military and political life always seem to take place late at night or early in the morning, and that the two endeavors usually went hand in hand. And now here she was once again, sitting in council with her cabinet, the old general droning on and on about the "impetus of war," her eyelids heavy with sleep, fighting to keep her head from drooping. It wasn't just that she had aged. Yes, she'd turn eighty this November, but she was still vigorous and alert. It was that she hadn't slept in twenty-four hours and it had been a long day.

"Goddammit, General, it's good money after bad! Good money after bad!" Cecil Hicks, Minister of the Exchequer, shouted, slamming his palm on the tabletop with a wet *smaaack.*

J. B. started at the sound. "Madam President," General Gonsalves Henricus, Chairman of the Mylex Joint Chiefs, implored, ignoring Minister Hicks's fierce scowl, "My only point is, we simply *cannot* withdraw our forces unilaterally from Ravenette without undermining General

Lyons's army, and if we cut and run now, the sacrifice of our men's lives will have been in vain."

"J. B., how can these people be so stupid?" Hicks interjected, referring to those in her government who demanded Mylex's troops remain on Ravenette in the war against the Confederation. "They all know that General Lyons initially refused command of the Coalition Army because"—he glared at the other ministers—"we cannot possibly defeat the Confederation in this war! We cannot afford the expense of this war, in treasure and in lives! And we are going to lose. That is a fact!" He again slammed his palm on the tabletop. "The Confederation commander on Ravenette, this General Billie, is a military genius! He's staved off General Lyons's forces while building up his own and when he takes the initiative, which he will, he will, he's going to overwhelm our army and end this war!"

"Billie's an idiot!" General Henricus shouted, slamming his own palm on the table. "Cecil, I know military idiots, and this Billie is one of them."

"Yes, you surely do." Hicks smirked.

General Henricus, face turning red, made to rise from his chair at that remark, but he was restrained by the Mylex Minister of Justice Carla Rappenthal, who placed a gentle hand on his shoulder. "Madam President, has anyone at this point considered what would happen to *us* if we do lose this war?" She smiled at the other ministers as she spoke softly. The question was rhetorical. "We'll be branded as traitors, J. B., and our fate will be certain and grim when the Confederation gets done with us."

"Carla, that's ridiculous!" Hicks shot back. "What are they going to do, take the governing bodies of *twelve* member worlds and put them all in jail? Besides, that won't happen to *us,* I guarantee you, if we withdraw from this enterprise and do it now. There are precedents: the Italian King and his entourage, the Finns in the Second World War when they withdrew from the Axis alignment, and so on."

Rappenthal smiled, "Cecil, we went along with the Ordinance of Secession, signed on like all the others. 'Caught with the crows, suffer with the crows.' "

The Minister of Public Information, Gabs Stukas, decided to join in. "Ma'am, there is the matter of, of, public opinion?" He spoke hesi-

tantly, glancing furtively at the Minister of the Exchequer, whom everyone in the room feared except J. B. herself and General Henricus, and
maybe Rappenthal. "Our last opinion poll shows thirty-six percent of
our people think the secession movement was a bad thing—"

"Yes, they think that now, with the embargoes and their men all off
at war," General Henricus said, interrupting, "but they were all for it to
begin with. Go back and check your polls the day after the news of the
massacre at Fort Seymour went public! You want to use the Second
World War as a precedent, Cecil? All right, take the Austrians. The
biggest hoax ever pulled on the world was them convincing everyone
that Hitler was a German! Goddamned public opinion is as fickle as a
whore in church. Oh, excuse me, madam"—he nodded toward J. B.—
"just an old soldier's phrase." He grimaced and cleared his throat nervously.

"This is a democracy, General," Stukas said, "and thirty-six percent
of the population is a significant voter bloc. Frankly, the longer this war
drags on, the higher the percentage of people opposed to it will rise."

"Gabs is right," Hicks interjected, "and there is an election coming
up. You—we—cannot afford to alienate our constituency."

"I want to go back to the Fort Seymour thing," General Henricus
said. "Cecil, I remember just after it happened, you were all for secession yourself. You made a public statement that the treasury was writing a blank check, as you called it, to finance an expedition to Ravenette
in support of General Lyons. Now you want to issue a stop payment on
that check, is that what you're telling us?"

"Indeed, I am," Hicks replied calmly. "You see, General, unlike your
hard-charging military men who spend money like water to support
even the most futile operation, I know when an investment has gone
bad, and when that happens, the prudent financier cuts his losses and
gets out of the market." Hicks folded his hands and smirked like the cat
who has eaten the canary.

Infuriated at the remark, General Henricus did rise out of his chair,
shouting, "Investment? Cut losses? Get out of the market? We're talking
about the lives of our soldiers here, Hicks, not one of your goddamned
penny-pinching budget-busting exercises! We're talking about the in-
dependence, the freedom of our people! We've had enough of second-
class citizenship in this Confederation and we're going to—"

"Oh, relax, General." Hicks gestured for Henricus to sit back down. "You sound just like that bourbon-guzzling backwoodsman, Preston Summers! I've had enough of his rhetoric. We Mylexans have never had much in common with the rubes on these other worlds and you know it." He turned to President Posterus. "We have to face up to facts, J. B. We rushed into this thing without thinking it through, but now we are thinking it over and our conclusion must be that it is time to get out."

"We lost thousands of lives already and you just want to toss them away like that?" General Henricus shouted.

"And we'll lose thousands more if we stay involved. For the ones who've already been killed, well, build them a monument in the capital and put all their names on it—"

"You goddamned coward!" General Henricus lunged across the table at Hicks and almost succeeded in grabbing him, but Hicks reared back at the last second and the other ministers were able to restrain the general.

"Dear friends," President Posterus said and sighed, "the hour is late, we all grow weary. I'm going to adjourn this meeting now. Let's gather again in the morning—oh, it already is morning! This afternoon, then, and at that time continue our deliberations calmly and in a professional manner." She nodded at General Henricus who sat breathing heavily in his chair. "So that's it," Posterus announced, "I'm hitting the sack, as they say."

Chloe Mayham lifted the bullhorn to her lips and shouted, *"Madam President, troops out now!"* The slogan was echoed by the hundreds of protesters gathered behind her holding placards and signs urging the government to withdraw its troops from Ravenette and quit the Coalition.

Mayham's son had been one of the first to fall in the assault on Fort Seymour. By all accounts he'd been a first-class infantryman and had died heroically. An officer had even come to her modest home and presented her with the medals her son had won. Later she threw them in the trash.

When her son, Taffyd, had volunteered for the reserve she had been upset, but at that time there'd been no war on the horizon and the extra money had come in handy paying for his education. Chloe came from a libertarian background and she believed the less government the better, especially when government proposed sending its citizens off to get killed. When Taffyd's infantry unit was mobilized for shipment to Ravenette, Chloe threw a fit. Since her divorce she had grown ever closer to and more dependent on her only child, and the thought that he might be hurt drove her to distraction, but he was of age and firmly set on going with his unit. His death had energized her, and she had changed almost overnight from a clinging vine to an avenging fury. From somewhere she had dredged up an ancient antiwar protest song which became her anthem at rallies:

> I didn't raise my boy to be a soldier,
> I brought him up to be my pride and joy,
> Who dares to put a musket on his shoulder,
> To shoot some other mother's darling boy?
> Let nations arbitrate their future troubles,
> It's time to lay the sword and gun away,
> There'd be no war today
> If mothers all would say,
> I didn't raise my boy to be a soldier.

Since then she had taken her antiwar protest from her small home-town of Centreville, three thousand kilometers from New Columbia, the capital of the Mylex Union, right up to the gates of the presidential palace. Along the way the ranks had swelled to thousands of Mylexans opposed to secession and the war, and Chloe's activism had propelled her into the virtual leadership of the movement. More to the point, per-haps, now members of Posterus's own political party were publicly urg-ing the president to withdraw their troops. It was not yet a significant majority, not enough to pass the vote of impeachment which many of the antiwar protestors wanted, but it was enough, she hoped, to con-vince President Posterus to reconsider her government's war policy.

At the rallies Chloe maintained her composure so well that her opponents labeled her heartless, an ice maiden, and speculated that her activism was only a stepping-stone to a career in politics. Others wondered just how devastated she'd been at her son's death. A media advisor she hired to orchestrate her appearances, once her movement caught on and people began to donate money, advised her to practice controlling her emotions. "If you go before the public as a grieving mother, people will say, 'Sure, no wonder she's upset, but we can't have grieving mothers running our war policy.' So keep your cool, show anger if you want, but keep the tears to a minimum." With effort, she followed this advice but at night, when alone, she thought about never hearing Taffyd's voice again or seeing his smile, and she could no longer hold her hurt inside her and collapsed.

"No More Of Our Children Must Die!" Mayham shouted, and that too was also taken up by a chorus of her supporters.

A cordon of riot police blocked the gates to the presidential palace, and other police units separated Mayham's antiwar group from the prowar demonstrators gathered about a block away. The prowar group was larger than Mayham's. Some held signs that said, TRAITOR MAYHAM and SUPPORT OUR TROOPS! Many in that crowd had also lost sons and daughters on Ravenette.

The Mylexan media outlets were concentrating on Mayham's group, hoping for a clash with the police or with the prowar demonstrators. Chloe Mayham was good for news: attractive, articulate, dedicated as only someone motivated by a great personal loss can be. Her former husband lived quietly, far away, and refused interviews. His opinion on the war and his former wife's activism against it remained unknown. The only comment he had ever made in public was to a reporter: "Leave me the fuck alone!"

Officer Calvin Riggs of the Capitol Police stood shoulder to shoulder with his fellow officers forming the cordon in front of the palace gates. The Capitol Police were responsible for the security of the Presidential Palace grounds and other government buildings in New Columbia. Officer Riggs had been on the force twenty years. His son, Calvin Jr., was a soldier in the Mylexan contingent on Ravenette. Like many fathers whose offspring go off to war, he suffered from the dilemma of intense pride in his child's courage and service to his country and the mind-numbing fear that he would become a casualty of war.

Officer Riggs remembered with silent pain the day he'd taken his own son to the reserve center where the boy's infantry outfit was mustering for shipment to Ravenette. They'd exchanged formal, awkward, good-byes. Neither man had ever shown much emotion toward the other; they simply were not used to public displays of affection. That did not mean their feelings for each other did not run deep. Riggs fought hard to act nonchalant and positive, as Calvin Jr., upbeat and anxious to be off, tried to show he harbored no thoughts of death, and was itching to prove himself in war.

At the time Riggs reflected that fathers and sons had been saying good-byes like this for many thousands of years, the old men trying not to infect their sons with the fear that grew from knowledge, the sons anxious to succeed in the age-old rite of passage. He would never forget the image of his boy's back dwindling into the armory. Wondering if he'd ever see his son again, he sat in his car for a long time after Calvin, Jr. had disappeared inside. He knew then how his own father had felt forty years before, when as a young man, Officer Riggs had gone off lightly to the Second Silvansian War. Alone in his car that morning, he buried his head in his hands and let the tears flow down his cheeks.

Since then he'd maintained a facade of stoic courage, and although he never admitted it even to his wife, when vid clips of the fighting on Ravenette were shown on the news, his heart always caught, especially when the reports showed casualties being evacuated from the front. But Riggs was used to not showing his true feelings. As a police officer he had practiced suppressing his emotions, the better to deal dispassionately with some of the vile and hateful people he encountered in his work. He had become very good at that, politely addressing people he really wanted to shoot. Once in a while he would slip up and address some criminal as a "motherfuckin' scumbag," but he never gave in to the strong urge some policemen feel to apply their truncheons to the heads of malefactors.

But one morning, driving himself to work, when the radio played a medley of patriotic songs, he almost lost it at the chorus.

> Brave boys are they!
> Gone at their country's call;
> And yet, and yet we cannot forget
> That many brave boys must fall.

So Officer Calvin Riggs supported the troops on Ravenette, but he also wished for the war to end and for his boy to come home safely. At times he hated Mayham and her supporters, but at other times he understood exactly how they felt about the loss of life the war had caused. If secession had been put to a vote, he never would have been for it, but since they were at war, as a loyal citizen he supported his government. But that day, festooned in riot gear, he stood facing Mayham and her people, feelings neutral, determined to keep order because that was his job.

Chloe Mayham stepped closer to the police cordon. "Do not cross that line," a police captain warned her, gesturing to a spot on the pavement a few meters in front of the officers in riot gear. Chloe ignored the command, and followed by a phalanx of her supporters, stepped even closer. Getting arrested, Chloe had come to realize, was the best propaganda for her cause and she was determined to wind up the day in custody.

Chloe stood upon the spot the officer had designated as the Rubicon. "TROOPS OUT! TROOPS OUT! PRESIDENT POSTERUS OUT! PRESIDENT POSTERUS OUT!" she shrieked through the bullhorn. She stepped across the line.

The police, transparent shields held before them, advanced on the protestors. Calvin Riggs now stood facing Chloe Mayham herself, his face not more than five centimeters from the mouth of her blaring bullhorn. "Please step back, madam, or I will arrest you," he tried to shout above the blaring voice. Riggs could see the spittle flecking Mayham's lips. Her face was flushed, the veins in her neck and forehead swelled with anger and determination. Actually, she looked beautiful, like an Amazon or a Valkyrie, filled with the justice of her cause. Riggs moved his shield to one side so he could be heard, "I said, back off or I will arrest you!"

Witnesses disagreed on what happened next. On the crystal recorded by several cameramen at the scene, it looked as if Chloe Mayham struck Officer Riggs with her bullhorn and that is what his fellow officers claimed they saw. Mayham's supporters, who were right behind her, swore the instrument slipped and struck Riggs by mistake. Riggs reacted instinctively, slamming his truncheon into the side of Mayham's head. People standing nearby actually heard bone shattering as he struck her. The police line surged forward. The media had a field day.

But Chloe Mayham's protesting days were over. And so was Calvin Riggs's career as a Capitol Police officer.

President Posterus's shoulders slumped. Gabs Stukas, her Minister of Information, waited patiently for her to continue. "Gabs, I called you here because I want you to prepare a very important press release." She took a deep breath. "I am going to sign an executive order withdrawing our troops from the Coalition army on Ravenette. I am composing a letter to inform Preston Summers now. I want you to read both documents and prepare a press release."

"A very wise decision, Madam President. Er, how is General Henricus going to take this? If I may ask."

Posterus put a hand to her brow. "Very badly, Gabs. When he learns of it, very badly."

"You haven't told him?"

The President shook her head slowly. "Nor anyone else in the cabinet. You're the first to know of it." She smiled weakly. "We've talked the issue to death," she said wearily, "and I'm tired of it all. I'm the commander in chief, Gabs, the chief executive of this Union. I made the decision to sign the order and I'm going to stick by it, come thick or thin." She handed Stukas a crystal. "The final versions of the order and the letter are on this crystal."

"Very well, ma'am." Stukas took the crystal and hefted it speculatively.

"Yes, is there anything else?"

"Uh, when will you send the message to Summers?"

"Directly. In your press release you can use the past tense and tell the public the order and the message were issued today. By the time I approve the release, our withdrawal from this war will be a done deal."

It was done, but too late for the Mylexan forces on Ravenette and too late for Corporal Calvin Riggs Jr.

CHAPTER SEVENTEEN

There was no space where the companies could assemble to be addressed directly by the company commanders. So Captain Conorado, like the other company commanders in the three FISTs going on Operation Backdoor, had the Marines of Company L assemble in the tunnel, wearing their helmets with all screens up, and addressed them via the all-hands circuit in his own helmet.

"I just got back from a commanders' call at FIST headquarters," Conorado said. "It's time to earn your pay again, Marines. I know we recently returned from a raid-in-force where we encountered more resistance than we'd been led to expect. I also know that not all of the injuries some of you received in our recent actions have had enough time to fully heal. But if that lack of full healing would endanger you, you would have been evacuated to orbit.

"As I said, we had some surprises when we went to Gilbert's Corners. I can tell you this: this time there are no surprises. This time we know up front we're going up against fresh troops who might outnumber us, might be better armed, and are more than likely better armored. We will engage them following an amphibious landing on what may be the most difficult beaches I've ever heard described. This time, we won't be on the defensive; we'll be on the offense. We will dictate the timing and the pace of the battle. And this time, we'll have all of our weapons with us.

"Here's what you need to know before we move out . . ."

* * *

It didn't take the Marines long to prepare themselves to board Dragons. Neither did they have to wait long once they were ready—General Cazombi's hastily assembled staff managed to get everything moving quickly. The Dragons splashed into the water at the southeastern corner of the peninsula, out of sight of the Coalition forces besieging the Bataan garrison, and headed toward the horizon at low speed to keep rooster tails from rising high enough to be seen from the land beyond the peninsula. Because of the relatively low speed of the Dragons crossing the ocean beyond Pohick Bay, it took more than an hour for them to rendezvous with the waiting Essays. The suborbital flight to 34th FIST's landing zone covered five times the horizontal distance, and much more than that on the ascent and descent, but took less than half as much time.

A squad from 4th Force Recon Company met 34th FIST at the LZ.

Sergeant D'Wayne Williams stood in the dark at the edge of a small grassland. Williams gave the infra flashers that marked the LZ a final look, then glanced at the infra wind cone his squad had erected. Satisfied that all was in order, he removed his helmet and gloves, and rolled his sleeves up to his elbows. He looked up at a distant roar and saw the exhausts of the first wave of three Essays in their final approach to the landing zone, even though he couldn't see the shuttles themselves against the dark sky. In another minute they were down and three Dragons set off their air cushions to rumble out of the Essays' rears. The Dragons sped away from the Essays, which lifted as soon as they were clear. Almost as soon as the first three Essays were gone, a second trio touched down. Williams estimated that it would take less than five minutes for all twenty Essays to land their Dragons and head back out to wherever they were headed. His mission briefing hadn't included information on where the Essays were going once they'd dropped the FIST that fourth squad, 4th Force Recon Company would be guiding.

Two Dragons, one from the first wave of Essays and one from the second, peeled off from the ones that were forming up behind the touchdown area and headed around the edge of the grass toward Williams. The Force Recon squad leader faced the Dragons and held infra panels out to his sides to make himself more easily visible. The first Dragon stopped fifteen meters away, the second just to its left and rear. The roar of their fans rumbled down to low, steady growls. The Dragons' rear ramps clanged open, then two Marines came around the side of each vehicle. Like Williams, they had their helmets and gloves off, their sleeves rolled up to their elbows. One of them marched directly at Williams, the other three hung back a pace and to his flanks.

"Sergeant D'Wayne Williams, sir," Williams said, saluting the lead Marine, "Fourth Force Recon. My squad will guide you to your first objective."

Brigadier Theodosius Sturgeon returned Williams's salute. He didn't look around for the other Marines in Williams's squad; he was certain that he wouldn't be able to spot them.

"I'm Brigadier Sturgeon," Sturgeon said. "Glad to see you, Sergeant Williams. What's the situation at Objective Alpha?" Objective Alpha, the encampment of the 7th Independent Military Police Company, and a POW camp—34th FIST's first objective on Operation Backdoor.

"Sir, it's three hours since we were last there, but at that time, everybody was drunk, getting drunk, or already passed out—even the sentries." He shook his head. "A platoon of pogues from Fleet Marine Headquarters could prance in and take the place without firing a shot."

Sturgeon chuckled.

"I left a couple minnies in place to keep an eye on things, sir," Williams continued, "but we're beyond their transmission range. I'll be able to give you an update when we get close enough."

"That sounds good to me, Sergeant." Sturgeon turned to the man on his right. "Commander Usner, as soon as the Dragons are down and in formation to move, move them out." Then back to Williams. "You and your squad are going to fly ahead of us, is that right?"

"Yes, sir. We can be in our puddle jumpers and hovering in front of your lead elements as soon as you're ready to go."

Sturgeon turned to look at the Dragons assembling several hundred meters away, then into the sky to see the final Essays approaching. "Better get your squad into their puddle jumpers now, Sergeant," he said. "We'll be moving out in a couple of minutes."

"Aye aye, sir."

* * *

The twenty Dragons moved in four parallel columns of five vehicles. Each column followed a Force Recon Marine who flew just below tree-top level through the thin forest land south of the landing zone. The chameleons worn by the Force Recon Marines were even more effective than those worn by the infantry Marines of the FISTs, but the exhausts from their puddle jumpers was very clear in infrared. The commander of each lead Dragon watched the flying Marines in infra, and gave verbal directions to the drivers, who watched their paths in visual. Except for one of the columns, which traveled along a "semi-improved" road. At least "semi-improved" is how the Marines characterized the road. The contractor who had built the road skimped on materials, so even though the road was little used, it was potholed and eroding at its edges.

Forty-five minutes after the Dragons bearing 34th FIST pulled out of the landing zone, Sergeant Williams called a halt, and the Force Recon Marines landed, Williams next to Brigadier Sturgeon's Dragon.

"Here we are, sir," Williams said when Sturgeon dismounted and joined him. He held his UPUD where the FIST commander could see its display. "This minnie is on a windowsill—about chest height. The other is on top of a barracks near the POW compound. This is what they're looking at right now."

Sturgeon looked at the display. "May I?" He held out his hand and Williams gave him the UPUD. The display showed what was obviously a temporary camp, even though it was composed of buildings rather than tents. The buildings had all the hallmarks of hasty construction: The structures weren't aligned in proper military manner, not all the walls were plumb, occasional gaps showed between roofs and walls, the roads were unevenly graded and they were oiled rather than paved, the street lighting was irregular. Maintenance was spotty at best. A door hung ajar on a barracks. Cracked and broken windows hadn't been repaired. Some streetlights were out. Litter marred the grounds.

"How do I get the view to move?" he asked.

Williams did something Sturgeon couldn't see, and the view began slowly oscillating side to side. Williams slipped off a glove and pointed to a touch key on the UPUD. "Sir, press that to toggle to the rooftop minnie."

Sturgeon watched the view move through a full 180 degrees and back, then toggled to the other minnie, which was already turning at Williams's command. "How do I get close-up views? Like I want to see that." Sturgeon pointed at an indistinct form on the ground in front of a barracks.

"I have to give commands to the minnie, sir," Williams answered. "Let me know what you want to see, and I'll have a minnie look at it." He used a control box to stop the minnie and refocus it on the form Sturgeon had indicated. Enlarged, it was a body, a soldier supine on the ground in front of a barracks, passed out or dead.

"Pull back and rotate more."

Williams did as Sturgeon ordered. He stopped the minnie and adjusted its focus on request so Sturgeon could take closer looks. All together, he saw more than a platoon's worth of soldiers on the ground or propped against building fronts. They saw only a few soldiers staggering about from one building to another, carrying bottles from which they occasionally drank.

"Drunk, getting drunk, or already passed out," Sturgeon finally said. "It looks like you characterized the situation exactly, Sergeant. Must have been a hell of a party last night. Now I want to take a look at the POW compound."

Williams worked his controls to give Sturgeon the best possible view of the fenced POW compound. Sturgeon studied it. The camp looked exactly the way it had in the intelligence briefings. The buildings were better constructed than the barracks buildings, the compound itself was surrounded by a razor-wire fence that might be electrified, two guard towers overlooked the brightly lit interior of the compound, and only one building was lit from within. Even the gate was slightly ajar as it had been when Force Recon first visited. Sturgeon looked at the guard towers. If they were manned, the guards were out of sight, likely as drunk as everyone else seemed to be. He handed the UPUD back and put his helmet on to contact his staff to plan their next step.

Company L went the last three kilometers on foot; three kilometers was as close as Brigadier Sturgeon thought the Dragons could get to the camp without making enough noise to alert people inside it.

First and second platoons were to enter the main camp from opposite directions, gather everybody who could be made mobile, and secure those too insensate to move on their own. Third platoon was responsible for securing the POW enclosure and gathering the POWs. The battalion's surgeon and BAS corpsmen accompanied third platoon, so they'd be on hand to give medical treatment to any POWs who needed it. The assault platoon set up security on the south side of the camp to stop any enemy forces that came upon them before the camp was cleared.

The sun was just peeking above the horizon when Company L moved in.

"On your feet, you!" first platoon's Corporal Wilson said loudly as he kicked the feet of a man lying sprawled on the bare dirt in front of a barracks. Wilson didn't look up at the sound of feet running past him and pounding up the short flight of stairs to crash through the door of the barracks. "Drop your cock and grab your sock, soldier!" Wilson said louder, and kicked the soldier's booted feet harder than before. He ignored the sounds of men being forcefully awakened inside the barracks. When the prostrate man at his feet didn't move, Wilson took a step closer and kicked him in the hip. "I said on your feet, you worthless scum!"

The soldier gave out a low moan and rolled away from Wilson's kicks. The Marine moved in closer and swung his instep hard at the soldier's buttocks. "I said get up and move, dammit!"

"Leemee 'lone," the soldier mumbled. " 'M sleepin'." He curled into a loose fetal position, but sprang straight when Wilson planted a boot in his posterior again.

"You *don't* want me to bend over and yank you to your feet, you sorry excuse for a soldier," Wilson said and kicked him in the ribs.

"Aw ri, aw ri," the soldier mumbled, and struggled to move around and raise his upper body. "Ah'm geddin' up." He looked up and saw Wilson's disembodied face hovering above him. He shook his head violently, then abruptly heaved, and bent lower to puke between his splayed legs. When he finished throwing up, he wiped a bare arm across his mouth, then looked up again. "Ah ain't wakin' up. Ah's still asleep. Ain't no ghost face hangin' inna air 'bove me." He dropped his head on his chest and started to topple over toward Wilson, who kicked him in the ribs hard enough to straighten him back up, but not hard enough to knock him over the other way.

"I'm not a ghost, you dipshit," Wilson snarled. "I'm a Confederation Marine, and you're my prisoner!"

"Ah ain't no pris'ner," the soldier said, his voice less of a mumble. "Ah's a MP. Ah *guards* pris'ners!"

"Not anymore, you don't," Wilson said. He reached down to grab the soldier's shirt collar, then yanked him to his feet. "You're not fit to guard a shithouse, you slimy turd! And now *you're* a prisoner of war." He shoved the soldier in the direction other Marines were herding other prisoners. The soldier stumbled and fell hard on his face. The fall did more to wake him up than anything else had; he scrambled to his feet and spun around, fists clenched and raised, looking for whomever had knocked him down. He ignored the blood that flowed from his nose and mingled with the vomit still on his face. He saw Wilson's face, and without noticing that he only saw the face, charged the Marine, milling his arms.

Wilson gave the charging MP a curious look, then stepped aside and put out a foot to trip him. The soldier squawked as he sprawled to the ground. In a flash, he was back on his feet looking for his tormentor. Fresh blood flowed from a cut on the corner of his forehead. He spotted Wilson's face and charged again, once more wildly swinging his arms. Wilson easily dodged the flailing fists and slammed the butt of his blaster into the middle of the soldier's back, knocking him down again.

Wilson moved quickly and planted a foot between the soldier's legs, high up so the front part of his boot pressed onto his testicles.

"You know," the Marine said, "we could keep this up until you seriously hurt yourself. Or you could just be a good boy and go with the rest of the prisoners."

The soldier flinched from the pressure on his scrotum, but didn't struggle. Instead he looked forward and saw other members of the 7th Independent Military Police Battalion walking along with their hands on their heads, toward a gathering place in the middle of the camp. At first, nobody seemed to be guarding them, but then he saw a hovering face. He looked around and saw other hovering faces. Carefully, so as not to agitate the man whose boot was putting pressure on his balls, he looked over his shoulder and saw a face hovering above his back.

"Confed'ral Marines?" he asked.

"Confederation Marines," Wilson confirmed. "And you're my prisoner."

"Yassah," the cowed soldier said. "You wan' me to git up and go wit t'others?"

"Yes, I do."

"Ahh, uh, kin ah move?"

Wilson stepped back. "You can move."

"Thank you, sah." The soldier eased himself to his feet, brushed himself off with as much dignity as he could muster, put his hands on top of his head, and joined the column of MPs shuffling toward the collection point.

Corporal Wilson shook his head sadly. "Those are soldiers?" he asked himself. "How the hell have they managed to keep us pinned up in Bataan for all these weeks?"

Wilson turned at a throat clearing behind him. His platoon sergeant, Staff Sergeant DaCosta, had come up without Wilson hearing him.

"I don't think the 7th Independent MPs is a representative unit for the Coalition army," DaCosta said. "You want my opinion, I think they got stuck way out here to keep them out of the way. That and we've got—" DaCosta suddenly stopped talking.

"You were saying, Staff Sergeant? We've got what?"

"Never mind, Corporal. We've been facing the effective part of the Coalition army." He looked Wilson in the eyes. "When we hit the 4th Division at Phelps, it won't be like this." He walked away, leaving Wilson wondering if what DaCosta didn't want to say out loud was ". . . and we've got that doggie general, Jason Billie."

CHAPTER EIGHTEEN

At the same time first platoon entered the camp of the 7th Independent Military Police Battalion from the coast side, and second platoon entered the camp from the inland side, third platoon silently slipped, one man at a time, through the slightly ajar gate of the POW compound. Inside, Corporal Dornhofer led his fire team directly to the guard tower to the left, and Corporal Dean took his men to the tower on the right; Sergeant Ratliff kept Corporal Pasquin's second fire team on the ground, watching the towers closely for movement. Sergeant Kerr led second squad past the two barracks buildings—sparing time for a quick look through the windows to make sure prisoners were still kept in them and to check for guards—and the sanitation building to the administration building. He kept his first and second fire teams by the main door of the admin building, and sent Corporal Doyle and his fire team to the interrogation building. The gun squad went to the barracks buildings to free the prisoners. As each fire or gun team reached its objective, the team leader sent a signal to Ensign Bass.

When every element of third platoon was in place, Bass signaled Dornhofer and Dean; the two corporals began climbing the ladders attached to the guard towers, followed by their men. Everybody else tensed, ready for instant action if the guards in the tower realized they were under attack.

When he got the signal from Bass, Corporal Joe Dean swallowed and took a deep breath, then began climbing. He kept his hands and feet at the sides of the wooden rungs, to reduce the chances they'd creak under his weight, but climbed as quickly as he could. He felt vulnerable on the ladder, more vulnerable than when he fought the implacable Skinks, almost as vulnerable as he did the first time he was in combat. On Bass's order, he'd left his blaster on the ground so it wouldn't impede his climb or make a noise that might alert the guards of his approach. The only weapon he carried on his climb was his combat knife, held between the thumb and forefinger of his right hand while he used the other fingers to climb with; he worried that the hilt of the knife would thud against the ladder, but he was very careful and made no noise while climbing, and no curious guard looked over the edge of the guard tower to see a knife making its lonely way up the ladder.

Dean stopped with his head just below the wall of the guard post, bringing his feet up another two rungs and moving into a crouching position. When he felt Lance Corporal Godenov's helmet against his right knee, he signaled Bass that they were in place.

As soon as Bass heard from Dean and Dornhofer that they were in place, he sent the *go!* signal. Dean lunged up and over; the time for silence was over. Godenov scrambled up the last few rungs and was over the wall almost before Dean landed on one of the tower's two guards. Both were sound asleep—or passed out, as the empty bottles littering the floor of the guard post suggested. Dean and Godenov secured them with wrist and ankle ties and gags before either gained enough consciousness to realize what was happening. Dean breathed a sigh of relief when the two soldiers were bound; he hadn't had to use his knife.

The other tower was taken just as quickly and quietly.

Looking through the windows, Sergeant Kerr had seen one soldier with sergeant's stripes on his shirt sleeves sitting at a desk in an office, half on the desk, obviously out cold. Two other soldiers were in the room with him; one was supine on a couch, the other sprawled on the floor. In another, unlit, room, his infra had shown four more soldiers sleeping on cots. The other rooms all seemed to be empty. When he got the signal, he sent his first and third fire teams rushing into the admin building. Corporal Chan's first fire team ran into the room with soldiers sleeping on cots; Corporal Claypoole and his second fire team went with Kerr, darting into the office.

Claypoole pounced on the sergeant at the desk, and had the man's hands twisted around behind his back and tied together in seconds. Then the sergeant emitted a massive snore. Claypoole looked at his men to see what they were doing. Lance Corporal Schultz had bound and gagged the soldier on the floor, and was helping Lance Corporal Ymenez bind the one on the couch.

Claypoole raised his screens and looked toward where his infra had shown Sergeant Kerr. "He's snoring," he told his squad leader. "Do you still want me to gag him?"

Kerr raised his screens, but he was listening to his helmet comm, then reporting to Bass. Finished with his report, he said, "Don't bother, the whole camp is secure. They can make as much noise as they want. I'm going to check on Doyle. Chan's in charge here until I get back."

"Aye aye," Claypoole said as his squad leader left the office.

While the Marines of Company L were closing in on the camp of the 7th Independent Military Police Battalion, Lieutenant Keesey, commander of the 1st MP Company, was the only member of the battalion neither drunk, getting drunk, nor already passed out. Keesey was a sober, serious man; he rarely drank alcohol and never with the drunkards of 7th MPs, and he was deadly serious with what he was about. Quietly, so as not to disturb anybody—anybody other than the one he wanted to disturb, that is—he eased the key he'd obtained into the lock on the rear door of Prisoner Barracks Two, the door that gave way to the women's squad bay. He unlocked the door and eased it open on hinges he'd earlier made sure were properly oiled, then closed it behind himself. He stood silent for a few moments to allow his eyes to adjust to the somewhat deeper darkness inside the barracks, then located his objective. He didn't really need to take the time for his eyes to adjust; the room was small, only a dozen bunks, and enough light came through the unshaded windows for him to see where he was going. His objective was, of course, a woman, but a woman he'd taken a particular interest in. Not only was Charlette Odinloc an attractive woman, something about her suggested to Keesey that she was more than the farm wife and refugee she claimed to be.

Keesey believed Charlette Odinloc was a spy. And he had his ways of dealing with spies. Particularly a spy who was also an attractive woman.

Creeping on soft-soled feet, Keesey approached Charlette's bunk. He withdrew a prepared knockout cloth from a sealed wrap he carried in his hip pocket, and in a flash, clamped it over her nose and mouth. Charlette reacted automatically, and in exactly the wrong way to defend herself—she bolted upright and took a deep breath to gather air to scream. Instead of air, she inhaled a heavy dose of the knockout, and fell back on the bunk.

Keesey stifled a snicker, and lifted Charlette to sling her over his shoulder in a fireman's carry. Walking silently despite the additional weight, he left the women's quarters, carefully locking the door behind him. Moments later he opened the door of the interrogation building and carried Charlette to a room he had already prepared. There wasn't much in the room; a washbasin, spotlights that were off, a straight-back chair, a long bed with bare mattress and manacles to hold wrists and ankles, and a drain in the middle of the floor.

He dumped his burden unceremoniously on the bed, and breathing a sigh of thanks for the condition of her clothing, stripped Charlette naked. He put the manacles on her wrists and ankles, making sure her arms were stretched tightly above her head and her legs spread wide, then turned on three of the spotlights; one on her face, one on her breasts, and one on her pubes. Then he sat on the straight-backed chair and waited for the knockout to wear off.

He waited for only a few minutes before he rose and went to the basin where he ran some water into a pan. Standing next to the bed, he waited for Charlette to breathe in and threw the water on her face. She breathed in some of the water and suddenly awoke, sputtering and shaking her head; she tried to sit up, but the manacles kept her supine. She gathered herself to scream, but Keesey slapped her across the face, hard.

"Now, now, missy, ya be quiet, ya hear? Ah'll gag ya if'n ya wanna yell. Ya wanna be gagged?"

Charlette looked up at him in shock, trying to blink the tears from her eyes—that slap hurt.

"Ah din't think so. Ah don' wanna gag ya anyhow. Ah needs to question you, and if'n yer gagged, ya cain't answer. Ain't that so now?"

He looked down at her body and tried to imagine what it had looked like before the ship she'd been on was sunk offshore near the MP camp, before she'd been half-starved as a prisoner. He liked what his imagination showed.

"Well," he drawled, running a clammy hand along her rib cage, "I don't really keer if you tell me the truth, 'cause what I'm about to do to you is find out the truth my own way, and this will hurt you a lot more than it'll hurt me." He smirked and stroked her silently for a moment.

The feel of Keesey's hand on her ribs told Charlette everything she had to know about what this monster meant by "my own way," and "this will hurt you a lot more than it'll hurt me."

"On second thought," Keesey continued after a moment of caressing, squeezing, and leering, "maybe you'll enjoy what's comin', honey. Most women do."

Corporal Doyle positioned his men by the entrance to the interrogation building and began a solo circuit of it, looking into the windows. Only one room was occupied, and it was well lit. What he saw when he looked inside appalled him; a naked woman manacled to a bed, a Coalition officer standing over her, molesting her. As fast as he could he finished his circuit. Fortunately, the well-lit room seemed to be the only one occupied.

Back with his men, Doyle quickly briefed them on what he'd seen and what they were going to do about it. He knew he was supposed to wait for the command to go from Ensign Bass, but he couldn't let that officer do what he obviously had planned for the woman. He tried the door. It wasn't locked. He pulled it open and crept in, heading for where he was sure the lit room was. A line of light at a door's bottom drew him to what he was certain was the right room. He positioned his men, then leaned his helmet against the door and turned up his helmet's ears to hear what was happening inside. He did his best not to fidget; he knew any noise he made before Bass's signal could cause problems for the platoon's mission. But, *damn* he didn't want to wait to rescue that woman.

There it is! Doyle stepped back and tapped PFC Summers on the shoulder. Summers lifted his right leg and put all his weight into kicking the door next to the latch. The door slammed open, and Summers almost fell through it.

Doyle managed to barge in without tripping on Summers and yelled out, "Freeze, asshole! You are now my prisoner!"

The officer, his pants down around his knees, spun around. "Wha' the—" he said, but got no farther; Doyle hit him in the head with a butt stroke, and the officer crumpled to the floor.

"Miss, are y-you all r-right?" Doyle stammered. He whipped off his helmet so she could see him, and looked around for something to cover her with. He plucked the discarded shift up from the floor. It wasn't much, but it would do the job.

Charlette was shouting with joy; as soon as she heard the voice out of nowhere, she knew the Marines had landed. "Marines! You're here. Oh, Goddess, you've saved me!"

By then, Doyle was examining the manacles, trying to open them, but they were locked. He turned to Lance Corporal Quick. "Quick, search that bastard; he must have the keys on him. Oh, and tie him up while you're at it."

"Huh? Oh, right," Quick said. Even though Doyle had told him and Summers that they were going to rescue a naked woman, the sight of Charlette Odinloc's naked body had momentarily stunned him. "Summers," he ordered, "give me a hand here."

"Miss, I'm Corporal Doyle, third platoon, Company L, 34th FIST. We've taken this camp and we're freeing all the prisoners. Do you know if anybody else is in this building?"

Charlette stopped laughing and crying with relief and said, "Corporal—Doyle did you say?—I don't think so. I think I'm the only one." She craned her head to look at Lieutenant Keesey where he lay trussed on the floor with his pants still down around his knees. "Me and that piece of garbage." She tried to spit at Keesey, but her position kept her from projecting the spittle beyond the edge of the bed.

"We'll have you freed as soon as we find the key, miss," Doyle said, looking toward Quick and Summers. "T-Take your helmets and gloves off," he told them; he found the sight of Keesey flopping about disconcerting. It became less so once he could see his men's heads, and their hands going through Keesey's clothing.

"Corporal Doyle," Charlette said, "I think the key's on the basin."

"Thank you, miss," Doyle said and stepped to the basin.

"My name's Charlette Odinloc. *Sergeant* Odinloc, Confederation Army."

But Doyle wasn't listening, he was looking for the key and not finding it.

It was Quick who found the key, on a corner of the bed, almost tucked under a corner of the mattress. He gave the key to Doyle, who unlocked the manacles that were keeping Charlette supine.

"Can—can you get dressed, miss?" Doyle asked as soon as he had the last manacle opened.

"Yes, thank you, Corporal."

"All right, turn your backs and give the lady some privacy," Doyle said.

"Thank you," Charlette murmured. A moment later she said, "You can turn around now."

They did. Doyle thought she looked better dressed than she had naked. Perhaps that was because now she was standing on her own instead of being bound.

"Where are the rest of the Marines?" she asked.

"Oh!" Doyle suddenly realized he hadn't reported what he'd found in the interrogation building. He knew Sergeant Kerr had given his fire team the assignment because he thought nobody was there. He radioed Kerr, and a moment later the squad leader came in, followed soon after by Ensign Bass.

"Sergeant Charlette Odinloc, Army G2, reporting, sir," she said when Bass arrived.

"Army G2?" Bass shook his head. "I'll bet this dummy didn't know what he had here, did he?" he asked, toeing Keesey in the ankle.

Keesey, conscious again, glared up at him, then at Charlette. If he hadn't been gagged, he would have said, "I knew there was sumpin' diff'nt 'bout ya!"

CHAPTER NINETEEN

"They're coming! They're *comiiiiiiiing!*" a female voice screeched in the street outside the headquarters building of the 4th Composite Infantry Division.

"What the hell's all that racket?" Major General Barksdale Sneed asked, looking up from the *Phelps Independent Courier,* which he read every morning. Because the paper had such a low circulation and Phelps, like most other places on Ravenette, was a somewhat backward place, technologically speaking, it was printed the old-fashioned way, on paper. Usually it was only four or five sheets in length but General Sneed enjoyed putting his feet up, sipping his coffee, and spreading out the sheets to read them. He read everything, even the advertisements. The paper was a morning ritual with him. He especially liked the editorial cartoons which often pilloried Cardoza O'Quinn, the self-important and sticky-fingered mayor of Phelps.

The 4th Composite Infantry Division had been stationed at Phelps for some time by then, and during that time General Sneed had come to despise the mayor who literally slobbered with joy over the presence of the soldiers in his town, who spent their pay in businesses mostly owned by himself and his extended family. But O'Quinn hated General Sneed, who imposed a strict curfew on his men and punished those who broke it or committed any other infraction of good order and discipline.

General Barksdale Sneed was an officer of the Old School, one who believed a soldier's duty was soldiering, not carousing and staying up late. He also resented being stationed at Phelps, which he saw as a backwater in the war against the Confederation. But no matter where General Davis Lyons sent him, Barksdale Sneed was going to do his duty. He kept his men in tip-top physical condition with road marches and calisthenics; they trained intensively, too, in small-unit tactics and battalion-size maneuvers, and when they weren't training, he found other work for them to do.

Sneed was the very picture of a professional soldier, tall, spare, closely cropped white hair, and a rocklike jaw that jutted aggressively out from his face. His battle-dress uniform was always spotless. He kept it that way by changing several times a day.

Today's cartoon showed "Hizzoner" O'Quinn, pockets stuffed with banknotes, being kicked down the street by an enormous boot attached to a skillfully executed caricature of Major General Barksdale Sneed, who was shouting after the departing notable, "Don't you know there's a war on?" Little figures clutching overstuffed cashboxes labeled with the names of his associates, mostly relatives, leaped out of the mayor's way.

"He got me down pretty good," Barksdale said with a chuckle, slapping the cartoon with one hand. "That artist, Olyphan, he's a genius! He-he! I bet old O'Quinn is choking on his coffee over this one!" A sudden ruckus outside caught his attention.

"What in the hell *is* all that screaming out there, Captain?" he asked his aide.

"I believe, General, it is, um, one of our soldiers," Captain Quang Nigh said from the window.

"Go on down there and find out what's up, will you, Quang? Find out who's coming and why that damned woman is screaming about it."

Captain Nigh groaned silently when he got close to the disheveled young woman swaying back and forth in the street. The General would not be pleased, he realized. Her uniform was soiled, her hair was in disarray, and she smelled awful, even from a distance. And her eyes were wildly bloodshot.

"They're coming!" she shrieked at the officer.

Captain Nigh could see she was a corporal. "What's your unit, soldier?"

The young woman pulled herself to a loose position of attention and saluted drunkenly, "S-Seventh MPs, shur, sir! Corp'ral Puella Queege, Fourth Comp'ny!"

"Have you been drinking, Corporal?" Then he did a double take and said, "Whaaat? Seventh MPs? What the hell are you doing here, and at this hour, and drunk?" Queege only stared back at him uncomprehendingly. "What in the hell is that *smell?*" He gasped.

"I was eatin' slimies, sir!"

"What?"

"Bet with my first sergeant, sir! He bet me I couldn't eat five of 'em." She burped loudly and gave a lopsided grin.

"Holy . . . okay, okay." Captain Nigh tried to get a grip on himself. "Who, precisely, is coming and why are you here, Corporal?"

"Well, I was takin' a shit down by my first sergeant's tent—"

"Why are you here?"

"The goddamn Marines landed! Thousands of 'em! So I pulls up my drawers and I hops into the company car 'n' I drives like hell down here to warn you"—she burped loudly—"but I ran off the road about a klick back 'n' hadda walk the rest of the way. Shu-Sir."

Captain Nigh blinked. "Confederation Marines have landed and taken the 7th MPs' positions on the coast? Is that what you are telling me, Corporal er . . ."

"Queege, sir, Puella Queege, company clerk, 4th Company, 7th Independent—"

Captain Nigh silenced her with a wave of his hand. By then several soldiers including two military policemen had gathered at the scene. "Take her," he ordered the MPs, "clean her up, sober her up, and when that's done, bring her to General Sneed's office." He turned on his heel and ran back into the headquarters building.

"I won the bet!" Queege yelled after him. The MPs held their noses as they dragged her down the street.

"Holy shitbirds!" Major General Sneed barked. "How reliable is her story?"

"I don't know, sir," Captain Nigh replied, "But, well, she came from there and something's going on out on the coast this morning. I think we'd better take her seriously."

Sneed wrenched open the door to his outer office and shouted, "Sergeant Major! Get the staff assembled! Right now! Move!"

In the division briefing room Sneed laid into his staff. "G2, what's going on out on the coast? What do you know? We had some drunken sot from the 7th MPs shouting in the street that the Marines have landed out there."

The intelligence chief shrugged. "All quiet on the Ashburtonville front, sir. Both armies still in place. No enemy activity reported in any other sector."

"Signals?"

The Signal Corps captain in charge of the division's communication network stood. "Sir, I've tried to reach the 7th MPs since last night. They never submitted their daily coast-watch report and they don't respond to messages. This is not unusual with them, sir, and I didn't think—"

"Sit down! Christ on crutches! That goddamned Cogswell." He was referring to Colonel Delbert Cogswell, commander of the 7th Independent Military Police Battalion.

"Sir?" It was the division operations officer. "I heard that Colonel Cogswell had declared, uh, well, a 'training holiday' for his battalion. They, uh, sent some men into town yesterday and picked up a lot of booze and some of the, er, ladies of the town. I didn't see them but someone told me they were over at Mayor O'Quinn's office and—"

"Oh, God save us all," General Sneed muttered, running a hand through his hair. "Why the *fuck* didn't anyone inform me of this mess?" His officers stared silently at the floor. "All right, all right. Plan Red is now in effect." Plan Red was an emergency defensive plan General Sneed had created just in case his division had to react to an invasion force coming in over the coast. "In case you don't remember Plan Red, gentlemen, here it is . . ." He paused in thought, then said to his intelligence officer, "But before anything else, G2, get whatshername, find out everything she knows."

"Probably won't know much, sir. She's drunk as a kwangduk at a sewer party." Captain Nigh chuckled.

"Try. Get on it. Maps!" He turned to the sergeant in charge of the trid displays, and a huge map of Phelps and the surrounding territory leaped onto the screen. "Aviation! Send hoppers to the coast, have 'em scope out the situation there but tell 'em not to engage! Operations! Send a recon platoon up the coastal road, get them as close to the 7th MP position as they can and report what they see up there. The remainder of the division recon elements, I want them spread out on both flanks along that coastal road, snooping and pooping. We can't afford to be flanked. 222nd Brigade"—he turned to the colonel commanding the 222nd—"I want you to send one of your battalions, mount 'em up, have 'em run down the coastal road to here"—he identified a spot on the vid display a few kilometers outside the Phelps city limits—"and set up a blocking position. If the enemy comes at them, they are to delay the enemy as long as possible, but no last-stand bullshit; withdraw them when you feel you can't hold any longer.

"Plan Red calls for a defense in depth. First Brigade will hold the town, armor will support you." The troop dispositions called for in Plan Red appeared on the screen. "Heavy weapons and aviation, with logistics and medical, will deploy behind the ridge bisected by the Ashburtonville road. The rest of the division will occupy prepared positions straddling the road with the ridge to their rear.

"Signals. Send a Flash message to General Lyons. Tell him we believe the enemy has crossed the coast, strength unknown at this time, and is probably moving inland. Send him updates every fifteen minutes. G2, G3, keep Signals informed as soon as you have more information.

"Civil Affairs. Get O'Quinn up here right now. I told that bastard to get an evacuation plan drawn up and he'd better have it. We can't have civilians encumbering our forces if this is really an invasion and not another reconnaissance in force like they pulled on Gilbert's Corners. I think it is a full-scale invasion, but we've got to know how big. Get moving, men!"

The briefing room was cleared in thirty seconds. Sneed sat there shaking his head, wearily. "I told General Lyons that the 7th MPs were the chink in his armor—oh, no offense Quang! But that coast is our Achilles' heel."

"Sir?" said Major Lucretia Spinoza, the division Civil Affairs officer, "Mayor O'Quinn's secretary says he is 'indisposed' and he will drop by after lunch? I told her of the urgency of the situation but she cut me off."

"The fat pig is drunk on his ass, Major. Okay. You get a detachment of military police. Go to his mansion—or wherever the useless bastard is—and bring him here. If anyone gives you any trouble, use whatever force you deem necessary to bring him to me. But be prepared to run the evacuation yourself. We have to assume that Hizzoner hasn't done jack squat about drawing up an evacuation plan. What's the population today?"

"Four thousand, give or take, sir."

"Damn. All right, go to Brigadier General Josephus of the 1st Brigade. Tell him I said to give you all the cooperation you need to get these people out of town. He doesn't need them around if he has to defend this place. I'll contact him in a minute and give him verbal orders. But do not make a career of moving them, Major. Those that don't want to move, want to hide in their cellars, let 'em. But warn everybody that once the fighting gets started they're on their own."

"Sir, why don't we just take over the evacuation now? Screw the mayor—excuse my language."

Sneed grinned. "Good thinking, Major. But protocol requires I advise the civil authority of the military situation and that they handle protecting the noncombatant population. You just get O'Quinn up here ASAP and we'll see what has to be done."

"Unhand me, you goons!" Cardoza O'Quinn struggled against the grip the two MPs had on his arms as they dragged him into General Sneed's office.

Cardoza O'Quinn was ugly even when sober and he was far from sober, still in his nightclothes, disheveled, breath reeking of alcohol. His normally ruddy complexion was inflamed that morning by what he'd consumed the night before and the outrage at being pulled out of his bed so early and so unceremoniously in the morning. The warts that covered his bulbous nose, face, and neck, quivered with anger.

"We pulled him outta bed, sir," the senior MP, a sergeant, reported. "The uh, lady, he was with never even woke up." He grinned.

"I apologize to your wife, O'Quinn," Sneed said.

"She weren't my wife, Gen'ral, 'n' don't think you kin get away with this! President Summers is a personal friend of mine and I knowed Gen'ral Lyons fer years! Yer gonna be in hot water over this!"

"Well, neither of those estimable gentlemen is present now, O'Quinn, so you have to deal with me. We have word the enemy's landed a force on the coast and it is probably headed this way. I want you to initiate the evacuation plan immediately."

"What 'vacuation plan?"

General Sneed regarded the mayor silently for a moment. "The plan to evacuate your bowels, O'Quinn, so you won't be so full of it! The evacuation plan I asked you to draw up in case Phelps ever came under attack! What the hell do you think I meant?"

"You gotta show me more respect, Gen'ral." O'Quinn drew himself up and tried to look haughty.

"You get what respect you deserve, O'Quinn."

"I ain't got no time for any such folderol!"

"You mean there is no evacuation plan, Mr. Mayor?" Sneed asked, his voice deceptively gentle.

"Aw, fuck you, you tin—"

Sneed turned to the MP sergeant. "Take this piece of dreck out of here."

"What do you want me to do with him?" The sergeant grinned.

"Throw him down a well."

"You cain't!" O'Quinn screamed, real terror edging his voice.

"On second thought, I don't want to poison our water supply, Sergeant. Take him home. You are on your own, Mr. Mayor. But you get in my way and I'll have you shot." General Sneed turned to Major Spinoza. "General Josephus is standing by, Major; he has troops to put at your disposal. Do what you can to get these people moving. Do *not* let anyone down the Ashburtonville road, though. We'll need that for our own movements."

"I'll commandeer all civilian vehicles in town, sir," Major Spinoza said, "and put them on the road south, away from the coast. There's a national park with camping facilities about twenty klicks in the direction of Gilbert's Corners. I'll get as many people there as I can."

"Very good, Major." They exchanged salutes and Spinoza left General Sneed alone with Captain Nigh.

General Sneed sighed and sat on the edge of his desk. "Quang, we're headed for some real action. Chow down and take it easy while you can because for the rest of the time we're here we'll be hopping."

"Sir?" It was the division intelligence officer.

"Yes, Burton? What's recon got for us?"

"Sir, it appears that the enemy landed at least a FIST-size element somewhere along the coast and managed to surprise the 7th MPs, rolled 'em up like a rug. They are presently consolidating their position and so far have not moved toward us."

General Sneed stood up and stretched. "Just a FIST? Good news!" He turned to his aide. "Quang, that female MP, whatshername?"

"Queege, something like that, sir."

"Yes. Well, put her in for an award. Screwed up as she is, she appears to have been the only soldier in the 7th MPs who kept her head. Write her up a decoration for valor and I'll present it to her as soon as she's cleaned up and sober." He laughed and patted his thigh. "Burton, keep tabs on those Marines!"

"Should we call off Plan Red, sir?" the G2 asked.

"Hell no, Burton! This is good training for them and for the civilians. Plan Red stays in effect until the threat is eliminated. Now, Quang, I'm going to the mess and have me some breakfast. Bring that award recommendation to me there. Gentlemen"—he stretched again—"just a FIST? Shit, I can handle a FIST with one fist tied behind my back!"

CHAPTER TWENTY

Senior Sergeant N'dolo M'kwazi stood at rigid attention before Major General Barksdale Sneed. Beside him was the commander of the 4th Composite Division's reconnaissance company, Captain Cangama. The company, known as the Trinkatat Scouts, had been assigned to the 4th Independent Infantry Division when it was formed and General Sneed considered them one of his best assets.

"At ease, gentlemen." General Sneed grinned and extended his hand. "Captain, you and your men have done good work for this division. Sergeant, they tell me you could track a fly across slate in a hurricane."

"Without a doubt, sir, he's the best tracker in this army!" Captain Cangama said, nodding at Sergeant M'kwazi.

"That a fact, Sergeant?"

M'Kwazi grinned and nodded. He did not need to confirm what the general had just said. He possessed the easy confidence of a man who knew he was so good at what he did that convincing others would be a waste of valuable time.

"Well, your fine reputation has preceded you. Now, here's the reason I called for you two. As you know, I've initiated Plan Red based on information we have received from a survivor of the 7th Independent MPs who apparently were overrun by Confederation Marines. I have sent the 319th Battalion of the 222nd Brigade up the coast road to block it here." He indicated the blocking position on the vid screen.

"The problem is this: Is this a raid, a reconnaissance in force, or a full-scale invasion? I have *got* to know. So far we've detected no other forces in this area"—he swept the entire coastline—"but that means nothing. I've got to have eyes out there to make sure we know what's facing us here. I *cannot* rely solely on electronics to tell me what's going on."

"Very wise, sir. Electronic surveillance, if you will permit me, sir, is unreliable," Captain Cangama said. "It can be fooled. I guarantee you"—he nodded at M'kwazi who pointed to his own eyes—"those peepers can be relied on."

"Deploy your entire company, Captain. I want every sector between here and the coast, in all directions, thoroughly searched. Senior Sergeant M'kwazi, the fate of this division and possibly the outcome of this war may very well depend on your skills as a reconnaissance man."

M'kwazi came to attention and saluted. "You can count on me, sir!"

Senior Sergeant M'kwazi had learned the rudiments of his trade by leading the way for gnuttle raids on neighboring kraals when he was a boy. After the first, disastrous raid he'd scouted for, he never again led a raiding party into a trap or had a raiding party lose a man because of him. Twenty years in the Trinkatat Scouts had honed the skills he'd developed in those raids. Nearly all of his peers and subordinates, as well as most of his superiors, considered him the best recon man in the Trinkatat army, and therefore in the entire Coalition army. As for M'kwazi's own opinion of his skills, he wished he'd been sent after the Confederation Marine Force Recon patrols that had ravaged the deep rear of the Coalition army. He knew he would have put fear into them. Any patrols he encountered would have been driven off—any he didn't manage to kill outright.

So it was inevitable that Senior Sergeant M'kwazi was assigned to lead a four-man patrol to locate the Confederation Marine infantry battalion that had apparently succeeded in overrunning the 7th Independent Military Police Battalion's position along the coast. Thinking of the MPs, Senior Sergeant M'kwazi sneered. Doughfoot amateurs, that's what they were! Had he and his squad been stationed along the coast instead, *nobody* would ever have surprised *them*. Oh, he'd find out what was out there!

He also thought it was well past time he was given something to do. He thought the 10th Trinkatat Scouts were being wasted performing routine tactical patrolling. Strategic reconnaissance, that was the name of the game, and "Strategy" was N'dolo M'kwazi's middle name! General Sneed had finally recognized that fact and M'kwazi respected him for making that judgment. M'kwazi would handle the rest.

The Marines had overrun the MPs, that much was known. M'kwazi's first stop before mounting out was to interview this Corporal Queege, the only known survivor of the raid on the MP positions.

"I hope you are sober now, Corporal." M'kwazi grinned as he took a seat opposite a somewhat composed Puella Queege.

"Unfortunately, I am," Queege answered. She sized M'kwazi up; tall, whipcord-thin, but he held his body like a coiled spring radiating not only enormous physical energy but strength. His teeth gleamed pearly white against his dark skin and his eyes regarded her with frankly intelligent appraisal. She knew instinctively that this man could see right through her.

"I am going out to your old camp, Corporal. Would you care to come along with me?" He grinned.

"Not only *no,* but *fuck* no!" Queege shouted, shifting her weight nervously and casting an apprehensive glance at the recon NCO. *Is this guy kidding?* she asked herself, licking her lips. She badly needed a beer.

M'kwazi laughed. The laughter came from deep inside his chest. "I want you to tell me everything you can remember about the 7th MPs' camp out there, where the units were, what kind of tents or buildings they occupied, everything you can remember about the layout and what you can recall from the attack. I don't have much time, so please be quick, but be thorough." He flashed her a grin and bid her begin with a gesture of his hand. The fingers on that hand were long and delicate, the fingers of a pianist, Queege thought.

"Well, okay. Y'see, I was out behind the first sergeant's tent, takin' a shit . . ."

M'kwazi left the interview smiling to himself. What a character the corporal was! He shook his head. Well, she was no fool; a drunk, yes, but not a stupid drunk, and she'd given him all she could and that would be a big help. M'kwazi wondered how in the world she'd ever convinced anyone she was an MP.

The question still to be answered was, where were the invaders going now and who might be with them? M'kwazi had little time in which to find the Marines. Therefore, he broke his normal operating procedure and took his patrol down the coast road, carefully paralleling the highway until he could smell the sea. Before they reached the late camp of the 7th Independent MP Battalion, he reached the ground where the Marines had most recently attacked. He dismounted his men and they crept carefully forward until they could see the battlefield. He spent only a quarter of an hour examining the ground. He saw where the defenders had thrown up an inadequate sandbag wall and where the Marines had attacked from, then where the Marines had swept along the abandoned defensive line at the end of the firefight. He saw where the main assault line had boarded air-cushioned vehicles and headed toward the coastal road, and where a second line had boarded aircraft—he had no way of knowing for certain where the aircraft had gone, but the coast road to Phelps was a good guess.

He boarded his men back onto their vehicle and headed out at speed.

Unlike the previous scouts and defenders who had faced the Marines this day, M'kwazi and his men had infrared capability. And used it. The scout vehicle skidded to a stop while it was still a kilometer and a half shy of the coastal road. M'kwazi saw infrared shapes through the trees ahead. Some were large, like vehicles, but most were man-size. He knew these must be the Confederation Marines he was seeking. They didn't seem to be doing anything, just holding in place as though they were waiting for something. And what could that something be? To him it was obvious—they were waiting for more forces to move toward them.

So where were the other forces?

The only way to find out was to go in search of them. M'kwazi had his driver turn north and circle around behind the Marine battalion he'd located. He did not forget to report the current location of the Confederation Marines he'd found.

Twenty minutes behind where the Marines were waiting, the recon patrol had to stop and go into hiding from an armored convoy coming along the road at speed. It was Confederation Army. M'kwazi read the markings on the lead vehicles, which was easy to do with the naked eye as the vehicles weren't painted in Marine chameleon, and identified them as belonging to the 27th Infantry Division.

Curious, M'kwazi thought. Part of M'kwazi's duty as the senior recon sergeant in the 10th Trinkatat Scouts was to keep himself informed on every aspect of the war. He did that by reading all the after-action reports generated by General Lyons's commanders. He followed very closely the action on Pohick Bay. The 27th was the division that beat off the amphibious assault against the enemy's flank from the bay. How had the 27th Division gotten off of the peninsula without General Lyons knowing about it? Or was the earlier intelligence that the 27th Division was one of the trapped units wrong? Privately, M'kwazi had thought that the Marines raiding behind the Coalition's lines had been freshly landed. But if the 27th Infantry Division had gotten off the Pohick peninsula, were these Marines also from the besieged garrison? If so, were there more Confederation forces that had managed to escape the trap now threatening the Coalition forces from the rear?

Senior Sergeant M'kwazi waited impatiently for the convoy—trucks, now that the armored vehicles had passed—to go by so he could get around to its other side and find out if any more units were closer to the shore. He reported the approach of the division.

When the column began to slow its passage, M'kwazi decided to stop waiting, as the division must be forming for an attack. He had his driver slowly back out of the hiding place and speed toward the back end of the column, staying just out of sight of the road. He hoped he wouldn't find another division behind the 27th Infantry. Soon, in fleeting glimpses through the trees, M'kwazi began seeing the self-propelled vehicles of the division's artillery regiment. Not long after that the patrol reached the end of the column. M'kwazi had his driver cross to the east of the road and take them closer to the division's rear. If another division was farther out, they'd be able to find it, and if it was there, it wouldn't block the patrol from the side of the road that he wanted to recon next.

When after two kilometers the patrol neither saw nor heard sign of a following unit, M'kwazi abandoned the original plan of reconning the 7th MP camp; the 27th Infantry Division was a more important quarry, and likely there was nobody left at the MP camp. He had his driver turn about and head back toward Phelps, close to the coast road. They went fast for a while before M'kwazi had the driver slow—he didn't want the noise of his own passage to alert any Confederation forces that might be ahead. After a short while longer, he had his driver stop and the patrol dismount. They continued on foot.

Half a kilometer farther, M'kwazi sensed his patrol was getting very close to someone. He stopped, had his men go to ground, and continued on alone.

Scouting for gnuttle-raiding parties had taught M'kwazi several valuable lessons at which he only became more expert with age and experience. Among them were how to move silently, and how to blend in with the background; in effect, how to be invisible even within sight of the enemy. M'kwazi firmly believed that he was every bit as undetectable as the scouts of the legendary Confederation Marine Force Recon units.

Of course, M'kwazi had never personally encountered the Force Recon Marines, he knew them only by their reputation. For that matter, he had never encountered *any* Confederation Marines. He knew what reputations were; the best reputations were always exaggerated.

Senior Sergeant M'kwazi never saw the Marine from 17th FIST who spotted him, and he didn't hear the *crack-sizzle* of the plasma bolt that Marine fired at him; the bolt that killed the one-time scout for gnuttle-raiding parties.

Half a kilometer back, his men *did* hear the *crack-sizzle,* and feared what it might mean. They waited the one hour M'kwazi had instructed them to wait, then radioed in their report. By then, though, it was too late.

CHAPTER TWENTY-ONE

The sun was not even up yet when a knock came on the door. "I have orders to evacuate you at once, sir," a military policeman announced when the door was opened. In the street outside of the Lee family home, other police, civil and military, were knocking on doors and rousing the inhabitants with the same message. The officer handed Burton Lee, the patriarch of the Lee family, a flimsiplast sheet. Lee held it out at arm's length to read it.

TO THE PEOPLE OF ASHBURTONVILLE!

IN VIEW OF THE MILITARY ACTION WHICH HAS BEEN UNDER WAY IN AND AROUND OUR GREAT CITY FOR SOME TIME NOW, IT HAS BECOME NECESSARY THAT ALL NONCOMBATANT PERSONNEL BE EVACUATED IMMEDIATELY TO LOCATIONS OUT OF THE WAR ZONE. YOU WILL BE ESCORTED TO STAGING AREAS AT ONCE AND THEREAFTER TRANSPORTED TO PREDESIGNATED CITIES AND TOWNS LYING WELL OUTSIDE THE ANTICIPATED ZONE OF OPERATIONS WHERE YOU AND YOUR FAMILIES WILL REMAIN IN COMFORTABLE CIRCUMSTANCES UNTIL HOSTILITIES ARE TERMINATED AND YOU CAN BE PERMITTED TO RETURN TO YOUR HOMES.

THERE WILL BE NO EXCEPTIONS!

EACH FAMILY MEMBER IS AUTHORIZED TO TAKE ONE BAG OF POSSES-
SIONS WEIGHING NOT MORE THAN 20 KILOS PLUS WHATEVER
VALUABLES AND OTHER ITEMS CAN BE CARRIED ON HIS PERSON.
WHATEVER ELSE YOU REQUIRE DURING YOUR STAY WILL BE SUPPLIED
AT YOUR DESTINATION. *NO EXCEPTIONS!* YOU WILL SECURE ALL REAL
AND OTHER PROPERTY LEFT BEHIND BEFORE DEPARTING. OUR MILI-
TARY COMMANDS WILL ENSURE ITS SAFETY AGAINST YOUR RETURN.
PLEASE BE ADVISED, HOWEVER, THAT THE CITY OF ASHBURTONVILLE
ASSUMES NO LIABILITY FOR ANY PROPERTY DAMAGES OR PERSONAL
INJURY SUSTAINED DUE TO MILITARY ACTION OR CIVIL DISORDER.

THE COALITION GOVERNMENT, RECENTLY RELOCATED TO GIL-
BERT'S CORNERS, HAS ISSUED A STRICT EDICT THAT ALL RAVENITES
WILL COOPERATE IN THIS OPERATION, OPEN THEIR DOORS TO ALL
EVACUEES, AND TREAT THEM GENEROUSLY AND WITH RESPECT.
THERE WILL BE NO EXCEPTIONS. VIOLATIONS OF THIS EDICT SHALL
BE REPORTED AT ONCE TO THE LOCAL MILITARY COMMANDER IN
CHARGE OF YOUR RESETTLEMENT DESTINATION.

DURING THE TIME OF YOUR ABSENCE FROM OUR CITY YOU SHALL
BE UNDER THE JURISDICTION OF THE MILITARY AUTHORITIES IN YOUR
TEMPORARY RESIDENCES. THEY HAVE BEEN ORDERED TO RENDER YOU
EVERY POSSIBLE ASSISTANCE. I BID YOU FAREWELL FOR NOW AND
GODSPEED.

GOD BLESS OUR COALITION! GOD BLESS OUR ARMS!
GOD GRANT US VICTORY! GOD KEEP YOU SAFE!
HENRY DINKUS
LORD MAYOR

"So, this is it." Burton Lee sighed. Rumors had been circulating for
days that Ashburtonville would be evacuated, but there had been no official word until that moment. Some citizens had already left the city
and Lee's business in the center of town had been closed for more than
a week. Until the arrival of the MP, he had considered his family safe in
the suburbs. He looked out the door, past the military policeman. The
huge pall of smoke and dust that had hung in the air over Fort Seymour

for days had taken on a menacing aspect in the early morning light, especially after the events of last night.

For days fighting had raged at Fort Seymour on the outskirts of the city. The citizens of Ashburtonville had been told the attack would be over in a matter of hours, but somehow the Confederation garrison out there had been holding on. The hapless citizens of Ashburtonville thrived on rumor because neither the Coalition nor the city government would or could tell them anything definite about how the war was proceeding. Rumor had it that huge reinforcements would be arriving soon and if that happened, the city itself would come under heavy attack. Each night since the fighting had started the Lees and their neighbors had assembled on the rooftops of their homes to watch the pyrotechnics of the battle raging in the direction of Pohick Bay. At first they had enjoyed having seats on the periphery of the fighting, but as the days dragged on and there was no end to it, many began to worry that the intensity of the battle would increase. The night before the evacuation order, that is just what happened.

For years the garrison at Fort Seymour had been an important part of life at Ashburtonville. Soldiers stationed there had married local women, spent their money in the city's businesses and entertainment spots, been welcome in the city's homes. It was still hard for Burton Lee to call them "the enemy" because until the attack they had been *allies,* servants of his own government. He still could not understand how those soldiers could have opened fire on the demonstrators. He had no idea why the garrison at Fort Seymour had been reinforced as it had been, but he never saw that as a hostile move against the people of Ravenette. If anything, it had been good for business. But the hotheads who wanted secession kept agitating that the troops had been sent to suppress the civil rights of the Ravenites and keep them in the Confederation against their will. Personally, he thought the Ordinance of Secession a mistake, and had it been put to a plebiscite, he'd never have voted for it.

Burton Lee and his son Brad were custom tailors and the business they ran had catered to many of Fort Seymour's military personnel. The Lees were experts at producing perfect regulation clothing items for the soldiers at the garrison, especially the mess dress uniform authorized for wear on formal occasions, but not an item of issue. Officers and NCOs who could afford a tailored mess dress uniform all wanted one and the Lees happily accommodated them. Yes, the Confederation soldiers were different and spoke standard English with accents it was sometimes difficult for a Ravenite to understand, but the Lees found that no obstacle to business, even entertaining, and they would laugh easily with the soldiers over the differences in their cultures. The young men and women from Fort Seymour were honest, decent people with cash in their pockets, and the Burton Lee family had prospered because they were there.

Then the real war had come to Ashburtonville. A little after midnight the night before the official evacuation notice, the entire city had been aroused from its uneasy slumber by a tremendous crashing and thunderous roaring. The very foundations of the citizens' homes shook and the skies overhead were split asunder by the brilliant arcs of landing transports and the flashing duel of ground and spaceborne weapons seeking one another out, while debris from destroyed ships rained down on sections of the city until then undamaged by the fighting, setting whole blocks of homes and businesses on fire.

The long-anticipated reinforcements had arrived.

"Bring your family into the street, sir. Lock up your house and remaining valuables before you depart."

"But where will you be taking us, Officer?"

"I have no idea, sir. Lorries will arrive momentarily to take you to your staging area. If you have friends or relatives living in other parts of the world, tell the processors at the reception center and they'll try to get you to them. Otherwise quarters will be found wherever available. Do not be left behind or we can't guarantee your safety. I have to be on my way now." With that he saluted smartly and walked over to the next house up the block. As if punctuating the man's words, a huge explosion from the direction of Pohick Bay rattled the windows in the neighborhood.

Burton Lee's family consisted of his wife of forty years, Marrilee, their son, Brad, his wife Janice, and their three children, Mary, thirteen,

Justus, twelve, and Lilly, seven. Lilly, a vivacious and intelligent child, was Burton's favorite. While the other family members tried to maintain their composure in order not to frighten Lilly, she knew perfectly well what was going on and was happily excited over the war and the sudden change in their lives. While her mother threw some things into a little suitcase for her, Lilly clutched her favorite doll, a lifelike baby slimie she called Hardee.

"Get rid of that horrid thing!" her mother said as she sorted through Lilly's clothes, picking out comfortable, practical items to take along.

"*No,* Mommy!" Lilly clutched the doll closer to her chest.

"Lilly!" Janice began, exasperated.

"*No!*"

"Lilly, what will you feed Hardee? We can't take much food with us on the trip," Janice said, trying to use logic on her daughter.

"Human flesh!" the child answered, beaming. She had heard from the news that the Confederation fortifications on Pohick Bay were infested by real slimies that fed off the dead and wounded, and since she thought those soldiers were the enemies of her people, she came to think of the slimies as true Ravenite patriots.

"*Lilly.*" Her mother advanced in a threatening manner.

"Oh, Janice, let her keep the thing," Burton said, as he walked into the room. "You pack her useful stuff, but let her keep the doll." he winked conspiratorially at his granddaughter, who grinned back at him. "Grandpa!" she squealed and ran to throw her arms around his waist.

Janice shook her head and went back to packing Lilly's things. "You spoil that child, Father," she said, but she smiled. Lilly knew what spoiled meant and she enjoyed every minute of it.

Other children Lilly's age played with regular dolls, bopaloos and other cuddly things and lifelike human figures they dressed and fed and talked to like they were real people, but Lilly had a *slimie* as her doll companion. To Burton that showed she had originality and could think independently, and perhaps even possessed a budding, wry sense of humor, which he admired. "Come on, come on!" He clapped his hands. "I hear the trucks outside now! We've got to get a move on."

* * *

The evacuation was very badly planned. In the first place, there were tens of thousands of people to be moved, and the government was trying to get them all out at once instead of in stages that could be better managed. There was also a shortage of transportation and no real arrangements had been made for their accommodations at their destinations, so many arrived in distant towns and villages like a desperate horde on the verge of panic. But worst of all, the roads leading in and out of Ashburtonville were crowded with military traffic, and Confederation fighters had raked the slow-moving targets with devastating effect, in some cases not distinguishing between the columns of evacuees and the advancing troops. Thousands of civilians died in the attacks.

The Lee convoy of several hundred people had been headed for a high-speed railhead, some kilometers south and west of Ashburtonville, that had somehow survived the bombings. With the attacks on the roadways in full swing, though, the refugees had been diverted to an empty warehouse outside the city, where they remained for several days with only the food the people had managed to bring along and with very little water. The officer in charge of the convoy, a quartermaster colonel from an Embata contingent, was frankly overwhelmed by the enormity of his responsibilities and the lack of both personnel and equipment to carry them out.

But Lilly Lee was enjoying every moment of the adventure. She made her way throughout the crowded warehouse, clutching Hardee and making friends with the other children. Her only moment of fear came when she thought she might not be able to find her way back to her own family, but that passed quickly enough. She was confident that if she got lost, someone would come looking for her. They always did.

On the evening of the fourth day, they were ordered to walk to the railway, which the colonel had been led to believe was still intact and operating around the clock. The trek there down pitch-black roads, people stumbling along in the darkness, took all night. Lilly's grandfather carried her most of the way. Toward dawn it had started to rain and the temperature dropped. It was already light enough to see when the van of the column reached the depot. Sure enough, there was the train, long and sleek and empty. People pushed and shoved and fought to get on the cars, thinking that they guaranteed warmth, safety, food, and rest. The press of desperate bodies was enormous, and many people were seriously injured. The few military escorts were helpless to impose order on the crowd and found themselves pushed aside. Burton Lee and his family had been about midway in the column and he had been holding on to Lilly's hand as they wearily slogged over a slight rise and saw the station before them. It was then the panicked rush began and he was swept forward by the crowd and instantly separated from his granddaughter.

At that moment the Confederation Raptors attacked.

The next thing Lilly Lee knew, someone was dragging her from under a section of the depot roof. She had no idea how she got there. The last thing she remembered was being dragged along by her grandfather and then waking up under the rubble. She had some scratches and bruises, but she was not seriously hurt. "Grandpa?" she whimpered, looking up at the man who'd rescued her.

"Are you hurt?" the man asked. She had never seen him before. "I heard you screaming. Quick, quick, we have to get out of here!" He pulled Lilly, still clutching Hardee, to her feet and dragged her along the platform.

Everywhere fires raged and people screamed in fear and agony and staggered about calling the names of their loved ones. The man's eyes were wild and the right side of his face was covered in blood. He muttered curses as he dragged Lilly along at his side and for the first time she began to feel terror.

"I want my grandpa," Lilly whimpered.

"All gone, all gone," the man said and groaned.

Lilly Lee's grandfather had always been the anchor in her life, a solid, dependable presence, always there with a kind word and a helping hand; now, in extremis, it was him she called for, not her parents, her older sister, or her brother. She sensed, vaguely, that at times her father resented the old man's influence over his younger daughter and she had learned how to exploit this when her father or mother wished to deny her something she wanted. Grandpa would always acquiesce and overrule. She had learned at a very early age what the word "spoiled" meant and she realized that she loved being "spoiled" and that Grandpa Lee loved spoiling her.

People and parts of people lay everywhere. The aircraft had struck the depot with devastating effect. Lilly glimpsed what looked like dolls lying scattered among the wreckage and flames, thin, sticklike dolls all black, arms flexed, parchmentlike black skin stretched tightly over their faces, teeth grinning weirdly. They had no hair on their heads and no lips. "Don't look!" the man screamed and ran faster.

Just as the sun cleared the horizon, they found their way into a grove of trees some distance from the destruction. The man fell down and began crying and beating his fists on the ground. Lilly lay in the grass and leaves and went to sleep. When she awoke it was dark and the man was gone.

Lilly got stiffly to her feet. It was cold and dark. She grasped Hardee ever closer for warmth. She was hungry and thirsty and had never felt more alone and frightened in her life. In one instant her great adventure had turned into hell. She cried out desperately for her grandfather.

"Whozzat?" someone shouted from above where Lilly was sitting. It was a man's voice.

"Grandpa!" she yelled, suddenly energized with hope, and scrambled up a slight embankment. In the light of the depot which still burned behind her, she saw that she was on a road crowded with people stumbling along away from the fires. No grandfather, only strangers. With no other alternative, Lilly fell in beside some people and walked along with them. She heard a woman say they were headed for the river, and once they got across they'd be all right. Lilly knew that south of Ashburtonville there was a river called the White River but she had never been there and she had no idea how far it was from the city.

All along the road Lilly constantly called for her grandfather, her father, her mother, even Justus, her twelve-year-old brother. She accosted people plodding along wearily, thinking they were her family, but always they turned out to be strangers who looked at her coldly and turned away. She was lost in a vast sea of desperate strangers who had other things on their mind than caring for someone else's seven-year-old girl.

At dawn, when the vast, bedraggled crowd at last reached the river, they found the bridge had been blown up. The White River raged swift and deep between its banks, and a stiff wind from the east was whipping the surface into whitecaps. Watching the foam from her perch high on the bank, Lilly reasoned that was probably why they called it the White River. A fleet of small boats was attempting to ferry people across one load at a time. One capsized as Lilly watched, the black heads of the people in the water visible for an instant as they were swept downstream with the current then disappeared beneath it. She wondered idly what had happened to them. "We don't want to get wet again," she told Hardee and shivered. The mishap did not stop anyone else from clambering aboard other dangerously overloaded boats.

Somewhere along the way, someone had given Lilly a candy bar. She was so ravenous she ate some of the wrapper. She fell asleep again and when she awoke it was almost dark. She could no longer remember how long it had been since the Lee family had left their beautiful home in Ashburtonville. She wondered if she would ever see her people again. It was quiet all around her. She concluded from the silence that most of the people had gotten across while she slept or they had gone swimming. She felt vaguely annoyed at that. She had slept away most of the day. Otherwise she'd be across the river and safe, like that woman had promised the night before. She wondered what had happened to the bridge, the remains of which lay partially submerged in the water where vast eddies swirled around the crumpled fragments. Cautiously in the gathering dark, Lilly made her way down to a tiny wharf at the water's edge. Some people were standing there arguing with a man in a boat.

"No more fucking room!" the boatman yelled when he saw Lilly approaching out of the dusk.

"I think she's alone," a woman said. "Where are your parents?" she asked gently. She bent down and looked searchingly into Lilly's face and smiled. She brushed the hair out of Lilly's eyes. "Are you alone, child? Where is your mother, your father?"

"Gone," Lilly squeaked in a voice that did not sound like her own.

The woman turned and said to the boatman, "She's going with us. Okay, Charles?" Charles was obviously her husband, standing with three smaller figures, their own children.

"Here," Charles gave the boatman something. "This is all we have. Take us and this orphan child across the river and it's all yours."

"You should be shot for taking our money like this, exploiting our predicament!" the lady shouted.

"Aw, fuck you, lady," the boatman replied laconically. "I ain't riskin' my life or my boat for you goddamned people lessen I get paid for it. Swim, if you don't like it. Hah hah!" His laugh was cruel and piercing above the rush of the water.

"All right," the man called Charles said. "Get on board." He ushered his children into the boat.

"Hurry it up! The wind's risin' and it's a good two kilometers to the other shore. It's gonna be a rough crossing, if we even make it!" the boatman shouted as he began casting off the lines.

"Hey, don't you have life preservers or something? I know the law. You're supposed to have that kind of equipment," the mother said.

The boatman shot her a look in the gathering darkness that clearly said he thought she was out of her mind to ask such a question. He laughed that mean laugh again and said, "Fuck no, lady! You think this is a luxury liner? We go over and you go into the fuckin' water, hold yer breath as long as ya kin." He laughed nastily again. "There ain't no fuckin' *law* no more lady. Yer on yer own and either you kin sink or you kin swim, all the same to me," he said, and spit over the side of his boat.

The family's name was Kincaid, Charles and Betty with their children, Arnold, thirteen, Daniel, nine, and Shannon, seven. Charles Kincaid claimed to have met Lilly's father once and said he thought highly of Brad Lee but had no idea what might have happened to the him or the rest of Lilly's family. "So many were . . ." He let the sentence trail off.

"Killed," Lilly finished the sentence for him. "I had a dog named Raymond," she volunteered, "and when he died we put him in a hole behind our house. Do you think my daddy's in a hole?"

"You are part of our family now," Betty Kincaid said quickly. They had long since reached the far side of the river and were well on their way south. "What is that you're carrying there?" She wanted to change that subject as quickly as possible.

"Hardee," Lilly answered in a tiny voice, afraid Betty would demand she throw Hardee away. No adult thought much of Hardee, who had by then become quite ragged and dirty. But when Betty reached down Lilly let her touch the doll.

Betty shook her head and smiled, "Well, child, we need all the help we can get, so tell Hardee he's welcome to come along with us."

Daniel Kincaid and Lilly became friends instantly, mainly because they were of almost the same age, and he successfully humored her by saying he respected Hardee.

The Kincaids had relatives, Charles's brother and his family, in a small town about one hundred kilometers southwest of Ashburtonville, and that was where they were headed. On the second night after crossing the White River they camped in a grove beside a farmer's recently harvested potato field. None of them had had much to eat that day or the days before. After the adults shared what little food Charles had been able to barter for along the way, Arnold whispered, "Let's go into the field. Maybe there's some potatoes left in the ground."

There *were* potatoes out there! Eagerly, the four children scrambled about the field, pulling the tubers out of the wet ground and stuffing them into their pockets. Occasionally one would stop, brush off the mud clinging to a potato, and bite into it. In the wild hunt for the tubers, they rapidly forgot where they were and what had happened to them.

Suddenly Arnold felt himself grabbed by the scruff of his neck and a hand slammed into the side of his head. Stars appeared before the boy's eyes and he shouted out in pain and fear.

"Goddamnit, boy," Arnold's father shouted, "put those potatoes back into the ground!" He was breathing hard. He shoved his son to the ground. "Do it, Arnold, put 'em back." He turned to the other children, "Go ahead, put those spuds back!"

Lilly stood there, open mouth full of potato. Charles came over to her. "Lilly, we Kincaids are not thieves. We will never take anything that doesn't belong to us. That's a rule we have in this family. Now put those potatoes back, go over to your mother"—he paused, realizing he'd forgotten himself and then smiled—"go over to your mother and clean off your face. Tomorrow I'll find the farmer who owns this field and ask him to let us have some of these potatoes."

In the morning boiled potatoes never tasted better to Lilly Lee, and all the rest of her life she would love them.

In later years Lilly was not sure how much of her ordeal she remembered accurately and how much of it she had imagined or dreamed, but the memories stayed with her the rest of her life. In the years to follow, the faces of her own family would fade into vague images and at times she would wonder if she ever had another family besides the Kincaids.

Later that morning beside the farmer's field, when they picked up their things and prepared to continue their trek, Lilly clutched Daniel's hand and held on to it confidently the rest of the way. In time Lilly would marry Daniel Kincaid, move far, far away from Ashburtonville, and raise her own family.

That morning beside the potato field was a turning point in Lilly Lee's life. She'd become too old to play with dolls anymore. She left Hardee behind.

CHAPTER TWENTY-TWO

While the Marines of the three FISTs were in transit from landing zones to their initial objectives, the Essays that had brought them returned to Bataan, via suborbital flights. This time, the Essays made combat landings in the Confederation base, rather than beyond the horizon. The thinking was that the Coalition would mistakenly believe that the Confederation was landing more reinforcements, probably in preparation for a fresh breakout attempt. The Coalition commanders would then likely rush reinforcements to the forces holding the line, and be slow to move forces to the northeast, to rebuff the Marine raids at the 7th Independent Military Police Battalion's camp, and at Cranston. Which also implied that the 4th Division at Phelps would likely not be further reinforced before the 27th Division, flanked by the 34th and 29th FISTs, attacked.

The Essays, loaded with troops and equipment from the 27th Division, launched straight up, and then went suborbital to a staging area ten kilometers northeast of 34th FIST and the completely demoralized 7th MPs. That first wave of Essays arrived shortly before dawn. Two of the first elements off the Essays were a military police platoon and a medical unit from the 27th Division. The MPs were there to take charge of the Marines' captives, and the medical unit to care for the freed POWs.

As fast as the Essays landed the elements of the 27th Division, Major General Koval got them into their route order. Only half of his men and equipment had arrived at the landing zone when the first elements began moving toward Phelps and the 4th Composite Division. The two FISTS covering the division's flanks had moved out as soon as 34th FIST handed its prisoners over to the army MPs. Thirty-fourth FIST had the right flank, the direction from which fresh reinforcements were most likely to come.

Second squad had the FIST's point, two hundred meters ahead of the rest of the column. Second fire team, not much to Corporal Claypoole's pleasure, had the squad's point. But Claypoole had known that would be the case even before any orders were given—Lance Corporal Schultz wouldn't accept anybody but himself in the position most likely to make initial contact with the enemy, so Claypoole was resigned to being the second-most exposed man in the entire FIST. FIST nothing, he was the second-most exposed man in the entire task force! He'd like to convince Sergeant Kerr or somebody else to give Schultz to a different fire team. But he had to, in the ancient expression, bite the bullet, and continue to trust Schultz's instincts, because neither Kerr nor anybody above him in the company seemed in the least inclined to reshuffle the fire teams so that Claypoole no longer had Schultz. At least Schultz was preternaturally astute at finding danger before it found him, no matter how exposed his position, regardless of the occasional wound he suffered. So there was nothing Claypoole could do except keep all his senses alert . . .

Yes there was.

His new man, Lance Corporal Ymenez. Not only was Ymenez on his first combat operation with the platoon, he was so new Claypoole and Schultz hadn't even had a chance to get acquainted with him. Not that Schultz ever expressed an interest in knowing anything more about a new man than that he was a Marine. As far as Schultz was concerned, every Marine had potential, but remained suspect until proven.

But Claypoole wasn't like Schultz; he had to know his new man, and the new man had to know what to expect of the other men in the fire team.

"Ymenez," Claypoole said into the fire team circuit.

"Yo," Ymenez answered distractedly. Claypoole heard nervousness in his voice. Understandable, Claypoole thought. After all, he was the third man in the FIST's column, headed toward unknown danger.

"There's something you need to know," Claypoole said. "We aren't out here in front of everybody else because somebody thinks we're expendable. We have the point because the Hammer is the best Marine in the entire FIST"—he paused because he knew Schultz was listening, and wanted to consider what he was about to say—"hell, the best man in the entire Marine Corps at knowing when there's trouble up ahead or to the flank. The fire team Schultz is in is always on the most exposed part of the formation."

Claypoole barely heard Ymenez's murmured, "Buddha's fuzzy blue shit. And I'm in *this* fire team?"

But Claypoole *did* hear the murmur, so he said, "Thanks to the Hammer, we're probably in the safest place in the FIST. Except for the pogues sitting back at Bataan."

The problem with talking to Ymenez on the fire team circuit was that there was no way to keep Schultz out of the circuit unless he had an equipment malfunction. Schultz grunted something that might have been, "Shut up so I can focus." At least that's how Claypoole interpreted the grunt, so he shut up so Schultz could focus on whatever or whomever might be waiting in front of them.

Sergeant Kerr trailed fifty meters behind second fire team, twenty meters in front of his third fire team—Corporal Doyle's. He wanted to talk to the man privately, but couldn't while they were on the move; the closest he could come to a private conversation was on the fire team leader's circuit or on the fire team circuit. He didn't feel like having Corporals Chan and Claypoole listening in, but Lance Corporal Quick and PFC Summers were different—after all, they'd been there when Doyle did what Kerr wanted to talk about.

"Doyle," he said into the fire team circuit.

"Y-Yes?" A hitch in Doyle's voice made Kerr think the corporal had jumped at unexpectedly being spoken to by his squad leader.

"How did you do that? Rescue that woman back there, I mean."

"Ah, uh, I s-saw what that, that officer was doing and, uh, I j-just jumped in and m-made him s-stop. That's all."

Kerr shook his head; no, that wasn't all, and he knew it.

"You had to have gone directly to the room the woman was held in," Kerr said. "Did you enter the building before the command came through?"

"N-No, Sergeant Kerr."

"You had to have, you couldn't have searched the other rooms before you reached that one if you hadn't already been searching before 'go.'"

"Tell him," Lance Corporal Quick said.

Doyle's sigh came over the comm. "A-All right," he said dully. "After y-you l-left us, I-I made a circuit of the building, looking in the windows to see if any of the rooms were occupied." His voice was becoming stronger. "I saw that officer with the woman, and what he was going to do to her. So after I made sure all the other rooms were empty, I went back and took my men inside. We set up outside the room so we could break in as soon as we got the 'go' command."

"You know, that building was supposed to be unoccupied. And there weren't any lights visible when I positioned you."

"Y-Yes, Sergeant Kerr, I know that's why you put me there."

Kerr had the grace to flush, even though his face couldn't be seen behind his helmet's chameleon screen.

"I saw all the rooms were empty except for the one," Doyle continued. "I took my Marines in and we waited for the signal. Then we went in."

"That was showing good initiative, Doyle, checking the windows before you went in the building. You did a good job there."

"Th-Thank you, Sergeant Kerr!"

"We'll make a proper fire team leader of you yet."

Now that he was off the Dragon and walking again, Lance Corporal Dave "Hammer" Schultz was in his element, holding the point of the unit on the task force's right flank—the most exposed position in the entire task force. It didn't matter to him that a Force Recon squad was several hundred meters to his front; Schultz still considered himself to be in the most exposed position in the FIST. Force Recon's job wasn't fighting, not yet: now, their responsibility was to scout the way and report back if they found enemy forces ahead. *His* job, Schultz's job, was to find any enemy along the FIST's route and kill them.

Now that Corporal Claypoole had stopped chattering, all of Schultz's senses were attuned to his surroundings. He wasn't thinking about Claypoole, but if he had he would have thought the man was a good enough Marine—even if he sometimes talked too much, and didn't always think before he did things. He'd also have thought that Claypoole was a good enough fire team leader; he'd never lost a man because of a mistake he'd made, anyway. It wasn't Claypoole's fault that Lance Corporal "Wolfman" MacIlargie got so badly wounded in that fight with the armored cars. Could have happened to anybody, even to Schultz. And, maybe most important, Claypoole stayed off Schultz's back, let him do what he did, the best way he could.

Of course, if Schultz had thought those things, he would have thought them in far fewer words. Most certainly he would have used fewer words had he spoken those thoughts.

Schultz knew exactly where he was going to place his feet as he walked—not only his next step, but the next twenty or more. He knew from step to step exactly where he would go for cover if the enemy attacked from the front, or where he'd take cover if they attacked from the side, or from any other direction. He saw for each place along his route exactly where an enemy unit might be lying in ambush. Or where an individual observer or sniper might be hiding.

Schultz knew these things not only for the places close to him, but he would have known the ambush, sniper, and observer locations all the way to the horizon had the FIST been moving through open land. But they were in thin forest, and he couldn't see to the horizon in any direction.

His senses were sufficiently attuned to his surroundings that Schultz wasn't in the least surprised that he felt the presence of the enemy in an area that Force Recon had already gone through without reporting them.

"Left front, three hundred," he murmured over the squad circuit.

Sergeant Kerr came back immediately with, "How many?"

"Wait. Don't see us." Which from the taciturn Schultz meant "I don't know yet. They don't know we're here yet." He continued advancing as though he hadn't detected enemy three hundred meters away.

Kerr reported to Ensign Bass. Bass relayed the report to Captain Conorado, then elected to listen in on Schultz's transmissions.

Three hundred meters. Schultz could see that far only in spots that shifted as he advanced. Whoever was there wasn't making enough noise to carry through the trees at that distance. Neither was anybody moving in a manner visible in the intermittent view Schultz had of the area. Nor were they cooking, or he'd smell their food. Schultz couldn't tell how he knew somebody was there, he only knew that he could. And so did every Marine who'd ever spent time with him in the field—particularly time spent when their lives depended on Schultz detecting enemy before anybody else could.

The line Schultz was following brought him within a hundred meters of the enemy. He stayed aware of his full surroundings, but gave particular attention to where he'd sensed them. It was a few minutes before he was able to make a follow-up report.

"Company plus. Maybe alert. Maybe more behind them," he said.

"How far, Hammer?" Bass asked.

"Hundred, hundred and fifty." Then, just to make sure, he added, "Left."

Bass switched to the platoon all-hands circuit. "Keep moving, but be alert. Schultz reports more than a company to our left."

Captain Conorado put the rest of the company on alert, ready to attack the enemy ambush at an instant's notice.

Corporal Reginald Thorntrip, a 4th Composite Infantry Division scout assigned to the 319th battalion of the 222nd Infantry Brigade, puzzled over his sensor displays. They'd been showing intermittent movement across the battalion's front for fifteen minutes, but he couldn't *see* anything through the trees where the sensors told him it was. He knew the Confederate Marines had raided the 7th MP Battalion's camp and were probably headed toward Phelps—that was why Major General Sneed had ordered the 319th of the 222nd to set an ambush along the route to Phelps. The battalion set up in a box, a reinforced company facing west and another facing east, along the Ashburtonville road. The remaining company was in the middle, ready to reinforce wherever it might be needed. Thorntrip knew that the Confederation Marines had field uniforms that made them invisible, which was why he'd set out motion detectors. But the movement his sensors were picking up was *intermittent,* which didn't make any sense. Unless . . .

Unless the Confederation Marines were moving on a line just *inside* his sensor line. After all, the motion detectors didn't have a 360-degree field of detection, just two hundred degrees. So if the Marines were closer than the detectors, but not *too much* closer, they might only show up intermittently.

Corporal Thorntrip wished he had infrared sensors, or at least infrared glasses, but he didn't, so he examined the motion detector display in light of the idea that the Marines were closer than the sensors. The intermittent movement was concentrated several hundred meters to his right, then faded out as it moved from right to left across his front. He puzzled over that for a moment. The change in frequency of detected movement could mean the Marine column was stopped, and accordioned in the place with the most movement, and the Marines were standing and moving about without advancing. Or it could mean that they were moving at an angle to the battalion's west front, with its point getting closer and closer with every moment. In either case, the scout needed to report to the battalion commander.

CHAPTER TWENTY-THREE

Lieutenant Colonel Farshuck listened to his communications man as the sergeant relayed Corporal Thorntrip's message. "Wall, gull durn it, he's a scout, fer cryssake! Whyn't he get his ass out thar an' do sum scoutin', fine out if'n anybody's thar?"

"Suh," the sergeant on the comm said, "wi' all due respec', suh, if'n they's Confed'ration Marines out thar, Scout Thorntrip won' be able ta see 'em, cause'n their invis'ble uniforms. But they'll sure 'n' shit be able ta see *him!*"

"If'n." Farshuck snorted. "An if'n they's Confed'ration Army, ain't nothin' goan stop him fum seein' 'em. Dang scout should get out thar an' *scout!*" He turned to his operations officer, who'd been listening intently to Thorntrip's report, and the exchange between Farshuck and the comm sergeant. "Ain't I right, Major Applegrate."

Applegrate cleared his throat. "Sir, I believe Sergeant Weyover is right." Major Applegrate had been educated offworld and affected a Standard English accent, rather than the patois common to the worlds of the Coalition. "The sketchy report Division received said that it was Confederation Marines, not army, that took out the 7th MPs. If it is indeed Marines that Thorntrip is sensing, he most certainly will not be able to see them unless he trips over one of them. Even at that, he won't be able to see the Marine, but rather merely *feel* him when the Marine takes him prisoner."

Farshuck cocked a suspicious eye at his S3—a Standard accent wasn't Applegrate's only vocal affectation. "Uh-huh. So's how's he goan know if'n thems Mo-reens out thar?"

"Confederation Marines are visible in infrared, sir."

"So he should look fer 'em in inf'red!"

Applegrate cleared his throat again. "Ah, sir, we don't *have* any infrared glasses in the battalion Table of Organization and Equipment!"

Farshuck shot Applegrate a look that Sergeant Weyover was glad wasn't directed at him. But the S3 wasn't affected by it. Either that, or he didn't notice.

"Suh," Farshuck snarled, "this hyar is *mah* b'talion, I *knows* we don' have any inf'red glasses in arn TO 'n' E. But the scout is fum *Division*, and Division do have inf'red equipment."

"Yes, sir, I, too, know that. However, Sergeant Thorntrip is assigned to Brigade, and I don't believe he brought any Division equipment with him."

"Wall, he shoulda." Farshuck turned to Weyover. "Aks thet scout he got hisself any inf'red 'quipment."

"Yes, suh," Weyover said, and bent to his comm. After a moment he looked up helplessly, swallowed, and said, "Suh, Scout Thorntrip says he ain't got no inf'red 'quipment."

"Dang it all t' blazes!" Farshuck swore. "How'ns we s'posed ta see if'n Confed'ration Mo-reens is out thar if'n we ain't got no inf'red cap'bil'ties?"

Weyover swallowed again and said, "Suh, Scout Thorntrip, he say he do believe the lead el'ment of thet Marine unit mus' be at the south end of the killin' zone. And gettin' closer, suh."

"He do?" Farshuck suddenly looked interested rather than annoyed. "Wall then, I thinks it's 'bout time we sprung this hyar ambush on them Mo-reens. Git me Cap'n—"

But before Farshuck could give the name of the commander of Easy Company, the company on the west side of the box formation, gun and blaster fire broke out along that front.

The Coalition forces lying in wait for the Marines had good cover in visual, but as the Marines approached closer to the enemy positions, they began picking up traces of them in the infrared. By the time Lance Corporal Schultz reached the far end of the ambush's killing zone, he could see the infrared signatures of three of the soldiers almost completely.

Schultz reported, "At the end."

Ensign Charlie Bass relayed the message to Captain Conorado, who replied, "Tell him to go twenty-five meters beyond the end of the ambush, then open fire on the nearest target. That'll be your signal to hit the ambush." He then contacted Ensign Antoni, whose first platoon followed third platoon, and told him to open fire to his left when third platoon opened fire. Second platoon's orders were to move briskly to the left and swing around to take the ambush from its flank.

Schultz got his orders seconds after giving his final report. He'd gone another five meters in the interval, so he picked a spot twenty meters to his front. When he reached that spot, he pivoted left, leveled his blaster, and fired two plasma bolts at the closest heat signature. He got off another bolt, at the next closest signature, before any of the other Marines got off their first bolts. The first soldiers of the 319th of the 222nd Brigade didn't get off their first shots until all the Marines of two companies were firing at them. By which time their strength was already down by almost twenty percent.

The ambushers fired fléchettes wildly, many of their shots going too high to hit the Marines even if they'd remained on their feet. But the Marines hadn't remained standing, they'd dropped to the ground as soon as they got off their first bolts. It did the ambushers little good to fire where they saw the bolts come from, because the Marines moved after nearly every bolt they fired. But the Coalition soldiers *didn't* move after firing, and their rifle barrels were warm enough to show in infra, which gave the Marines better targets to fire at. Casualties mounted.

Lieutenant Colonel Farshuck may have acted a buffoon when he received the first report from Corporal Thorntrip, but once the battle was engaged he demonstrated that he knew his business. The sounds of fire told him the company being engaged by the Marines was in serious trouble and suffering heavy casualties. The first thing he did was order Fox Company, his reserve, into the line to bolster Easy Company, which was having anything but an easy time of it. Then he ordered George

Company, facing east, to send a reinforced platoon around the north side of the box to hit the Marines from the flank.

After that, all he could do was report the contact to Brigade, and sit back to listen to the sounds of battle and the stream of communications from his company commanders—and hope the movement along the west side of his box wasn't a diversion, and that a larger force wasn't coming along the Ashburtonville road.

Second platoon got into position to rake the flank of the ambush, but held its fire, waiting for Captain Conorado's order to open up. That's what saved it from being hit by the reinforced platoon from the 319th's George Company when it came barreling through.

Corporal Patricus, whose fire team held the left of second platoon's line, was startled to see Coalition soldiers running past, just a few meters in front of him. But he recovered almost immediately, and reported to Ensign Molina. "It looks like a reinforced platoon," he answered when his platoon commander asked how many there were. "And they aren't in a straight column," he added as he took a step back to avoid one of the soldiers running by.

"Second platoon," Molina said laconically, "take them out. Grab a few prisoners if you can."

Patricus looked to his left, saw more soldiers running his way, took a step forward, and stuck out his foot. A running soldier ran into the extended foot and went flying, to land heavily on his face. Patricus turned to face another onrushing soldier. Holding his blaster across his body, he slammed it into the soldier's abdomen below his arms, which were holding his rifle at port arms.

While Patricus was dealing with that soldier, one of his men used wrist ties to secure the soldier Patricus had tripped, and his other man tackled another surprised soldier. In seconds, Patricus's fire team had taken three prisoners. The fire team leader then ordered his men to open fire on the soldiers still coming their way.

When Lieutenant Colonel Farshuck heard about the trouble the platoon from George Company ran into, he commanded Sergeant Weyover, "Fine out if'n the scout wit Jojeh Comp'ny got hissef any sign a

Confed'rates." Then to Major Applegrate, "If'n nobody's comin' on thet side, I wan' the res' a Jojeh Comp'ny ta go roun' the noth flank a Easy Comp'ny, an' go through shootin'!

"In a meantime, ah'm goan for'ard, take a look-see fer mahsef."

Major Applegrate watched his commander head west, with three riflemen for security. If the S3 knew his commander, those three riflemen would shortly join their fire to that of Easy and Fox Companies. Not that three extra rifles would do a lot of good if the Confederation Marines were seriously hurting the battalion—and from the changing gunfire he heard, it sounded like they were. When Farshuck was far enough away, Applegrate looked at Weyover, who was just finishing talking to the other scout.

"Well, Sergeant?" he asked.

"Suh, ain' nobody comin' on a east side," Weyover reported.

"Get me the George Company commander." Applegrate held his hand out to receive the comm unit. He'd accompany George Company on its movement.

Commander van Winkle, the commander of 34th FIST's infantry battalion, had his command element located between Company L and Mike Company, with Kilo Company trailing. Unlike the companies, which weren't able to use their UAVs while on the move so far from their home base, his UAV squad rode in a Dragon, so the controllers could operate their birds.

"Pull one of them back. I want to see what's happening on the north side of the enemy force," van Winkle told Ensign Qumell, the UAV commander.

"Aye aye, sir." Qumell looked at the monitors to see which UAV was closer to the north end of the action, then told its operator to head north and sweep to the east.

"Coming up."

Van Winkle examined the monitor over the operator's shoulder. "Head east, toward the road," he said once he'd seen the dead and captured Coalition soldiers who'd run into Company L's second platoon. "I just know there are more troops in that direction."

In little more than a minute the UAV, swooping through the treetops, disguised as a local avian carrion eater, found the rest of George Company forming on line to sweep through the area held by Company L's second platoon.

"XO," van Winkle said to his executive officer, Captain Uhara, "alert Conorado that his flanking platoon has a superior force assembling to advance toward it." As Uhara said, "Aye aye, sir," van Winkle turned back to the UAV operator. "Swing to the south, let me see where they came from."

The UAV operator did as van Winkle said, and came across the command post of the 319th Battalion.

"Good work, Marine." Van Winkle clapped him on the shoulder. "Keep an eye on those troops assembling to the east, let me know when they start moving."

"Aye aye, sir." Van Winkle next watched the UAV that was prowling above the ambush line that Company L was fighting and saw the south end of it was completely out of the battle. He turned to Uhara again and said, "Contact Conorado. Tell him to have his point squad start rolling up the flank of that company."

Sergeant Kerr listened to the orders from Ensign Bass, then relayed them to his men. "Second squad, listen up. According to higher, there's nobody facing us now. We're moving in to roll up their flank. Everybody, use your infras. Hammer, lead the way one hundred meters to the right, then circle in. Questions? Let's do this thing."

Lance Corporal Schultz rose to a crouch and headed south at speed, leaving it up to the others to keep up with him. They did but not all were able to move as fast while crouched. It didn't matter, as none of the ambushers had infra glasses to see them with—and the Coalition troops were too busy shooting at the Marines firing at them to notice one squad moving away anyway.

A hundred meters to the south of his fighting position, Schultz slowed enough to make sure Corporal Claypoole, the next man in line, saw where he was turning, then swung right to head for the flank of the ambush. When he reached a spot where he heard firing from the ambush line, he paused briefly again to look back. The whole squad was trailing him.

"Go beyond?" Schultz asked on the squad circuit.

"Five meter intervals," Kerr said. Hammer, go twenty meters farther. When we're all on line, I'll give the word to go forward."

Kerr's position was in the middle of the squad's line. When he reached the midpoint of the sound of fire from the ambush, he looked to his right and left, along the line of the squad, then ordered, "At a trot, go! Watch your dress."

Second squad moved out as commanded and quickly came in sight of the former south end of the ambush. Farther ahead, they heard battle sounds suddenly reach a crescendo.

"Ignore that, people," Kerr ordered. "That's probably reinforcements at the far end. Mike Company's taking care of it, let's worry about doing our own job." Seconds later he saw the red splotch that marked an enemy soldier and called the squad to a halt. "Three Actual, three-two is in position," he said on the platoon circuit.

"Stand by," Staff Sergeant Hyakowa said.

Kerr told second squad to hold in place and hold their fire. He waited impatiently for orders to advance.

Then Ensign Bass's voice came over the comm. "Third platoon! Second squad is about to advance on the enemy flank. Watch for their fire, then roll yours in front of them. Be careful not to hit our Marines. Second squad, secure anybody who surrenders. First squad, stand by to move up and take control of prisoners once second squad passes you. Second squad, go now!"

"Let's go!" Kerr ordered. "Secure anybody who surrenders, kill anybody who doesn't."

Second squad moved out at a brisk walk, firing at every infrared signal they saw. Here and there, a Coalition soldier threw his weapon away and raised his hands, shouting, "Don' shoot, ah surrendah!"

"Second fire team, secure the prisoner," Kerr ordered when the first Coalition soldier surrendered.

Corporal Claypoole led his men behind first fire team and got ties ready. Lance Corporal Little stepped over to the first soldier to surrender, and Claypoole pounced on the man before he could try anything, wrenching his arms behind his back to secure his wrists. Lance Corporal Ymenez went with Claypoole and secured the man's ankles with another tie. After a quick glance to make sure the prisoner wasn't going to try anything, Schultz ignored him, to keep watch on the squad's exposed flank and rear. By the time second fire team had secured the first prisoner, third fire team had secured the next soldier to surrender. Second squad had to join in to help secure the surrendering soldiers as most of them gave up the fight when they saw their line was being rolled up.

Fire died down on the far end of the ambush as Mike Company devastated the 319th Battalion's George Company when it tried to advance around the flank of the ambush.

Lieutenant Colonel Farshuck stood dumbfounded. He'd been certain his battalion could damage the Marine FIST badly enough to drive it off before it could fight back. Instead, his battalion was wiped out, nearly all of its soldiers dead or captured. He didn't know how many of his men managed to escape once the battle was lost—if any. He was still standing there, a stupefied expression on his face, when a voice said out of the air, "Sir, I'm Captain Lew Conorado, Confederation Marine Corps. You are my prisoner. I would be grateful if you would hand over your sidearm."

Farshuck blinked in the direction from which the voice had come, then numbly reached for his sidearm. He briefly considered firing it rather than handing it over, but he couldn't be positive of where his target was. Shooting at a ghost would be a futile gesture that wouldn't benefit himself or his men. He shook his head sadly, and handed his weapon over.

"What would you have me do, sir?" he asked.

CHAPTER TWENTY-FOUR

"Major, are you telling me—?"

"Decimated, wiped out, dead or prisoners. All of them, sir." Major Applegrate, late the operations officer for the 319th Battalion of Brigadier General Josephus's 222nd Brigade, shook his head wearily. "All," he added. He put his head into is hands. "All," he repeated.

General Josephus was speechless for a moment. "Colonel Farshuck?"

"I don't know, sir. H-He went out to one of the companies and we didn't hear from him afterward. We lost contact with all the companies, sir." He looked up and his expression pleaded with the brigade commander to try to understand what it had been like out along the coast road. The 319th had been sent there to block any advance by the enemy from the 7th MPs' overrun position along the coast. They had left Phelps with confidence high, not quite bands blaring, but with total confidence that they would successfully block the highway. Now Major Farshuck was telling the brigade commander the battalion had been wiped out?

"Marines, you say?"

"Y-Yes, sir. They-they came at us out of nowhere! It had to be Marines, with those special camouflage uniforms they wear." Major Applegrate beat a fist against his knee. He was almost in tears. "I-I pulled the command post out of action to avoid being overrun, sir. It was all I could do! We didn't have infra capability, sir! We were not prepared to go up against them!"

"You estimate they were battalion-strength?"

"Yes, sir. Based on the volume of firepower they used against us and the lack of supporting arms, I'd say a light-battalion-size element."

"Major, I know you've been through hell this morning, but pull yourself together, man! We're going up to report this to General Sneed."

Corporal Puella Queege had always wanted to be a military policeman. In her own mind her service as a company clerk with the 7th Independent Military Police Battalion actually qualified her to be an MP. She'd picked up a lot about MP operations during her time with the battalion's 4th Company. So once sobered up, cleaned up, and presented before Major General Sneed to receive her Bronze Medal of Heroism, she had told everyone she actually *was* a military policeman. *What the heck,* she thought, *it was only a tiny white lie.*

"We need brave, quick-thinking soldiers like you, Corporal," the general had said as he pinned the medal on her tunic. He turned to a lieutenant colonel standing by, the CO of the division MP battalion. "Colonel, get this gallant soldier some gear and put her out there on the streets and back to work. You're going to need every man—and woman—you've got to keep order during this evacuation." Sneed smiled at Queege, shook her hand, looked at the cameras, and departed.

Queege did not think it would be very wise to admit to her new company supply sergeant that she did not know how to use half the equipment he issued her. Somehow, though, she got it all on her in the correct position. She knew what the stuff was intended for; handcuffs, stun sticks, and so on, but she'd never been taught how to use any of it in an actual confrontation. Likewise the huge M26, 10mm semiautomatic caseless fléchette handgun strapped to her equipment belt. No one showed her how to charge the weapon. She knew she had to work the slide to chamber the first huge round of the ten in the weapon's magazine. She also knew the weapon had a decocking lever and a magazine release stud, devices common to the older handheld weapons, but she'd never fired the thing. But, she reasoned, she'd probably never need to use it on any of the civilians in Phelps, so what the heck. Just having it should be deterrent enough. Besides, the huge MP brassard on her left arm was probably all she'd need to assert her authority.

Her new platoon commander introduced her at roll call and the other MPs were suitably impressed. None of them had ever been so close to a winner of the Bronze Medal of Heroism; besides, she'd seen real action, which none of them had. If only they'd served alcohol at roll call, Queege would've been in heaven.

"Men—and lady—our job is to keep order in the streets while the civilians are being evacuated," the company commander said, "make sure there's no looting, no vandalism."

The platoon sergeant gave out the individual patrol assignments. Queege was left for last. "Corporal," he told her, "I want you to position yourself at the Bank of Phelps, it's on the corner of Quimby and Cruller streets, here"—he pointed to a trid display of the Phelps street system— "five-minute walk from here. Don't let no one in; anyone already in there, roust 'em out and secure the doors." He gave her a heavy lock and chain. "Oncet you done that, stay on guard until yer relieved. Any- one gives you any shit, call for backup." He indicated the tiny radio at- tached to her equipment belt. "Otherwise, do not hesitate to open fire. Here"—he handed her another magazine of 10mm fléchette ammo— "two mags ain't enough fer patrollin' anywheres, but mos' likely you won't need all three. Now git up to the bank. I'll be roaming around me- self. I'll bring you coffee later." He grinned.

The walk to the bank was, as the platoon sergeant had said, a short one. The streets were full of people hurrying to get under cover or out of town. Queege strutted along importantly, wondering what all the civilians thought of her in her new role as a law enforcement officer. She paused before a bar. The door was open. She hesitated, looked around, and then stepped quickly inside.

"I was just leavin'," someone said from the back of the bar. "We're gettin' the hell outta town!" A middle-aged man emerged from the shadows at the back of the bar, his arms full of things. "Oh, Officer, I own this place," he said quickly, seeing Queege silhouetted against the bright sunlight in the street. The man was fully aware of the penalty for looting.

"Thass okay," Queege responded in her most convincing command voice, which sounded to her like a squeak, "but I was wondering if I could get something to drink. It's mighty hot out there—"

"Oh," the man said, relieved he wasn't going to be arrested for looting, which is just what he was doing in the bar. "Hep yerself, Officer, hep yerself!" He grinned and pushed past her out into the street.

Queege stepped behind the bar. Whiskey or beer? she pondered. Well, it was a hot day in Phelps, so beer should do the trick. She found the robo-server, punched in her request, and the machine duly poured her an ice-cold liter of ale. Queege drank thirstily. With a deeply satis-fying belch, she wiped the foam from her upper lip, leaned against the bar, and burped contentedly one more time. She wondered what had happened to her first sergeant and the others in the 4th Company. She shrugged. Dead or POWs, she figured. Nothing anybody could do about that! But she'd liked her first sergeant. When he wasn't verbally abusing her, which was a game they played, he was amusing her, and they both loved their beer. She drank two more liters before she felt good enough to finish the walk up to the bank.

When she arrived at last at the Bank of Phelps she found the mas-sive front doors wide open. Someone was inside, that was for sure, making quite a racket too. Probably depositors, demanding their ac-counts be cleared. Strange, though, they were laughing. Well, she squared her shoulders, burped loudly, mounted the steps and walked into the cool interior of the building. She squinted, getting her vision back after the bright sunlight outside. She thought she saw three men with large bags coming from the vault. One was huge, struggling to drag several bags behind him.

"Who the *fuck* are you?" the huge man rumbled, stopping in the middle of the gallery. Queege burped loudly by way of response. "I am Cardoza O'Quinn, the mayor of this here town, 'n' I am removin' the municipal funds to a safer location, so I'm tellin' you, get yer skinny ass outta my way! *Gawdam*," he exclaimed suddenly and turned to the men behind him, "this'n smells like a brewery!" He turned back to Queege. "Now git out'n muh way!"

"No, you ain't," Queege squeaked, undoing the flap on her holster, but someone else fired first.

"A *light* battalion, you say? Our *entire* battalion rendered combat-ineffective?"

Major Applegrate nodded affirmation. "Yes, sir. Judging by the vol-ume of fire, they had at least a third fewer men than we had—and no supporting arms." He shook his head now. "If we'd only had infras, sir—" General Sneed waved him into silence with a gesture.

"Marines for sure," Brigadier General Josephus added.

General Sneed drummed his fingers on his desk. "This changes the whole situation, gentlemen." He addressed his entire staff, or those he was able to assemble on such short notice. "G2, what's the word?"

Brigadier General Burton shrugged. "Recon reports only the Marines that the 319 ran into, sir. It seems to be only the infantry battalion from a single FIST."

"Am I to believe they landed only *one* Marine battalion just to harass the 7th MPs?" General Sneed looked in turn at each officer.

"They've done it before, or at least they've sent in limited forces to harass us. We all remember the attack on Gilbert's Corners—"

"Yeah, yeah, I know all that. But is this the spearpoint of a major invasion? That's what I need to know, gentlemen, and right now."

"I'd say no to that, sir," the division operations officer said, while several other officers nodded their agreement. "In the first place, if this were an all-out attack, they'd be coming at us with a lot more than a battalion. I'd describe this more as a reconnaissance in force, sir. I doubt frankly they'll proceed much farther down the coast road now they've brushed the 319th aside."

"But more could be coming? This is just a probe?" General Sneed looked at the other officers and they all nodded their heads.

"That's my opinion, yes sir," the G2 responded.

"Very well, then. Triple Deuce," Sneed addressed Brigadier Josephus, commander of the 222nd Brigade, "I am very sorry about what happened to the 319th. I knew Colonel Farshuck, a gallant officer. Now, infras." He nodded at Major Applegrate. "This was a 'come as you are invited' war, gentlemen. Most of us left our home worlds short of a lot of authorized equipment. We all know that and we all know how much we've had to scrounge to make up the differences. I want what infra devices we do have redistributed immediately. I don't know what the inventory is, but I want those devices in the hands of the maneuver units ASAP! Depending on how many you can lay your hands on, I want them distributed at least to company level if that's possible.

"Signals." He turned to his communications officer. "Send this message to General Lyons immediately: 319th Battalion, 222nd Brigade, engaged enemy on coastal road. Heavy casualties. Enemy estimated to be a battalion-size element from a Marine FIST. Feel this is a probe of our strength in this sector. Send infra equipment if can be spared. Am prepared to defend this position. Will keep you informed. Send it at once.

"Gentlemen, eyes and ears open, fingers off your triggers until we know precisely what we're up against. Major Spinoza," he said to his civil affairs officer, "how goes the evacuation?"

"Badly, sir. The 222nd's MP battalion's been a great help, but most of these people do not want to evacuate. Following your orders, we have not forced them to."

"Well, do so now, Major. Get them all out of the way. Use whatever force you deem necessary. Goddammit, I've lost a *battalion* of my men! We'll turn this miserable town into a fortress and I'll be damned if I'm going to let a bunch of candy-ass civilians muck up my battle plan!"

"Sir, we've managed to keep looting at a minimum, but something's going on at the Bank of Phelps—"

"Probably just O'Quinn withdrawing his ill-gotten gains." General Sneed chuckled. "Let the MPs handle it. All right, folks, hop to it! It's gonna be a long day in Phelps."

General Davis Lyons read Sneed's message a second time and looked up at his staff. "An attack by an element this small has got to be a probe. Is there any sign of seaborne activity?"

"None, sir, at least none we've been able to detect," the G2 responded.

"Ummm." Lyons drummed his fingers on his desk. "All right. Get what infra equipment you can scrounge and send it up to the 4th Division, priority. Christ on a shitter, if a single Marine battalion without supporting arms can wipe out one of our battalions in such short order, we'd better hope there aren't more on the way, or that our guys have the equipment they need to see those boys in their chameleons."

"Shouldn't we reinforce the 4th Division, sir?" the G3 asked.

"No! Sneed is a capable commander. He hasn't asked for reinforcements. Let's not panic. Remember, we sent the 7th MPs down there to be a tripwire. Well, the wire's been tripped, all right, but until I'm sure this is a full-scale maneuver against our rear, I am *not* going to deplete my army's strength here."

General Lyons sat by himself after the staff had been dismissed. He remembered now all too well what someone on the Committee on the Conduct of the War had said when he appeared before them at Gilbert's Corners, that the 7th MPs on the coast-watch were the army's Achilles' heel. Well, that pesky committee was no more and the government had been transferred to the Cumber Mountains. And now the 7th MP position had been overrun. Were things beginning to fall apart? No! The bulk of the army was still intact, full of fight, ready to move against the fortifications out on the bay! Lyons's opposite number, this Jason Billie, had proved himself to be an idiot so far, playing right into Lyons's hands. He was just not bold enough to mount a backdoor assault on Phelps. What was happening down there was a diversion, nothing more.

General Davis Lyons sighed. "Well, I hope so," he quietly murmured.

Corporal Queege was not sure what kind of weapons were being fired at her. All she saw in the dim light were several brilliant flashes. Something, the first round, glanced powerfully off the chain the platoon sergeant had given her, which still hung around her neck. It struck so hard she was momentarily stunned and fell to the ground. The rest of the rounds went zipping through the air where she'd been standing, screeching and caroming off the walls in a shower of sparks and chips of masonry.

The Bank of Phelps did business the old-fashioned way, with paper, despite the fact that throughout most of the Confederation member-worlds electronic banking was the preferred way to store and access funds. So at intervals in the lobby there were convenient marble-topped writing tables stocked with styluses and various forms for deposits, withdrawals, and so on. Not knowing what else to do, Queege crawled under one of these. The fire directed at her now ricocheted off the marble, shredding the paper like confetti. The noise was so terrific she could not hear her own voice shouting into her radio for assistance.

Queege fumbled her M26 out of its holster. She could clearly see the fat man from under the table, from his feet up to about the middle of his bulging belly. She leveled the gun and squeezed the trigger. Nothing! She'd forgotten to charge it! She cursed and pulled the slide back, putting the weapon into battery. Caseless ammunition produces virtually no recoil, so the rounds go precisely where the shooter points them. Each round fired by the M26 releases twenty-six tiny, razor-sharp fléchettes at a muzzle velocity of approximately 450 meters per second. Queege's magazine was loaded with two different types of alternating rounds: five designed to fragment or be released when they entered a target, then five that discharged from the barrel like pellets from an old-fashioned shotgun in a dispersal pattern that grew one centimeter per meter traveled. The latter rounds did not have much range and were designed for shooting in close, confined spaces. Both types of ammunition were intended for police use because, while deadly, they would not threaten anyone other than the intended target through overpenetration.

The first round she fired was designed to penetrate. It hit the fat man right in his navel. He was no more than three meters from Queege. The round entered his abdomen and sent the twenty-six fléchettes tearing through his intestines. He emitted a high-pitched shriek. His handgun, which he had been shooting into the marble top of the desk under which Corporal Queege lay, clattered to the floor. The man's voice rose to an impossible falsetto, like a woman in hard labor, and he thudded wetly to the floor, where he twitched and spasmed like a fish out of water, his hands clutching to his stomach. *"Ahaaaaaaa!"* he shrieked.

The other men stopped shooting momentarily. Queege thought she'd seen three others, so she emptied the remaining nine rounds in her magazine, three at each figure she thought she could see in the dim light. She slammed another magazine into the gun, but there was no answering fire. Her ears were ringing from all the concussions, but she thought she could hear more screams. She lay panting under the desk. A long, black tendril of blood flowed toward her from beneath the fat man who now lay silently on the floor. Queege scuttled away from the blood. She shook her head to clear it of the loud ringing.

Someone said something over her radio. "Bank!" she gasped. "Shooting! Help!" She became vaguely aware of people outside the building creeping up to the doors, peering cautiously inside and exclaiming at what they saw, but she ignored them as she staggered to her feet. Her eyes had now adjusted to the dark interior. Her helmet was gone and the right side of her head felt funny. When she reached up she found to her horror that her ear was gone; then she noticed the burning pain of the wound.

She had the weird sensation she was outside herself, detached, watching everything on a trid.

It was deathly quiet in the Bank of Phelps. The four bandits, including Hizzoner, the mayor, were all quite dead. Queege had killed them all. Bags of banknotes lay scattered among the bodies and the congealing pools of blood. Cautiously, she examined the bodies. All of her hits had been above the chest, and the men's faces were reduced to masses of unrecognizable gore. She was reluctant to touch the bodies. Besides, with wounds like those, surely they were all dead. She walked to the door, her boots squeaking in the already drying gore.

Corporal Puella Queege, late company clerk with the 7th Independent Military Police Battalion, blinked in the bright sunlight outside the Bank of Phelps. Curious citizens parted before her as she wobbled down the steps.

"One of 'em's the gawdam *mayor!*" someone cackled. "She sliced 'im open like a ripe tomato!" he shouted gleefully. "Yessireee! Tom Gritchens 'n' Hank Weatherby's in thar too! They heads is awmos' tore complete off! Ah, haaa! Ain't see ennythin' so wunnerful sinct the hawgs et muh little sister! Ol' Cardoza, he fin'ly got what was a-comin' to 'im!"

Several men dashed up the stairs and into the bank. They were her fellow MPs. Someone put a hand on Puella's shoulder and gently relieved her of the M26, which dangled forgotten from one hand. It was her new platoon sergeant. "Gawdam, girl!" he said, "You gonna get a medal for this, you sure'n hell will!" He put an arm around her shoulder and guided her gently to a waiting landcar.

Puella felt a violent throbbing in her head but it didn't bother her. She grinned up at her platoon sergeant and thought to herself, *I wonder if I coulda done any of that if I was sober?*

CHAPTER TWENTY-FIVE

"Move, people, move!" Ensign Bass shouted.

"Move, move move!" Staff Sergeant Hyakowa echoed.

The Marines of third platoon scrambled onto the Dragons that had been brought up after the firefight. The enemy now knew that the Marines were in their rear, and 34th FIST had to move fast to get deeper behind the enemy before General Lyons could begin moving maneuver forces after them. Behind the Dragons that picked up Company L and most of Mike Company, the Marines of Kilo Company boarded hoppers. The remainder of Mike Company and the prisoners from the 319th Battalion squeezed into other hoppers for the short flight back to the task force's landing zone so the 27th Division's military police company could take charge of the POWs.

Brigadier Sturgeon sent his three UAVs and the infantry battalion's two on ahead to scout for enemy units. The birds had to stay below the woodland canopy most of the time and track back and forth to cover the FIST's entire front; only when they encountered a clearing large enough to be called a meadow could they rise high enough to get a wider view. It was slow going, but the UAVs found the first enemy positions some six kilometers north of Phelps. A reinforced battalion was in a lightly built defensive position.

Thirty-fourth FIST had to move fast to take fullest advantage of the enemy's flimsy positions; reinforcements might be on their way. Sturgeon had no time to plan his attack, he'd do that on the run. He didn't waste any time wishing he had his Raptors or his artillery with him, he'd make do with what he had. He issued his commander's-intent orders for the coming assault. After that, it was mostly up to Commander van Winkle, the infantry battalion commander.

The Dragons lurched to a stop two kilometers short of the northernmost Coalition position, dropped their rear ramps, and the Marines boiled out.

"Company L, columns of squads," Captain Conorado ordered over his all-hands circuit. "Line 'em up and begin moving out. We want to get there before they're ready for us." Throughout 34th FIST's infantry battalion, the other company commanders gave the same commands.

"Second squad, on me," Sergeant Kerr said on the squad circuit. He raised his right arm and let the sleeve of his chameleon shirt slide down so his men could see where he was. "First fire team, second, third." He watched in the infrared as his squad got in line. As soon as they were, he spoke. "Chan, move it out. I'll be between first and second fire teams. Go!"

Moments after dismounting from the Dragons, Company L and most of Mike Company were moving at a rapid walk toward the Coalition's hastily prepared blocking position. Eighteen squads, each with a gun team attached, advanced in rough order, separated by seventy-five meters. Assault squads with their heavier weapons followed behind the blaster platoons. The hoppers, having deposited the prisoners with the 27th Division's MPs, landed Kilo Company and the remainder of Mike Company behind the advancing squads. Kilo and Mike-Bravo quickly formed up and followed the first wave. The hoppers remained grounded, waiting for the battle to join.

"Watch your dress, squads," Captain Conorado said over the all-hands circuit. The platoon commanders echoed him, and the squad leaders repeated on their squad circuits. All along the line, the squads' point men looked to their left and right, using their infras, to make sure they weren't getting too far ahead of or behind the squads seventy-five meters to their flanks.

Except for third platoon's second squad.

Lance Corporal Schultz held point for second squad, and second squad held the FIST's right flank. Schultz only looked to his left to check his dress.

Four hundred meters from the enemy positions, van Winkle issued an order to his company commanders: "Columns of fire teams." All along the battalion's front, company commanders relayed the order, echoed by platoon commanders, and finally squad leaders, who moved their fire teams second and third in their columns up to the right and left of their point fire teams. Except for third platoon's second squad; Sergeant Kerr moved both of his trailing fire teams to the left of his second fire team, to keep Schultz on the rightmost flank. Schultz, in turn, moved twenty meters right to keep proper interval between fire teams. The gun teams and assault squads closed the gaps ahead of themselves, keeping close behind the blaster squads.

At 250 meters, van Winkle ordered his battalion's fire teams to get on line.

"Y'all think they's comin'?" Private Willie Sawshank nervously asked his squad leader.

Corporal Waylon Drummel chewed for a few seconds, then spat a long, dark brown spume over the low wall of camouflaged sandbags in front of his squad's position. "Reckon so," he drawled.

"Them Confed'ration Marines?"

"Parbly, parbly." Drummel nodded. " 'Magine so, Wee Willie."

"Don' call me Wee Willie," Sawshank snarled. "Ain't ma name, ain't right t' call me thet."

Drummel looked at him and nodded again. "Reckon it ain't right t' call ya Wee Willie. Could call ya Big Willie, though."

Sawshank didn't like Big Willie any more than he liked Wee Willie, and said so. Willie Sawshank stood little more than a meter and a half tall, and was sensitive about his height—or lack thereof. He certainly didn't like any name that called attention to his shortness. Corporal Drummel called him Wee Willie or Big Willie because Drummel stood well over two meters tall. It felt to Sawshank as if his squad leader was making fun of him, putting him down. And that was *wrong*. Sawshank was as good a soldier as anyone in Drummel's squad, and Sawshank knew the bigger man knew it. He didn't understand that Drummel gave nicknames only to men he thought were better than average soldiers.

The two soldiers were quiet for a long moment, then Drummel asked, "Ya eber come up 'gainst Confed'ration Marines?"

Sawshank shook his head.

"Ah trained with 'em oncet," Drummel said. "They got these field uniforms they calls kam-lions. Guess the kam's fum camouflage, an' the lion's is cause thet's how they fights—mean as lions. Anyways, they wears their kam-lions, an' ya jist 'bout cain't see 'em."

Sawshank screwed up his face. "If'n ya cain't see 'em, how kin ya fight 'em?"

Drummel shrugged. "Same as ya fights anybody else—ya puts out as much farpower as ya kin an' hopes ya hits sumpin'." He looked into the distance, and then at Sawshank. "Here's sumpin' mos' sojers ferget when they fights Confed'ration Marines. Ya kin see their shots. Ya see, they uses plasma blasters, shoots out thangs lak a bit of star-plasma. Real bright like, ya kin see where they comes fum. What mos' sojers do is, when they sees the plasma bolts, they shoots back at whar they come fum. But all that does is it wastes ammunition. Ya see, what mos' sojers fergets is, the Marines *move* after they shoots mos' times. So if'n ya shoots where the shot come fum, t'ain't nobody thar fer yer shot ta hit. So what ya do is, ya figure out how far a man'll roll between shots, an' thas how far fum the shot you shoots."

Sawshank screwed up his face at his squad leader. "Whatch way d' ya shoot oncet ya figures out how far?"

Drummel shrugged. "Doan matter. You shoots either side a where the shot come fum, you got a better chance a shootin' some'un than if'n ya shoots where the shot come fum."

Sawshank mulled that over, and decided Drummel had a good point. "Got'cha," he said, nodding.

"Good. Now ah'm goin' thataway ta tell the rest a the squad the same thing. Ah wants yo ta go t'other way an' tell the mens that way the same thing. Then we goes t'other way and does the same. Thet way they'll hear it fum the two of us, an' mebbe it'll sink in ta one of 'em what they should do when they starts fightin'."

Sawshank nodded. "Tha's why yer squad leader an' I ain't. Ya thinks a thet kind a shit."

"Thinkin' thet kind a shit is why ah've lived long as ah have. Now you do the same, Big Willie."

"Doan go callin' me no damn Big Willie. T'ain't ma name!"

* * *

Two hundred meters from the Coalition line, the Marines of Company L and half of Mike Company were on line, with the enemy in view. The Coalition soldiers were well concealed, invisible through the thin wood at that distance—in the visual. But few of them understood infrared, and most of them showed themselves to the Marines in infra.

"Battalion, halt," Commander van Winkle ordered. The company commanders echoed the order on their all-hands circuits. Any closer than two hundred meters and even half-trained soldiers would be able to hit targets through the wooded land. "Prone. Wait for the order to fire," van Winkle ordered, and the company commanders repeated.

The platoon commanders and squad leaders amplified the battalion commander's last order: "Pick your targets. Let's hit them so hard and so fast they'll break and run instead of fighting back." Many of them added, "I don't want any of us getting hurt, people, so make every one of your bolts counts." All along the line, the fire team leaders made sure every one of their men had targets. The guns and bigger assault guns prepared to open fire.

Fire team leaders reported, "Ready," to their squad leaders, the squad leaders reported, "Ready," to their platoon commanders, who reported to their company commanders, and finally the company commanders back to Commander van Winkle, who ordered, *"Fire!"* and a company and a half of Marines opened fire on the hapless defenders.

Corporal Drummel was as surprised as everybody else when the plasma bolts hit the Coalition line. But he was one of the Coalition soldiers who understood about infrared cover. So was Private Sawshank. And, between them, they'd managed to get most of the squad into infra cover—all the way down behind the sandbag wall. Still, three of the eight men in the squad became casualties in the Marines' opening salvo because they'd insisted on looking over the sandbags, exposing themselves to the Marines' infra vision.

Drummel hunkered low, out of the way of the fusillade pouring at him and his men, until the fire stopped impacting near his position. Then he poked his head and fléchette rifle through an embrasure in the sandbags so he could see where the Marine fire came from.

" 'Member what ah tole ya 'bout the Marines movin' after they shoots!" he yelled at his squad.

" 'Member, the Marines shoots and moves!" Sawshank called out, to make sure the men at his side of the line heard Drummel's command. He also poked his head and rifle into an embrasure. *There!* He saw the sunlike flash of a blaster firing. He flipped a mental coin and rapid-fired three shots a few meters to the right of where the shot had come from. Then he switched and fired three more quick shots at the other side. He watched for another plasma flash, saw one, and fired to both sides of it. He didn't take the time to look to his sides; for all he knew, he and Drummel were the only ones in the squad shooting to the sides—he didn't even know if anybody other than himself and Drummel were firing back at all.

"Yowww!" Lance Corporal Ymenez yelped—a fléchette had just torn its way along his right forearm. Then he ignored the minor injury and fired again. Rolled, prepared to fire a third time. Flinched when fléchettes struck the ground mere centimeters to his right. "What's going on here?" he yelled.

Corporal Claypoole hadn't been hit by a fléchette, but he also noticed how close they came when he changed position after firing. What was going on? It looked like somebody was using aimed fire, and most armies didn't use aimed fire, they settled for massed fire and hoped that if they put out enough, they'd hit something. More than aimed fire, whoever was doing it knew about the Marines moving after they shot. Claypoole picked a likely target and sent a plasma bolt at it. Then he stayed in position and watched.

When the Marines first opened fire, they took the defenders by surprise, and return fire was spotty. The return fire built up to something less than a crescendo, and began tapering off as the Coalition soldiers' casualties quickly mounted. By now, not much more than two minutes into the firefight, the return fire was rapidly ebbing. So it was easy for Claypoole, through his infra, to pick out fire coming his way. He saw the flash of a round being fired an instant before fléchettes peppered the ground two meters to his left, then another flash an instant before more struck to his right. He sighted in on where the flashes came from and fired three rapid bolts at it. No more fire came from there. He looked for more flashes.

* * *

Corporal Drummel heard a scream to his right and paused in his own firing to listen to his squad. After the scream, he heard nothing to his right. Neither did he hear anything to his left. "Sawshank, report!" he shouted. Private Sawshank didn't respond. He started calling out his other men's names, one at a time with a pause after each. Nobody answered. Drummel swore under his breath, then scrambled to his left to check on his men. He found two of them, dead. The other man who should have been there was gone. He didn't see anybody beyond his squad's section of sandbagged wall. Still staying below the tops of the sandbags, he crawled to his right, beyond his previous position. The first man he came across was alive but in shock from a plasma bolt that had taken his arm off at the shoulder. Drummel wasn't sure it was a blessing that the plasma had cauterized the wound instead of leaving the soldier to bleed out and die. Sawshank was next in line. He was dead; a blackened hole bored through his head, another gouged his shoulder. There should have been two more men beyond Sawshank. There was only one, and he was dead, sprawled on top of the sandbags he should have stayed behind. Again to the right, Drummel saw nobody beyond his last man.

He lay prone, his shoulders propped up on his elbows, and let his head hang to touch the ground, thinking what to do. His entire squad was gone, dead, or missing, except for the one man in shock. Nobody was on either of his flanks. What should he do, continue fighting until he was killed as well? He didn't see any point in that. He twisted around and returned to the soldier in shock, did what little he could for him, then pulled him over his shoulders and began low-crawling away from the sandbag wall. He left his weapons behind.

"Cease fire!"

"Cease fire!"

"Cease fire!"

The command went down the chain of command, from Commander van Winkle all the way to the fire team leaders. In seconds all the Marines had stopped firing. They lay waiting for what came next as silence settled over the battlefield.

What came next was an order for a squad from the right flank to sweep through the enemy position and make sure the fight was over.

Company L's third platoon was on the battalion's right flank, and second squad's second fire team on the platoon's extreme right. As far as Lance Corporal Schultz was concerned, it was only right and proper that he and his squad were the ones to sweep through the enemy positions and deal with anybody who was left. Except for a few stunned soldiers who were curled into pathetic balls, second squad found only dead men. They bound those soldiers hand and foot for later pickup.

The infantrymen of 34th FIST remounted Dragons and hoppers to join in the assault on the main Coalition forces outside Ashburtonville.

CHAPTER TWENTY-SIX

Brigadier Ted Sturgeon was out of breath. He had just come into General Cazombi's command post from the ridge above Phelps where 34th had succeeded in breaking the defensive line of the enemy's 4th Division and sent them scampering up the Ashburtonville road, one of the most successful attacks in a career filled with them. "We busted their line!" he shouted, wiping the perspiration from his forehead and grinning at the officers and NCOs. He turned to General Alistair Cazombi, came to attention and saluted. "They're running back up the Ashburtonville road in complete disorder, Alistair!" forgetting momentarily that military protocol required he address the commanding general by his first name only in private. "The back door to Bataan is swung wide open!"

"Good God almighty, Ted, you've done it! Good work, good work!" Cazombi pounded Sturgeon on the back. "Lieutenant!" he shouted at his communications officer, "Get General Billie on comm!" He turned back to Sturgeon. "We're going to push those guys right up the road"—he smacked a fist into his palm—"and end this war *today*. I *knew* you could do it!" He draped his arm around Sturgeon's shoulder. "Come on, Ted, I want old Jason to see you standing with me when I announce that you've won his war for him."

But it was Major General Balca Sorca, Billie's chief of staff, whose face popped up on the comm's screen. There was a faint haze of cigar smoke about his head, but Cazombi noted he wasn't smoking himself. "Get Billie!" Cazombi said. "We've busted through the 4th Division's lines and we're pushing them back up the Ashburtonville road. Now's the time for you to break out of Bataan! Dammit, Sorca, where's Billie?" Nobody had ever seen Alistair Cazombi so excited.

Sorca hesitated a moment before he said, "Well, sir, he's, er, indisposed at the moment."

"He takin' a shit or what, Balca? Goddammit, go *get* him! We can't afford to waste another second! Lyons is no goddamned fool like"—he almost said Jason Billie—"some people think he is! He'll see what's coming and shift his troops around to meet us! Goddammit, Balca, go get the son of a bitch and do it right fucking *now!*"

A look of embarrassment crossed Sorca's face as he glanced furtively sideways. In that instant Cazombi *knew* Billie was standing right there, just out of the vid's view range. Suddenly Sorca was thrust aside and General Billie's face, livid with rage, came on the screen, a Clinton clenched between his teeth. "Who the hell you calling a son of a bitch, General?" he growled.

"Billie, I've called you worse than that, you son of a bitch!" Cazombi yelled back. The veins in his neck bulged and his eyes flashed with anger. He was no longer Cazombi the Zombie, but a warrior in full tilt after a defeated enemy, and Jason Billie was standing in his way.

"You forget yourself, General," Billie responded calmly, removing the cigar from his mouth.

At first Cazombi did not know what to say. He could not believe Billie was just standing there chewing on his cigar. He had just announced a stunning victory that if followed up immediately would break Lyons's army and end the war, and here his commander was telling him he'd forgotten himself? Cazombi controlled himself with effort. "General, we have broken through the 4th Division's defensive line and they are in full retreat. The road to Ashburtonville is now open. This is your opportunity to break out of Bataan and split Lyons's army in two. We'll defeat them in detail—"

"I'll be the judge of that, General," Billie responded calmly. "The time is not yet ripe for the breakout. Hold your positions until further notice." The comm screen went dead.

Cazombi stared at the screen openmouthed. The eyes of every man in the command post were focused on him now. Some of the men shook their heads in disbelief, but no one dared to utter a single word. For a long, long moment the only sound was the static of the communications systems connecting the CP with the infantry units.

"I'll be goddamned," Sturgeon whispered at last.

"Not you, Ted, not you," Cazombi said through gritted teeth, "but somebody else is going to think *he* is." Cazombi sighed and his shoulders slumped. "We both know he sent Godalgonz out to Gilbert's Corners to get rid of him, and he sent us down here for the same reason. But instead of tripping over our swords, we've won the damned war for him and the goddamned bastard will sacrifice us so he can get the credit all to himself. He is going to sit up there until the opportunity is lost and then he'll break out in his own good time at the cost of many lives, Ted. And we can't have that." Everyone in the CP heard what he'd just said. Normally, an officer like Cazombi would *never* have made such a statement about his commander in front of his troops. But Lieutenant General Alistair Cazombi had finally arrived at a point in his life when he'd had enough.

"What do we do now, sir?" Sturgeon asked quietly. He noticed that every man in the CP was grinning and nodding his head in agreement with what Cazombi had just said, which was only what they all knew and were all thinking.

Cazombi straightened his shoulders. The anger and dismay disappeared from his face and he was suddenly back to being Cazombi the Zombie once again—calm, unruffled, thinking fast. He spoke now with the authority these men were used to from him. "You turn 34th FIST over to Colonel Ramadan, Ted. You're coming with me." He turned to the colonel commanding his aviation battalion. "George, get me a hopper." He swung around to face the army major general who was his second in command, standing nearby. "Phil, you're the next senior officer of this task force. You take command. Ted and I are going to Bataan. I want you to press the enemy with everything you've got, drive him straight back up the Ashburtonville road, do not ease up on him. You *will* have support from the army on Bataan. Is that clear?"

"Yes, sir!" Koval snapped to attention, grinning fiercely. He knew

Billie's orders had been to stand fast, but Cazombi was his commander and he'd carry out Cazombi's order with vigor.

"Okay, Ted, you and I, we're gonna pay General Jason Billie a little surprise visit."

Sturgeon grinned. "About time. But how are you going to get him to change his mind?" Sturgeon had a feeling he knew what was coming.

Cazombi passed a hand over his closely cropped head. "Well, I'm going to grab that bastard by his stacking swivel and jack his ass up once and for all, and if that don't work, well"—he hesitated and then grinned—"I'm going to *really* get pissed off at him!"

Formally, as if taking a change of command ceremony on the grinder back at Camp Ellis, Sturgeon drew himself to attention. If Cazombi was going to do what Sturgeon suspected, there'd likely be a new commander of 34th FIST by the end of the day. He saluted smartly. "Brigadier Sturgeon requesting orders, sir!" he said in his best parade-ground voice.

The men in the command post broke into cheers.

"Corp' Queege, you take up your position here, you see? This here's a very important road junction. You direct all military traffic up to the ridge there, all civilian traffic thataway,"—the military police captain pointed to the road leading off to the southwest of Phelps—"to the park, where all the civvies are bein' camped. You don't let no one but military personnel up the Ashburtonville road, unnerstan'?"

Queege nodded. "But all by myself, Cap'n? What if someone tries to brush by me?"

"Sheeyit, Corp', you jist shot three men dead this mornin'! Shoot 'em, girl! Yew kin handle this! Tha's why I'm puttin' you here."

"How long I gotta stay here?" Queege asked, glancing apprehensively back at Phelps, which she could see clearly in the distance, about five kilometers toward the sea.

"Until you are relieved," the captain replied quickly, climbing back into his landcar. The rest of the company was already far ahead of the officer. He glanced nervously back toward Phelps and then ahead at the dust of the disappearing vehicles.

"When will that be, sir?"

"Dammit, Queege, when the last elements of the brigade clear the intersection! You jump on the last vehicle and rejoin us on the other side of the ridge.

"Well, Captain, I ain't—" she almost admitted that she'd never pulled MP duty before. Traffic control was one of an MP's main functions, she knew. She wished now she'd stayed a mere clerk. Ahead of her the division was digging in, preparing for a pitched battle; behind her, in the town, the enemy was advancing. Pretty soon she could get caught in the cross fire. But finally she only said "What if I get thirsty?" Before the captain could answer his driver, a wild look in his eyes, slammed the vehicle into forward and left Queege standing in a cloud of dust.

She hefted the canteen on her belt. Damn, it was half empty and the sun wasn't even up to its zenith yet. And she was still hungover from earlier that morning.

Corporal Puella Queege hefted the traffic wand her first sergeant had given her. She ran a hand nervously over the M26 in its holster. She jiggled her canteen. Those items were all that stood between her and . . . what? She didn't want to think about it.

During the next hour, as the sun rose higher in the sky and the intersection grew hotter and dustier, military vehicles roared by. She soon realized they didn't need her to direct them to their positions on the ridge beyond town. They already knew where they were going. She was there to keep the civilians out of the way. Several private cars, some lorries, and buses rumbled down the road to the southwest without hardly even slowing down. They, too, knew precisely where they were going. Puella groaned. Typical military screwup! They needed her here like a mouthful of turds, she reflected sourly. She wondered if she should just start walking up the Ashburtonville road or wait for the next military convoy and hitch a ride.

She licked her lips. Boy, did she need a drink, and not water either!

From the direction of Phelps suddenly came the ripping roar of small-arms fire interspersed with the heavy *thud-thud-thud* of artillery followed almost immediately by blossoming explosions in the town. That was followed almost instantaneously by answering, indirect, and preregistered fire from behind the ridge. In seconds the town was partially obscured in clouds of dust, smoke, and fire.

Puella experienced a horrible sinking sensation in the pit of her

stomach, and she felt an urgent need to rush into the bushes and defe-
cate. There were no bushes along the road from Phelps, but there was a
vehicle coming, roaring along at top speed, a huge rooster tail of dust
billowing out behind it. As it got nearer she could see that it was a civilian landcar. Puella stepped into the intersection, her wand raised trembling above her head and extended to the southwest.

The car screeched to a halt. Puella stepped in front of it.

"Git outen the way!" the driver, a middle-aged man, shouted. His
eyes bulged out of his head and his face was bathed in perspiration that
ran through the dust on his cheeks in dirty rivulets. "I gotta git to Ashburtonville right now!" he yelled.

"Nope, no civilians allowed up that road, sir."

"I got important dispatches fer Gen'ral Lyons from Mayor O'Quinn,
the mayor of Phelps! Now stand aside or you'll be in *big* trouble, missy!"

"Nope. Mayor O'Quinn, didja say, mister?"

"Yes! Important dispatches! Now, let me through or I'll run you
down where you're standin', military police or no military police!"

Puella drew her M26, checked the loading indicator with her
thumb, and leveled it at the man's head. "The mayor's dead, mister. I
shot him myself only this mornin'. Now, you get yer ass on down that
road to the park or I'll shoot you down like I did him 'n' his buddies."

The man squawked, threw the car into reverse, and spun off down
the road to the southwest. "Hey!" Puella shouted after him, "You got any
beer?"

Puella continued standing in the intersection. The intensity of the
battle for Phelps increased dramatically. Suddenly vehicles and running
men began to emerge from the closer outskirts of the town, fleeing pell-
mell toward the division positions on the ridge. She could clearly see
some of them throwing their hands up into the air. An armored vehicle
came tearing up the road from town. Ah, my ride! Puella thought. Less
than a kilometer from where she was standing, the vehicle burst into a
greasy orange ball of flame and crashed into a ditch. No one got out.
Puella swallowed hard. "Time to leave!" she muttered.

"Not so fast!" someone shouted. Puella froze in her tracks and
looked around. No one there. She shook her head. The sun and the
beer had finally gotten to her. She turned to go up the Ashburtonville
road when the voice came again, louder and more insistent. "I said,

Halt! Confederation Marine Corps! One more step and I open fire!"
Someone shoved Puella hard to the ground where she lay stunned in
the dust. Invisible hands disarmed her, bound her arms behind her
back, and hauled her to her feet.

"You are now my prisoner," a harsh male voice said, then the man
laughed.

CHAPTER TWENTY-SEVEN

The flight to Bataan from Phelps was circuitous. First the hopper pilot had to head far out to sea, at wavetop level to avoid ground surveillance systems, then dogleg at very high speed back to land to make it into the sally port at Bataan without getting shot down by the many antiaircraft batteries set up in and around Ashburtonville. But the time the flight took was valuable for Lieutenant General Cazombi because it gave him a chance to talk to Brigadier Sturgeon.

"Ted, we're stepping into a hornet's nest doing this. Billie's going to be very highly upset to see us arriving unannounced at his headquarters. He will most certainly accuse us of abandoning our posts. I know you meant it when you said you'd back me up, but are you truly ready to take the shit he's going to hand us when we get in? Truly?"

"I am. But Alistair, what *will* you do if he refuses to budge, arrests us even, for deserting our posts?"

"I am through taking any crap off this guy. I will do what has to be done, Ted. Before this little visit is over, we could be charged with a lot more than just desertion in the face of the enemy." He threw a hard look at Sturgeon as he said this.

"You mean—?"

"I am not taking any more off this tin soldier, Ted. He is either going to mount his breakout and support our men at Phelps or . . ." He gestured with one hand.

"Or?"

"I am."

Sturgeon did not reply at once. He let the implication sink in first, and then said with a shrug, "In for a penny, in for a pound, as Grandmother Sturgeon used to say."

Cazombi grimaced. "Caught with the crows, you suffer with the crows, as Grandmother Cazombi used to say." The hopper made a violent jink toward land. "Tighten your cheeks, Ted. Once more unto the breach, as Henry V once said."

The chief bosun's mate sitting in his control tower was astonished to see two flag officers, uniforms stained with the dust of combat, jump out of the hopper as it came to rest inside the aerial sally port. The pilot had radioed ahead that two VIPs were coming in, but he hadn't said who they were or what their business was except that it was top priority, so the chief had cleared all traffic until they touched down.

Cazombi tapped on the tower window and shouted, "We're here to see General Billie. Where can we find him? Word I had last night was he'd be in the command center all day today. Still valid, Chief?"

Major General Sorca, the army's chief of staff, issued to all elements of General Billie's army a daily roster showing every principal staff officer's whereabouts for the entire day, every day of the week. This was a routine peacetime practice in every headquarters, one that General Billie had continued even though he was commanding a field army in combat, where schedules changed frequently and without warning. The chief consulted a display. "Quadrant 54G, sir, until 1043, then he's meeting with the chief of staff."

"What? I thought—" Cazombi consulted his chronometer. It was 1020; they'd have plenty of time to get to Quadrant 54G. "Probably having a cigar smoke-in," Cazombi said to Sturgeon. "Who's he with, Chief?"

The chief consulted his vid screen again. "Says here G1 and some other staff members, sir. Something about Morale and Welfare, it says."

"What time did the conference start?" Cazombi asked.

"Zero eight forty-five, sir."

Cazombi and Sturgeon exchanged glances. That was where Billie had been when Cazombi called him from Phelps to announce the breakthrough and he'd put him off to talk about "morale and welfare" matters when the fate of the army hung in the balance? "I don't remember this on the goddamned schedule Sorca sent us last night," he said to Sturgeon.

"Sez here it was changed first thing this morning, sir."

"And we weren't informed," Sturgeon added, exchanging a significant glance with Cazombi.

"Chief, where, exactly, is Quadrant 54G?" The chief swiveled his display around so Cazombi could see it. "Jesus." Cazombi sighed. "Way the hell down in the bowels of this place. Thanks, Chief! Ted, let's get started."

But when they got to Quadrant 54G they found that Billie had left early for the command center. They were both perspiring heavily when they finally reached him. General Billie, sitting at a console in the middle of the room, was in the middle of a meeting with what looked like his full staff variously sitting and standing around him.

"Sir, you've got to attack *now*!" Cazombi shouted, barging through the door, followed closely by Brigadier Sturgeon. Heads swiveled in surprise. General Billie's head snapped up from a display as if he'd seen Banquo's ghost.

Wh-What the hell?" General Jason Billie, face instantly flushing a bright red, shouted. "General, what are you doing here?" The staff officers and commanders sitting around Billie shifted uncomfortably in their chairs. Personnel elsewhere in the army's command center, startled by the outburst, and Cazombi's unexpected entry into the room, stopped what they were doing to eavesdrop on the argument.

"Sir." Cazombi leaned over Billie's console. "You've got your hammer and anvil, Task Force Cazombi is pushing up the Ashburtonville road. You've got to attack *now*, before Lyons moves his army!" he pleaded. "You've got to pin him in place. Sir!"

"General, is that why you deserted your post?" Billie responded calmly, "Return at once to your men and I will not charge you with desertion! The time is not yet ripe for us to mount our breakout. We have to wait until the Marines get farther along the road—"

"You goddamned fool!" Cazombi yelled, having lost every shred of his famous self-control. "The son of a bitch has taken out the string-of-pearls so the fleet can't follow his movements! If you sit there on your ass and let Lyons get away, this'll turn into a war of maneuver and you'll have lost whatever chance you ever had to crush him here! If he gets away we'll have to go after him and fight him on his own ground. The dumbest private soldier in this army knows that, General. So what's your excuse?"

General Billie's chair went clattering to the floor as he leaped to his feet. "You black bastard! You have opposed me ever since I took command here! You are a scheming, disloyal officer," he screamed. "I'll have no more of this! You are relieved, General!" he thundered.

Cazombi moved swiftly. He reached across the desk, grabbed Billie by the front of his well-tailored uniform blouse, pulled him off his feet and partly over his desk. "Now you listen to me for a change," he said. "I am relieving *you* of command of this army. You have done nothing but screw up this war and get our boys killed, and I am officially taking over. Sergeant"—he turned to the military-police sergeant in charge of the security detail who was standing by, gaping at what was happening—"escort General Billie to his quarters and stand guard over him there until you are properly relieved."

"Yes, sir!" The sergeant snapped to attention.

"Cazombi, what are you doing?" Billie shrieked, "This is *mutiny*! Sergeant! Stand fast! No, no! Do something, man! Arrest this officer! I order you to arrest this traitor! Do it! Do it now!" he screamed. The other officers in the staff meeting had jumped to their feet and were now standing nervously around the room, as if afraid they'd catch something if they interfered in any way. All except Brigadier Ted Sturgeon, who took up a stance beside the MP sergeant.

"Sir, what do I *do*?" the MP whispered to Sturgeon.

"Sergeant, you're the cop, it's your decision," Sturgeon whispered back, "but if I were you, I'd *arrest the bastard!*" Those words penetrated into every corner of the command center, burning into the memory of every man present.

Billie and Cazombi stood in a frozen tableau in the center of the room. "Balca! Balca!" Billie screamed at his chief of staff. "Do something! Don't just stand there, *do something!*" he demanded.

General Balca Sorca shifted nervously from one foot to the other and looked at the floor.

The MP sergeant glanced first at one officer and then at the other, not sure which one to obey, but sure he knew who the "bastard" was.

Already two of his men were standing by, looking to him for orders. Suddenly he felt a sickening weakness in his colon. After weeks of twiddling his thumbs on this deadly boring security detail, he had to make a decision. Often in the affair of war chance decrees that the action of one man makes the difference between victory or defeat. Now the entire outcome of the war against the secessionists depended on what Sergeant Maximilian Heck, 716th Military Police Company, would do next.

Sergeant Heck stepped forward to where the two generals stood, came to attention, and saluted smartly. All eyes were on him at that moment. "General Ca-Cazombi," he stuttered, "uh, I mean, *General Billie,* sir, would you please come with me?"

Billie screamed threats all the way to his quarters.

"Sir." Brigadier Ted Sturgeon stood at attention, facing General Cazombi. "What are your orders?" From somewhere in the back of the command post someone started a cheer.

"Unmask the laser batteries!" General Davis Lyons ordered. "And give me a 1:25,000 of this grid." He zoomed in on the northwestern portion of the huge topographical vid that covered one wall of his command post. "Here." He pointed to a small village at the foot of the Cumber Mountain Range about 150 kilometers northwest of Ashburtonville. "Here's where I want to set up my command post. Rene," he said, turning to Colonel Raggel, "start packing for the move!"

The shock that had frozen Lyons's commanders and staff into statuary at the news that the enemy had landed on the coast and taken Phelps vanished instantly at the sound of his voice. "General," he said to the army's artillery commander, "I want your laser batteries trained on those satellites. Take them out! We can't have their fleet observing our movements." Acknowledging the command, the artilleryman saluted perfunctorily and departed for his post. Lyons had wisely kept several powerful batteries of antisatellite lasers hidden around Ashburtonville just in case he needed them to take out the string-of-pearls that were the Confederation's eyes on his army.

"Ops?" Lyons turned to his operations officer.

"The 4th Division is retreating up the Ashburtonville road, sir. General Sneed reports the enemy is hard on his rear and pressing him vigorously."

"Can he hold them at all?"

"No, sir."

Lyons thought for a moment. "You"—he gestured at one of his mechanized infantry division commanders—"take your division down the road toward Phelps and reinforce Sneed's troops, or what's left of them. You *must* delay the enemy advance, if only for an hour or two." Lyons regarded his commanders. With this attack on their rear, the entire war had suddenly turned against the Coalition forces. Suddenly the air was broken by the unique *cra-a-a-ak* of the laser cannon. Lyons smiled. He might just pull this off. "Gentlemen, I want the 24th Embata and the 3rd Sagunto divisions to remain in place here. Raise as much hell with Billie's defenses as you can. He must be convinced this army is intact and ready to oppose him when he tries to break out.

"Everyone else"—he pointed again to the map—"the Coalition government has already removed to the Cumbers from Gilbert's Corners. They've made considerable improvement to the limestone caverns out there. We'll fortify ourselves up there and make the Confederation come to us and we'll cut them to ribbons. Engineers?" He turned to his G4 officer. "Get them out there *now!* Deepen and improve the fortifications. They have their work cut out for them." The grim-faced army logistics officer hurried off to get his engineers moving. "Gentlemen," Lyons said to his remaining commanders, "return to your commands and get ready to move to, to"—he turned back to the map and located the village at the foot of the Cumber massif—"Austen. Oh, G5," he said to his civil affairs officer, "you'd better get on out there and evacuate the civilians, everyone but the government officials holed up in the caves. The residents don't need to be involved in this, and since the Coalition wanted this war, set the damned thing up on us, they can stand with my army. Take an MP battalion with you; we'll need them in place when the traffic picks up." Lyons clapped his hands together. "I'll have a movement order to you in a little while, gentlemen. Now get moving and good luck!" With a scraping of chairs and a gathering up of equipment, General Lyons's commanders departed the CP in a rush.

"Sir? What about the government out in the Cumbers? Should we let them know we're coming?" Colonel Raggel asked.

Lyons stuck the stub of a Davidoff between his teeth and regarded his aide out of one eye. "Fuck 'em. They'll know when the MPs get there. If this maneuver doesn't work, Rene, it's not them we'll have to worry about, it's *them!*" He nodded toward General Jason Billie's fortifications on Bataan—unaware General Jason Billie was no longer in command there.

CHAPTER TWENTY-EIGHT

General Billie's screams of protest could still be heard clearly, receding down the corridor, when General Cazombi slapped his thigh with one hand and said to the assembled officers who still stood, frozen at the recently concluded spectacle, "Okay, people, let's get this show on the road!"

As if brought out of a spell, the staff came back to life and crowded around Cazombi. "I'm making some changes in the army's organization," Cazombi announced. "First, Brigadier Sturgeon, you will immediately assume duty as my chief of staff. Get a message to Colonel Ramadan that 34th FIST is his until further notice. General Sorca," he said grimly to Balca Sorca, formerly General Billie's chief of staff, who had stood by silently relieved that Billie had been removed from command, but now anticipated his own disgrace, "you are now the deputy commander of this Army." Cazombi permitted himself an amused grin at the expression of surprise that now crossed Sorca's face.

"Th-Thank you, sir," Sorca stuttered. Sorca knew very well that the position of deputy commander was essentially a dead end, that it was the chief of staff who really controlled an army, but he was thankful Cazombi hadn't had him dragged off to a detention cell along with Billie. For his part, Cazombi had not forgotten how Sorca had come to him and advised him to relieve Billie, an act of considerable moral courage.

"Ted, a message to General Koval." Cazombi turned to Brigadier

Sturgeon. "He is now in command of Task Force Cazombi, which we will now rename Task Force Koval." Cazombi actually smiled when he said this. "He is to push on up the Ashburtonville road with all possible speed. We will break out and link up with him on the outskirts of the city—"

"Sir!" It was Captain Bulldog Bukok, the Task Force 79 liaison officer. "Word just in from Admiral Wang: Lyons has taken out the string-of-pearls again. He must have kept antisatellite batteries masked around Ashburtonville for an emergency. The fleet won't be able to track him if he tries to regroup outside the current area of operations."

"Map, 1:50,000," Sturgeon ordered, and a tactical map of the Ashburtonville area of operations sprang onto the vid screen. "Captain, didn't Fleet inform General Billie that an interrogation had revealed a plan to move the Coalition government to . . .?" He glanced at Bukok, who nodded at Brigadier General Wyllyums, the army's intelligence officer.

"That's true, sir. They were moved to the town of Austen in the Cumber Mountains. Zoom in on that section, please," Wyllyums said to the operations sergeant running the display.

The staff studied the overlay silently for a moment and then General Cazombi whistled. "That's where the old fox is headed, gentlemen!" He slammed a fist on the table. "I'll bet he's long ago sent an advance party out there to fortify the place. Used to be an old salt mine in those foothills, right, General Wyllyums?" Wyllyums nodded. "It's a great place for a last stand, gentlemen." Everyone fell into another moment of silent contemplation. "That's why Lyons kept those batteries in hiding around Ashburtonville and that's why he used them to take out the string-of-pearls. He's going to retreat to the Cumbers!"

"Sir," said Brigadier Wyllyums, "please note the road network between here and Austen. It runs mostly through a very dense forest populated with some enormous trees, some of them a hundred meters in height or more. They'll use those forests to screen their movements."

"Makes good sense. General Thayer." He turned to his operations officer. "I want everything that can fly in the air over the route to Austen, everything. Attack every target along the way, I don't care of it's a shithouse, put ordnance on everything including bridges and the roads themselves. Crater them and knock down the bridges."

"We'll lose aircraft and pilots, sir. Lyons has a very strong air-defense capability."

"I know, I know, but it's got to be done. We've got to hurt Lyons as much as we can before he can consolidate his forces in those mountains. If he gets there unscathed this war could drag on forever, and frankly I don't relish the thought of an assault on the Cumbers. Meanwhile, gentlemen"—Cazombi turned to the rest of the staff—"goose your subordinate commanders to stand by and prepare for action. Billie never prepared an operations order for a breakout, so we're going to have to do that right now. And somebody take out those goddamned antisatellite batteries! All right, let's *move!* We're already a day late and a dollar short."

The officer commanding General Davis Lyons's antisatellite laser batteries and all of his men bravely volunteered to stay behind to cover the army's withdrawal to the relative safety of the mines in the Cumber Mountains. That one act of heroism was probably what saved the bulk of the Coalition's forces from utter destruction.

Wellford Brack, now a sergeant in the Mylex Provisional Infantry Brigade, sat in the lead vehicle of his company convoy, Private Amitus Sparks driving. Normally an officer would've had that honor but casualties had been high among the brigade's officers and now sergeants performed many of their duties. Their orders were not to use the main highway but to travel offroad as much as possible, keep their stealth suites in a high state of performance, and maintain a sharp lookout for Confederation Raptors which everyone was sure would pounce on them as soon as the army on Bataan realized Lyons was withdrawing his forces.

"Hunnert klicks to go in this shit," Sparks muttered as their tactical vehicle bounced over the rough ground. A lighted Capricorn hung from one side of his mouth as he drove.

"Put that gawdam thing out!" Brack ordered, reaching over and snatching the cigarette. "Damned things'll kill you, Amie."

"Sarge!" Sparks protested.

"Amie, you dumb shit, you can't drive this thing 'n' smoke at the same time! Keep your eyes on the terrain!"

"Geez, Wellers, we're in a friggin' combat zone, might die any minute, 'n' you worry about me dying of cancer from these cigarettes?"

"I ain't worried about you, Einstein. You lower-ranking enlisted swine are expendable. I jus' don't wanna get ashes on my clean uniform. You oughta take up a *clean* habit, like chewing." Brack spit tobacco juice into a small, splashproof container.

"Clean?" Sparks grimaced. "That gawdam Deadman weed you chew?"

"It's called Redman, you ignoramus."

"We hit another bump like the last one 'n' that shit'll fly all over the inside of this vehicle. When the Raptors get us we'll be parboiled in your friggin' tobacco juices! Raptors ain't got no respect even fer you higher-ranking noncommissioned swine. Yeah," Sparks said, suddenly hit by another thought. "They calls it Deadman 'cause you'll die of cancer of the mouth, you chew enough of that shit. Well, mebbe not, they kin always do a mouth transplant on ya. Be a big improvement over the piehole you was born with."

"Amie, why don't you shut yer yap 'n' kiss the opposite end of my alimentary canal?" Brack chuckled. The banter relieved somewhat the tension he was under, but his uniform was still soaked with nervous perspiration.

They were plowing through scrub where the ground was particularly uneven, probably from the furrows of an old crop field, and driving over it was extremely difficult in the pitch darkness even with the vehicle's night-vision optics at full power. "Watch for them trees, Amie," he warned. There weren't many of them but they were big. "Be my ass if I let you run this convoy into a friggin' tree."

"Yeah? You got enough ass to go 'round for everybody, Mr. Tons of Fun," Sparks muttered. For some reason he thought of Suey Ruston, the third member of their original fire team, killed some weeks before. He was having difficulty remembering what Suey looked like.

Brack, firmly secured to his seat, busied himself checking the stealth and aircraft surveillance systems. They were not using the highway that ran parallel to their route because the macadam retained enough heat from the day to show up as a bright ribbon of light on an aircraft's infrared sensors. Were vehicles, even vehicles with stealth systems turned on to full capacity, to drive along the road, they would present a contrasting image and give attacking aircraft potentially juicy targets. As it was, Brack worried that once the enemy's fighters got airborne they might just do a reconnaissance by fire, strafing and bombing at random along the shoulder of the road. The convoy was spread out for ten kilometers behind him with plenty of interval between each vehicle, but a lucky secondary explosion could still expose them.

The vehicle bounced violently. "Amie, slow down!" Brack shouted. "You damned near ruined my family jewels!"

"Sorry, Sarge, but sooner we get to Austen sooner we can get under cover. Ah, screw it!" he muttered, fumbling another Capricorn out of its pack. Brack sighed, leaned over, and gave him a light.

Cruising at 2,600 meters, just under the sound barrier, Ensign Bondo Kano, Falcon Four, in his A8E VSTOL Raptor fighter-bomber was the first and only pilot in his squadron to get airborne. He was fragged to pursue the enemy toward the Cumber Mountains and attack any target of opportunity. The antiaircraft fire from the enemy positions around Ashburtonville had been particularly intense as he climbed for altitude. His defense array had successfully deflected several direct hits from the enemy's laser cannon; Falcon Three had not been so lucky and had gone down.

The highway to Austen stretched out below him, a bright green strip in the darkness. He fired four of his sixteen onboard AGM34 missiles into the strip to crater the roadway. They exploded with brilliant flashes in the darkness. He made a wide arc west-to-east and came in to cut across the road at a right angle. There was a bridge down there; he could see it clearly through his infrared optics. He drew no antiaircraft fire on his pass. Was it undefended or were the AA batteries masked, waiting for a better shot? It was not a long bridge. It could be replaced quickly if the enemy had bridging equipment. No matter, it was a target and he was going to take it out. He climbed for altitude and doubled back, going into a steep dive. Suddenly the entire landscape below lighted up with AA fire. "Holy shit!" he exclaimed. "Falcon Four, bridge at XT945231 is hot, repeat hot!" he informed his controller. He let the onboard computer system guide the Raptor now, jinking it wildly to avoid the probing fingers of energy reaching out to him from the batteries protecting the bridge; the aircraft shuttered violently as its defensive system bled off several direct hits from the laser batteries.

Kano took back control of his Raptor and dived for the deck, skimming along twenty-five meters above the ground at Mach 2. "Okay, motherfuckers," he whispered, "I am going to light you up now." He gained altitude as soon as his instruments told him he was out of range of the guns and headed back to the southeast, toward Ashburtonville, unloading his munitions along the west shoulder of the road. Then he doubled back to cover the opposite shoulder. When his missiles were gone he strafed with his laser cannon. Suddenly a huge plume of greasy orange flashed by behind him. "Gotcha!" Kano exulted. He zoomed in low for another pass and was gratified to see more secondary explosions. He'd found an enemy convoy! He blurted out the target coordinates, zooming along at treetop level now, his laser cannons winking and flashing death and destruction onto the vehicles strung out below. *"Ah-haaaaaaaa!"* he screamed. This was what he was born to do! He'd never felt better in his life. It was at that moment Ensign Bondo Kano flew smack into a tree that towered fifty meters above the scrub.

"Enemy aircraft approaching! Disperse! Disperse!" the convoy commander shouted over the tactical net.

"Move! Move! Move!" Brack shouted. Frantically, Sparks spun off away from the road. A terrific roaring noise passed overhead as the fighter-bomber made its first pass above the convoy. Now the tactical net was alive with shouting and screaming. Somewhere very close behind them a vehicle burst into flames, momentarily dimming the night-vision optics in the glare of its destruction. "Jesus!" Brack whispered. He was beginning to perspire heavily. Sparks grunted. Their vehicle bounced and jumped over ruts and underbrush, literally flying through the air in some places, coming to earth in a bone-jarring crash. Only the vehicle's excellent suspension system kept the occupants from sustaining serious injury.

"We're being slaughtered," Sparks squeaked, his voice several octaves above its normal pitch. Brack thought about making some snide remark about "family jewels," but he was too scared to get the words out.

"Faster, goddammit!" Brack screamed, his voice coming back. "Get the hell away from here!" The pair bounced up and down in their restraints but they didn't care; their only thought was to get away from the enemy aircraft that was savaging the convoy. Suddenly Brack screamed a warning. Right in front of them was *another* vehicle stopped dead in its tracks. Sparks saw it too but not soon enough to avoid it. They ran into its rear at thirty kilometers an hour. They hardly had time to brace themselves for impact.

Brack sat in his seat, stunned. Sparks had banged his head hard against the instrument panel and slumped unconscious in his harness. Had he not been securely strapped into his seat, the impact might have killed him. Brack sat there controlling his breathing. He dared not dismount from the vehicle and expose himself to the attacking aircraft's IR system or both vehicles would be fired on. *Well, here is as good as any-place to wait out the attack,* he thought. Suddenly the vehicle they'd run into burst into fire. The crash had ruptured its fuel cell, and flames roared up and began engulfing both vehicles!

Brack sat frozen into his harness. Flames were everywhere. He could see Sparks's clothes beginning to burn and felt himself catching fire. He fumbled at his harness. He felt no pain, only horror. He was going to burn to death, he knew it. *Aw, fuck it,* he thought, *may as well just die right here.* Then he felt the pain. *No, goddammit, I'm not going to die here!* He released his harness and opened the door. He put an arm up to shield his face and noticed his hands were on fire. But he was not going to die there, not if there was a chance to live. Clothes on fire, he stumbled out of the burning vehicle, staggered a few meters and flopped to the ground where he began rolling in the dirt to put out the fire. Someone ran up to him, grabbed him under the arms and dragged him away from the burning vehicles as they exploded in a huge ball of flame.

Someone flashed a light and muttered, "He's dead, poor bastard's dead!"

"*No I am not!*" Brack gasped.

Private Amitus Sparks died in his vehicle but Sergeant Wellford

Brack made it back to a field surgical hospital in Austen along with a few survivors from his unit. No more aircraft came back that night, but Ensign Bondo Kano had effectively decimated what was left of the Mylex Provisional Infantry Brigade. That was just a taste of what was in store for the rest of Davis Lyons's army.

CHAPTER TWENTY-NINE

Lance Corporal Dave "Hammer" Schultz toggled his helmet comm off and allowed himself to groan. The wound he'd aggravated a week earlier when he left the hospital to help repulse the Coalition's attempt to penetrate the Bataan defenses hurt from the shaking of the Dragon he rode toward fresh combat. But damned if he was going to admit to *anybody* that the Hammer was in pain. If only they'd *get* where they were going—once they were off the Dragon and he took his rightful place in third platoon's most exposed position, the adrenaline and endorphins surging through his bloodstream would blot out the pain. But the ride seemed to be taking forever.

The ride wouldn't have been so bad by itself, but it was the third ride that day. The first was the longest, with the Dragons in the bellies of Essays in flight from Bataan to north of the camp of the 7th Independent Military Police Battalion. There hadn't been enough action at the camp for Schultz's body to pump enough adrenaline and endorphins to overcome the pain he'd suffered on the flight. The two subsequent firefights hadn't been enough, either. So he was in pain, but *damned* if Hammer Schultz would let anybody know!

Suddenly, the roar of the Dragon's fans shrieked higher, then rumbled down, and the armored vehicle settled to the ground. Its rear ramp dropped and the Marines surged out and to both sides. Then Marines scrambled to get out of the Dragon's way as it rose back up on its air cushions and spun about to head off to pick up Marines from a company in another FIST.

Schultz already had his infra screen in place by the time he exited the Dragon. As soon as the beast was out of the way, he looked to his sides and saw the red blotches of chameleoned Marines on his flanks, and beyond them. He raised his infra to take in the terrain. It was prairie that reached several kilometers, to what looked to be a dense forest. The undulations of the ground were barely visible through the vegetation, mostly grasslike and mixed shrubs that seemed seldom more than waist high. The land was higher to the right, and sloped almost imperceptibly to the left.

Schultz toggled his comm back on before he growled. Nine of the thirty Marines of third platoon had already been wounded on the campaign, and two others were killed. That was too damn many good Marines down; somebody was going to pay. And Hammer Schultz was just the swinging dick to collect the bill.

Twenty meters to Schultz's left and rear, he made out the command group. Ensign Charlie Bass was on comm, talking to Captain Conorado. The platoon commander said something to Staff Sergeant Hyakowa, then Hyakowa's voice came over the platoon circuit.

"Third platoon! Second squad has point. Then guns and first squad. The word is we've got them on the run and we're getting close to their tail-end Charlie. So Hammer, step lively. Move out."

"You heard the man, people," Sergeant Kerr said on the squad circuit. "Second fire team, me, first team, third team. Move it."

Schultz lurched to his feet and barely bothered to check his direction before he stepped forward, leading Company L toward the last known position of a Coalition army brigade. Schultz's pain was forgotten; he was where he was supposed to be, and doing his proper job. He barely heard Corporal Claypoole say, "Hammer, me, Ymenez." That was the order the fire team always went in. Schultz grinned; his back was usually covered by the two worst goofballs in the company. He grinned wider; he also knew they were two of the the company's best fighters. His grin vanished; MacIlargie was out, badly wounded, and he didn't yet know how good a Marine Ymenez was. He stepped off between a tuft of grass and a shrub, disturbing neither in his passage. Claypoole followed fifteen meters behind.

Schultz hadn't gone far enough for all of Company L to exit the drop zone before he felt a tingling at the base of his neck. Without stopping, he turned to look toward the source of his sudden perception. Through the ground cover, he could just barely make out a long, low rise two hundred meters to the right. It was an ideal position to set an ambush. But was anybody actually there?

Schultz slipped both his magnifier and infra screens into place and scanned the rise. *There!* Seventy-five meters ahead he spotted a small red blotch in the brush right at the top of the rise. He watched it for a few seconds—it could be a small prairie grazer—until he saw the glint of a reflection in the middle of the red blotch. He hadn't heard of any animal on Ravenette that reflected light the way glass does. So it had to be a man, mostly hidden behind the rise. But was the man an observation post, an artillery observer, or an officer preparing to give the command for his troops to come up from hiding and open fire on the Marines passing below?

"Rock," Schultz said into the squad circuit, knowing that everyone in the squad, the platoon command group, and someone in the company command group would hear what he said to his fire team leader. He recalculated the distance. "Ahead, six-five mikes, right two hundred. Observation." He used a minimum of words, but everybody who heard would know exactly where and what he meant.

"How many?" Claypoole asked as he scanned the area Schultz indicated.

"See one." Schultz continued examining the rise. *There!* He saw another, fifty meters to his rear. "Two. Kerr's flank."

"I have him," Kerr said a few seconds later. "Keep moving."

"Are they using infras?" Claypoole asked.

Schultz grunted, how could he know? But he thought the observer must be using some sort of infrared lens or filter on his optics—otherwise he wouldn't be able to observe the Marines. Schultz looked back and saw that the observers didn't need infrared optics; most of the Marines behind him weren't carefully stepping between grasses and shrubs—they were making a visible trail through the vegetation.

Captain Conorado listened in and silently swore. Mike Company was moving in column a klick to Company L's right, which was why he hadn't sent flankers along the rise. "Two Actual, this is Six Actual," he said on the command circuit. "Who do you still have at Delta Zulu?" Second platoon was bringing up the company's rear and part of it was still at Delta Zulu, the drop zone where the Dragons had let the company off.

"Six Actual, Two," Ensign Molina answered immediately. "Two Five, one squad, and"—he checked his UPUD—"one gun team."

"Send them to flank the back side of the rise on the right. I want to know what's there."

"Will do, Six." Molina switched to the platoon command circuit. "You get that, Chway?" he asked.

"We're on it," Staff Sergeant Chway, second platoon's platoon sergeant said. He had begun moving the half-platoon still in the drop zone looping back as soon as he'd heard Conorado's order. His idea was to swing beyond the near flank of whoever was behind the rise before approaching them.

"Everybody keep moving," Conorado ordered on the company command circuit. "I've sent flankers, they'll let us know what's there." He turned to Lance Corporal Escarpo, his comm man, and told him to get an infra feed from the string-of-pearls, or whatever surveillance the navy had of the area.

"I'm trying for it, sir," Escarpo said. "There are big gaps in the string-of-pearls coverage."

"Keep trying."

"Aye aye, sir."

Conorado toggled to the battalion circuit and reported the situation to Commander van Winkle. Van Winkle said he'd see if he or Brigadier Sturgeon could goose the navy into getting some infra coverage. Conorado thanked him and signed off, but he knew that unless the navy could simply flip a switch, there was no chance of getting infra coverage in time to do the company any good in the current situation.

On the point, Schultz kept scanning the rise with his infra and magnifier screens. As far ahead as he could detect, there seemed to be an observer every seventy-five to one hundred meters. He reported every one he saw with a terse, "Up one hundred. Up one-eighty," or whatever the range was from his current position.

Conorado listened in, but kept silent. He plotted each position on his map as Schultz reported it. If the point man was right—and Conorado had no reason to believe otherwise—and each known observer was a platoon commander, there had to be an entire battalion on the high ground, waiting for Company L to get too far into the ambush's killing zone for anybody to be able to back out. He looked along the line of the company's route; the trail the Marines made through the grass and shrubs was obvious. Even without using his infra screen, he could make out where individual Marines were by the way the vegetation moved. One of the Marines' major advantages, the virtual invisibility conferred on them by their chameleon uniforms, was negated by the vegetation.

He looked at his map again. If each plotted position was a platoon commander, the enemy was set in a very tightly packed line, too tight for the Marines to be able to charge across the two hundred meters of prairie and break through them. *Buddha's blue balls,* he thought, *when the enemy on the rise opens fire, Company L is going to be chewed up before Mike Company can close in and hit the ambush from the rear. Then the Coalition troops will turn about and chew up Mike Company.*

"Oh. My. God." Conorado heard Chway's voice on the command circuit. "They're almost shoulder to shoulder for more than a klick and a half, maybe two klicks."

"Two Five," Conorado said tightly. He knew that he couldn't wait for infra images from above. "What weapons do you see?"

"Six Actual, mostly fléchette rifles. They seem to have one assault gun per platoon unit."

"Two Five, can you lay down enfilading fire?"

"That's an affirmative, Six."

Conorado knew that he didn't need the infra images, not unless the Coalition had other forces in the area that his Marines hadn't yet spotted. "Get into position to do so. Let me know when you're in position, then wait for my command." But he knew that the Coalition army was on the run, so it was unlikely that this unit had reinforcements nearby.

"Aye aye, Six."

Conorado switched to the all-hands circuit. "On my command, drop to your right and open fire on the rise to the right. Until then, continue moving." He looked back and saw the tail of the company, less the squad and gun with Chway, was entering the ambush's killing zone.

It didn't take long for second platoon's Bravo unit to get into position.

"Six Actual, Two Five. In position," Chway reported little more than a minute after receiving the order.

"Now hear this," Conorado said over the all-hands circuit. "When the flanking element opens fire, everybody go down to the right and use volley fire on the rise." Then to Chway, "On my mark. One. Two. Three!"

Fire from the assault gun and ten blasters with Chway erupted into the near end of the enemy line and began racing along it. The nearest Coalition soldiers screamed and died as the plasma bolts burned through them. The next were surprised and failed to return fire before the continuing rain of plasma reached them and they started dying. Farther along the line, many of the soldiers heard fire and began shooting before their officers gave the command. Many but not all, and the hesitation of some saved many of the Marines.

When the first bolt went off, Claypoole shouted, "Down to the right!" echoing the squad leaders all along the company column.

Schultz was on the ground and firing before the last of Claypoole's words were out.

"Second squad," Sergeant Kerr ordered into the squad circuit, "volley fire. Five meters below the top. *Fire!*"

The ten blasters of second squad went off almost simultaneously, making a ragged *crack-sizzle*. The bolts didn't hit in a straight line, but were closer when Kerr shouted *"Fire!"* the second time. The bolts hit the ground five meters below the top of the rise and broke apart to fan out across the top of the rise. Screams came faintly to the Marines as the spattering bits of starstuff from their blasters found men scrambling to the top of the rise to fire down on the Marines. Kerr ordered another volley, then ordered, "Move left!" The Marines of second squad rolled three or four meters to their left and tried to find faint ripples in the ground to give them some cover from the tiny darts buzzing their way. The Marines had to move; there was no mistaking exactly where blaster fire came from. Anybody who saw the light trail of a bolt could return fire to its point of origin and hit the shooter.

All along the line, other squad leaders also had their men move. In many cases, fléchettes or fire from assault guns plunged into the ground a Marine had just vacated. The assault guns had a harder time moving; they were crew-served weapons mounted on tripods. Two Marines had to pick up the platoon-level guns to move them; the bigger guns of the assault platoon had to be dismounted from their tripods before they could be moved. The guns fired long bursts, spraying a wide swath of the rise just before they moved. Then they had to change overheated barrels before they could resume firing.

Here and there along the line, a Marine screamed and a squad's fire slackened slightly as fléchettes found their marks. But the fire from the top of the rise slackened more—the disciplined fire from the Marines sent many of the Coalition soldiers back down behind the top where they couldn't return fire, and the spreading fans of the plasma bolts hitting just in front of the top hit those who dared rise high enough to fire down on the Marines.

"On my flank," Schultz growled into the squad circuit.

Kerr poked his head up high enough to see over the grass and shrubs. "Claypoole, move your people," he ordered—more than a platoon of Coalition soldiers were maneuvering from the far end of the ambush line toward the end of the Marine line.

"Oh, shit," Claypoole murmured when he looked to his left and saw the soldiers, now only a hundred meters away. "Ymenez, let's move it!" He scuttled to the left of Schultz, who had turned to face the new threat. A glance to his own left told him Lance Corporal Ymenez was with him.

Kerr reported the situation to the platoon command group, then ordered Corporal Chan to move his fire team to the left of second fire team.

Ensign Bass reported the situation to Captain Conorado and made a suggestion, which the captain approved. Bass radioed Kerr. "Tim, move your entire squad into a blocking position and stop the flanking element."

"Will do, boss," Kerr replied, then moved his third fire team onto line with the rest of the squad.

* * *

At the back end of the ambush, where the first bolts had been fired, Staff Sergeant Chway requested permission to move his squad and gun forward, to get closer to the soldiers he was engaged with. Conorado checked his situation map, and ordered Ensign Molina to take the rest of his platoon to join with the Bravo element and begin rolling up that flank of the Coalition line. Little fire was coming now from the first five hundred meters of the ambushing battalion, so he ordered first platoon's Ensign Antoni to move one of his squads so it could bring fire down the length of the rise.

When all of second squad was on line, Kerr ordered his men to pick individual targets and take them out. A few of the advancing soldiers dropped, obviously hit, and the rest of them went down, taking advantage of the concealment of the grasses and shrubs.

"Kneeling position, Marines," Kerr ordered. "I'll make a mark, then volley fire." Kneeling, the Marines could see over the grass. Kerr aimed his blaster where he thought the bolt would strike about twenty meters in front of the hidden enemy soldiers, and said, "On my mark, *fire!*"

Ten plasma bolts flashed out from the short line of Marines and struck in a line, burning swaths through the ground cover. Manic, undisciplined fléchette fire came back from the enemy, but all the darts missed.

"*Fire!*" Kerr commanded, and ten more bolts flashed out, burning new tracks through the grass. "*Fire!*" Again and again, until an area of ground the width of a platoon was bare and seared, beginning seventy-five meters away and extending nearly forty meters deep. Some soldiers lay writhing on that ground, in agony from their wounds. Others lay motionless in death. The remainder of the flanking element was running away.

Before Kerr could decide whether to pursue by fire, or turn the squad back to fight the soldiers on the rise, Ymenez yelped and fell over. "Back on line," Kerr ordered. "Kill that son of a bitch!"

"Already got him," Schultz growled. "Get his friends." In seconds, second squad was back on line, firing volleys at the rise.

A cheer from his right drew Kerr's attention. He looked and his infra screen showed second platoon advancing at a trot along the top of the rise, and most of first squad racing across the prairie at an angle to join up with first platoon. The enemy was on the run. The Marines had walked into an ambush and turned it back on the enemy. The battalion that had intended to hit Company L with a death blow instead joined in what was becoming a general rout.

Lance Corporal Ymenez wasn't badly injured; a single fléchette had torn a gouge along his shoulder. Doc Hough slathered the gouge with antiseptic and slapped some synthskin on it, and Ymenez continued in the hunt for stragglers.

Hammer Schultz's pains were long forgotten.

CHAPTER THIRTY

Doctor—now Colonel—Ezekiel Vance stood up wearily as General Lyons entered his tiny cubicle at the entrance to the long tunnel that housed the 24th Base Hospital facility. "Zeke, how you doin'?" Lyons asked, placing his hand on the doctor's shoulder.

"Shot at and missed, shit at and hit, Davis." Vance smiled. "How's Varina?" He meant the general's wife. "We haven't had a chance to talk much since . . ." He almost said since Tommy, General Lyons's son, had died of the psittacine tuberculosis.

"Since Tommy died," Lyons finished the sentence for him. "I can't let memories of Tommy worry me now, Zeke, not with all these men of mine . . ." He gestured helplessly at the long rows of cots along the walls, each with a seriously wounded or dying soldier lying on it. "I thought I'd come down and talk to some of them. Okay with you, Doctor?" Lyons had frequently visited the hospital when it was situated back at Ashburtonville but that marked his first visit since it had relocated to the Cumbers.

"Talk's about all I got for most of these boys, General."

Years before the war, the little town of Austen had prospered from the salt mines that had been burrowed into the heart of the Cumber foothills. Getting the tunnels ready for the Coalition's forces had been a fairly easy job for Lyons's engineers. They made an ideal fortification, so deep in the rock they were virtually immune to attack. For the most part, the engineers had only to restore the power and ventilation systems left behind when the mines shut down, but the job was done in such haste that often one or the other system failed. Then the long tunnels and chambers might be plunged temporarily into darkness or the air would gradually grow foul and the temperature would rise uncomfortably with all the men crammed into them. Disposal of waste was also a big problem, and each day it became worse.

But nowhere in the mines did it smell worse than in the hospital tunnel. There the smell of blood, feces, vomit, and dead flesh hung over the place like a pall. The doctors, nurses, and corpsmen became inured to the odor, but to visitors it was like running into a wall. Soldiers in nearby tunnels and chambers were also affected by the smell but they endured it well enough because, after all, they were safe and not themselves in the hospital. And besides, everyone knew that it was only a matter of time before the war would be over.

A makeshift morgue had been set up in a huge chamber located in the far reaches of the mine, but there was no refrigeration and it was rapidly filling up with corpses.

"General, we don't have anything to treat these boys with. I don't even have a working stasis unit, can you believe that? And what I need are dozens of the goddamned things. The medical supply depot where we stored them is in enemy hands now. Some asshole didn't get the order to evacuate in time." He shook his head. "That damned ten percent that never gets the word. Our casualties increased tenfold when we got hit coming out here, and what supplies we had were used up mighty quick. Half the other medical units in this army never made it here or are still out there somewhere. This"—he gestured at the cots—"is all this army has left. Goddamn, Davis, can't you arrange a truce to get some of these men out of here?" Dr. Vance implored Lyons.

"I'm going to do better than that, Doctor," Lyons answered, but he said nothing further. He didn't have to.

Vance sighed, smiled, and straightened his shoulders as if a great burden had been lifted from them. He knew what the general meant. "If there is a God," he whispered, "and he cares about us and can do anything to help us, then thank God. How soon?"

Lyons glanced around, took a breath, coughed, and said, "Not soon enough for some of these guys, I'm afraid. But take me to see some of your more severely injured men, will you?"

They stopped at a cot where a man lay swathed in dressings. "That lad's under heavy sedation," the chief nurse told Lyons. "He's got full-thickness injuries to thirty percent of his body."

"That means third-degree burns, General," Dr. Vance added. "In some spots the fire burned all the way into the poor man's muscle tissue, what some call fourth-degree burns. They were so bad on his left leg, his inboard leg, he was sitting in the passenger's side of a vehicle, we had to take it off. Burns as bad as this guy's got heal more slowly than second-degree burns, they're more difficult to treat, and they're more likely to result in complications. Infection's a killer in these cases and down here"—he grimaced—"I'm surprised we're not all down with something."

"The seriousness of burn injuries depends on how deep they go, General," the nurse added. "And how much of the body's surface has been burned. This patient's got first- and second-degree burns also, but if we had the technology we could treat those successfully in a matter of hours."

General Davis regarded the nurse, a Lieutenant Colonel probably in her mid-sixties. Her face was lined with weariness and her uniform soiled. From somewhere nearby a man screamed so loudly it penetrated the overlying hubbub of cries, curses, shouts, and conversation that never stopped in the hospital tunnel. The nurse snapped her head and half turned in the direction of the scream, but another nurse and a corpsman rushed to the soldier's side.

"What's your name again, Colonel? Excuse me for forgetting, my mind is elsewhere, I suppose."

"Ginny Guks, General. That's okay. We survive down here by focusing our minds elsewhere when we can." She smiled weakly.

"Ginny, is there anything you can do for this man?" He reached for the chart hanging at the foot of the cot and read the man's name. Sergeant Wellford Brack.

"If we had proper facilities we could put him back together again. It'd take a while but we could do it," Dr. Vance answered for her. "For right now we're using old-fashioned methods just to keep him alive—silicon and collagen dressings, thymus oil to retard the spread of nitrous oxide."

"Nitrous oxide is produced by the body in larger amounts than normal following burn injuries," Colonel Guks explained. "It reduces the supply of blood and oxygen to the wounded area. Thymus oil is an ancient remedy for burns. It has antioxidant and antiseptic properties that help."

"We're out of synthskin grafts and he doesn't have enough skin of his own for the grafts we'd need to repair the burned areas." Dr. Vance shrugged. "We're also using polychromatic light-emitting diodes to stimulate the flow of blood. That's primitive stuff too, but it's all we've got."

Suddenly Brack stirred on his cot. "Shit, he's coming to. Medic!" Dr. Vance gestured to a corpsman nearby. "Put this man back under again!"

"Unnnn," Brack moaned. Then he opened his eyes. "I ain't dead yet, goddammit, an' doan tell me I am!" he shouted. "Anyone sez I am, he can kiss my ass!" The medic administered a sedative and Brack fell back on his cot, unconscious.

Dr. Vance grinned and nodded. "General, I think that's one patient who just might make it. Once these lads give up hope they're gone, but those who still have spirit, I think they'll make it despite what we're doing to kill them."

"Aw, Zeke, Ginny, you're doing as much as anybody can under these circumstances. Come on, let's see some of the other men." General Lyons saluted Brack before he left his bedside.

Suddenly the lights went out, plunging the hospital into total darkness. "Who forgot to pay the fucking light bill?" someone shouted. A chorus of laughs echoed up and down the corridor. Men who had nothing to laugh about were laughing!

"Looks like someone around here has a lot of that spirit you just mentioned, Doctor," Lyons said with a grin. The emergency lights flashed on; weak, but generating enough illumination to see by.

General Lyons walked up and down the long corridor, pausing to talk to patients who were conscious, asking questions about those who weren't. Dr. Vance observed his old friend closely. The more Lyons talked to the men the paler and more haggard he seemed to grow, but he also noticed the effect their commander's visit was having on the wounded. It was as if Lyons was transmitting his own energy to them at a great cost to himself. Men sat up or tried to when they recognized who he was. Others called out to him from their beds: "Have those bastards surrendered yet, Gen'ral?" "Kin I have a three-day pass when I git outta here, sir?" "Shit, Gen'ral, I don't need *two* legs to kick ass!"

The lights came back on as they neared a side tunnel. "What's in there, Zeke?"

Dr. Vance and Colonel Guks exchanged a nervous glance. "That's our surgery, sir," Guks responded.

"Let's take a look." Lyons started down the side tunnel, Dr. Vance and head nurse Guks close behind him.

"Sir, maybe we shouldn't disturb the surgeons."

"I won't."

The tunnel widened into a good-size circular chamber. Operating tables, at least a dozen of them, were arranged in a circle around the walls. Each was occupied while teams of surgeons plied their bloody work. One man had been hit by numerous fragments, one of which apparently had severed his left leg above the knee. He lay conscious on the table while doctors worked on his wounds. A medic held an oxygen mask over his face, which the wounded soldier was trying unsuccessfully to rip away. A nurse, her hands red with blood, cut the few tendons that were still holding the man's leg on, pulled the leg to the foot of the table, and covered both legs with a sheet. A medic lifted the man's torso so a surgeon could examine a wound in his back. The wound was deep and dark and ugly, and extended from just behind his left shoulder down his back where it disappeared somewhere above his pelvis, but it had stopped bleeding.

The floor was covered with bloody dressings, body parts, and dropped instruments. Men were heaved off the tables onto gurneys when the surgeons finished, but before the blood on one table could be wiped away, another casualty was hefted up onto it and the doctors began their work all over again.

"There's been an attack somewhere; that's why all these men are being brought in here," Dr. Vance commented. "It's like that. There's a steady stream of wounded, sick, and injured that we can normally handle, but when an attack hits, they flood in on us. It was bad enough back at Ashburtonville when we had all our equipment and supplies, but now, hell, we've lost track. I don't even know if anyone's bothering to fill out morbidity reports anymore. I don't even know what happened to our admissions and dispositions people. They left Ashburtonville after we did, but I guess they didn't make it. Neither did some of our clinicians, like epidemiology." He laughed bitterly. "Not that anyone's worried now about insect vectors and water purification."

"I've seen enough," Lyons muttered. "We're only in the way here."

Back at Dr. Vance's "office," a partition set up in a corner across from the chief nurse's station, Lieutenant Colonel Guks excused herself to return to her duty and the two old friends sat down. Dr. Vance lighted a Capricorn and sucked the bitter smoke deep into his lungs. He exhaled loudly. "Smoking these things is a bit of a dirty habit and they foul the air, Davis, but they sure help calm the nerves down here."

"Normally I'd warn you about cancer, Doctor, but this is a war zone, and we could all be dead in five minutes."

"Davis, are you going to end this misery?"

"Yes. They've got a new man over there now, Cazombi or something like that. I understand he's a fair man. He's sure cleaned my clock." Lyons smiled ruefully.

"You did what you could. You did what you had to do, Davis."

"What I should have done, Zeke, is I should have arrested that whole bunch before this got started! What I should do now is bring every one of those goddamned politicians down here to visit these boys, see what their 'secession movement' has cost us in terms of lives."

"Preston Summers was here this morning. He's the only one of those people who's ever come down here, Davis. He went away looking like an old man."

"He is an old man." Lyons chuckled. "He's a good man too. Of them all, he's the only one I won't hang when this is over." He told Vance what he'd learned about the riot at Fort Seymour that had been deliberately staged to precipitate the secession movement.

The doctor was too tired and too disillusioned to be surprised. All he said was, "Davis, when you talk to this Cazombi fella, will you see if he can get us the vaccines we need to treat that TB?"

"I will and he'll come through and he'll also help us with our casualties, Zeke." He stood up. "I'm going back to my headquarters." He punched the doctor lightly on his shoulder. "And I'm gonna put an end to this war. You tell that Sergeant Brack when he comes to again to hold on. We're going to give him back his life."

The drugs Sergeant Brack had been given apparently were not sufficient in strength to keep him sedated, because at that moment he woke up again and shouted, "Fuck 'em all!" before lapsing back into unconsciousness.

CHAPTER THIRTY-ONE

The grizzled old infantry colonel ran a gnarled hand through his closely cropped white hair. "Well, your story checks out, Sergeant. You check out; the fingerprints, retinal scans, all came back positive for Sergeant Charlette Odinloc, recently assigned to the Confederation Army's 3rd Division's G2 section. Welcome back to the fold, from wherever the hell you've been." He extended his hand to Charlette Caloon, née Sergeant Odinloc. "Uh, and just where *have* you been, Sergeant?" he asked. "And who is this young man?" He gestured at Donnie Caloon.

Charlette stood at rigid attention, staring just over the top of the colonel's head. She saw by the embroidery above his left battle dress pocket that his name was Maricle.

Donnie Caloon shifted his feet nervously by her side. "Well, sir, ya see, it's kinda like this," he glanced at Charlette and mumbled something.

"What was that? Speak up, young man, speak up!"

"You see, sir, uh, Colonel Maricle, Donnie and I, well, we're married, sir," Charlette answered, the side of her mouth twitching slightly, "and, er, um, I guess I'm pregnant." Her face turned red. She licked her lips.

"Sweet Jesus on skates, Odinloc, we thought you were dead!" the colonel shouted, sounding like he was disappointed she wasn't dead. "They are officially carrying you as missing in action, presumed dead! Now you're back, rescued from a POW camp run by those MPs, married, pregnant, dropped on me by the Marines to decide what to do with you. Sweet Mary Eddy's tits on a platter, don't I have enough to do?" He cast an appealing glance at his sergeant major, George Ganzefleisch, who, regarding the pair through gimlet eyes, towered silently in one corner of the room.

"Well, sir," Charlette began, "it's like this." Briefly, Charlette explained what had happened to her since the war started, including her and Donnie's precipitous flight from Bibbsville with Lugs Flannagan's hoods in pursuit, their precipitous enlistment in the Loudon Rifles, their capture by the 7th Independent Military Police Battalion along the coast, and their liberation by the Marines.

"Those bastards treated you pretty rough, didn't they?" Sergeant Major Ganzefleisch asked. He meant the men of the 7th MPs, who had practiced their primitive interrogation skills on the pair. Donnie's face still showed the effects of the burns inflicted on him during that ordeal.

"That they did, sir," Charlette answered, her face turning red. "But I never told them squat and for the rest of my life I'll cherish the expression on that bastard's face when the Marines busted in and caught that sumbitchen lieutenant with his pants down. The Marines interrupted my interrogation at just the right moment, sir." She gave a lopsided grin, "And that, sir, is about what happened."

"Well, things are right as rain now," Sergeant Major Ganzefleisch said, a wry expression on his face. *This girl's got grit,* he said to himself, nodding.

"About?" The colonel shook his head. "Sweet Jesus on a rail, what haven't you told me?" Immediately he shook his head, indicating he did not want to hear any more of the story. "And you said you *guess* you're pregnant?" He squinted up at her.

"Yes, sir."

"Well, Sergeant, no guessing about that." The colonel sighed. "Your medical exam revealed the truth. You are two months into your pregnancy. I presume this chap here is the father?"

"Ah, shore am, Cunnel!" Donnie replied enthusiastically. "We ain't exactly decided on a name fer it yet, though." Donnie came to attention and saluted smartly.

The colonel stared in disbelief at the pair. "Sweet Mary on a toilet seat! Okay, let me get all this straight, Sergeant. You were sent into Ashburtonville as an agent handler, developed this young man as your source, got stuck in the city with him when the war started. I got that? All right. Then you fled the city, sailed fifteen thousand kilometers away with this young man here, got married, got mixed up with gangsters, had to join the militia to escape, your troop ship was sunk off the coast, you got yourselves captured and tortured, and then rescued by Marines, and now here you are, standing in my office. Oh, and somewhere during all these adventures you found time to get yourself pregnant. I'm amazed you found the time to do that, Sergeant. Did I miss anything?" The colonel reached into a pocket, pulled out a cigar stub and lighted it. Through the smoke he glared at the pair.

"No, sir," Charlette said, nodding, "that's it, just about entirely."

"That's what I was afraid of." The colonel sighed around his cigar. "I have not heard a story as fantastic as this since, since, hell since I don't know, since Caesar was a road guard!" He drummed his fingers on his desk. "Dammit, Sergeant, stand at ease," he muttered, waving his cigar at the pair. "You make me nervous, staring off into space like that. All right, I've got to figure out what to do with you two love birds. And I will. They don't call me Miracle Maricle for nothing. Have a seat outside." He gestured for them to leave. "Sergeant Major, you and me need to confer on this."

Charlette and Donnie sat before Colonel Maricle's desk, nursing hot cups of army coffee. The colonel puffed on a new cigar, a satisfied smile on his face. Sergeant Major Ganzefleisch stood off to one side regarding the pair a little more sympathetically.

"Higher headquarters advises me to go easy on you, Sergeant Odinloc, er, I guess Caloon now, huh? The way they see it, and I agree, you got caught in Ashburtonville through no fault of your own and you did what any enterprising NCO would have done—you took advantage of the situation." He nodded at the sergeant major. "Isn't that right, George?"

"Right as rain, sir," the sergeant major barked.

"Now I've downloaded your service record, Sergeant. I see you've got 120 days of ordinary leave coming. That right?"

"Er, 120 days? I suppose so, sir. I've taken no leave since I was assigned to Ravenette. Yes, I guess that'd be about right."

"This young man has family back in this Cuylerville place?" He glanced at Donnie, who nodded vigorously. "Well, they're your family now too, Sergeant. Suborbital flights have been restored to that part of the planet. We've been in touch with the authorities in Bibbsville, the county seat, and they inform us that order has been restored in Loudon County, whatever that means. I guess it means that Flannagan character who gave you so much trouble has been dealt with." He glanced over at Donnie. "I don't know about your folks, son, that's something you'll just have to deal with, okay?" There was genuine sympathy in the colonel's voice.

"So here's what's going to happen. I've assigned you to the town commandant's office here in Phelps. He will carry you on his morning reports. I'm moving on to join the rest of the army and I don't have any slots for overhead in any of my units. I'm also puttin' you on 120 days of ordinary leave to be followed by maternity leave. I expect that now that General Cazombi's chased the rebels into the hills, this war will be over by the time your leave expires—if it isn't already. But there'll be a garrison force left behind for some time to come, so when you're ready to come back to duty, Sergeant, contact your unit. Uh, I see you have eighteen months until expiration of your term of service. You'll probably still be here then, so you'll have a decision to make, reenlist or get out. Sergeant Major?"

"Right as rain, sir," the sergeant major answered. He was very pleased that the colonel had followed his advice in this matter.

"You have any questions?" He turned back to Charlette and Donnie. "No? All right, you are dismissed. Report to the Phelps town commandant, just across the street in that old school house, get your personnel records updated, your travel orders, and your back pay."

Both gulped their coffee, came to attention, saluted, and about-faced.

"Oh, one more thing, you two!" Sergeant Major Ganzefleisch stepped forward and put his hand gently on their shoulders as he guided them to the door. "Welcome back. Things'll be right as rain for you two from here on out."

Phelps was too small to have a spaceport but it did have an aerial port that could accommodate suborbital flights. What the Caloons did not know when they arrived there, tickets in hand, was that there were only two flights a week between Phelps and Loudon County, and theirs, if it departed on schedule, wasn't due for two more days.

They sat disconsolately in the run-down terminal building. "What next?" Donnie asked.

"Find a place to stay, I guess." Charlette shrugged. "Keep checking back until our flight leaves."

"Um." Donnie nodded. He looked out over the tarmac. "Wisht we knew who was flyin' *that* thing." He gestured with his chin at a gleaming Bomarc 36V Starship. "Them things kin travel suborbital or deep space. Maybe we could ask the pilot to give us a lift—*hey!*" He jumped to his feet. "Charlette, my eyes playin' tricks on me?"

"What do you mean, Donnie?" She squinted in the direction he was pointing, then jumped to her feet. Emblazoned along the fuselage of the Bomarc were the words Caloon Enterprises, Ltd.

"I bin lookin' all over for you kids," someone said from behind them. They whirled at the sound of the voice. Eyes fairly bugging out of their heads, they beheld Timor Caloon, Donnie's father, standing there, hands casually thrust into his pockets, a lopsided grin on his face. "The army tol' me you two was up here an' ready to come home, so I come to take you there." He held out his arms and embraced the pair.

Later he told them that Colonel Maricle had made inquiries of the authorities in Bibbsville, in Loudon County, checking up on Charlette's story, and through them he had discovered that his son and daughter-in-law were alive and well at Phelps. The Bomarc, he explained, had belonged to Lugs Flannagan. When asked what had happened to the Flannagan gang he only replied, "Well, them boys, they never could shoot straight when someone was shootin' back on 'em. An' once the smoke cleared, well, I took over the whole operation and made it legitimate. We've taken over his distribution system and we're sharin' the profits equally among all the folks back in Cuylerville," he announced, proudly. "Ever'one is jist tickled pink.

"How's about you, Charlette?" he asked.

Briefly, she explained her status.

"You gonna stay in yer army, once the baby's come, or you gonna take that discharge? Before you answer, girl, you know you always got a home with us back in Cuylerville, an' Mother Caloon'd be tickled pink to have you back in the family. But I gotta tell ya, Flannagan's operation was big, Charlette, too big for an old hick like me to run by myself. I need good help. I need someone with brains and get-up-'n'-go to market our thule products, someone who knows what it's like beyond this ol' rock an' kin travel an' deal with folks. I kin use you an' Donnie in the business. Think about it."

Sergeant Charlette Caloon, née Odinloc, Confederation Armed Forces, didn't need to think about the offer. She knew where her place was now. "Father," she said, and the three embraced warmly as the tears ran down her cheeks.

CHAPTER THIRTY-TWO

"Third platoon, form on me!" Ensign Charlie Bass called over third platoon's all-hands circuit. He had his helmet and gloves off and did the sleeve thing. Third platoon was spread along a two-hundred-meter line, so it took a couple of minutes for everyone to reach the platoon commander and form up in front of him. Bass stood with his back to the west, the direction of the enemy. Four or five flights of Raptors from the airfield at Bataan zoomed overhead while Bass waited for his men to assemble.

"Show yourselves," Bass said when his men were assembled. The thirty Marines of third platoon removed their helmets and gloves.

"It appears that we've got the Coalition on the run. Evidently, they're running so fast that we can't keep up with them on foot." He paused while his Marines chuckled. "So Lieutenant General Cazombi—I believe you know that General Cazombi replaced General Billie as overall commander of this war—" He paused briefly again as the Marines reacted loudly and enthusiastically to the mention of Billie being replaced by a general whom they respected, even if that general *was* just a doggie. After a few seconds, he held up his hand again and the platoon fell quiet. "As I was saying before being so rudely interrupted"—which caused another, briefer outburst—"Lieutenant General Cazombi, in his wisdom, has decided that we Marines need to ride for a bit. He has deployed a convoy of army lorries to pick us up and convey us to where we can again come into contact with the rear of the Coalition army."

Until now, Bass had been speaking drily. Now his voice went hard. "And when we catch up with them, we're going to make them sorry they didn't run faster. We'll make them sorry they started this war in the first place!"

"*Oooh-RAH!*" the Marines cheered.

More flights of Raptors passed overhead, some heading out to pound the fleeing enemy, others returning for fuel and munitions.

As hard as the Marines had been pressing, they weren't able to keep up with the retreating Coalition army; General Lyons's army had enough vehicles for all its personnel to ride, but the Marines didn't have enough Dragons to carry more than half of them. General Koval's 27th Division had enough to carry itself, but not enough to haul Marines. Hence the lorries being dispatched from Bataan. So the wait was welcome; the hard-pressing Marines were tiring out after so many hours of pursuing a mounted enemy on foot.

"Corporal Claypoole," Lance Corporal Ymenez asked, "where do you think they're going to? The enemy, I mean."

Claypoole didn't look at him. "Out there someplace," he said with a vague wave of his hand.

Ymenez looked where Claypoole waved. He'd caught an occasional glimpse of mountains out there. The mountains looked high and barren. He shivered; he had no experience in montane warfare, and nearly no training in high mountains. "What's it like?" he asked. "Fighting in the mountains, I mean."

Claypoole shrugged. "Damned if I know. Never fought in mountains. Not real mountains like them, anyway."

Schultz rumbled, "Same as on flats. Fight. Kill." He paused long enough that the other two thought he wasn't going to say more, then he added, "Win."

Claypoole had nothing to say after that, and Ymenez decided to let the question drop. Moments later, they heard the approach of the lorries from Bataan. Soon after that, 34th FIST's infantry battalion and the Dragon company were headed at speed after the fleeing Coalition army.

* * *

"Jim Ray, cain't you drive this thang enny fastah?" Sergeant Helm Knickers of the Mylex Provisional Brigade shouted, pounding on the rooftop of the lorry he rode in. "Ya saw what happened ta Sergeant Brack's truck back thar. Ya want thet ta happen ta us too?"

"Goan fas' as ah kin, Sarge," PFC Jim Ray Robbins said. "We ain't on no paved highway, ya knows!" To demonstrate his point, Jim Ray increased power, and the jouncing of the lorry over the uneven ground knocked Knickers off his feet.

"Ya did thet on purpose, damn you, Jim Ray!" Knickers shouted when he'd managed to pull himself to a kneeling position behind the cab.

Jim Ray eased back on the power, and the jouncing smoothed to a lesser degree of violence.

"Hey, Sarge," a voice called from the rear of the lorry's bed, "Ah think we got more problems!"

"What kine problems?" Knickers yelled, looking to see who spoke up.

"Back thar." Private Vilhelm Crustman pointed to a dust cloud barely visible through the trees to the rear.

"I'll be buggered Brigham Young!" Knickers swore. He *knew* there were no Coalition vehicles to the rear, that the dust being kicked up *had* to be from pursuing Confederation vehicles. He turned back to the cab and pounded on its roof again. "Go faster, Jim Ray. Ah doan care *how* rough the ride gits. Confed'rations is ketchin' up with us!" He held on firmly and didn't lose his footing when the jouncing increased. He wasn't sure his kidneys and spine would survive the ride, but that was a small price to pay to stay alive. The lorry gained on the vehicles racing ahead of it.

"Heads up, people," Ensign Bass said into third platoon's all-hands circuit. "We're gaining on somebody, and you just know there's no friendlies ahead of us."

The suspension of the Confederation Army's lorries was better than that of the Mylex Brigade's vehicles, so they gave their passengers a smoother ride than Sergeant Knickers and his men suffered. Still, the lorry bed swayed side to side, sometimes jinked hard, bounced up and down, twisted in what felt like corkscrews. The Marines whose earlier wounds weren't yet fully healed felt them again; in some cases Marines were surprised when they checked their wounds and found they hadn't broken open once more. So, many of the Marines were relieved to hear they were gaining on somebody; pretty soon the lorries would stop and they'd dismount to fight. Fighting and risking fresh wounds had to be better than riding those vehicles. There was general grumbling about the damn army and how it gave its worst trucks to the Marines to ride in. Of course, the Marines had no way of knowing that the soldiers of the 27th Infantry Division, somewhere to the left of 34th FIST, were being jounced more violently because their lorries were in worse shape than the fresh lorries that had come from Bataan to pick up the Marines.

"Thrush Lead, I have a convoy on the ground." The excited call came from Solitaire, the most junior pilot in Thrush Division.

"I have it too, Lead," chimed in Wood, Lead's wingman.

Hermit, Solitaire's flight lead, kept his own counsel.

"I see it, Solitaire," Thrush Lead answered drily. "So what?"

"So it's a target of opportunity, Lead! We can get them all!" Solitaire's voice had gone from merely excited to nearly orgasmic ecstasy.

Wood was just about as enthusiastic as Solitaire in declaiming the joys of hitting the speeding convoy below and getting closer. Hermit continued to keep his counsel to himself.

"Solitaire, Wood, take a look in the infra, about a klick behind the convoy. What do you see there?" Thrush Lead said.

There was a moment's radio silence while the two junior Raptor pilots did as their lead bid.

"Ah, Marine vehicles?" Wood finally said.

"That's right, children," Thrush Lead said. "And they're gaining on the convoy. Let's leave the stragglers to our muddy-booted brethern, whilst we continue on to blast the blazes out of our assigned targets."

"But . . ." Solitaire objected weakly.

"Lead, won't the Marines on the ground want our help?" Wood asked.

Hermit finally spoke up: "Chillins, we're at angels twenty-five, those mud Marines down there can't even see us. They don't know we're here, they don't expect our help."

Neither Solitaire nor Wood had anything to say to that.

Thrush Division continued on its way to its assigned target, an artillery base in the making outside Austen.

"Hey, Sarge," PFC Jim Ray Robbins called from inside the cab, easing back on the power and slowing the lorry, "ah jist got a call fum the Cap'n. He say we supposed ta stop an' git out, fight them Confed'rations comin' up, slow 'em down."

"*What?*" Sergeant Knickers squawked. "Us an' what army? We stop an' try an' slow 'em down, we gits kilt! Keep goin' an' doan you dare slow down none." He pounded on the roof of the cab for emphasis.

"You tell 'em, Sarge!" Private Vilhelm Crustman shouted. "Ain't no call fer us ta commit no damn suicide."

"Thas fer damn sure," someone else muttered.

"But the cap'n—" Jim Ray started to protest.

"Bugger the buggerin' cap'n," Sergeant Knickers shouted. "He ain't here, *his* precious ass ain't on the line. *Mine* is, an' so is *yourn! You* wants ta try an' stop the Confed'rations, ya move your fat ass over so's I kin crawl in thar an' take over drivin', then *you* jump out an' try by your own sef. Ah'm gittin' out'n hyar alive!"

"*Me* try an' stop 'em?" Jim Ray squeaked. "Nossir, Sarge!" He hit the power harder, and the lorry surged forward. It would only be a few more minutes before he caught up with the lorry to his front and passed it by. Then let the Confed'rations catch up with somebody *else!* He reached over and turned off the radio so he wouldn't have to listen to the captain's harping voice, demanding that he stop his lorry and try to get Sergeant Knickers to dismount the troops to fight for a forlorn hope. Hell, as far as he could tell, all the other drivers were ignoring the captain's orders as well. Jim Ray's mama might have raised herself a soldier boy, but she didn't raise no death-wish dummy.

Lance Corporal Hammer Schultz stood in the front of the lorry that had picked up half of third platoon. He stared ahead, looking at the dust cloud raised by the convoy they were chasing. At first they'd been gaining on the enemy vehicles, but for the past quarter hour the dust cloud seemed to be maintaining its interval, neither receding nor getting closer. Schultz was impatient for action; he was one of the Marines with incompletely healed wounds who wanted the lorry to stop so he could get off and fight. Of course, Schultz would have wanted that even if he *wasn't* in pain. So he stood in the front of the lorry, up against the back of the cab. His right hand held his blaster across the top of the cab, aimed toward the distant lorry; the fingers of his left hand beat an impatient tattoo on the cab's roof.

Corporal Claypoole stood on Schultz's right. Not because he particularly wanted to be next to Schultz when the big man was impatiently waiting for the chance to shoot someone, but because Schultz was *his* man, and he believed a fire team should stick together in the field. Lance Corporal Ymenez was to Claypoole's right. Again, it was the fire team sticking together. But Ymenez was glad that Claypoole was between him and Schultz; the big man made him nervous.

Ymenez wasn't the only man Schultz was making nervous. Everybody else nearby was getting the jitters, waiting for something to trip inside him, and they were afraid of what he might do if he didn't have a proper direction in which to vent his desire—need?—to fight and kill.

Ensign Charlie Bass was on that lorry. Normally, when a platoon was split between two lorries, the platoon commander would ride in the cab of the lorry that carried the first squad, and the platoon sergeant would do the same with second squad. But Bass chose the back of the lorry with second squad. The reason for that was Hammer Schultz. Bass knew Schultz would be anxious to get into action, to extract vengeance for the injuries inflicted by the Coalition army on third platoon. Not to mention for his own wounds. And Bass didn't have any great expectations of such opportunity rising soon.

So after a time, when he saw Schultz getting more impatient and agitated, Bass rose from the left side of the lorry and gingerly made his way to the front, where he leaned against the back of the cab to Schultz's left. He moved in close so he could talk privately.

"Don't worry, Hammer," Bass said into Schultz's ear, "we'll catch them."

Schultz grunted.

"Then you'll do what needs to be done."

Schultz made as though to spit, but didn't.

"How's your back doing?"

Schultz grunted again, but there seemed to be a word hidden in it: "Hurts."

"This war's almost over, Hammer. Then we'll get some proper care for your back. You'll be back to your normal irascible self by the time we get back to Camp Ellis."

Schultz turned a gimlet eye on Bass, a look that had made many strong men blanch and back off. Bass didn't budge. "Right," Schultz snarled, and turned back to stare after the fleeing convoy. But he stopped drumming his fingers on the cab roof, and some of the tension eased out of his body. The Marines nearby began to breathe more easily.

Not long after that, the retreating army reached the prepared positions outside Austen. General Cazombi arrayed his army in front of the defenders.

CHAPTER THIRTY-THREE

General Davis Lyons sighed. There was only one thing left for him to do. The terrible devastation his army had suffered on its move to the Cumbers had reduced his combat strength enormously. What happened to his air-defense capability, he wondered. Well, he could not hold out much longer. "Rags?"

"Sir?" Colonel Rene Raggel had been standing nearby watching his commander stare at the trid overlay of his opponent's dispositions around the town of Austen. The command center was oddly hushed, each man's senses attuned to the lull that had fallen over the fighting. It was as if the army now confronting them had paused in its forward advance to take a deep breath, and was flexing its powerful muscles one more time in preparation for its inevitable, inexorably overwhelming assault. All eyes not on the enormous screen were on their commander. Even the lowest-ranking enlisted man in the center knew what was coming.

"Rags, get Admiral DeGauss, the rest of my staff, and as many of my commanders as can come on such short notice, and have them assemble here. Get President Summers and his cabinet too. While you're doing that"—General Lyons reached into a cargo pocket and took out a Davidoff—"I am going into my little cubicle and smoke this here last cigar." He bit the end off the cigar, grinned, and parted the curtains to his private retreat.

* * *

"Ted, Balca, gentlemen," Cazombi addressed his staff. They were head-quartered in abandoned buildings on the outskirts of the little town of Austen in the foothills of the Cumber Mountains. It was a brilliant day. Sunlight gleamed off the snowcapped summits of the taller peaks ranged in serried rows beyond and above the town. "I want the army to stand down."

A soft murmur ran through the assembled officers. "Sir, we're ready to mount the final assault," Major General Sorca ventured. He had been given the job of deputy army commander upon Billie's relief, a position he filled with great efficiency because it required no decision making on his part.

Brigadier Ted Sturgeon had been temporarily assigned as Cazombi's chief of staff. "I think I know what's coming, Balca," he said. "Unless you want to lead the first assault wave." He grinned at Sorca, who winced but remained silent.

A sign of good humor, a slight muscle spasm, creased Cazombi's face. "I think old Davis Lyons has had it. I'm going to sit here for a while and see if he takes the hint. I don't fancy frontal assaults on fortified po-sitions, especially when the enemy occupies the high ground. Ted, pass the word to our combat commanders to stand fast until further notice. Now, gentlemen"—he produced a box of cigars—"General Billie left these behind when he, er, departed. They're Clintons but they'll smoke. Help yourselves, light up, and take it easy for a while. We may have a little wait before us."

"I am going to request surrender terms," General Lyons announced to the assembled staff and government officials. The military men uttered a sigh of relief, and some even smiled, but the Coalition cabinet officers, all but Preston Summers, blanched at the announcement and protested loudly.

"Gen'ral, that leaves our asses hangin' out high an' dry!" the finance minister protested. He'd had no part in anything since the war had started, but as a high-ranking official of that government and a coward, he was worried about being arrested as a rebel. Several other cabinet of-ficials protested loudly.

"Gentlemen, pipe down," Preston Summers demanded. "You was all in favor of goin' to war with the Confederation an' Gen'ral Lyons here, he warned us first off that we could never win. An' now we all know the incident at Fort Seymour was a gawdam setup." His voice turned bitter now and his face flushed. "It's time to ante up and take our knocks. Gen'ral," he said, turning to Lyons, "save what's left of your army and get the best terms you kin. For me, I only ask for an escort out of these mountains. I want to go home an' drink some o' my bourbon before they haul me off to jail." He paused. "Oh, one more thing." He handed Lyons a small box. "Here's some Davidoffs. You deserve 'em, an' mebbe you kin take 'em along with you to jail."

General Lyons, Admiral DeGauss, and Colonel Raggel stood in the center of General Cazombi's command center. "I am Alistair Cazombi, General, this is Ted Sturgeon." They shook hands all round.

"I am here to surrender my army, General, and end this fighting. I only ask for fair terms for my men under the articles of war."

Cazombi regarded Lyons carefully. "Yes. Well, I only wish we'd met under more pleasant circumstances, General."

"As do I, sir," Lyons responded.

"Well, all right." Cazombi glanced at his officers. "Here are my terms, if you'll accept them. Return to your army and have your men stand down all military operations at once. We will make arrangements to transport your men and their equipment to their home worlds—"

"Uh, you mean their weapons and equipment?" Lyons asked.

"Yes, General. But first each will sign an oath of allegiance to the Confederation and promise never to take up arms against us again. When we round up your politicians, I'll do the same with them. Once all this is properly taken care of, will you and your staff join me and mine in a farewell dinner? We got bigger fish to fry and have to be on our way, now that this little unpleasantness is over."

Lyons nodded. "Those terms are most fair and honorable, General. I must tell you though, I have proof that the incident at Fort Seymour, the tragedy that sparked the Ordinance of Secession and started this war, was a setup by some of our politicians. Our people fired the first shot."

Cazombi raised an eyebrow, an expression, for him, of great surprise. "So. Well, General, that is your problem. Deal with the varmints as you see fit."

Now it was Lyons's turn to be surprised. He nodded his agreement. "One more thing, sir. Our children are suffering from a variety of TB. You have developed not only a vaccine but a cure. Can you please get that stuff to us as quickly as possible, now the war's over?"

"You bet. Have your surgeon get with mine and we'll have the medicine shipped in immediately." He offered his hand. "You fought a good fight, General." They shook. "Since every soldier is measured by his enemies, you make me look like some tough sumbitch. Now if you'll go back to your army and make the arrangements, I'll have my judge advocate get with yours to draw up the formal surrender terms. I'll need the president of your coalition to cosign them."

"He's already left, sir, gone home to get drunk." Lyons chuckled.

"Can't say as I blame him. Well, I'll send someone over to his place when you and I have signed the terms."

"Oh, I almost forgot, General," Lyons said, reaching into a cargo pocket. "President Summers gave me this travel humidor before he left. There are five fresh Davidoffs in there. I want you to have them."

"Well, thank you, General."

"Sir? One final question?" Cazombi nodded. "What happened to your General Billie?"

Cazombi did not answer at once. He stood there, turning the humidor over in his hands. "Well," he responded at last, "he went on home, just like you and I are going to do."

After Lyons and his party had departed, Cazombi gestured for Sturgeon to join him in private. "Earlier today I received this back-channel message from Marcus Berentus. I thought you'd be interested in knowing what it says: 'Defeated worlds *must* be allowed to defend themselves when returned home. You are herewith ordered to return to Earth as soon as hostilities are concluded to face a court of inquiry into your conduct.' " Cazombi shrugged. "I'd have let Lyons's troops take all their weapons with them anyway."

"Billie's been busy." Sturgeon grimaced.

"Yep. To be expected. Ted, I'm not going to involve you in this mess." He held up a hand as Sturgeon began to protest. "You take your Marines home and drink a lot of beer and eat a mountain of that reindeer steak you're always bragging about. I'll face this inquiry on my own. Besides," he said, and broke into an actual grin, "I have this get-out-of-jail card." He produced another back channel. "It sez, 'Good job. Senate asked to confirm your fourth star' and it's signed by President Chang-Sturdevant, Ted. Long as I got that old girl in my corner, I can give the Marines a rest."

"Sound an alarm, your sil-ver trumpets sound, and call the brave, and on-ly brave, and on-ly brave a-round." The rich tenor voice filled Preston Summer's music room. More than half the contents of the bourbon bottle on the side table were gone and he was feeling no pain. "What a way to go," he muttered, his head wreathed in a rich cloud of cigar smoke. "Nuttin' like a little Handel to get a handle on . . ." *On what?* he wondered. What had this mess come to? The government had dispersed, each slobbering politician with his tail between his legs running for his worthless life.

But he was home at last. No one was there, of course. Summers had long before sent his family and household staff to a remote corner of Ravenette where they'd be out of the fighting. The empty halls echoed his footfalls as he walked through the house. Dust lay everywhere, the furniture covered by white linens, reminding him of a mortuary. That thought made him smile. *"Sic transit gloria mundi,"* he said with a sigh.

He poured himself another glass of bourbon. "To you, Mr. Handel." He toasted the soaring music.

"Jus-tice with courage, jus-tice with courage, is a thou-sand men," the voice sang. Summers shook his head. Courage they'd had all right, but justice? No justice after what Lyons had found out about the incident at Fort Seymour. The bitterest disappointment about the war for Preston Summers was not that it was lost but that nobody would ever believe he didn't know about the plot. *Well, that's how the chips fall,* he thought, and finished the drink in one huge gulp. The only consolation—and the only courage—he had now was of the liquid variety.

A tremendous roar penetrated from the front of the house, the unmistakable thunder of military vehicles drawing up outside. "Damn," Summers muttered, getting unsteadily to his feet, "didn't take 'em long to get here." He straightened his clothes and brushed off the dust. He patted his vest. Yes, he had a few cigars in there. Would they let him keep them? Maybe not. He opened the humidor and stuffed more into his pockets. He paused, considering. "Ah, Mohammed's golden toilet water," he mumbled after a moment. "A peace offering never hurts. Hope those boys are smokers." He thought they would be. He'd heard that Marines love good cigars. Sticking the humidor under one arm and squaring his shoulders, he walked slowly, ponderously, but with dignity toward the front door which was now being vigorously assaulted by a pounding fist.

He paused. "What a way to go, out on Mr. Handel!" He fumbled for the control in his pocket and turned the volume up on the music until the dust on the floor began to spurt in little fountains. "Sing it out, Georgie, you old bastard," he shouted to the empty house. "Sound the trum-pets! Beat the drums! See, the conq'ring he-ro comes!"

The knocking persisted. Staggering a little, Summers flung the door open to see a Marine colonel in dress reds standing on the threshold. "Mr. Preston Summers, late President of the Coalition of Independent Worlds?" the colonel asked.

"The shame, er, I mean, the same!" Summers blinked and swayed slightly. "I am yer prishoner, sir," he announced with drunken gravity.

"Sir, I am Colonel Festus Grimaldi, General Alistair Cazombi's judge advocate, and I have something here I wish you to sign. General Lyons has already signed. It is your army's capitulation. May we go inside?" He paused and tilted his head to one side. "Wonderful music, sir. Handel, isn't it?"

Late that night Cazombi and Sturgeon sat sipping whiskey and smoking one of the Davidoffs General Lyons had given Cazombi.

"Al, despite the president's support, our asses are grass and the Confederation Congress is the lawn mower. You'll never get away with letting Lyons and his men go like this, and you know sure as death Billie's filed charges of mutiny against both of us. And there are those politicians in the Confederation Congress, sitting safe in session back on Earth, they'll want your head for being so generous with these people." Despite himself, Sturgeon had to laugh. "But by the Virgin's hangnails, I'm glad to be along with you for that long, long slide down the razor blade of life!"

"Getting yourself into hot water seems to run in your veins, Ted." Cazombi chuckled. "In the future, if there is one, you'd be advised to pick your associates more carefully. But I'm not taking any more of this

Darkside nonsense, this damned cloak of secrecy our government's put over things. Lyons put the blame for this war on those bastards who engineered that massacre at Fort Seymour, but Ted, it was our own policy that led us into war; we set up the conditions, the secessionists only took advantage of them. Let me tell you now, Ted, nothing's going to happen to you or me over any of this, let Billie scream all he wants to, let the fat cat congressmen holler for an investigation. The time is just right to clear the decks, my friend."

Cazombi drew on his cigar. "Ah, damned fine smokes, these!" He exhaled luxuriously. "I said earlier today we have bigger fish to fry." He reached into a pocket and pulled out a folded sheet of paper. "This is a printout of a back-channel message I got this morning from a friend of mine at the Heptigon, someone very high up in military intelligence. In view of what's on this paper, Ted, everything else is on hold." He grinned as he passed the slip to Sturgeon. "They aren't going to pasteurize two old warhorses like us, Ted. They have one more mission for us to perform."

Carefully, Sturgeon unfolded the flimsy, eyeing Cazombi quizzically as he did. He spread the paper out on his knee, took a deep drag on his Davidoff, and squinting through the aromatic cloud of smoke wreathing his head, read the very short sentence written there.

"The Skinks are back," he said softly.

CHAPTER THIRTY-FOUR

"Gentlemen," Admiral Joseph K. C. B. Porter, Chairman of the Combined Chiefs, smiled broadly, "I give you"—he snatched the lid off the steaming dish dramatically,—"*macaroni!*"

Porter's luncheon guests eyed the steaming heap of greasy white macaroni suspiciously. "Dig in!" he chortled, serving himself a heap of the glutinous mass. "Steward, serve 'em up!" he commanded. He shoveled a spoonful of the stuff into his mouth. "Hmm, needs a bit of salt," he murmured, reaching for a shaker. "Maybe some pepper as well. Steward, tell the cooks to add some salt, pepper, and butter to the next batch."

"Very good, sir," the mess steward replied. "They aren't very familiar with the recipe, sir."

Anders Aguinaldo, Commandant of the Marine Corps, used a fork to toy experimentally with the mess the steward had just deposited in the middle of his plate. He glanced sideways at the newly appointed army chief of staff, Frank Wanker, who was cautiously tasting the concoction. The army four-star grimaced slightly and winked at Aguinaldo. Luncheons in the chairman's mess often consisted of meals of ancient, long-forgotten cuisine that for some reason Admiral Porter relished. So-called hot dogs were another favorite of his. Thank God they weren't having any of *those* things this afternoon, Aguinaldo thought. God only knew what went into them. They tasted like sawdust to Aguinaldo.

"Joe, do you think," Aguinaldo ventured, "that this, er, macaroni might go down a bit better with, say, melted cheese?"

"Huh? Cheese? Oh, no, Anders, cheese won't do."

"But Joe, I think Anders has a point there, cheese might do very well," Wanker said.

Admiral Porter glared at General Wanker and then turned to the messboy, "What do you say, steward?"

"Cheese? Oh, no, sir! Definitely not, sir. Why, er, it'd just ruin the um, *bouquet.*" He knew from experience that it was not wise to disagree with Admiral Joseph K. C. B. Porter on culinary matters, about which the admiral considered himself an expert.

"Well, there you have it, gentlemen. Ah, Anders, when does your new appointment take effect again?" He was referring to the president's recent appointment of Aguinaldo as commander of the task force she created to deal with the Skinks.

"A couple of weeks, sir."

"Well, shame you won't be making these luncheons for a while, Anders. Eat up! Eat up!" Porter shoveled another mass of the macaroni into his mouth. "Perhaps some hot sauce?" he mused, reaching for a bottle of Tabasco with which he sprinkled his macaroni liberally. He tried another forkful of the pasta. Carefully, he sipped ice water, trying manfully not to scream at the searing pain on his tongue; he'd been a bit too liberal with the hot sauce. He wiped his lips with a napkin and coughed, a bit too hoarsely. "Gentlemen," he squeaked, but his voice soon came back to its normal level, "what you are sampling here this afternoon is known as *pasta secca,* the dried pasta made from Triticum turgidum, variety durum or hard wheat. Taxonomists believe durum developed as a mutation of emmer around five or six thousand years B.C." He paused to sip more ice water.

"Macaroni," he continued, "was a staple dish in households throughout the world until that goddamned food prohibition fad about 150 years ago, when the World Health Council banned it as an unhealthy food. Same time they banned tobacco, the goddamned fools. We've learned better since then, but in the course of time people forgot how to prepare macaroni and it just went out of style. Not tobacco though, thank God!"

"Macaroni," General Wanker turned the word over in his mouth, finding the word more palatable than the macaroni itself. "Sounds foreign to me, Joe. Where's it come from?"

"Italian," Admiral Porter answered, now in his element, explaining the origin of arcane words. "In the Italian language it's *maccherone,* which some lexicographers trace back to a Greek word, *makaria,* meaning 'food of the blessed.' Another possible origin"—he shrugged scholastically— "is from *maccare,* archaic Italian meaning 'to knead.' " He smiled, "I prefer *makaria,* since I think we are blessed to have such a dish now in revival, if only in my mess here at the Heptigon. But who knows, maybe it'll catch on again."

"Perhaps it will, sir," General Wanker replied without conviction, "but too bad the CNO couldn't join us this afternoon." He winked at Aguinaldo.

"We'll get him another time." Porter shrugged. "But now, gentlemen, I have a special surprise for you, a fruit dish for dessert, a delightful twentieth-century gelatin concoction called Jell-O! I got the recipe off a box in an exhibit at the National Museum!"

A navy captain came into the mess at that point and leaned over Admiral Porter's shoulder, whispering something and handing the admiral a sheet of flimsy. He then discreetly withdrew from the mess. "Excuse me a moment, would you?" Porter asked his guests, scanning the flimsy. "Jesus fucking Christ on a crutch!" he screamed, dropping his fork with a clatter and jumping to his feet.

"Joe, what is it?" General Wanker asked, glancing nervously over at Aguinaldo as if to ask, *Does he do this often?* Porter's face had gone brick red with rage and his hands were shaking.

"That goddamned fool!" he spluttered. "That fucking idiot! I'm getting him back here and I'm going to nail his balls to the shithouse door, I am!"

"What is it?" Aguinaldo asked.

With difficulty Porter gained control of himself. "Cazombi," he rasped, shaking the flimsy at Aguinaldo, "has relieved General Jason Billie of command and taken over the army on Ravenette!"

"Joe," Aguinaldo said calmly, "maybe you'd better leave Cazombi's balls alone until he's won that war for you." He'd been reading Ted Sturgeon's back-channel messages so this event came as no surprise to him—delighted him, in fact. "May I see the message?"

Porter had crumpled the flimsy into a little ball, which he now tossed across the table to General Aguinaldo. "I was going to send *you,* Anders, instead of Billie," Porter commented ruefully. What he didn't say was that he had wanted to give Anders the command to get rid of him. "But Billie talked me into sending him instead," he added.

Carefully, Aguinaldo unrolled the flimsy. "Yes, Joe, but during the meeting with the president, when she asked why Cazombi had been sent to Ravenette, you covered that very nicely." Aguinaldo smiled archly and read the message silently. Porter, to cover up having sent Cazombi to Ravenette as punishment for talking back to him, had told President Chang-Sturdevant he'd been sent there as a "steady hand" in a tumultuous situation. Aguinaldo noted that the message had not even been addressed to Admiral Porter, but to President Chang-Sturdevant; Porter was only an "information" addressee. "Well, I'll tell you this, Joe." Aguinaldo offered the flimsy to General Wanker to read. "Now that Cazombi's in charge, the war is as good as over. Given the length of time it takes for messages to reach Earth from Ravenette, he may well have won the war by now and be on his way home as we speak."

"*Hrumpf.* Yes, that may well be true, as you say. But another war is about to start! Did you read that last sentence? Billie's coming back here. He's going to demand an investigation, a court of honor or some-such nonsense, Anders. You know Jason, he'll raise as big a stink as he can over being relieved." Porter was cooling down now.

Aguinaldo shrugged. "Cazombi could hardly keep him there, Joe. But you can handle him. Joe, you might go a little easy on Cazombi. He's got the president's ear, you know."

Admiral Porter harrumphed a couple of times, shook himself, and resumed his seat. "Do you really think so, Anders? Hmmm. Yes, yes. Well, he doesn't go into any detail on why he relieved Billie. Maybe we'd best wait until we see if he can end the war before I court-martial him. Um. Yes. Steward, the fruit dishes, please?"

Aguinaldo leaned forward and tapped the table. "You know, Joe, I really do think that macaroni of yours could do with a little bit of cheese next time."

"Marcus, what General Cazombi did is unprecedented in my experience. What do you think happened out there?"

Marcus Berentus, Cynthia Chang-Sturdevant's Minister of War, shrugged. "Something unprecedented, ma'am." He chuckled, gently kneading Chang-Sturdevant's neck.

"Marcus," Chang-Sturdevant said, her voice dripping with sarcasm, "if Cazombi screws up the war on Ravenette, it'll be the Congress with their hands wrapped around my neck, and they won't be as gentle as you are, my dear, so please, take this seriously."

"Cazombi's a tried combat commander, Suelee." Only Chang-Sturdevant's most intimate associates ever used her middle name. Marcus Berentus was one of those associates. "He would not have made such a move unless he was forced into it for the good of the army. We'll just have to wait until Billie gets back here to explain—"

"No. What we wait for is the next battle report. If he cracks the Coalition's army on Ravenette, that puts a whole different light on this, this act of mutiny. That's what it amounts to, right, Marcus? Mutiny?"

"Well, my general counsel and the Ministry of Justice have looked into this, and there are justifications for military subordinates relieving their superiors—chief among them mental or physical disability preventing them from performing their duties. I should think one or both of those conditions prevailed when Cazombi took command of the army. But whatever happened, there will have to be an investigation, Suelee." Berentus ran his thumbs down the muscles in the side of Chang-Sturdevant's neck and under her shoulder blades. "How does that feel?"

"Mmmm. When you're done let me work on you for a while, Marcus."

Gently, Berentus rocked her head back and forth. "Promises, promises." He chuckled. "Now it's *you* who has got to get serious. But Suelee, you know Billie has friends in the Congress—"

"That doesn't surprise me. I'm already beginning to hate him. You know, when we met that time, before I sent him out there to Ravenette, well, there was something—he was just a bit too slick to be good, know what I mean?" She sighed. "Well, Marcus, when will General Billie get back here? A week, two weeks? That message is a week old and he departed sometime after it was sent. So he should arrive back here about the same time the next battle report comes from Cazombi." She shook her head. "For all we know, Cazombi might already have won the war by the time we get that message. Anyway, I want a press release put out that General Billie has become a casualty and General Cazombi has taken over the army in his place. You get ready some kind of an award for Billie, the Presidential Legion of Honor, something vast and meaningless like that; you know, the kind of thing we give someone to avoid a scandal just before kicking him out to pasture. I do *not* want a scandal over this."

"You won't, certainly not if Cazombi beats Lyons. And if he does conclude this war, I'm going to recommend you appoint him Chairman of the Combined Chiefs, retire that old windbag Porter."

"Marcus," Chang-Sturdevant murmured sleepily as he kneaded her right shoulder blade, "you took the words right out of my mouth. Yes,"—she sat up—"that's a damned good idea! With Cazombi the chairman and Aguinaldo in charge of the anti-Skink task force, we'll boil those damned lizards alive in their own teacups!"

"But if he screws up?"

"Promote him anyway. But then, my love, I'll need your firm hands to put my cervical vertebrae back together again after the Congress hangs me."

The headlines in the morning edition of the *Fargo Dispatch* two weeks later screamed, *LYONS SURRENDERS! BILLIE CLUBBED!* Below was an interview with General Jason Billie along with Cazombi's latest dispatch from Ravenette containing the liberal surrender terms he'd given the Coalition forces.

"That bastard went to the media!" Chang-Sturdevant exclaimed. She had already known about the surrender terms and had approved them. She also knew why Cazombi had relieved Billie, and approved of *that*. Immediately after his arrival back on Earth, Billie had been presented with the Legion of Honor and ordered to retire. The reason given for coming back home early was ill health.

"He was put on the retired list and told to keep his mouth shut in public." Marcus Berentus shook his head. "Now this."

"The Senate Armed Services Committee is calling for a full investigation." Chang-Sturdevant sighed. "And they'll have it. There's nothing we can do about it."

"Send Billie to Darkside?" Berentus chuckled.

"I've had enough of that, Marcus. No, we'll just have to tough this one out. I want you to ensure that General Cazombi has all the help he needs to prepare his testimony. He can call whomever he needs as witnesses and I want your ministry to see that's done. I'll have the attorney general appoint a legal team to assist him. After he's had a chance to explain his actions, this whole thing will blow over. Dammit, you'd think Billie would be smart enough to figure that out! He's going to destroy himself over this. Good heavens, Marcus, just based on Cazombi's report, we should have given Billie a court-martial, not decorated him!"

"They'll also be looking into whether Cazombi had the authority to give the Coalition forces such liberal surrender terms. Or you the authority to approve them without the consent of the Senate."

Chang-Sturdevant grimaced. "I know, I know, but Marcus, I know of a precedent: Cazombi is U. S. Grant to my Abe Lincoln. That ought to take care of the military end of things, and I'll handle the political end. Since the attack on Fort Seymour was a setup in the first place, those who did that are the only ones who deserve to be punished, and I think Preston Summers is just the man to do that. Let them wash their own laundry."

She paused for a long moment. "And on top of everything else, Marcus, we have to share the responsibility for what happened. You know what I mean about that." She got up and poured herself another dollop of Scotch from the bar. She held the glass to the light and admired the amber fluid. "Lagavulin," she murmured. "The only Scotch I've ever been able to drink without a mixer to kill the taste." She saluted Berentus and sipped the whiskey. "I have a decision to make, Marcus, and I'll need your advice."

"You have it, Suelee. But don't tell me you're thinking of resigning again."

"Umm, maybe later, but right now, Marcus, I have to decide something very big." She finished the whiskey in one gulp and smiled as it warmed its way down into her stomach. "I think the time has finally come to tell everyone about the Skinks."

"And why might that be?"

"Ah, yes, you haven't seen this yet. Be a dear and get my comp for me."

Berentus stepped around Chang-Sturdevant's chair to her desk to retrieve her personal comp, then handed it to her. She fiddled with it for a moment, then handed it to him.

"Read this."

Berentus gave her a curious look before taking the comp and beginning to read.

OFFICE OF THE PLANETARY ADMINISTRATOR
HAULOVER

FROM: SPILK MULLILEE, PLANETARY ADMINISTRATOR
TO: ROBIER ALTMAN, UNDERMINISTER OF STATE
SUBJECT: ODD OCCURRENCES

ROB,

I NEED SOME ADVICE. THERE HAVE BEEN SEVERAL RECENT EVENTS HERE THAT NEITHER I NOR ANYBODY ON MY STAFF CAN QUITE MAKE SENSE OF. AT LEAST, NONE OF US HAVE HEARD OR BEEN ABLE TO FIND INFORMATION ON SIMILAR INCIDENTS EITHER IN THE (ADMITTEDLY BRIEF) HISTORY OF HAULOVER, OR ANYWHERE ELSE IN HUMAN SPACE. MAYBE YOU OR SOMEONE ON YOUR STAFF CAN ADVISE ME ON WHAT WE ARE UP AGAINST, AND WHAT TO DO ABOUT IT.

OVER THE PAST TWO MONTHS, TEN REMOTE FAMILIES HAVE DISAPPEARED FROM THEIR HOMESTEADS. IT'S NOT AS THOUGH THE FAMILES PICKED UP AND MOVED WITHOUT TELLING ANYBODY, EITHER. IN EACH INSTANCE, THE HOMESTEAD WAS BURNED TO THE GROUND, NOTHING WAS LEFT. IN THREE INSTANCES, SHARDS OF BONE WERE FOUND IN THE SIFTINGS OF THE ASH. OUR ANTHROPOLOGIST BELIEVES THEY ARE HUMAN BONE FRAGMENTS, THOUGH THEY WERE SO THOROUGHLY DAMAGED BY THE FIRES THAT OUR LABS HAVE BEEN UNABLE TO GET ANY USABLE DNA FROM THEM TO VERIFY THE ANTHROPOLOGIST'S PRELIMINARY FINDINGS. THE MOSTLY MELTED REMAINS OF A COMM UNIT WERE FOUND IN ONE SITE, AND THAT POINTS

EVEN MORE THAN THE SUSPECTED BONE FRAGMENTS TO FOUL PLAY.
THERE HAVE BEEN NO—ZERO—REPORTS OF ATTACKS ON HOMESTEADS.
EVEN THE TEN DESTROYED HOMESTEADS NEVER REPORTED ANY
PROBLEMS BEFORE THEY SIMPLY DISAPPEARED.

DURING THESE THREE MONTHS THERE HAVE BEEN A FEW REPORTS
OF UNUSUAL METEORITES. METEORITES ARE COMMON ENOUGH IN THE
NIGHT SKY OF HAULOVER, BUT THESE WERE REPORTED TO NOT FLASH
OUT LIKE NORMAL METEORITES, AND IN SEVERAL CASES THEY WERE
REPORTED TO HAVE ABRUPTLY CHANGED DIRECTION IN FLIGHT. SOME OF
THEM WERE ALSO REPORTED TO BLINK OUT AND THEN IMMEDIATELY
REAPPEAR AT DISTANCES TOO GREAT FOR THEM TO HAVE TRAVELED IN
THE INTERVENING TIME. ONE OBSERVER, A FORMER STARSHIP CREWMAN,
SAID IT LOOKED LIKE THEY BRIEFLY TRANSITTED INTO BEAM SPACE. BUT,
OF COURSE, EVERYBODY KNOWS IT'S IMPOSSIBLE TO GO INTO OR OUT OF
BEAM SPACE IN A GRAVITY WELL. THERE HAVE BEEN NO INSTRUMENT
READINGS TO CONFIRM THESE REPORTS, WHICH HAVE ALL BEEN IN
REMOTE LOCATIONS AND OBSERVED VISUALLY BY ONE OR ONLY A FEW
PEOPLE. SEVERAL OF OUR SCIENTISTS HAVE DISMISSED THE REPORTS AS
"SWAMP GAS," IF THAT ANCIENT REFERENCE MEANS ANYTHING TO YOU.
I'D BE INCLINED TO AGREE WITH OUR PSYCH TEAM, WHO DISMISS THE
REPORTS AS THE RESULT OF OVERACTIVE IMAGINATIONS OF SOCIAL
MISFITS WHO GO INTO THE WILDERNESS, ONLY TO DISCOVER THAT THEY
NEED SOCIAL ATTENTION, SO THEY MAKE UP FAR-FETCHED STORIES TO
TELL THE FOLKS THEY LEFT BEHIND. WHAT I FIND DISTURBING ABOUT
THESE REPORTS IS THAT EACH OF THEM HAPPENED WITHIN DAYS BEFORE
WE LOST CONTACT WITH ONE OF THE HOMESTEADS.

ONE FINAL DETAIL. TRACES OF AN ACID WERE FOUND AT SEVEN
OF THE BURNED-DOWN HOMESTEADS. OUR CHEMISTS DESCRIBE IT
AS, "SOME KIND OF PHOSPHORIC ACID . . . POSSIBLY WHITE PHOSPHORUS.
MIXED WITH ORGANIC SOLVENTS LIKE CARBON DISULFIDE OR BENZENE."
WHATEVER THAT MEANS. I DO KNOW THE HOMESTEADERS HAVE NO
USE FOR SUCH AN ACID AND, INDEED, THE CHEMISTS ASSURE ME
IT'S NOT EVEN KNOWN TO BE IN THE INVENTORY ANYWHERE ON
HAULOVER.

IF YOU HAVE ANY INFORMATION THAT WOULD HELP ME WITH THIS PROBLEM, I'D MUCH APPRECIATE IT. I HOPE YOU AND YOUR FAMILY ARE DOING WELL.

From there, the message contained personal details.

Berentus whistled after reading the message. "That certainly does sound like the Skinks," he said.

"And it's our secretiveness about the Skinks that caused this war. I believe it is past time we went public about them."

Berentus looked at her long and solemnly before saying, "Let's drink to that." So they did.

CHAPTER THIRTY-FIVE

Jason Billie glared at Admiral Joseph K. C. B. Porter, who looked away as he fiddled nervously with the third button on the front of his tunic.

"Ahem, Jason—" Porter began.

"I *demand* a court-martial! I *demand* you court-martial that goddamned nigger and his asshole buddy, that Marine!" Billie rose halfway out of his chair as he spoke. Admiral Porter reared back in his own seat, half afraid Billie would come across his desk at him, he was so enraged. He held his hands out in a gesture that both suggested Billie calm down and warded off an assault if he didn't.

"Jason, the president has ordered—"

"That fucking Chink cunt!" Billie almost screamed. "Goddamned bitch! Goddamned bastards, all of them! They were all against me! From the start, nothing but trouble from those people. I was sent out there to fail, I know that now. They were out to destroy me!" Billie sank back into his seat, breathing heavily, virtually exhausted by his outburst. He wiped his brow and lips with a handkerchief. He had conveniently forgotten that he had asked Admiral Porter for the command of the army on Ravenette in the first place, and it was he himself who convinced the president to give it to him.

Porter said nothing for a while. *So,* he thought, *now I begin to see why Cazombi relieved this madman from command.* Cautiously, during the prolonged silence, an aide stuck his head in the door and raised his eyebrows at the admiral, silently asking if everything was all right. Porter shook his head briefly, indicating that everything was under control. Quietly, the aide withdrew, but had two burly MPs stand by in the anteroom in case they were needed. Admiral Porter knew nothing about the MPs, but he might have been more relaxed than he was if he did.

"Jason, old friend," Porter began, "the president has accepted Cazombi's surrender terms on behalf of her government." He paused, waiting apprehensively for the violent response he expected from Billie, but the four-star general just sat there silently, his handkerchief to his lips. "She has ordered that there shall be no, uh, scandal over what he did to you out there." Again Porter paused, expecting another outburst and enormously relieved when it didn't follow. When he was sure Billie had calmed down he went on. "I have my orders. You had to resign your command due to ill health, Jason; that announcement has already been made. You have been placed on the temporarily disabled-retired list effective today, full pay and benefits. I want you to return to your quarters now, get a grip on yourself, and be back here at fifteen hundred for your retirement and award ceremony."

"You're going to give me one of those goddamned meaningless attaboys and put me out to pasture." Billie shook his head slowly. "Joe, I don't know what the service has come to, letting these cunts and niggers—"

"*That'll be enough of that talk, Jason!*" Porter said sharply. "Fifteen hundred. You be here. You behave yourself during this ceremony, do you understand? Any more talk like that out of you and I guarantee you, Jason, I'll court-martial you and dismiss you from the service for disciplinary reasons! What happened on Ravenette is over." Porter meant what he'd said.

Billie sighed. "Admiral, I am fucked, but let me tell you something. I'm not done. You haven't heard the last of me." He saluted formally and departed.

Porter let out a long sigh and slumped in his seat. His steward came into the office. "Sir, lunch?"

"Is it lunchtime already?" Porter frowned, but instantly brightened somewhat at the prospect of eating. "What's on the menu today?"

"What you ordered, sir. Your favorite—hot dogs with a dessert of orange sherbet and green pepper slices!"

"Um. I'm not very hungry. Take it away. Uh, no, wait, leave the sherbet," he added quickly. He sampled the sherbet and took a bite of the green pepper. He understood this had been a favorite dessert dish during the twentieth century, enjoyed particularly by the people living in the subtropical areas of the former United States and called the "Fort Lauderdale Trots." He never understood what that name signified, but he enjoyed the dessert. He summoned his aide and ordered the steward to bring back the hot dogs. *What the hell,* he thought, *I'm not going to let Jason Billie screw over my appetite!*

The Green Lizard was a dark and sleazy bar at all times, but darker and sleazier that night than usual, and sparsely occupied at that late hour. Just the place for conspirators to meet. It was also situated in a Fargo suburb guaranteed not to attract anyone who might know Jason Billie, dressed in nondescript civilian attire, or his guest.

"This crystal is my report on what *really* happened on Ravenette. I want you to read it and share it with the members of your committee." Billie shoved the crystal across the table.

"Well, General, I'll read it but I can't guarantee you the committee will do anything about it. Most members are happy the war's over and that our side was victorious," the little man replied. He hefted the crystal in his palm. "You've heard, haven't you, that Alistair Cazombi's name is going to be put forward as the next Chairman of the Combined Chiefs?" The little man smiled wryly at Billie, calculating what effect the news would have on him.

"*What?* Cazombi, *chairman?*" Billie gasped. "You're joking? They're jumping that, that, *man* over all the eligible four-stars? I'm telling you now, Senator, in our world of today, virtue is punished while criminals and traitors are allowed to prosper."

The little man sitting opposite Billie did not know him very well, but he knew him well enough to understand that he was far from having any virtues himself, that he was in fact a manipulator who'd do anything to advance his own interests. He permitted himself a mental grin. Jason Billie would make a good politician. "I am not joking, General, and furthermore, if the president submits his name, he'll get the appointment. There's hardly anyone in the Senate who'd oppose her on this. Cazombi's star, er, *stars,* have risen."

"The Virgin's slimy boogers, you say!"

The little man winced at the curse. "It's a fact, General. So why should I stick my neck out for what's on this crystal of yours?"

"I'm not a general anymore, Senator," Billie said bitterly. "I'm just plain old Mister Billie now." Briefly but with feeling, Billie gave his version of the war on Ravenette. "Mutiny, treason, that's what it amounts to," he concluded. "Treason because he let those war criminals off and she went along with it! There's an election coming up, Senator. This should be an issue. Your hearings could swing the vote. You could be Chang-Sturdevant's successor to your party's leadership." He shrugged and left the rest hanging.

"Ummm. General, did you know that General Anders Aguinaldo has been appointed to head up some kind of special military task force? Rumor has it he's already departed to form it up on Arsenault. Rumor has it that Cazombi's appointment as chairman has got something to do with Aguinaldo's new command. Any idea what's going on?"

"I've heard about Aguinaldo getting a new job." Billie's response was noncommittal. He was perplexed. What did Aguinaldo's new assignment have to do with his problem on Ravenette? " 'Nother goddamned Marine," he added dismissively. "But what's on that crystal, handled properly, can unseat Chang-Sturdevant's administration, Senator."

"Ummm. Well, General, we'll see." He pocketed the crystal. "Have you retained counsel?"

"I am going to, Senator."

Senator Kutmoi scribbled a name on a napkin. "Call this man tomorrow. He's a senior partner in a very famous law firm here in Fargo. He could get Judas Iscariot off."

"I don't know if I care for that comparison, Senator," Billie said, his face turning red.

"Oh, no offense, General! Just an expression. Well, it's getting late. You must excuse me." He extended a thin, clammy hand. "I will be in touch." And with that he departed.

"Thanks for coming," Billie muttered to the senator's back. Billie sat there for a long time after the senator had departed, nursing a glass of beer that had long gone flat. Everything had gone flat, he reflected. He rubbed a hand across the five-day growth of beard on his jaw. *He'd* gone flat. "Goddamned politician," he muttered. He doubted the senator would even read his report. "Damn asshole." He stood up, threw some bills on the table and walked painfully to the door. The events of the last weeks had prematurely aged Jason Billie and the devil of it was he wouldn't even be eighty until next month.

Jason Fosdick Billie sat in his hotel room, his fists pressing hard into his temples. Tears of bitter disappointment stained his cheeks. He had been a soldier all his life. He had risen to the very pinnacle of military success with his appointment to lead the army on Ravenette. Now he was down, out, disgraced, and his enemies had been put over him.

Why? he asked himself over and over again, *Why?*

At Billie's elbow was a tumbler half full of the very best Scotch available in Fargo. He had consumed the missing half, but in his present mood it had tasted like bad water and did nothing for him. A Clinton lay in an ashtray beside the Scotch, burned out only one-third of the way down. Usually so delicious, this evening it had only scorched the inside of his mouth and left a taste of dried excrement on his tongue.

And now, after having suffered unimaginable disgrace, he had fallen even further, to the despicable level of consulting with the two lowest forms of human life, a ward-heeling *politician* who had recommended he see a *lawyer.*

Even though Jason Fosdick Billie had more in common with lawyers and politicians than he was willing to admit, he still had the quality of competence on the plus side of his ledger. He was very good at what he did. He understood the military service, which in one important aspect was a bureaucracy. Field commanders worked in a fluid environment, one where rules and regulations often did not apply and where individual initiative was required to overcome problems and where delay could be fatal; make the wrong decision in the field and that could be the end of an officer's career. That is the main reason why as a junior officer Billie had avoided field command, especially in war, which by itself could be very damaging to one's health.

But in the bureaucracy of an army staff, Jason Billie was in his element. He could obfuscate, delay, confuse any issue before the staff, postpone important decisions until behind the scenes he had politicked the ones he wanted. He was an expert at the give-and-take of the conference room. He could dominate and be subservient at the same time, browbeat those who disagreed with him and suck up to those in authority. He could think fast and no one ever caught him at a loss for words, his command of repartee, the only kind of "command" he was really good at, was devastating. Few would dare to cross verbal swords with Jason Fosdick Billie.

Except that goddamned Alistair Cazombi. *Cazombi!* The name coursed through his brain like a hot poker. How he *hated* that man! Cazombi, a former *sergeant* who had risen somehow to flag rank without ever attending a military academy. Unthinkable! How could such an ordinary man have achieved three stars, much less a nomination to be the next Chairman of the Combined Chiefs of Staff? That had been Billie's job! He should have been the next chairman! He'd have had the job too, until that damned man came along. He groaned audibly and smashed his fists into his head repeatedly as he remembered with burning cheeks how Cazombi had him *arrested* in front of the entire staff, had *him, a full general,* hauled off like a disobedient brat for picking his nose at the dinner table!

It was all due to that old bitch, Chang-Sturdevant. Could Cazombi have been porking the hag? How else could she have taken to the man so readily? No, he thought, that wouldn't have been possible; Cazombi had been on Ravenette too long, no opportunity. Then it occurred to him. Both of them were dirty *wogs*! Well, one was a wog, the other was a nigger. But that was it! The racially inferior types always ganged up on the pure Aryan. That had been the case for centuries and Jason Fosdick Billie was only the most recent victim of such schemes.

Jason Fosdick Billie had never married. His career had been the only interest in his life. He had a sister; she lived elsewhere on Earth and would have nothing to do with her brother. He came from a family with a long history of distinguished military and public service. His ancestors had been commanders and statesmen and to some extent his illustrious name had aided him in his rise within the army hierarchy. No matter what kind of man he had become, he was the descendant of a long line of valiant military men. And he was rich, not just because of old family money but because he was a shrewd investor. He could take his retirement now and live in splendor the rest of his days. Any other man would have consoled himself with that. But not General Jason Billie.

No, there is only one way to end this disgrace. He got up from where he was sitting and took a bag out of the closet. Inside was an antique semiautomatic handgun. It had belonged to his great-great-great-grandfather, who'd retired as a major general, covered with decorations for valor. It was a .32 caliber Colt which had once been standard issue in the old United States Army for the exclusive use of flag officers. Years ago, at some expense, Billie had had fifty bullets specially manufactured for it and he had actually fired the old gun several times. He had kept it in good condition and it still worked perfectly. There was some pitting in on the slide, but otherwise it was in almost-new condition.

General Jason Fosdick Billie pulled the slide and inserted a brass cartridge into the gun's chamber. He put the barrel into his mouth. The strong taste of steel spread over his tongue. He squeezed the trigger lightly. One second, one instant, and it'd all be over. He closed his eyes. *Me, consult a lawyer? Make my disgrace a matter of public record? Better death.*

But . . . A thought suddenly occurred to him. He paused. He took his finger off the trigger and removed the barrel from his mouth. What if that lawyer could do something to resurrect his reputation? What if that senator's hearings turned things around? He, Jason Billie, could hold his own! Who'd be watching and listening? Plebeians, politicians, people naturally inferior to himself, people who could be swayed. Yes! Yes, he could do it!

Jason Billie laid the pistol down and sipped his Scotch. He relighted his Clinton, sucked the smoke into his lungs and exhaled luxuriously. "Alistair," he said aloud, "watch out, you black bastard! Jason Billie is not done with you yet!"

CHAPTER THIRTY-SIX

"Do you think," Senator Haggle Kutmoi said, glancing around the sleazy bar with disgust, "we might have met in a more, um, *congenial* environment?"

"General Billie recommended the Green Lizard. He said you'd been here before, Senator," Sanguinious Cheatham replied, smirking. "Besides, Senator, we can't quite conduct our business in one of Fargo's more upscale bistros, can we? We, ah, don't want your colleagues to know you're meeting with Billie's lawyer, do we?" He shifted from smirk to smile.

"And just what is our business, Counselor?" Cheatham was a senior partner in the law firm of Feargut and Cheatham, which General Jason Billie had retained to represent him in a suit he planned to bring against President Chang-Sturdevant and Marcus Berentus over the war on Ravenette. Feargut and Cheatham was a well-known firm that specialized in high-profile cases. Their fees were high but so were their settlements, and they had a nearly perfect record at winning controversial cases. Often merely the announcement they'd been retained in a case was enough for their client to win an out-of-court settlement.

"Ah. Well. You've read the statement General Billie gave you?"

"I have."

"And will you use it?"

"I will."

Cheatham nodded his approval. "You see, the General has decided to go after the principal architects of the Ravenette fiasco. This Cazombi fellow, he was a mere instrument of President Chang-Sturdevant's misguided policy. It was Chang-Sturdevant who pardoned the rebels, after all. She could have overturned Cazombi's surrender terms but she did not. I presume you will call Cazombi to testify when you hold your hearings?"

"I will, of course. I would call the president herself if I could, but that is out of the question, as you very well know. Now where does that leave me, Counselor?"

"As President of the Confederation of Human Worlds, of course. If you play to your advantages."

Kutmoi permitted himself a barking laugh. "You can't be serious, Counselor. That's not possible." He grinned and folded his stubby little fingers sanctimoniously.

"Politics is the art of the possible," Cheatham replied airily. "Your hearings could bring down Chang-Sturdevant's government, certainly weaken her party, excuse me, *your* party, in the next election. You could stand as an independent in the primary. Party loyalty, Senator, like ethics in the legal profession, is a matter of expediency, pure expediency." He smiled expansively.

"And how am I to do that with my hearings?"

"Surely, Senator, I don't have to explain that to a man of your experience."

"Try me."

Cheatham shrugged. "Pack the panel."

"Everyone does that, so what?"

"Select the right witnesses to testify."

"Anyone can testify before my committee; all they need to do is apply to the clerk of the senate and they'll be put on the agenda."

Cheatham grinned. "Select the right witnesses."

"Ah. But you realize the president will have reports and affidavits submitted in advance, already has in fact, that could be very damning to your client's case. I might have to take a bath on this, Counselor. Oh, I'm going forward with it, that's my job," he added quickly, "but I don't know how many of the senators on the panel I can get to agree on my final report or how many members of the full committee will go along with our recommendations and support legislation."

"Screw the affidavits and your final report, Senator, if you will permit me such language. It's how you appear during these hearings that the public will remember come election time. Do you think the voters will *read* your report? Don't make me laugh. Control your witnesses—it's all theater and you know that."

"But this Cazombi, he's a reputable, highly respected officer. His testimony can be damaging."

"Of course you'll have to subpoena this Cazombi fellow, but no one else from his side, you see? None of the senior commanders who were on Ravenette. As to those of the public who volunteer to testify"—Cheatham shrugged—"all you'll get there are assholes. Their testimony won't count for beans. Shoot Cazombi down and you shoot Chang-Sturdevant down. Use these hearings to get the Congress to pass legislation limiting the use of presidential powers and you come out as the man who saved the Confederation from that dictatorial harridan. If the legislation ploy flops, no matter, you proposed it and that'll count heavily in your favor. Blame its failure on the timidity of your colleagues."

"I voted for the war, don't forget."

Cheatham permitted himself another shrug. "Yes, but you saw the light, Senator. You were one of the few who did. Capitalize on that. Nothing impresses a judge more than honest contrition, and in this case the voters will be your judge."

"You should be a politician." Kutmoi grinned.

"And you, Senator, should be President."

Kutmoi laughed.

"And here, sir"—Cheatham passed a crystal across the table—"is a generous contribution to your election campaign, all legal and aboveboard. The code on this crystal will give you access to an account established in your name and you can draw upon it as necessary to finance your campaign expenses."

"What goes along with this contribution, Senator?"

"Bosch Feargut wishes to be appointed Attorney General in your administration."

"And?"

"And perhaps, when the time is right, a seat on the Supreme Court."

"And you, counselor?"

"Ah, me, a mere atom on the scales of justice?" he asked, waving a hand airily. "Well, with dear old Feargut away serving the citizens of the Confederation of Human Worlds, I become *the* senior partner in our firm."

Kutmoi raised an eyebrow in surprise. The first was a modest request, the second one not at all unusual or that hard to get confirmed. "I hope the money in that account is not contingent upon my winning the election."

"It is not, Senator."

"Then consider it done."

"Then I shall bid you good evening, Senator." Cheatham rose to go.

"I'll see you around." Kutmoi grinned up from his seat.

"You certainly will, Senator. I'll be sitting right beside General Billie when he testifies."

Munchin' Donuts was a popular eatery on the corner of Lincoln and Washington Streets in downtown Fargo. Its windows looked out on the crowds of shoppers and office workers hurrying to and fro, and the eatery was usually crowded during the daylight hours. People in the streets frequently stopped to gaze longingly through the windows, eyeing the culinary displays set out there, the huge varieties of donuts, cakes, pies, breads, and sandwiches for which the establishment was famous throughout the city of Fargo.

Alistair Cazombi casually dipped his plain cake donut into his coffee and regarded the stocky, bald-headed man sitting across from him. "What can I do for you, Senator?"

"Back home, when I was younger," Ubsa Nor began, "I worked in the mines. Gave me an appreciation for what it's like to work with your hands, be low man on the pole. I've never forgotten that, General. I think you know what I'm talking about."

Cazombi laughed briefly. "Worst duty I ever had in the army was kitchen police in a consolidated mess hall. I was on pots and pans, Senator. When the day was done my fingers were so wrinkled from the hot water they looked like raisins."

"I opposed the war on Ravenette, General. I oppose Chang-Sturdevant's government."

"I know that, Senator. So why don't you tell me why you asked for this meeting."

"I'll come straight to the point now."

"I'd appreciate that, sir."

"When you come before my committee for confirmation to be the next Chairman of the Combined Chiefs, I will support your nomination. I'll do that because you're the best man for that job. You did what you had to do on Ravenette. I'm also on Haggle Kutmoi's panel 'investigating' the Ravenette war and I've read all the reports and statements. Kutmoi's going to use that investigation as a springboard to support his candidacy for president when his party holds its next election convention. He wants to replace the Old Lady. That I cannot stand for, General. Yes, he is the greater of two evils, in my eyes. We'll run someone against Chang-Sturdevant and maybe win, but Kutmoi cannot be allowed to run for president. Anyone, even the Old Lady, is preferable to that man. So when you testify before that committee of his, you've got to hit him between the eyes. If he carries this hearing off and gets the publicity he's seeking, that may be all he needs."

"So he's not interested in finding out the truth about what happened on Ravenette?"

"No. Privately, he thinks Jason Billie's an idiot, an incompetent braggart who should never have reached the rank of private first class. But Billie's a showman, you can count on it that his testimony will play like a Shakespearean tragedy. You've got to counter that."

Cazombi shrugged as he bit into his donut. "I'm no actor, Senator. I'm going to tell the truth, and let the chips fall where they may."

"But, General," Nor said and gestured helplessly, "you've *got* to loosen up, you've *got* to show some, well, *emotion* in your testimony. I know they call you Cazombi the Zombie, but you've got to lighten up, billions of people will be watching."

"I never learned how to express emotion very well, Senator. That, and these damned donuts, are the only personal shortcomings I'm aware of. It's too late for me to reform now." He popped the final piece of donut into his mouth, "I'll do what I've always done, speak straight to the truth of what happened. You see, Senator, I don't need vindication, I won't play politics, and frankly, it's all the same to me who's president. I'm a soldier and it's my duty to follow orders to the best of my ability."

"But you know right from wrong, General! I've studied your record. I know what happened on Avionia Station with that scientist, and on Ravenette you stepped in and acted. I mean, you put *everything* on the line out there."

Cazombi reached for another donut. "These are my worst sin, Senator. Have one?"

Nor shook his head. He knew there was no use coaching the man. "Have you retained legal counsel, General?"

"Yes."

"May I ask who that is?"

"Sure, Lieutenant Judie Dorman, from the Combined Chiefs Judge Advocate's office."

"Jesus' bloody nails!" Nor exclaimed and ran a hand over his head in frustration. "Billie's retained the finest attorney in Fargo, maybe the world! And you're going in there with a *lieutenant* JAG officer?"

"Yes. Her military bearing impressed me."

"Military bearing?" Nor groaned. "Aw, what the hell, General, gimme one of those donuts."

With a bang of his gavel, Haggle Kutmoi, the Confederation Senator from Bulon, senior member of the Senate Armed Forces Committee and chairman of the panel hearing testimony relating to the recently concluded war on Ravenette, convened the committee's first session.

Kutmoi was in his element. In the public eye. Running things. Asserting himself over the president, her cabinet, and the armed forces of the Confederation of Human Worlds. He was joined by seven other senators, three from his own party, nominally supporters of President Chang-Sturdevant's policies, and four from Ubsa Nor's party. Recently Nor and Kutmoi had made news when they came to blows in the Senate steam bath, fighting over the war on Ravenette, but for the hearing they seemed to have put their differences aside.

That Kutmoi was chairing the committee was extraordinary in itself because its avowed purpose was to gather evidence to sponsor legislation limiting the president's war powers, and possibly to establish grounds for impeachment proceedings over the way in which she had pardoned the secessionist leadership. Since Kutmoi was seen by many as a possible successor to Chang-Sturdevant as President of the Confederation, many watching the hearings realized they were merely a grandstand for Kutmoi's political aspirations. They also expected the hearings to be grand theater.

Above the chest, Haggle Kutmoi looked the perfect image of a senator—white, wavy hair, distinguished facial features. But from the chest down, he resembled a turnip with matchsticks for arms and legs. That morning he was visible only from the chest up.

"Ladies and gentlemen, I now call these hearings to order," Kutmoi intoned. "Our purpose here this morning and in the days to come is to hear testimony relating to the war on Ravenette, the summary and illegal relief of the army commander in that war, the president's pardon of the war's instigators, and a review of the President's abuse of her war powers in violation of the Confederation Constitution. Our first witness this morning will be General Jason Fosdick Billie, lately commander of our ground forces on and around the world known as Ravenette."

After being duly sworn, Billie and Sanguinious Cheatham took their place before the panel. "I will keep my remarks short." Billie smiled up at the senators as he made a show of unfolding a thick sheaf of papers, which brought a laugh from the spectators in the gallery. He conferred briefly with Cheatham, nodded at the panel, and began. "I have been a soldier all my life. It is with heavy heart I take this seat today to testify in these hearings. My heart is heavy not because of anything that happened to me on the world known as Ravenette, it is heavy because I must bring to light certain events that will no doubt embarrass deeply certain members of this government, and more particularly, some of my erstwhile comrades in uniform, men of valor and reputation who, because of a totally misguided government policy, were forced to make decisions in keeping with neither military tradition nor the ethics of the military profession."

Billie spoke for more than an hour. During the entire performance the gallery was rapt in total silence. Billie's words rolled off his tongue in mellowed tones, and occasionally his voice vibrated with profound feeling. He used allusion skillfully, referring to the heroic deeds of the past in such a way that without saying so, he compared himself with those heroes. Many watching compared his speech with that of Douglas MacArthur's "Old Soldiers Never Die" performance. He referred only obliquely to those who had relieved him on Ravenette, and never once did he accuse them of anything but bad judgment arrived at on the spur of the moment while under extreme duress. He was magnanimous and generous and totally controlled. General Cazombi, who sat awaiting his turn to testify, shook his head in amazement. The last time he'd seen Jason Billie he was screaming and cursing and frothing at the mouth. Now here he was, John Wilkes Booth in his finest role.

Billie wore his uniform as he was entitled to as a retired flag officer. It was resplendent with rows of ribbons, all for meritorious service, of course, but none of the senators and few others watching knew the difference. Later there would be much comment in the media about Billie's wartime service compared with that of Alistair Cazombi's, but what stuck in the public's mind was his live performance before the panel.

"In conclusion, gentlemen, I now publicly acknowledge that if I made mistakes in my command, they were entirely my own. I take full responsibility for the lives we lost on Ravenette. I regret only that I was not able to execute my strategic plan in time to save more of my men's lives. I ask you, the people of this Confederation, and almighty God to understand and forgive me."

Congressmen and observers in the public galleries stood and cheered when he had finished. There were no questions.

Next Cazombi was sworn and took his place before the panel, the buxom Lieutenant Dorman at his side. She wore no decorations on her uniform because she had not been in the service long enough to earn any. Cazombi wore only the Army Good Conduct Medal that he had earned as an enlisted man. Millions of former enlisted personnel throughout Human Space took notice of that simple decoration.

"Mr. Chairman, senators," he began, "I did what I had to do." Lieutenant Dorman whispered something in Cazombi's ear and he shook his head. "I obeyed General Billie's orders faithfully. I carried out my mission to the best of my ability. I relieved General Billie when, for whatever reason, he refused to take advantage of a strategic breakthrough of the enemy's lines. I saw the opportunity for victory and took it. The sworn testimony submitted by the other officers present at that time will amply justify my actions. I deeply regret I had to relieve General

Billie of his command, but I believe I had no other choice. I have nothing further to say at this time."

Lieutenant Dorman appeared to be suffering an attack of apoplexy. Cazombi laid a hand on her arm, said something, and smiled.

There were no questions from the panel. "You, you may retire now, General," Kutmoi muttered. He seemed perplexed, like the man waiting for the other shoe to drop. "Ah," he murmured, looking nervously at his colleagues, "we may recall you later, sir."

Alistair Cazombi stood, gave a nod to the senators, and with one hand on the small of Lieutenant Dorman's back, left the gallery. They sat silently in the senate shuttle that connected with an underground station in the center of Fargo, where they could avoid the press corps waiting outside the Great Gallery.

When they emerged onto the street it was raining. They stood in the shelter of the underground entrance, watching the rain fall. "You could have bombed them, General," Lieutenant Dorman said at last. "But gee, that Billie." She shook her head. "It was an award performance."

"Aw, he's just full of hot air, Judie. People will catch on quick enough. They always do." He laughed. "You should have been there when I relieved the bastard! Best thing I ever did."

"But sir, we have all the evidence." She patted the small container of crystals in a uniform pocket. "We could have displayed it all right there, put an end to this whole thing today."

"Judie, we have all the ammo we need. The senators have copies of all those testaments too. They or their staffs can read them later. There are times in war when it's wise to let the enemy come to you. Now, my dear, would you join me in a cup of coffee and a donut? Donuts are my only vice." He put an arm around her shoulder and they stepped out into the rain.

CHAPTER THIRTY-SEVEN

Marcus Aurelius Berentus had been a soldier all his life, with the possible exception of the recent past during which time he had served in the cabinet of Cynthia Chang-Sturdevant as her Minister of War. Perhaps, then, it would be better to say he had devoted his life to public service, because the warrior in a democracy such as the Confederation of Human Worlds serves as the bulwark ensuring the freedoms of its citizens.

Chang-Sturdevant had selected him to be a member of her cabinet early in her administration. She had tapped him for the position based on the recommendation of her massage therapist, Karla Grabbentao, whose husband, Barton, had served in Berentus's squadron during one of the Silvansian wars and virtually worshipped his old commander. Desperate to find someone who actually knew something about war and the military service, someone more qualified than the political hacks appointed to the office by her predecessors, she had called Berentus out of retirement for a chat. She liked his easy, relaxed manner and his honesty. So, despite some misgivings on the part of her staff and other cabinet members, she put his name before the Confederation Senate to be her next Minister of War.

The senators had debated endlessly. All, even those of her own party, had been dismayed at her choice, but none could find any dirt on Berentus that would disqualify him from such a high office. Instead, they debated his qualifications. "Doesn't know his way around Fargo!" "No experience in government!" "No political affiliation!" "Not even married!" But in the end they had confirmed him.

For once the politicians had made the right decision, because no better man could have been made for the job.

Marcus Berentus sat alone in his office awaiting the imminent arrival of General Anders Aguinaldo. He had asked the Marine to stop by on his way to his personal interview with the president, just to chat. He liked Aguinaldo and, of course, the president had selected him to head up the Skink task force partly on his recommendation—and her own instinct.

His favorite music played quietly in the background, some tunes made popular by an ancient string band of the early twentieth century. His secretary announced that the general had arrived. "Don't keep him waiting, Connie," he responded. He stood, came around his desk, and met Aguinaldo in the middle of his spartan office. "General." He extended his hand and they shook warmly.

"Excellency, thank you for inviting me."

"Call me Marcus, General. Confucius's calluses, General, if they hadn't made me Minister of War, you'd outrank me all to hell!"

Aguinaldo laughed softly. "Call me Andy, sir." Berentus nodded and indicated a comfortable settee on one side of a coffee table. The table itself was a beautifully carved piece of slate depicting in three dimensions several types of fighter aircraft. Aguinaldo ran a hand over the carvings. "You fly any of these, sir?" He knew that in his younger days Berentus had been a hotshot fighter pilot, in fact an ace in both deep-space and aerial combat.

"Yup, made as many landings as takeoffs."

Aguinaldo cocked his ear to the music. "That's a catchy tune, sir— I mean Marcus."

"Yes. I'm a fan of that old-fashioned stuff, being a dinosaur myself. The tune they're playing now is 'Pass Around the Bottle and We'll All Take a Drink,' to the tune of 'The Battle Hymn of the Republic.' You listen carefully enough and you can actually understand the words." He laughed. "Speaking of which . . . ?" He nodded at a cabinet against one wall.

"A battle hymn or whiskey? I've had more than my share of both. Oh, no, sir." Aguinaldo laughed. "I can't go in to see the president with booze on my breath!"

"Don't you worry about that," Berentus said, getting up and opening the cabinet. "You'll probably leave with booze on your breath; the Old Lady's liable to offer you a libation herself." He began mixing two drinks. "I refuse to own or use, if I can do it myself, one of those goddamned robo-servers." He chuckled. "Two things no real man leaves to a machine: his sex partner and mixing his drink. How do you like your Scotch, Andy?"

"Oh, maybe one finger, couple of rocks?"

"Man after me own heart!" Berentus poured two drinks and returned to the table. He raised his glass to Aguinaldo. "General, you are about to depart on a mission of the greatest importance to all of us, possibly the greatest task ever assigned anybody. Your Marines proved on Kingdom they could handle these bastards and the president and I both know you'll clean their clocks for good." They sipped their drinks in silence.

"This is damned good Scotch!" Aguinaldo said at last.

"It ought to be. Sue, er, the president herself recommended it to me." Berentus's face turned slightly red and he looked away sharply to cover the near slip. Aguinaldo caught it, however, and suppressed a slight smile. The Minister of War was as embarrassed as a schoolboy stealing his first kiss. Aguinaldo liked that kind of irrepressible honesty in a man, since so few people these days could be embarrassed by the plain truth about themselves. Everyone knew that Marcus and the president were very "close," if that is the proper word to describe their private relationship. "Well," Berentus continued, "I just wanted to ask you over here before you saw the Old Lady. You'll never meet anyone as straightforward and accessible as the president, Andy. If she'd chosen the military service as her career, she'd be wearing four stars now. As it is, she outranks us all anyway. Andy, we—you and I and any soldier worth his pay—are damned fortunate to have her as our Commander in Chief."

"I'll drink to that, sir!" They toasted the president.

"Andy, you need anybody to fly one of those newfangled A8E

VSTOLs, you give me a call. Why, couple of months retraining, maybe a few new organs, and I'll be ready to wax some of those Skinks for you."

Sensing that the interview was over now, Aguinaldo finished his Scotch and stood up. "You bet!" he replied. "We can always use a bold pilot."

"Let me tell you something, Andy. There are old pilots and bold pilots but there ain't no old bold pilots!" Berentus laughed. "Good luck, Andy." They shook again.

"Uh, sir?" Aguinaldo nodded at the music. "Just who *are* those guys?" he nodded at the music which was still playing in the background.

"Oh, that's Gid Plunkett and His Sand Sifters, an old Georgia string band." Berentus laughed.

"Well, what in the hell are they singing about?"

"They're singing an old novelty tune about a boardinghouse somewhere. The idiom is very old American English but if you listen carefully you can make out most of the words. Here, I'll translate.

"Oh, the pork chops, they was rare,
The potatoes had red hair
Fido had all his feet down in the soup.
Oh, the eggs they would not match,
If you cracked one it would hatch
In that awful hungry hash house where I dwell!

"They ought to make up a song about me, Andy. I told you, I'm a dinosaur, a connoisseur of the ancient and improbable. Just the man to be Minister of War in a time of universal crisis."

"Marcus, you and Porter with his hot dogs, macaroni, and Jell-O would hit it off just fine."

Berentus laughed. "I've heard about those luncheons of his. Fortunately, I've always had business to keep me away." He paused and looked steadily at Aguinaldo for a moment, then said, "Andy, we're counting on you and we know you'll pull this operation off successfully, but just in case you need a little extra assistance, God bless you and your troops."

* * *

"General, I won't wish you luck, but success."

"Ma'am, thank you, but if it weren't for luck, well"—he smiled—"I'd probably still be an ensign."

They were sitting in Cynthia Chang-Sturdevant's private office sipping Lagavulin. She smiled. She liked General Anders Aguinaldo's self-deprecating sense of humor. It only confirmed to her that appointing him to head the Joint Task Force was a wise decision coming even as late as this. "When do you leave?"

"Tomorrow. My staff is already on Arsenault, assembling some of the specialized units I'll need as the cadre for the force."

"General, sometimes I think that anything I don't screw up I shit on. I should have appointed you to head this task force long ago instead of appointing you commandant, as much as you and the Marine Corps deserved it. I could've given you your fourth star right then as task force commander and—"

"Ma'am, if I may? You had a lot on your plate at the time. Besides, once we chased the Skinks off Kingdom, we thought we'd cleaned their clock permanently. There was no urgency then to implement the task force."

"Thank you, General!" Chang-Sturdevant laughed. "Well, to the matter at hand. Your orders give you the powers of a plenipotentiary. Use them. I have instructed every ministry in my government to assist you to the fullest extent possible. Tolerate no bureaucratic bullshit, General. I'm retiring Admiral Porter and appointing General Cazombi to his post. You've met Cazombi?"

"Yes, ma'am. He is the perfect choice. But let me add, please, that old Admiral Porter, well, he's not a bad sort. But he belongs in retirement. This situation calls for a man like Cazombi."

"Porter will be retired with full honors, General. One more thing. I may not be in office much longer."

"What?"

"I'm addressing a joint session of the Confederation Congress tomorrow. I'm telling them everything." She shook her head. "I think the reports we've had that the Skinks are back are accurate. I'm releasing to the media the vids and all reports generated after the encounter on Kingdom. We cannot keep this under wraps a day longer, General. We have *got* to mobilize and you will be at the sharp end of the stick. But the politicians may not be happy I've waited this long to tell them about the Skink threat. I could be impeached over this."

"I hope the hell not!"

"Whatever happens to me is of little importance. Time is of the essence, General. Get out there, put your forces together, and deal with these bastards. You do that and my conscience will be a lot lighter."

Aguinaldo finished his drink. "Damned good Scotch! Well, Madam President, it'll be a big day for all of us tomorrow. I'd better be off. Do you have anything else for me tonight?"

Chang-Sturdevant rose and held out her hand. When Aguinaldo took it she kissed him lightly on the cheek and whispered, "We're all depending on you. God bless you and your troops."

President Cynthia Chang-Sturdevant was perspiring. "Marcus," she said, "this is going to be an ordeal, a debacle, if I don't handle it just right." She was referring to the joint session of the Confederation Congress that she would address in only a few minutes. "The whole shebang will be out in the open, Marcus. Back where I come from we have an old saying, Marcus. Today the cucumber is in your hand; tomorrow it may be up your ass. In a few minutes I'll know where it's going." She took a deep breath. "I'm as nervous as a bride on her wedding night." She grinned.

"Well, you shine today like a young girl walking down the aisle, Suelee," Marcus remarked. She did, she looked positively radiant—to Marcus. She was wearing a military-style tunic that buttoned closely around her throat and on her left breast shimmered the Order of Military Merit she'd earned as a Reserve Second Lieutenant in the Second Silvansian War. It was not her only decoration, but it was the only one she ever wore. "Shall I change into my old uniform and be your 'husband' and accompany you?" Marcus asked.

"Are you proposing?" she responded, archly. "Not now, Marcus, but thanks just the same." She kissed him lightly on the cheek. "We can talk about the husband part later."

Berentus's face had turned red with embarrassment. Now might not have been the best time for such a proposal, but Chang-Sturdevant knew how he felt about her and he figured since the target was in his sights he should fire away. "Well, okay then, Madam President, will you marry me?" he blurted out. "I'd have asked a long time ago," he hurried on, "but you've been keeping me so damned busy lately!"

Chang-Sturdevant laughed. "Okay, Mr. Minister, let's do it! Damn, you beat me to it! But Marcus, isn't a proposal supposed to be more romantic? Nice of you to pop the question just before I go down the shitter. Give me *something* to be happy about as I slide down the razor blade of political disaster."

"We'll hold hands and go down together. Ah, well." Berentus chuckled. "We've known each other too long for any romantic stuff. But going back to the crisis of the moment, Suelee, sure you don't want one friendly face out there to back you up?"

"No, I got us into this and I'm going to have to get us out or take the well-deserved consequences." She smiled briefly. "I can always count on you, can't I?" she added. Her expression had become serious. What she was about to do would be the turning point in her career. She'd had so many turning points recently she was getting dizzy.

"You bet."

"Well, when they throw me out will you still love me, Marcus?"

"You bet, Suelee! Hell, you goddamned better count on it, Madam President," he replied with feeling and kissed her back. "I wish we would get tossed out, then I'd have you all to myself. Damn, Suelee, Mary Baker Eddy's toenails, we sure gummed things up this time, didn't we?"

"What's this 'we,' Marcus? You got a kwangduk in your pocket?" She laughed.

Berentus grinned. She was beginning to talk like a warrior now. He knew nobody in that Congress could handle *this* president. "Little girl, want me to walk you to the hall, carry your books, buy you an ice cream?"

"Nope. Just give me a hug." He did, and a long one too. "See you later?" She smiled and hummed the words from an old, old song they both knew so well:

> Will you come and plant some flowers
> Round my cold eternal grave?
> Will you come and sit beside me
> Where the lilies nod and wave?

Cynthia Chang-Sturdevant waved nonchalantly and walked out into the Great Hall of the Confederation Congress.

When the sergeant at arms announced President Chang-Sturdevant's entry into the Great Hall, half of the members did not even bother to get out of their seats; the other half were already up, shouting and arguing with one another. After a long call to order, a restive silence finally engulfed the assembled legislators. In fact, most of the members of both houses of the Confederation Congress were present since it had been announced earlier that President Chang-Sturdevant would deliver an important address that day. The media were there also, covering the entire session, happily recording the antics of their elected representatives.

"Madam Chang-Sturdevant, President of the Confederation of Human Worlds, will now address this Congress," the old sergeant at arms announced in a stentorian voice. Bowing to the dais, he took his own seat beside the President of the Senate.

Chang-Sturdevant had never looked better. Her blazing white tunic perfectly offset her black hair with its single strand of white and the Order of Military Merit glittered brilliantly in the lights. She was very proud of her Merit award and, besides, it intimidated other politicians, most of whom had never worn a uniform in peace or war.

"Madam President! Madam President!" It was Haggle Kutmoi, the Senator from Bulon, an early and vigorous supporter of the war against the Coalition. "Madam President!" His voice thundered without amplification. Chang-Sturdevant wondered how such a little man could have such a powerful voice.

"Be seated, Senator! The president is about to address this Congress!" the sergeant at arms thundered, half rising out of his seat.

Kutmoi ignored him, a dangerous thing to do, and kept on anyway. He advanced toward the podium, one hand held high. "Madam President, I do not need to tell you and the august members of this legislative body that the hearings I am presently conducting into the scandalous, nay, *mutinous* events on Ravenette in which you, Madam President, are complicit, are now a matter of public knowledge and comment. They will reveal how you have let the Ravenette traitors off the hook! When all the facts are in I shall demand, *demand* legislation limiting your War

Powers authority as well as commence impeachment proceedings against you and Minister of War Marcus Berentus!"

"Senator," Chang-Sturdevant replied calmly, "I have nothing further to say about Ravenette. That matter is closed so far as I am concerned. Let your hearings proceed as they may, Senator, but you can expect no cooperation from anyone in my government. As to your committee's recommendations, whatever they shall be, well, Senator, you can take them and shove them straight up your—" What she said was drowned out in the cheers, howls, and laughter that engulfed the Great Hall.

The settlers in the far-flung reaches of Human Space did not receive vids of Chang-Sturdevant's momentous speech for many days after it was delivered and what she said to Senator Haggle Kutmoi, although old news by then, still made them laugh and cheer and pound one another's backs, and swear they'd vote for this woman in the next election; they'd already seen vids of both Billie's and Cazombi's testimony before Kutmoi's panel and opinion was running high on the side of the plain-spoken Cazombi.

Chang-Sturdevant did not need a high-priced lawyer to tell her about the advantages of being honest with the voters, of admitting mistakes openly. That is what she was about to do, and after she was done, Haggle Kutmoi's hearings would collapse like a pricked balloon. But what she told them made their blood run cold.

Chang-Sturdevant told them about the Skinks.

Several days later, sitting disconsolately in his hotel room, Jason Fosdick Billie put the muzzle of his antique pistol in his mouth and pulled the trigger.

EPILOGUE

The Marines of 34th FIST weren't bedraggled when the Essays landed them at Boynton Field, the combination airfield, Essay field at Camp Major Pete Ellis, and 34th FIST's home on Thorsfinni's World. Two and a half weeks on board the CNSS *Lance Corporal Keith Lopez,* where they'd been able to clean their weapons, their bodies, their uniforms, and their equipment, and heal their wounds, had seen to that. Still, aside from isolated whoops of joy, they were a somber band as they dismounted from the Dragons that rolled out of the Essays that had borne them from the orbiting starship and formed up by platoons to board lorries for transport to the barracks.

When the lorries dropped off Company L, the Marines formed up behind the barracks. Captain Conorado didn't make his Marines wait for him to come out of the company office; he went directly from his lorry to stand in front of his assembled Marines. The Marines didn't move fast, but it didn't take them long to assemble and straighten their ranks. They stood at attention, waiting patiently for their company commander to say what he had to say.

Conorado looked over his company. In garrison utilities, all were visible. Remarkably, considering the severity of the action they'd so recently seen, there were no holes in the formation. Even First Sergeant Myer, who rarely attended formations, was present. The lack of holes in the formation wasn't because the casualties were light on Ravenette; it was because of the replacements they had gotten from the Whiskey

Company that Commandant Aguinaldo had provided for 34th FIST well before the war. Conorado had mixed feelings about that. On the one hand, each hole in the formation would have been a reminder of a member of Conorado's Marine family who was dead or severely injured. On the other hand, there were too many faces he didn't recognize, or barely recognized, men who'd already replaced the company's dead or severely wounded.

"Marines of Company L," Conorado finally said. He didn't speak as loudly as he normally did when addressing his company, but his voice carried well enough for every man to hear. "You did an outstanding job, one in the highest tradition of Company L, 34th FIST, the Confederation Marine Corps, and the Naval Services. I want you to know that I am proud to be associated with men such as you.

"I don't know yet how long we have before a new training cycle, or what we will be training for. When I dismiss you from this formation, you are to retrieve your belongings from the company supply room and take them to secure in your squad bays. You have one hour to do that, and then the company will reassemble here to march to the battalion mess hall, where base personnel are preparing a meal to welcome us home. I will have information about liberty when we reassemble after that."

Conorado stood tall, looking over his company again. He hadn't indulged in hyperbole—he really was proud to command these Marines. He filled his chest, then bellowed, "COMP-ny, dis-MISSED!"

The Marines broke ranks and headed to the company supply room. Even though they weren't in formation, they lined up by platoons and squads to get their belongings.

Brigadier Sturgeon declared five days liberty for the entire FIST, effective immediately. Not everybody took off immediately.

Ensign Charlie Bass was one who didn't. He went to the officers' club for a drink, then returned to the barracks and made the rounds of third platoon. Most of the Marines were in their fire team's room, sleeping, watching trids, reading, studying, or simply staring into places only they could see. One room was occupied by only one man.

"Lance Corporal Ymenez," Bass said. "How ya doing?"

"Sir!" Ymenez said, jumping to his feet to stand at attention.

"As you were, Lance Corporal." Bass patted the air and indicated Ymenez should sit down again. He pulled a chair out from one of the minuscule desks in the room and sat himself. "As I said, how ya doing?"

"I-I'm good, sir."

Bass cocked a disbelieving eye at him, but let it ride. "That's good, Ymenez." He looked around the small room, and listened for sounds from the adjoining head that second squad's second fire team shared with the third fire team. "Where are Corporal Claypoole and Lance Corporal Schultz?"

"They went out on liberty, sir."

"And they didn't take you with them?"

"N-No, sir. C-Corporal Claypoole said something about personal business."

Bass nodded. He had a good idea what the personal business was.

"Are you going on liberty?" he asked.

"Yes, sir, I think so. Later. With some other men from the squad. Or the platoon."

"Very good. You *should* get out and blow off some steam." Bass stood to leave.

"Sir?" Ymenez stood and returned to attention. Bass looked at him. "Sir, what's going to happen to me? I mean, if Lance Corporal"—he tried to remember the name he'd heard, couldn't, and used the nickname he'd heard instead—"Lance Corporal Wolfman comes back?"

Bass looked at him soberly for a moment. "I don't know. First I have to find out if Lance Corporal MacIlargie—and Lance Corporal Longfellow—are coming back at all. Once we know that, then a decision will be made. Why do you ask?"

"Sir, I know I haven't been with third platoon very long, but I think this is a good platoon. I'd rather stay here than be sent back to Whiskey Company."

Bass studied Ymenez for a few seconds, then nodded. "Thank you, Lance Corporal. I accept that as a compliment to me and to the Marines of third platoon. I don't know what's going to happen, but I'll find out as soon as I can—and I'll do what I can to keep you in third platoon."

"Thank you, sir!"

Bass reached out a hand and shook Ymenez's. "Don't forget to get out of here," he said as he left the room.

His next stop after the barracks was the base hospital, where he visited MacIlargie and Longfellow. Staff Sergeant Hyakowa had already been there, as had Top Myer and Gunnery Sergeant Thatcher. Both were doing well and looking forward to returning to the platoon. The other platoon commanders were there about the same time Bass was. Captain Conorado arrived as Bass was leaving.

After he left the hospital, Bass checked on the location of a couple of his men who'd already left for liberty—the ID bracelets each Marine wore transmitted his location. As Bass had suspected, Corporal Claypoole was at a small farm in Brystholde. Bass knew that's where Claypoole's girlfriend, Jente—what was that young woman's last name? He'd have to find out—lived. Bass had to look up the address of Schultz's location. He grinned when he found it; it was the home of the new cook at Big Barb's, Einna Orafem.

"Speaking of women," Bass told himself, it was time he took off himself. Katie would be getting anxious.

Ravenette wasn't a small campaign like so many that 34th FIST embarked on; it had been a full-fledged war. For the vast majority of the Marines and sailors in the FIST, Ravenette was the biggest campaign they had ever been on—even those who had been in the Diamundian War. The Marines, sailors, and soldiers who'd been deployed to Ravenette weren't going to get another campaign star for their Marine, Navy, or Army Campaign Medals. No, Ravenette rated its own campaign medal, which would be issued as soon as one was designed and struck.

Brigadier Sturgeon finally made good on a promise that had been implied when Charlie Bass had been shanghaied into finally accepting a commission: Sturgeon promoted Bass to lieutenant. But he left him in command of third platoon rather than moving him into a proper lieutenant's billet.

Oh yes, one more detail. The Marines of 34th Fleet Initial Strike Team didn't know it yet, but the Skinks were back and had to be dealt with. But that's another story.

ABOUT THE AUTHORS

DAVID SHERMAN is a former U.S. Marine and the author of eight novels about Marines in Vietnam, where he served as an infantryman and as a member of a Combined Action Platoon. He is also the author of the military fantasy series Demontech. Visit the author's website at www.novelier.com.

DAN CRAGG enlisted in the U.S. Army in 1958 and retired with the rank of sergeant major twenty years later. He is the author of *Inside the VC and the NVA* (with Michael Lee Lanning), *Top Sergeant* (with William G. Bainbridge), and a Vietnam War novel, *The Soldier's Prize*. He recently retired from his work as an analyst for the Department of Defense.

ABOUT THE TYPE

This book was set in ITC Berkeley Oldstyle, designed in 1983 by Tony Stan. It is a variation of the University of California Old Style, which was created by Frederick Goudy. While capturing the feel and traits of its predecessor, ITC Berkeley Old Style shows influences from Kennerly, Goudy Old Style, Deepdene, and Booklet Oldstyle, all of which were also designed by Goudy. It is characterized by its calligraphic weight stress, and its x-height, now described as classic, is smaller than most other ITC designs of the day. The generous ascenders and descenders provide variations in text color, easy legibility, and an overall inviting appearance.